*The Pan Book of*
# HORROR STORIES

*The Pan Book of*
# HORROR STORIES

*Edited by*
HERBERT VAN THAL

*With a new foreword by*
JOHNNY MAINS

PAN BOOKS

This collection first published in Great Britain 1959 by Pan Books Limited

This edition published 2016 by Pan Books
an imprint of Pan Macmillan, a division of Macmillan Publishers Limited
Pan Macmillan, 20 New Wharf Road, London N1 9RR
Basingstoke and Oxford
Associated companies throughout the world
www.panmacmillan.com

ISBN 978-1-5098-2889-0

Copyright © The Estate of Herbert van Thal
'A Brief History of the Horrors' copyright © Johnny Mains 2010

The acknowledgements on page 297 constitute an extension of this copyright page.

All rights reserved. No part of this publication may be reproduced, stored in or introduced into a retrieval system, or transmitted, in any form, or by any means (electronic, mechanical, photocopying, recording or otherwise) without the prior written permission of the publisher. Any person who does any unauthorized act in relation to this publication may be liable to criminal prosecution and civil claims for damages.

The Macmillan Group has no responsibility for the information provided by and author websites whose address you obtain from this book ('author websites'). The inclusion of author website addresses in this book does not constitute an endorsement by or association with us of such sites or the content, products, advertising or other materials presented on such sites.

A CIP catalogue record for this book is available from the British Library.

Typeset by CPI Typesetting

This book is sold subject to the condition that it shall not, by way of trade or otherwise, be lent, re-sold, hired out, or otherwise circulated without the publisher's prior consent in any form of binding or cover other than that in which it is published and without a similar condition including this condition being imposed on the subsequent purchaser.

Visit www.panmacmillan.com to read more about all our books and to buy them. You will also find features, author interviews and news of any author events, and you can sign up for e-newsletters so that you're always first to hear about our new releases.

# Contents

*Introductory Note by Herbert van Thal*   vii

Johnny Mains – *A Brief History of the Horrors*   ix

Joan Aiken – *Jugged Hare*   1

A. L. Barker – *Submerged*   9

Oscar Cook – *His Beautiful Hands*   28

George Fielding Eliot – *The Copper Bowl*   37

Jack Finney – *Contents of the Dead Man's Pocket*   50

Peter Fleming – *The Kill*   68

C. S. Forester – *The Physiology of Fear*   81

L. P. Hartley – *W. S.*   98

Hazel Heald – *The Horror in the Museum*   110

Hester Holland – *The Library*   141

Fielden Hughes — *The Mistake*  *152*

Nigel Kneale — *Oh, Mirror, Mirror*  *158*

Noel Langley — *Serenade for Baboons*  *164*

Hamilton Macallister — *The Lady Who Didn't Waste Words*  *175*

Chris Massie — *A Fragment of Fact*  *182*

Seabury Quinn — *The House of Horror*  *190*

Flavia Richardson — *Behind the Yellow Door*  *213*

Muriel Spark — *The Portobello Road*  *222*

Bram Stoker — *The Squaw*  *246*

Anthony Vercoe — *Flies*  *260*

Angus Wilson — *Raspberry Jam*  *269*

Alan Wykes — *Nightmare*  *287*

## *Introductory Note*

Why do we like reading about torture, sadistic monsters, cruel people? Why do we like frightening ourselves by reading about events which we would hope never to see, let alone participate in? Is it not the memorable and agelong custom that we like 'being taken out of ourselves'? And is there not a slight feeling of smugness, that while sitting in our (we hope) comfortable armchairs we can safely read of the ingenious and terrifying things men do to men?

Despite the so-called advance of civilization, we have witnessed wars, revolutions and crimes that are often more terrifying than fiction; as witness C. S. Forester's story.

In short, truth is stranger than fiction. Even so, we feel that the stories in this book are such that if your nerves are not of the strongest, then it is wise to read them in daylight lest you should suffer nightmares, for these authors know their craft, and they have not hesitated to expound it with little thought of sparing you from the horrifying details.

H. van Thal

Johnny Mains

# *A Brief History of the Horrors*

When *The Pan Book of Horror Stories* first hit the shelves in 1959, the last thing on the editors' or indeed the publisher's minds was that for the next thirty years the book would become an annual staple for the horror-hungry aficionado.

But apart from a brief hiatus in 1961, a new volume of the Pan Horrors was published each year until 1989. Their place in history as the longest running horror anthology in the *world* has yet to be beaten.

And now, you hold in your hands the book that started it all, *The Pan Book of Horror Stories* (X 45), originally published on 11 December 1959. It was edited by Herbert van Thal, a prolific anthologist and biographer whose breadth of work in the horror genre is impressive.

Van Thal edited twenty-five volumes of the Pan Horror Stories and was also responsible for at least a dozen other horror anthologies. Before his own company Home and van Thal was sold he reprinted Mrs J. H. Riddell's *Weird Stories* and Rhoda Broughton's *Twilight Tales*.

Herbert (or Bertie as he was known to friends) was brought to work for Pan by Clarence Paget; one-time literary agent who had previously worked for publishing house Cassell's. In 1957, the enigmatic sales director Ralph Vernon-Hunt suggested to Paget, now Pan's Chief Editor, that publishing a horror anthology might be a success. He asked if Paget knew of an editor. Paget did; turning to van Thal who was said to have been an old friend. Even though he was working for publishers Arthur Barker at the time, van Thal agreed and work began on finding stories for the book.

Bertie didn't have to look too far. Most of the tales for the first Pan Horror came from the benchmark of genre anthologies of the day, the 'Not at Night' series – edited by Christine Campbell Thomson and published by Selwyn and Blount from 1925–1937. Over 100 stories from the 170 in those books had previously been selected from *Weird Tales* magazine in the U.S. Christine herself would go on to contribute to the Pan Horror series; one tale under her own name and two by her nom de plume, Flavia Richardson.

It has been suggested that Christine may have advised van Thal on which stories from the 'Not at Night's should go in to the Pan book but with a lack of evidence, whimsy takes centre stage. The choices made, though, are excellent ones. 'The House of Horror' by Seabury Quinn is taken from *You'll Need a Nightlight*. 'The Copper Bowl' by George Fielding Eliot comes from *By Daylight Only*. 'The Horror in the Museum' and 'Behind the Yellow Door' by Hazel Heald and Flavia Richardson respectively, come from *Terror By Night*.

Indeed the first five books of the series contained mainly reprints, with 'Not at Night' being replaced by the 'Creeps' series as the source of gruesome tales which was edited anonymously by Charles Birkin. Charles, like Christine, saw his stories appear in the Pan books, with three under his own name and two under his pseudonym Charles Lloyd.

Van Thal's masterstroke, and the decision that would see the series last as long as it did, was to open the doors to submissions. And soon a steady trickle of original stories began to appear in the books. Names such as Basil Copper, John Burke, Alex Hamilton and Martin Waddell cut a swathe in an unknown landscape, offering new stories that a buying public greedily accepted. Sales were high and the blurbs on the back covers proudly declared they had sold millions of copies.

Another draw to the books were the instantly recognisable

covers. The first seven books had the 'Horror Stories' logo surrounded by a bold yellow box. In pre-Photoshop days every single letter would have to be painstakingly painted on by hand. These early covers had specially commissioned paintings; while the artist of the first volume is unknown, the second volume was painted by S. R. Boldero. The third, fourth, sixth and seventh volumes were all painted by the little-known William Francis Phillips, with the fifth book being one of their first dips into 'trick' photography. As the series progressed a new, almost hip, logo was used briefly on books eight to twelve (it was the late sixties…) and the covers would veer from the absurd 'portrait' shots to beautifully painted covers. Renowned 'Discworld' artist Josh Kirby supplied the talent for the thirteenth, fourteenth and possibly fifteenth books. It has to be said that, towards the end of the series, the covers became more violent and outlandish with the twenty-seventh volume (bearing a man's head being cleaved from his shoulders, by the late South African artist Stuart Bodek) and the thirtieth and last in the series (a rendition of Stephen King's 'Lawnmower Man' painted by prominent Fantasy artist Melvyn Grant) being the two main culprits.

In its teenage years 'The Pan Book of Horror Stories' was at its peak with startling talents emerging from the shadows. Names such as Conrad Hill, Dulcie Gray, Harry E. Turner, Roger F. Dunkely, Norman P. Kaufmann and the pseudonymous Alex White provided stories that really did amp up the scares. But it was also during this time that the rot started to set in. Many stories showed an almost cavalier attitude to horrendous violence, tossing aside the supernatural and psychological tales that had gone before in favour of cheap sadistic thrills, rape and extreme body torture.

It was this Jekyll and Hyde aspect to the Pan Horrors that would eventually see the series plummet into a dramatic decline in sales. Though van Thal as editor was to blame for the stories that made it into all volumes until twenty-five, it was already apparent that readers preferred their visceral horror on the big screen or home video. One could argue that if the latter Pan volumes were released today, in the era of 'gorenography' and films such as *Hostel* and *Saw*, no one would have batted an eyelid. In this regard, van Thal glimpsed the future, but the horror reading public, ironically, didn't have the stomach for it.

Bertie and Clarence pushed on regardless. However, Pan baulked at the multitude of stories by a single author van Thal would try to put into one volume. So much so that he would persuade authors to use a pseudonym. One author, Ian C. Strachan appears four times in *The 25th Pan Book of Horror Stories* as Strachan, Carl Schiffman, Curt Pater and Thomas Muirson. Van Thal even created the pen name of Alex White and used several of his Pan authors to write stories based on ideas and themes that he himself had come up with to get round Pan's embargo.

Van Thal and Paget's relationship must frequently have been a tense one. Both Herbert van Thal and Clarence Paget received royalties from the first book. Paget was likely to have been responsible for taking over the reins for books eleven and twelve (all acceptance and contractual letters to authors indicate this) though van Thal's name still appears on these volumes. Van Thal may have been in America or working on other projects at the time. In all other volumes, and after a cursory chat with Paget to discuss which stories he had, Herbert was left to get on with it alone. One wonders if Clarence Paget felt that his name should have appeared on the books along with van Thal, but Herbert van Thal was the trademark, the name you could trust to deliver the scares. The brand could have been damaged otherwise, and this presumably was recognized.

Another decision that did the then struggling Pan Horrors no favours was the inclusion of Stephen King in the line-up. It was a misguided attempt by van Thal to ride the wave of popularity that the author was creating at the time. King's stories in several of the volumes were readily available in his own collection *Night Shift* and his popularity was such that any horror reader worth his or her salt had bought and read the collection already. Why read them again so shortly after initial publication? The decision had the reverse effect, with sales dipping once more.

When van Thal died in 1983, many thought that the series would die with him. But in 1984 *The 25th Pan Book of Horror Stories* appeared; the last one to bear his name, though the feeling is that Clarence Paget finished editing the volume with 60 per cent of the stories being 'locked in' by van Thal.

Paget took charge of the last four books and the series quickly plummeted both in style and substance. Only a handful of gems appear, but these are hidden in amongst some terribly garish stories which in all honesty should have been thrown straight into the bin.

So with the publication of *The 30th Pan Book of Horror Stories* in 1989, the king of anthologies was finally dead after thirty bloody years on the throne.

Or so one would have thought.

There was to be one last throw of the dice, when editor Stephen Jones, along with Clarence Paget, brought out a retrospective collection called *Dark Voices: The Best From the Pan Book of Horror Stories*. The stories contained were by the most famous authors from the series and came complete with introductions to each tale from James Herbert, Shaun Hutson, David Cronenberg and others in the horror field.

The book sold phenomenally well, and this in turn led to Dark Voices being commissioned as a series. During this time, Clarence Paget passed away, and Stephen Jones worked along side David A. Sutton. Together they produced a further five best-selling volumes for Pan with a score of the old Pan authors contributing stories, but it was the turn of fresh talent to break free from the shadows of the old masters of the macabre.

After *Dark Voices 6* was published in 1994 the series was dropped, but was subsequently picked up by the publishers Victor Gollancz and re-named as *Dark Terrors*. The books from both series were no longer reprinted and in time could only be found in charity shops and at car boot sales.

So what of 'The Pan Book of Horror Stories' legacy? If the series was a stone thrown into a pool, the ripples they created are still visible today, fifty years after the series was first introduced to the public. Other publishing companies at the time, seeing the instant success that Pan was having, instantly jumped on the bandwagon. Fontana published *The Fontana Great Book of Horror Stories* first edited by Christine Bernard and, after she left, by Mary Danby. In fact Fontana were the closest thing that Pan had to a rival; a 'Ghost' series was also published, edited by Robert Aickman and R. Chetwynd-Hayes. Arrow, Panther, Orbit and others brought out their own anthologies and for a while the selection of new stories and reprints that were available to the reader was overwhelming. But none of these publishing companies had the name, drive or money behind them that Pan did, and even though the 'Fontana Great Book of Horror Stories' ran to an impressive seventeen books, the record that the 'Pan Book of Horror Stories' holds looks like it will remain unbeaten for the foreseeable future.

Another proud achievement that the Pan Horrors have attained is the amount of readers who turned into writers as a direct result of reading these books when they were children or teenagers. The stories were nothing if not impressionistic, and they definitely left their mark!

It seems that 'The Pan Book of Horror Stories' has been ingrained into the nation's psyche, the literary world's dirty little secret. But you can still find authors such as Clive Barker, Shaun Hutson, Mark Morris, Philip Pullman and Muriel Gray talking about the books and the effect that they had on them. And the interest hasn't abated, with the small print press eager to emulate the style of the series. *The Black Book of Horror* sometimes comes close to mimicking the feel of the series and has featured stories written by a handful of original Pan Horror authors. Other books have been volumes one and two of 'Humdrumming Horror Stories', a series that completely missed the mark on what the Pan Horrors were all about, two volumes of 'The BHF Book of Horror Stories', a gentle horror anthology entitled *The Panda Book of Horror* and *Back From The Dead: The Legacy of the Pan Book of Horror Stories* which showcased sixteen brand new tales and five reprints from the original series, the first time Pan Horror authors had appeared in an anthology en masse since 1989.

The internet has helped to deepen the cult that surrounds the series; websites dedicated to the books have sprung up, and online auction sites have turned the last two volumes in particular into sought after collectibles. 'The Pan Book of Horror Stories' lies in a restless grave and it doesn't want to stay dead.

So now we come back, full circle.

The stories that you are about to read are not for the faint-hearted. You will find tales of the quietly disturbing such as Oscar Cook's story of flesh rotting in 'His Beautiful Hands'; George Fielding Eliot's 'The Copper Bowl' in which the Mandarin Yuan Li demonstrates to Lieutenant Fournet that his beloved Lily doesn't have a strong stomach; and Angus Wilson's bone crunching 'Raspberry Jam' will certainly leave you disquieted for a long time to come. Rest assured that the other nineteen stories contained in this volume are of an equally high standard and show why the series became as popular as it did.

For old friends of the series…a hearty welcome back. It certainly has been a while. For new readers, beware the untold horrors that lurk in the following tales.

You have been warned!

**Johnny Mains**
*www.panbookofhorrorstories.co.uk*
*Norfolk*
*September 2010*

# Joan Aiken

## *Jugged Hare*

'You look sumptuous.' He said it with dispassionate admiration, and she nodded, lazily agreeing. On the bleakest winter day, with her great ramparts of corn-coloured hair and magnificent petal skin, she could seem to any man like an evocation of summer; she was an orchard in bloom, with promise of fruit, a wheatsheaf, an armful of lilies...

'You've established yourself very handsomely; were you expecting me?'

'You? No. Why should I? I just like to be comfortable. Nobody comes here, you should know that. Henry has quarrelled with them all. And you had better not stay here gossiping; he is somewhere about shooting, and he's been getting so jealous and queer lately that it makes me nervous.'

Her provocative smile, however, belied the words, and Desmond Colne continued to linger and eye her appreciatively.

She had slung her metal-and-silk hammock beside the towering hedge of guelder rose and Queen Anne's Lace, which supplied her with a frothing background of white blossom. Against it she idly swung, one ankle dangling, the month's epitome, while June arched overhead. 'What's this, crochet?'

'Tatting,' she corrected, taking the spider webbing from him and beginning to flick the shuttle in and out. 'What for?'

'Lace scarves, frills for petticoats...'

'Frills!' he said, and, suddenly chuckling, 'What are those great shiny sweets, honey humbugs? No, satin cushions. That's what you remind me of, a satin cushion. Gorgeous and golden and curving and brittle and hard.'

She was delighted. 'No one's ever compared me to a honey humbug before. Doesn't it sound like the last line of a poem?

> *My mistress is mad about judo, no holds barred.*
> *She's gorgeous and golden and curving and brittle and hard.'*

They were still laughing when something flew between them with a savage whip and whine of unexpected sound. It anchored itself dithering in the ground beside her hammock.

Colne jumped back with a sharp exclamation.

'You see what I mean,' said Sarah flatly, though the shock had driven all the blood from her face. 'One of his little accidental-on-purpose games.'

She glanced with revulsion at the thing beside her – a three-foot arrow, which had pinned her cloudy tangle of tatting to the grass.

'But, good god, the man's not safe, he might have hit us…'

'Oh, heavens no. Henry's a marvellous shot. If he'd wanted to hit either of us, believe you me, he would have. This is just a gentle hint that you've come here to sell him machinery, not to gossip with me. Better get on with it.' She pulled the arrow out with a jerk as Henry Hargreaves came towards them, unstringing his bow. 'Here,' she called, 'take your blasted thing; you've ruined my afternoon's work.'

'So sorry, my dear. The wind must have caught it. But look at my afternoon's work. Tender eating, eh?' He dangled proudly at them the long, *limp*, gingery body of a hare, its ears dabbled with blood.

Sarah turned her eyes away.

'I don't know how you can,' she said. 'One's just about able to endure the thought of shooting them with a gun, but with an arrow – ugh!'

'You don't understand it at all,' Henry said shrilly. His eyes were shining. 'I only wish we had some deer – there'd be twice the satisfaction in shooting something so big. You could really choose your mark – the neck, the flank, the eye. As it is, you have to shoot at anything you see.'

'Oh, shut up,' Sarah said angrily.

'Where did you bag the hare?' Desmond asked in polite diversion.

'In what we call the hidden road. When they cut the new highway they left the old lane that goes through my woods. No one uses it now, it's nearly grown over, and it makes an excellent game run. Well' – he flipped the hare's ears dismissingly – 'got the specifications with you, Colne?'

'In my car,' Desmond said. The two men turned across the grass towards the car, which stood beside the house. Sarah, with a flash of petticoats marked by Desmond out of the corner of his eye, swung herself out of the hammock, gathered up her tatting, and followed them.

'Is this your car?' she said, yawning, as Henry studied the papers Colne gave him. 'It's very pretty, but what a melodramatic number, HEL 999. Is that help, murder, or the Mark of the Beast?'

'Neither, I trust.' He was not good at this fooling with Henry's eye upon them.

'*I* think it's ominous.' She yawned again. 'A good journey to you, anyway. Didn't you say you were driving up north tonight? And Henry's running down to Aylmouth to catch the ten o'clock tide for his yacht race; what busy, purposeful lives men lead.'

Her husband shot her a narrow glance. He was a thin, hot-eyed man, with crusted lips and hands that trembled continuously and nervously, except when he was holding a bow or a tiller; then they calmed and steadied.

'And what will you do with yourself, my dear?' he inquired.

'I shall have a delicious, solitary evening. I shall go to bed early and *curl* up with a box of chocolates and several thrillers, and then I probably shan't read a word. I shall go to sleep thinking of you energetic people speeding through the night, and how much more I am enjoying myself than either of you.'

And it was true, too, Desmond thought in exasperation. He could not ever convince himself that when he was out of her sight she spared him a single thought, or that, if she did, he was regarded as anything more than a pleasant garnish to a comfortable existence.

'Goodbye, Mr... Colne,' Sarah said, indolently moving towards the house. 'Supper when you want it, Henry.'

'You'll let me know, then, as soon as these are available,' Henry said to Desmond, tapping the papers.

He watched the car go, following it with his eyes until it was out of sight, like a suspicious watchdog who has as yet no proved grounds of enmity. Then he walked indoors, staring at the ground as if he hoped to see spoor on it.

'I've put up your sailing food in the canvas bag,' Sarah called. 'It's all ready for you.'

After Henry had driven off to catch his ten o'clock tide, Sarah fulfilled her programme to the letter, dozing over the thrillers and the chocolates until she smiled and roused herself and went to bed. She switched off all the lights and listened for a moment to the trees; the wind was rising. Henry will have to reef right down, she thought, and felt in imagination the rasp of wet, stiff rope on her fingers. Then, dismissing both men from her mind, she went to sleep.

She was roused by the cold touch of lips on her arm: lips that had come fresh from exposure to the wind outside.

'Hullo,' she said, half waking. 'Oh, it's you; how very pleasant.'

'Weren't you expecting me?'

'I had no idea; I thought you might have been put off by Henry's arrow.'

'But he's well away by now, surely? Rocked on the deep. Rocked is the word, I may say; he'll be lucky if he finishes without some broken spars. Listen to it.'

She lifted her head from the pillow and listened to the wind.

Desmond was moving quietly about the room. He was a big man, with intent, staring, sardonic eyes, which were often so preoccupied, watching faces for revelations of hidden motives, that they missed the obvious. Sarah was a perpetual enigma to him because she was so simple.

'Wouldn't it be curious if Henry were to drown?'

'Most curious. Should you be pleased? I suppose he'd leave you quite well off?'

'It would be a relief,' she said reflectively. 'He really has been most trying lately, snarling like a savage dog if I so much as pass the time of day with any other man; he was quite vile about a couple of books he found that Eric Ames lent me.'

'It's lucky I'm not in the habit of lending you books,' said Desmond, chuckling. He kissed her ear and picked up a handful of the honey-coloured hair. 'But why does Ames lend you books, anyway? Haven't you enough to read here?'

'How absurd you are. Don't say you're starting to get jealous, too?' She turned to him, leisurely smiling, unambiguous as the sun on a field of barley.

'Of course not,' he said, stifling the thought. 'Look, I brought a bottle of Beaune. Shall I put it down near the fire?'

'Marvellous; but pour me a glass first. Just listen to that wind. Heaven help poor sailormen on a night like this.' She raised her glass to him. It winked red in the firelight.

A couple of hours later Desmond looked at his watch.

'Better be off,' he said.

'Do you have to?'

'I really am going up north. Have to be in Stockport by eleven tomorrow morning.'

'How long shall you be gone?'

'A month, two months,' he said, picking up the empty bottle, tilting it against the light, and tossing it into the wastepaper basket. 'I shall be bored.'

'Still, if Henry's acting suspicious and odd, it's probably quite a good thing. He'll have simmered down when I come back.'

She made no reply, but lay idly watching him as he knotted his tie. 'Where did you leave the car? You're going to get wet,' she remarked, as a gust of rain slapped the window.

'Out in your hidden lane. Not far to run. It makes a grand hiding place. Well—'

'Well.'

He raised his eyebrows, briefly kissed her goodbye.

When he was gone, Sarah rolled over in drowsy luxury and stretched, thinking, 'How delicious to have the bed to oneself from time to time.'

She had nearly dropped off to sleep again when she was woken by a splitting, tearing crash, followed a few seconds later by another, equally loud. Then silence, except for the hushing of the wind.

Sarah looked at her watch. The tiny green gleam showed three o'clock.

'If this was a thriller,' she thought sleepily, 'it would be important to remember the time. If this was a thriller I'd seize my torch and revolver and dash out to investigate...'

A tidal yawn engulfed her, she slid an arm beneath the pillow into her accustomed position, and slept.

Next morning, in the glimmering watery light of the dying gale, Henry came home. He was tired, unshaven, and hollow-eyed; his mouth was framed by two deep grooves like geological faults.

'Weather conditions hopeless,' he told Sarah. 'The race was scratched. Just as well for me. Mainsail split while we were still in harbour. Hell of a mess.'

'It did blow,' Sarah said placidly. She glanced out at the lawn, covered with broken wreckage of trees. 'I wondered about you.'

His eyes flickered at her, and the twitch at the corner of his mouth that might have been a smile or just a muscular spasm jerked twice. He strolled out into the porch, picked up his bow and quiver, and said tonelessly, 'I'm going through the wood. Always some injured birds after a gale like that.'

She nodded without reply and twirled her filament of tatting.

If the thought of possible tyre marks came to her, she ignored it. He watched her inimically for a moment or two: fresh, graceful, composed, she sat in the window seat among her gossamer artefacts. Her nimble wrists and smooth, capable forearms emerged from the drooping Restoration sleeves of a corded silk housecoat, but there was nothing provocative about her today; she was as self contained and aloof as a cat embarking on its morning toilet.

He shrugged and went out into the wet garden.

The grass was bent and silvered; heavy drop-laden spider-webs swung and dangled from bush to bush. In the hidden road the scent of broken, wet greenery was strong and steamy.

A hundred yards along the overgrown lane a brighter flash caught his eye among the wet leaves and he nodded sourly to himself in acknowledgment of his unexpressed suspicions: Colne's car stood there. Two huge elm boughs had dropped across it, pinning it as securely as a beetle to an entomologist's board.

'HEL 999,' Henry said aloud, still with his sour smile. 'The Mark of the Beast, eh?' He walked up to the car, wondering what excuse Colne would offer for its presence, and then his smile grew fractionally wider as he saw that the owner was still inside. He must have made an attempt to get out when the first bough fell, and had been caught half in and half out. It would not have been comfortable. He must have lost a considerable amount of blood; quite a pool of it had dripped into the leaf-filled rut below the car. Looking at him attentively, Henry saw that he was not yet dead, though unconscious; perhaps it was even possible that he could be saved.

'Still, we won't bother about that,' Henry murmured; he often talked to himself when he was in the woods. 'No one else ever comes this way; we'll just leave him to cool, eh?'

His eye caught a chattering grey squirrel among the branches, and he drew out an arrow but changed his mind. He had wished for larger game, and now he was presented with it. He thought of Sarah, lolling so composedly, her wrists flashing among the lace; thought of her with a hunter's voluptuous possessiveness. He was quite prepared to wait; he would give her six months, perhaps a year even, until Colne's tragic accident was out of people's minds and would not be connected. Then – an accident in the garden, a freak of wind as she swung in her hammock, a horrible mischance for which, knowing Henry to be a devoted and uxorious husband, no one could have anything but the deepest sympathy.

He swallowed deeply, savouring this prospect, took, with keen enjoyment, a last look at poor Colne who had met such unexpected retribution, and then turned back towards the house, mentally making an inventory of all his arrows and trying to decide which was the best for his purpose. The ironwood, perhaps; or the teak; or the rowan he had made himself, fitting on it for fun a flint arrowhead he had picked up in the park.

And then at last, slowly and with infinite satisfaction, he began pondering the choice that was to take him through so many months of long-drawn-out pleasure, the choice of which mark to aim at: the neck, the heart, or the eye?

'Lunch, Henry,' Sarah called through the porch window. 'Jugged hare.'

# A. L. Barker

## *Submerged*

Diving into the river, Peter Hume always felt he was entering something of his own. The brown water never rebuffed him, even the first chill on his skin had a curious softness, like snow; everything crisp and taut in his mind relaxed and was drenched.

It was a mild river, dropped into a steep slot between its banks and thatched over with trees. Some instinct for secrecy kept it at work, quietly shifting the soil, settling with the persistence of a hermit into a deeper, browner bed. The colours here were not the bright mirror colours of a river. Loosestrife, with its carnival purple, strong yellow ragwort and red campion, all had a diffidence; softened, almost brumous, they enriched without decking the river bank. Round the occasional eddies, bright beams of sunlight jumped and jazzed until late evening, and then all that was left of their energy was a thin, milky mist.

Peter couldn't often stay so long, he had to go home to supper or there would be questions. He wasn't supposed to swim in the river anyway, there was some talk about its being dangerous because of the submerged roots of trees. Peter knew all about those, they added the essential risk which made the river perfect. He had been careful never to give any promise, for his conscience was lively and would have kept him to it. His mother supposed he swam in the quarry, and Peter's code, which was rigid enough within the letter of its law, did not require him to disillusion her.

The other boys rarely came to the river. They preferred the quarry which was twenty feet deep in places and ideal for diving. Peter sometimes went with them, but there was nothing to see under water, whereas here, once you had the knack of diving between the roots, it was like being in a bony world of dim arches and aqueducts, caverns and slanting forests. Peter did not try to persuade anyone else to his way of thinking, he preferred to keep the river to himself.

For his first dive, he always went to the left of the willow, where there was nothing more exacting than a couple of stumps which could knock every breath from his body at the slightest miscalculation. That first plunge, with the water roaring in his ears and the mud smoking up from his outflung hands, was the moment of relaxation. The world was at once bounded by a bank, the sky was a fragmentary blue between the leaves, and until it was time to put on his clothes again he felt no distinction between himself and the river dwellers – the otters, water rats, minnows, and frogs. He was as contented as they, plundering the mud or floating on his back and beating up a white spray which looked, on that sober water, surprising as a glimpse of petticoats under brown homespun.

This was a Saturday afternoon. From early morning the distance had never been still, the heat quenched all movement save a small, tireless jig of solid and motionless things. Peter's skin was thirsty for the river even while he went, meekly, to have his hair cut and, fuming, for his music lesson. But the afternoon was his own, and that first plunge, to the left of the willow, past the stumps and up through ribbons of cool weed, absolved him of the morning's sufferance.

He came up breathless, shaking the wet hair out of his eyes. Ripples were widening round him, already they had reached the bank and were moving the grasses. It was nice to make himself felt like that, he wished he could see it happening in the air as he moved about, although he wouldn't care to have other people's ripples getting mixed up with his own.

He lay on his back, and the noise of the water in his ears was like the intermittent singing in a shell. When he thought about the river, he could always remember that sound and the way his hair was gently lifted from his scalp and floated.

Looking up, he saw that the blue sky was trying to burn through the leaves and get at the river. Had it ever been dry? How much hotter would it have to be before the sun could suck all this water up and bake the mud? It was supposed to have happened once to the earth, and there were cracks so big that you would need a bridge to cross them, and looking down, you'd see the fires burning at the middle of the earth. That must have been some heat wave. Peter let himself sink like a stone.

Of course, there could be two opinions as to the delights of the river bed. Peter was not squeamish about the soft fleshy mud creeping round his ankles or about the things which slid from under his feet. He trod firmly, feeling the weight of the water on his eyeballs, seeing only a little way through the greenish gloom. There was one thing he needed now, and that was a knife, carried between his teeth like a sponge diver. He had almost saved enough to buy one.

Under water was no solidity except in touch. Banks and tree roots had no more substance than the reeds, they moved together as in a tiny draught. Peter could see what appeared to be the ribs of a huge skeleton, greening and forgotten on the river bed. They formed a narrow black tunnel with an arched opening which reminded him of a church door.

Peter shot up to the surface, drank in air and blinked in the violence of the sunlight. He stayed where he was – treading water – his wet head shining like glass. It was as well not to move away because he was positioned exactly for his performance. As usual, he was dubious about it, his heart began to knock. A certain excitement was permissible, due to the occasion as a whisper to a church. Any other, lesser emotion belonged to some girlish self which he would gladly have detached and drowned.

This performance was partly a pleasure, partly an endurance test. Until it was accomplished, Peter felt he had no more rights over the river than any of the myriad gadding gnats. Afterwards, by the law of possession of the tamed by the tamer, he considered himself established beyond deeds or bonds.

The ribs under water were tree roots left arched and empty by the river's delving. They were big roots, thicker than Peter's wrist, and there were enough of them hooped over to form a short, tortuous tunnel. Peter had explored it and found he was just able to squeeze through before his breath gave out. It was a foolhardy trick, that was its great attraction. Peter knew that if he ever got wedged in that bony tunnel, he would drown as miserably as a cat in a sack.

But danger was a saving grace. Without it, Peter would not have been able – nor would he have needed – to establish his suzerainty over the river. He was convinced that if he ever swam here without going through the submerged tunnel, the river would be estranged from him, his sense of property and kinship would be lost.

He looked down at his hands, pawing the water like a dog to keep himself afloat. If he came often enough he might get webs across his fingers and his blood might cool. Then he could live here without any trouble, and explore the river from beginning to end. He could follow it down to the sea, and when he was tired of swimming he could make a boat with a cabin and a couple of guns in the poop. A boat was always useful – if he stayed in the water all the time his skin would probably go green and pimply like a frog's. That thought troubled, not his vanity, but his dread of the conspicuous.

A bird flashed past him and vanished in the shadows. For a moment the brown homely river was fired by something tropical – a flicker of cobalt, bronze, and scarlet. The improbable kingfisher.

Sight of that pure violent motion inspired Peter. He dived fiercely. The tunnel rushed to meet him, the dark entrance quenching the image of the kingfisher. Then his head and shoulders were under the first root. Twisting, levering, held fast in a green skeletal gullet, with mud clouding round him, shins and elbows scraped, he yet found some sizeable satisfaction in the ordeal. He was proving himself and the more desperate the struggle, the more splendid and impeccable the proof. All scars were honourable, his lungs withheld not only the river but the force of a mighty and malignant enemy.

The tunnel ended in a last twisted hoop with a clump of shadowy weed beyond. Peter squeezed his head and one arm and shoulder through first. His hand slipped, then grasped the weed. Some of it came away, mud boiling up with it, but the main clump was firm and he hauled himself free by it. Then he was moving upwards, and a dim, gnomish world dropped away under his feet.

It was like coming in out of the dark when the sun beat down on his head and shoulders. He swam grunting to the bank, pulling the water aside familiarly as one who casts off his tangled bed sheets.

For a few moments he lay stretched out on the bank until his skin felt sticky and partly dry. Then he sat up, looked behind him at the empty blond fields, still juddering with heat, and back again at the river. There was wild angelica growing on the far bank, green umbrella ribs blown inside out and ending in a frivolous froth of white. The water did not reflect it, there were too many bright beams just here, but Peter thought it looked cool and eatable. He wished now that he had brought something to eat, he began to tease himself with visions of ice cream – enough to fill a decent-sized bowl, and a spoon in the middle, leaning a little sideways as the ice cream came to the rich liquefying stage which he loved best.

But he was not inclined to hanker after hypothetical pleasures with real ones to hand. As he slipped back into the river there was no splash, only the slow ripples moving out. His mood was now leisurely and relaxed. He followed the ripples, letting himself sink slightly in his laziness before he would lift an arm to make a stroke. Pursing his lips, he blew fleets of bubbles along the top of the water, snuffled it, floated and enjoyed it with the intensity of a very young animal. Ice cream was forgotten, even when he saw the angelica again it did not remind him of something to eat. There was a faint lilac tinge on the flowers and the stalk was flushed a rich purple. It was prettier than any of the flowers his father grew in the garden, but then, he conceded as he floated idly into midstream, it was only right that his own river should have the best flowers.

The sun, the stillness, the drowsy boom of water in his ears, lulled him into a half doze which the river's slight chill would not allow to become complete. Drifting from shadow to sunlight and back to shadow again, he watched the burnt-out blue of the sky, thickly figured with fiery leaves. Thoughts that were partly dreams slipped through his mind. Imperial, childish dreams. The mild river fostered them as school and home never did. Brittle, boy's bones stretched in a flash to the shape and substance of a man; his child's mind – bigoted and unsteady – was great with the sum of wisdom; fame, honour, wealth, were all got as glibly as prizes at a fair.

Peter was strictly practical. This mood being past, he would drop his fantasies and go back to the business of life as he found it. Daydreaming was part of the river, and that was so much his province, he had every right to fill it with himself, lifesize – and beyond.

A sudden noise, a thrusting among the undergrowth, jerked him wideawake. Someone coming. Still on his back, he stared from under his hand. The bushes were snatched aside, an odd, ridiculous figure burst through and almost overbalanced into the river.

It was a woman in a red mackintosh. No longer very young, and so plump that the mackintosh sleeves stretched over her arms like the skin of scarlet saveloys. A green crescent-shaped hat with a spotted veil had tipped over one eye, leaving the other glaring round the polka dots. She would have been funny, but there was something chilling about her, about the steep expanse of speckled red chest heaving under her torn blouse, about the brassy hair tumbling down on her neck, and the skin of her face dreadfully, darkly suffused.

She stood there, too breathless to speak, turning her hands towards Peter with an awful beckoning motion. He stared in horror, and her one visible eye glared back at him. He was frightened by her, by the contagion of her own deadly fear. He thought she was mad; his skin prickled and he backed away through the water.

She cried thickly, 'Come out! Come out of there for God's sake!'

As he gazed, open-mouthed, she was looking over her shoulder back the way she had come, and her hands were moving towards him as if they could draw him ashore bodily.

Peter did not move. Those hands, that huge, speckled bosom bursting from the flimsy mackintosh, revolted his maidishness. He tried to avert his eyes, but he was almost mesmerized by her physical power – not of muscle and sinew, but the power of animal, abundant flesh.

'Come out! Come out, you idiot!' She stood on the very edge of the bank, leaning towards him. 'You've got to help! Do you hear? I've got to have help!'

Slowly Peter moved in to the bank, but when she reached out and tried to snatch at him, he drew away.

'Please turn your back while I get to my clothes.'

His voice sounded thin and ridiculous; the woman's one eye narrowed. 'So's you can make a bolt for it? Think I want to look at a tadpole like you? Get out!'

Peter stayed where he was, treading water, his face scarlet but stony. She swore at him, using words and threats which heightened the colour in his cheeks. He would not move, he stared past her at a disc of sunlight trembling on a tree trunk.

'Oh, for God's sake!' She turned her back. 'Get out and get your trousers on. Unless you're so modest you want to dress in the water!'

Peter said nothing. He was scrambling up the slippery bank towards his clothes, draped over a branch. She swung round as he stepped into his trousers; with flaming cheeks and a horrible sickness in his stomach, he hauled them up over his wet skin.

She stared at him from between the leaves, and he had a feeling that she was staring right through his body and seeing something beyond.

'There's a man coming to kill me,' she said, and put a leaf aside with terrifying gentleness. 'I can't run any more, I've got to stay here. So have you. He won't lay a finger on me if there's a witness and a chance he'd swing for it...'

He heard; before she did, the thudding of feet on the baked earth. She saw his look, and turned to face the opening in the bushes through which she had come.

Instinctively, Peter crouched out of sight, screwing his shirt into a ball and pressing it against his chest. The man, when he came, was almost as bad as the woman. Almost, but not quite, because he was a man, and although he was frightening, there was not that strange undertow of fascination. He was huge – to Peter it seemed both the man and the woman were mountainous while he had dwindled to something tiny and bloodless like a gnat, and the river was just a brown ditch.

The man stood on the top of the bank staring down at the woman. He had hardly any neck, and he must have weighed about fifteen stone. His little flat head was stuck between his shoulders; there was something of the tortoise about him, the same ponderous air of trouble and defeat, just now opposed by his mood.

People often got angry, and Peter found it amusing to watch, especially if they danced about, like his father. This man was angry, but it wasn't funny. His rage was quite outside him, as the woman's fear had been. It moved his hands for him, as her fear had moved hers. Over and over again they rehearsed an action inspired, not by the brain but by the blood. The fingers were drawn in, the fists thickened until they were bunched solid, and the grip expended on itself.

Peter shivered, he longed to run, but the impotence of nightmare kept him still. Very slowly the man came down the bank. As he passed through a patch of sunlight, his face showed glistening wet, his bushy brows were loaded with the sweat streaming from his forehead.

The woman waited calmly. She had one hand on her hip, and she did not seem to be so frightened now.

'Well,' she said scoldingly, 'you've got yourself into a fine old paddy, haven't you?'

The man came on, his expression unchanging, his hands

rehearsing their action. Then, just before he reached her, she sprang forward, flung her arms round him and put her mouth on his. His hands came up, the thumbs spread wide, and fastened round her neck.

And now, at sight of those two figures, locked together, the dread of the unspeakable was added to Peter's fear. Trembling, he waited for the man's hands to perform what they had practised, to close and crush as they had crushed the air. They stayed where they were, round the woman's neck, almost hidden by the coil of brassy hair. After one convulsive grip, they fell away and just rested there, heavily.

Peter did not relax. He had been staring too hard, the figures of the man and woman dodged in front of his eyes, coloured solid blue and sometimes red. He knew that the worst was yet to come. There was no peace between them, only something violent which this embrace was muffling for a moment.

The woman drew away gently; put up her hands and took the man's loose fingers from her neck.

'Well, then,' she said, smiling, 'what did you do with the knife?'

The man's size was of no account now, his rage had been snuffed out, and all that was left him was an odd, tortoise-like defeat. He looked at his empty hands and touched his pockets.

'You dropped it somewhere, didn't you?' She laughed at him. 'You would! You lose your savings, so you think you'll knife me in case I took them. But then you lose the knife – does it sound sense?' She eyed him, head on one side, like someone considering an awkward child. As he only stood there, looking dazed, she sighed and began to pin up her hair under the green hat. 'I've taken it very well, considering – accusing me of pinching your money and chasing me with a knife! Why, I've never touched a farthing – is it likely when you carry it round with you all the while? You've lost it somewhere. That's you all over.'

She stood there, her plump arms held up, fastening the last strands of hair in place, and she didn't seem to be looking at the man. But Peter could see that she was watching him with sideways glances which didn't go at all with what she was saying. Peter wondered when she would call to him to step out and be a witness. She seemed to have forgotten all about him, and although he was terribly cramped, he dared not move in case he made a sound and reminded her that he was there.

'Yes,' she went on, briskly tightening the belt of her mackintosh, 'that's what's funny about you – the way you lose everything. Though, I must say you did yourself a real good turn when you lost that knife. Others aren't so careless as you – they don't lose the rope they keep for hanging, you know!'

She thought that was a good parting shot, and with hands thrust into her pockets, turned her back on the man and started to clamber along the bank.

'Where are you going?' He asked a question, but there was no question in his tone. Rather was it as if he could not believe even in his defeat until she stated it.

She looked back over her shoulder at him, still standing bewildered by her kiss, almost searching for the fury which had driven him here and then dwindled like vapour. Perhaps she saw something of the troubled tortoise in him, because she laughed.

'Just one more thing you're losing – little me! So long!'

Still laughing, still looking back, she pushed her way through some clumps of purple loosestrife. Her scarlet mackintosh was overlaid with purple flowers, her face, all screwed up with laughter, looked back over the blossoms and then, just as Peter was thinking of making a dash for the open fields, the face seemed to drop out of sight, the red was suddenly blotted out, leaving only purple loosestrife, violently shaken. At the same moment, a scream and a great thudding splash froze Peter's first tentative stirring. The woman had fallen in.

In that moment, the river won back all Peter's esteem and affection. From his hiding place only part of the water was visible, and he dearly wanted to see what was happening. But he was naturally wary, he stayed still, contenting himself with the huge brown ripples brimming on the surface and lapping high up the bank.

After the splash it was very quiet. The man stood there, gaping at the loosestrife expectantly, like someone watching a conjurer's hat. The tall flowers settled back into stillness, there was only the stealthy chink of water as the eddies spread wide.

Peter wondered what the woman was doing. He held his bunched shirt against his mouth to stop himself from shouting. Why didn't the man move? He must be an idiot.

Peter was scornful of him now. If he had only a tiny brain like a pea, then his huge body was all the more ridiculous. It was nasty, too, as the woman's big speckled chest had been nasty – because there was too much of it.

The man trampled slowly into the loosestrife, parting it uncertainly with his hands. Peter followed him, dodging low out of sight.

It was easy to see where the woman had fallen in. Earth on the edge of the bank had powdered under her foot, leaving a scooped hollow. It was just here, by a great clubbed root, half submerged, that Peter took his bearings for his 'performance'. The tunnel lay almost immediately below, it was even possible to dive to it from here because the bank dropped away into deep water.

Mud was still clouding up from the river bed, colouring the water like strong coffee, and the surface was not yet quiet. But there was no sign of the woman except that among the loosestrife lay the odious green hat with its spotted veil. The man picked it up gingerly, as if he expected her to be underneath. He turned it over in his hands, looked wonderingly at the river and then called out 'Eh?'

The sound of his voice startled him, he swung round, staring, and Peter only just had time to crouch out of sight. The woman was having a fine old game. Either she was under water, waiting to bob up and startle the man, or she had swum downstream and climbed out farther along.

When next Peter stretched his neck and looked over the loosestrife, the man had gone to the water's edge and was leaning down, hands on his knees, peering in. Peter would have gone and given him a brisk shove from behind, so wiping out the memory of his first ignoble fear, but the rustling loosestrife would have betrayed him before he got near enough.

The creature went down on his knees, rolled up one sleeve and plunged his arm into the water. It was so unexpectedly deep that he nearly overbalanced, and he muttered in alarm. But he kept on, groping about under water, first with one arm, then the other. Obviously he was searching for the woman, and just as obviously, he wasn't able to swim. That completed his ignominy in Peter's eyes.

After a while the man had an idea. He searched about and found a long stick. With this he was able to prod the steeply shelving earth immediately below the bank. Farther out the water went deeper than the length of the stick. He stood up and, with the dripping stick in his hand, called out 'Eh?'

Once again he was shocked by the loudness of his own voice. He called 'Eh?' twice more, the third time desperately. There was no answer. His face darkened, his lips grew loose and trembling – if he hadn't been a grown man, Peter would have sworn he was on the verge of tears.

He looked at the river for several minutes, then with a sudden movement flung the stick away and charged up the bank, breaking and trampling everything in his way. All at once he was in this violent hurry, and when Peter climbed to the top of the bank and looked after him, he was thudding across the field in the white sunlight.

He had only just realized that the woman must have stolen a march on him, climbed ashore farther downstream, and run home. How could a man be so stupid? There was a boy at school, Girlie Thomas, who was a famous dunce, but he wasn't as slow as that.

Peter watched the man out of sight. He was waiting in case the woman had hidden instead of leaving the river. He was ready to run if she appeared. Standing in the sunlight, he pulled on his shirt, scraping indifferently with his finger nail at the patches of dry mud.

He left the tails hanging outside his trousers for coolness, and wandered round like a Russian boy in a smock.

The heat was changing. It was heavier now, oppressing the lungs instead of burning the skin. And the hills which had been blue all day were a thick vegetable yellow. There was a storm coming.

Peter concluded that the woman must have gone. There were one or two places where she could have climbed out while the man was fishing for her with his stick. The banks were pretty steep – you had to know where to get out, or you'd have no more luck than a frog trying to climb up a glass jar.

Peter walked along the bank looking, out of curiosity, for the spot where the woman had left the river. It would be easy enough to see, the grass would be flattened and the dry brown earth wet from her drenched clothes. He did not care what became of the woman, he hated and feared her, but his was a precise mind and here was an event which was not finished. Until it was complete, he did not know how he would confront it, how he would remember it, or whether it would be an advantage not to remember it at all. Those two had done something to his river, he knew he would need to make so many adjustments in his own mind that finally it could not be the same river. It was not such a hermit, perhaps; in some obscure way it had allied itself with them, and he was mildly surprised, as one who discovers an old and sober friend in some cheap vulgarity.

But it was still better than anybody else's river, the underwater tunnel was still particularly his, and the bony aqueducts and the forests of tenuous weed. He would still want to come, even if he had to treat the river differently.

He frowned with his proprietor's frown, glancing along the bank. There were no signs of anyone having climbed out recently, no wet patches, no draggled grass. Had she gone to the other side? If she had, she must have been easily visible to the man, and besides, the river was narrow enough for Peter to see that the opposite bank was just as dry and untrampled.

Funny. He climbed on to a willow branch overhanging the water and from this vantage point, stared up and down the river. A rat pottered by in the shadows, refusing to quicken its pace when Peter hissed. The water and the gnats were the only other things that moved; leaves and grasses were pinned under the heavy air.

Unwillingly, he went back to the spot where the woman had fallen in. The broken loosestrife was already limp and dark, and there were some flies crawling on the green hat. The water was very deep here, so deep that looking up from the bottom you could only see a pale blur of light far above...

Suddenly he ran and seized up the stick which the man had thrown away. He flung himself down on his knees and poked about in the water. He could never touch bottom with the stick, but he might find if there was anything floating under the surface.

The thought was admitted, his skin grew greenish, a weight dropped and rolled in his stomach. He let the stick fall, knowing that either he would run away now, leaving this horror entrenched for ever in his river, or he would prove for himself that it was non-existent. There was only one way to prove it.

He came up, fighting, from the first wave of dread. Sight of the slow familiar waters made it so ridiculous that he stripped off his shirt and trousers with a fierce grin at his mawkishness.

All the same, he had never felt less like swimming, so he gave himself no chance to baulk at the water's edge. Even as his shirt – flung out behind him – settled on the grass, he dived deep.

When the water closed over him he was immediately reassured and didn't believe any of it. Deep down, nothing was changed, it was green and gnomish, the mud fumed up from his feet and his outstretched hands, the coolness braced his whole body.

The real river, the dim miniature landscape beneath the surface was still the same. There could be no invasion of his province here, he was a fool to think people on the bank above could make any difference. As for the man and woman, he decided as he stroked through the reeds that he cared nothing about them, except that they should never come again; the unfinished event he could finish – when he was sufficiently interested – in his own way.

It was time he went home, but he felt the need of some act which would express his happiness at finding the river his own again. He had not forgotten the purpose of this dive, and now that his dread was groundless, he had every reason to be pleased with himself. As a formal conclusion and to set the seal to his prowess, he decided to go through the underwater tunnel once more.

At the surface he breathed the heavy air and kicked a lacing of foam on the broad waters. Murmurous and still distant, he heard the thunder and wondered how he would feel if that were artillery and a battle on the other side of the hills. He decided to pretend it on the way home, and dived just as the lightning stripped the sky like a blade.

At first Peter thought it had affected his eyes, because he could not see the tunnel until he was nearly on it. The dark church-like entrance appeared and then was unexplicably blotted out. Not until the moment of collision did he understand that there was something between himself and the tunnel.

Under water was no solidity except in touch, but he knew, before his outflung hands confirmed, what it was hovering in front of him. His fingers slid on something soft; his dive carried him violently against a heavy mass. The impact swung it a little away, but then, as he crumpled on the bottom, it bore down on him from above with a dreadful, leisurely motion.

Peter had never fainted, he had never been under sufficient strain. Now, on the river bed, he came so near it that even the green underwater gloom was blacked out. He saw nothing, he scarcely knew what he did. His mind ceased to calculate; it was his body, reacting to physical nausea, swamped and drowning, which made him strike out blindly, seeking to batter and break the web of water. His fist hit something yielding, he turned and hammered it with hands and feet and it gave like pulp. But it swung aside and he was free. Still fighting, still blind, he shot up to the surface.

Above water he heard, as if from some other person, the harsh see-sawing of his own breath. Without respite he struggled to the bank and dragged himself out. Never had the earth felt so brisk and salutary or the daylight so clean. His skin still crawled with the touch of soft and slimy things; he lay panting and shuddering.

It was the thunder which roused him and the glare of lightning. He rubbed himself down with his hands and began to huddle into his clothes. The very dailiness of dressing reassured him more than anything else, and by the time he had tied his shoe laces he was engaged – squeamishly but logically – with the method, instead of being obsessed by the result.

The mystery of how the woman left the river without a trace was solved. She had never left it, she was down at the bottom, out of sight. But drowned people usually floated on the surface. She must be caught up, perhaps by one of the roots probably – Peter coldly conceded it – a foot or an arm was wedged in the vaulting of his tunnel. If that were so, why hadn't she struggled and freed herself? She could have, easily. Once he had wedged his foot under a root – only a sharp twist was needed to loosen it.

He went cautiously to the loosestrife and peered over. There was the clubbed root jutting from the bank. She might have hit her head on that as she fell and been unconscious. Or she might have got her foot or arm so tightly fixed that she couldn't get away, and so she just drowned down there while they watched for her on the bank above.

Peter found that deduction could have a purely cerebral excitement stronger than squeamishness. He so far forgot his diffidence as to push through the loosestrife and stand on the very spot where the woman had last stood. He examined the clubbed root for marks which might bear out his theory. To his disappointment, the dry, horny wood showed no signs of having been struck by anything recently. He went down on his hands and knees to look more closely, and was wishing he had a magnifying glass when he caught sight of the woman's green hat. It still lay there, and flies still crawled on it as if it were something that had been alive and was now dead.

All at once Peter realized what had happened. He scrambled up and stared at the river with loathing. It was knocking away a little earth from the bank, carrying it off, delving deeper into its quiet hermit bed. It had always looked secretive; it still did, only now it had a secret to keep. There would be something else, something strange, to move under water with the reeds and the solid roots, turning, dipping with a slow, waltz-like motion.

Peter ran all the way home, but the storm broke before he was indoors.

At first, Peter thought intermittently about what had happened. He never spoke of it to anyone. There was something shameful about it and, anyway, it was none of his business.

He had the weapon of youth, the power to bury deep that which was more profitably forgotten. In a few days, not only the event but the place of the event – the river – dropped out of his mind for long periods. And the river had been important to him. When he was unable to go and swim there, he had kept it as a retreat, a place of his own, and at rare moments – rare because he was not given to daydreaming – he would summon the memory and use it as a panacea for some grievance or a vehicle for indolence.

He hardly noticed the loss. It was as if he had closed a lid on the river. If by chance it was lifted, he did not remember the brown, soft water, the quiet colour, the jumping beans of sunlight. There came only a pang of alarm, a warning not to invite memory. This he prudently heeded, the lid was replaced on the river and all its associations.

When the woman's body was found, weeks later, local gossip boiled over, and some of Peter's school-fellows went to look at the place by the loosestrife. Peter usually fidgeted when they discussed it, and turned the subject by some violent horseplay. As he had considerable authority among his friends and set for them the fashion of their interests, they soon followed his lead and talked no more about the drowned woman.

It was his parents who really irritated him by their transparent tact. They treated the subject as too extreme to fall within his knowledge or understanding. It confirmed his suspicion that there was nothing but a great deal of wilful mystery in adult affairs.

If the boys had dropped the matter, there were others who had not. Peter was cleaning his bicycle one morning when Girlie Thomas ran up and hung over the garden gate.

'Say, Hume! Heard about the murder?'

Peter looked up with interest. 'What murder?'

'That woman they got out of the river – she was murdered.'

Peter straightened, oily rag in hand. 'Who says?'

'Who?' Girlie Thomas hooted indignantly. 'Everyone knows she was. Anyone could tell that. She was hit on the head and thrown in the river, besides – they've got the man that did it!'

Peter resented hearing news from Girlie Thomas, especially this news. With his thumbnail he began to prise a flint from his tyre and refused to look impressed.

'It was a blacksmith from Mulheath way,' Girlie Thomas went on, his boots scraping the gate panels. 'My pop says he'll swing for it, unless its manslaughter. How many years do they get for manslaughter?'

'Don't know,' said Peter shortly.

Girlie Thomas looked over his glasses. 'You used to go swimming in the river, didn't you, Hume?'

'So what?'

'Well, you might have been there when it happened.'

Peter grunted. 'I never go to the river now. I don't like it. And stop kicking that gate, Thomas. My father doesn't like that gate being kicked.'

'Who'd tell him?'

'I would.'

'Yes, you would, squealer,' agreed Girlie Thomas, and when Peter made a dive at him, ran off, whistling amicably enough.

Peter went back to his bicycle. He stood frowning and spinning the cranks. It was quite true about not liking the river. He didn't. He hadn't been there since the day, and he wouldn't be going again. He preferred to swim in the quarry with the others.

Those two had done something to the river. He couldn't swim there any more, his skin crept at the thought of the brown water, the soft, pulpy mud. And the underwater tunnel – it belonged to the fat woman now.

They thought the man had killed her. That wasn't right, he should have thought anyone would know it wasn't. For a moment he was shocked at adult fallibility. Came again the pang of alarm, the warning not to remember, not to resurrect that pitiful self, shrinking in the lee of a nightmare. It had been ugly and stupid; most of all, it had been shameful in a way he could not understand. There was in it the very substance of those whispers, innuendoes and stories which he heard often at school, which he did not disbelieve, but did not care to verify. It was not his affair and there was no part which he would wish to claim as his.

The lid was replaced, and it was almost as if there had never been any river. Whistling, he wheeled his bicycle into the road. He was going to swim in the quarry.

# Oscar Cook

## *His Beautiful Hands*

I was not grumbling. I had given that up a long while. I was merely contemplating the rain, wondering what a whole dry day would be like. And I came to the conclusion that such a phenomenon was impossible – at least until the forty days of St Swithin were up – that the age of miracles was past. And then, without warning, I shuddered and felt that cold, creepy feeling which premonates a horror spread over me, or rather down me, from my head to my feet.

A presence was drawing near. I realized that immediately, and almost as quickly knew whose that presence must be. It must be Warwick – he being the only living soul capable of awakening such sensibility in me. I turned reluctantly from watching the rain to look at the far end of the club smoking room. Warwick had just entered the door and was approaching.

Before he reached me I had pressed the bell knob in the wall close to my chair. I knew the necessary adjunct to Warwick's presence was inevitable.

He spread himself over a chair, which he drew close to mine, lighted one of his beastly Philippine cigarettes, blew a mouthful of smoke into my face, and, leaning forward with hands on knees, elbows out at right angles, barked out:

'Well!'

For a moment or so I said nothing. I knew that ambiguous monosyllable, half question, half assertion, and the tone in which it was made. A story was coming – and it would not be a pleasant one. While I was still silent, the waiter arrived.

'Two whiskies and soda,' I ordered.

'Doubles,' supplemented Warwick.

I nodded and, looking him squarely in the eyes, paid him in his own coin.

'Well?' I asked, and waited for him to make the next move.

'A yarn,' he said, succinctly and succulently. 'As good as any I've heard for many a day.'

He chuckled. I continued to face him squarely.

'A beastly one,' I slowly asserted, 'judging from your tone.'

He nodded, and at that moment the waiter returned.

Warwick took his glass and I took mine.

'To "His Beautiful Hands",' he toasted. 'They've earned me fifty guineas and so saved my bacon for a few days. Would you like the yarn, or—'

I made a gesture, so non-committal as to mean assent; at least, that is how Warwick read it.

'Listen,' he began, looking round to see that we were alone and drawing his chair still closer to mine. 'It's a tale of revenge and passion—'

'With a capital, purple "P",' I interpolated.

Warwick paid no heed. '...about as sweetly gruesome and gruesomely diabolic as I know.'

He put out the half-smoked cigarette, took a long pull at his whisky and soda, and began.

'Did you see that piece in the paper today about the sculptor johnny who lost his right arm?'

I nodded.

'Well, it's that sort of story, only—'

I put out a hand quickly to interrupt him. If I must hear the story, I'd hear it properly with full names and details, not shorn of its 'curtains' and suspense.

Warwick took the hint.

'I'm going too fast,' he muttered, 'but even now it rather gets me, and... well, it's like this. About two years ago I was in the habit of frequenting a lady barber's – there was a craze for them then; now there are only one or two left – and one of the assistants was head and shoulders – metaphorically speaking – above the other girls for looks and personality. She never had a spare moment. I was one of her regulars, and there was a fellow, a customer, more than twice her age, always hanging around, whom I grew to hate.'

'And he comes into the story?' I asked.

'He *is* the story,' Warwick answered forcefully. 'He and Paulina and his violin.'

'A musician,' I couldn't help saying contemptuously, for, rightly or wrongly, instrumentalists are my *bêtes noires*.

Warwick grunted annoyance at my interruption and continued.

'Well, he was dead nuts on Paulina, and she, to my disgust, played up to him, or so it seemed. He was always bringing her presents, giving her tickets for his concerts, taking her out of evenings, and generally going the whole hog.'

Something in his tone and in the choice and emphasis of his last expression seemed to convey a deeper meaning than just the words.

'You mean...?' I asked, and then broke off, for I hate talking lightly of a woman, even an unknown one.

Warwick has no such scruples.

'Exactly,' he replied. 'She went to be his "keep", although she stayed on at the shop. But of course this establishment was not set up all at once. It evolved, so to speak, out of what appeared quite natural, though unfortunate circumstances.'

Warwick paused to take another drink.

'And the situation annoyed you?' I asked. 'You felt aggrieved, slighted?'

He nodded. 'In a way, yes. I'm no saint, and I'm a bachelor, and Paulina was—'

'Was?' I queried quickly.

For a moment he made no answer. Then, indifferent churchman though he is, he crossed himself.

'She's dead,' he said flatly. 'Died in childbirth, ten days ago. I went to the funeral – a double one – hers and the child's. Thank God it died – and they both died,' he added with a sudden fervour, and then slumped back into the chair and relapsed into a silence as inexplicable as his sudden change from ghoulishly journalistic delight.

I waited. This new mood intrigued me, and I sensed a tragedy more real and personal than Warwick had meant to lay bare. It was obvious that he needed a safety valve.

'Sorry for that display,' he said, when presently he pulled himself up in his chair and smiled. 'It shan't occur again, but I loved her, in spite of the fact that five generations ago a coloured strain got introduced to the family. It was that, of course, which... but I go too fast.'

I offered him a cigarette.

'A story is easier to follow,' I suggested, 'if it begins at the beginning and not half way through. So far, all you've really told me is that there's a musician and Paulina and his violin. And you mentioned one more thing, or rather two, "His beautiful hands". How do they come in?'

Warwick laughed, an ungodly sound.

'They don't,' he said at length, 'they don't. That's the cream of the story, the point of the – ' He started to laugh again, and pulled up short.

'I'm off colour tonight,' he muttered, 'but it's like this. This Mr A. – we'll call him that – was a celebrated violinist, and apart from realizing the value of his hands he was inordinately vain of them. They were his passion. But I couldn't stand them. They weren't a man's hands, and they weren't a woman's. They were... were—'

'Ethereal,' I suggested.

Warwick's hand suddenly gripped my arm tightly, and his face came close to mine.

'The very word,' he said. 'Ethereal. And it was one of Paulina's jobs to take care of them, tend them, worship them; for that is what he demanded of her – worship of his hands.'

I nodded.

'She was a wonderful manicurist, with a cool, soothing touch that somehow seemed to linger on your fingers long after the treatment was over and urge you back to her, till you were conscious of a semi-physical, semi-spiritual longing. All of us customers experienced that feeling. And the curious thing is that it wasn't sexual or sensuous but just caressing.'

Warwick paused and looked at me with, for him, a curiously appealing glance, as much as to say: 'You *do* understand, don't you?'

I nodded. 'The touch of the East,' I said gently. 'I suppose your Paulina had Javanese blood?'

Warwick smiled his thanks. 'You're right,' he went on. 'And it was really on account of that – taint – that the trouble arose. They're revengeful, the Javanese; they never forget an injury to themselves or to those they love. Though they're all fire – and Paulina was passionate – they're capable of slow smouldering, like a station waiting-room fire.'

Again Warwick paused, and I begin to think we never should get to the story. I looked at my watch. The time was 6.30 pm. In a quarter of an hour I should have to go and dress – I was dining out. I leant across to him.

'So far,' I said, 'you've really told me little – hardly enough to make me even a trifle curious. Of course, if you'd rather not... I'll respect your wish... on the other hand—'

That was enough. I had touched him on the journalistic raw.

'Wait,' he almost barked at me. 'Wait. It's a short story, but... Well, one day, just a year ago, Mr A. came into the establishment with the little finger of his left hand bound up. Of course, Paulina had to be in attendance. I'd just been finished, and stayed on to have a cup of tea. Naturally, I could not help hearing their conversation – mostly about the finger. The nail had become discoloured, and all round the cuticle was puffy and sore. Mr A. could hardly bear to let Paulina touch it, yet he longed for the caress of her massage.

'She suggested a doctor, but he would not hear of that. She and she only must look after his hands. We could all understand that in general, but not in this case, when medical advice was sorely and obviously needed. He was adamant, infatuated beyond belief.

'A week later he was back. The finger was worse, much worse, and the third finger was beginning to become affected!'

'And he was still adamant?' I could not help putting the question, for I was rapidly beginning to put two and two together and making four.

'Yes, and so it went on till all the fingers of both hands were in varying stages of affectedness. It was horrible – I say – bloody. Day after day he would come in with his filthy, bandaged hands; undo his bandages, expose his rotting fingers, and talk about them till we customers and the other girls were utterly sick.'

'You had your remedy,' I interrupted. 'Even if the girls hadn't.'

Warwick looked at me pityingly. 'That's just what we hadn't got.' He spoke in a most matter-of-fact way. 'Something held us, drew us. Of course, the proprietress was doing a roaring trade, but we didn't care. We sensed something; what, we did not know, but we meant to be in at the death.'

'And Paulina?'

'Was her usual sweet self, controlled, gentle, amusing, sympathetic, efficient. Without a flinch, at least an outward blench, she attended to the ghastly sights; passed from Mr A., to whom she was all kindness, to other customers. So matters went on till one day, just after Mr A. had gone out, one of the girls was crossing the room and slipped on something on the floor. It rolled under her feet. She thought it was a pencil, and stooped to pick it up. Then an awful scream rang through the room and she fell down in a faint. We rushed to her; by her side, where it had fallen from her grasp, was the middle, rotting finger of a man's hand.'

'Severed?' I gasped, gripped at last.

Warwick shook his head. For a moment or so he could not speak.

'No,' he managed at last. 'No. It had just rotted off – and the stink as one touched it was enough to... to – ' He put his hand to his nose and shivered all over.

By a freak of the weather the rain had ceased, and the evening light flooded through the smoking-room window. It brought us back towards normal.

Warwick shook himself.

'Do you want the rest?' he asked.

'I've just time,' I said, looking at my watch.

Warwick drained his glass.

'We picked up the girl and carried her out, leaving for the moment only Paulina in the room. I was the first to return. As I entered, she quickly put her hands behind her back, but she had not been quick enough, for I distinctly saw that she was holding the rotting finger.

'I went up to her and put a hand on her shoulder, horror-struck though I was.

'"Paulina," I cried. "Tell me truly ... in spite of ... of ... you love him?"

'Her immediate answer was to laugh hysterically. Then she held out her hand on which lay the filthy, rotting finger.

'"Could you love *that*?" she asked.

'I couldn't answer, but my whole face expressed volumes.

'"Then why insult me?" she spoke very bitterly. "That's what I think of him... and all men... fit for the scrap-heap," and as she spoke she carelessly flung the horror into the wastepaper basket. It fell with hardly any thud, but the fall sent up a cloud of stenchful vapour. Paulina seemed not to notice it. "I only wish..." she began, then stopped as the others came back.

'That was the beginning of the end. Paulina gave notice – the proprietress would not dissuade her – and consequently Mr A. gave up coming. The last time he came he showed us both hands, devoid of fingers and thumbs... and all the time he raved of Paulina.'

'And you – kept up with her, married her – the dead child was yours?' I put the question very gently.

Warwick spread out his hands.

'You'd think so,' he said, a trifle grimly. 'And it should be so, according to the best novels, but you'd be wrong. No. I lost sight of her, too, till just before the end she sent for me and told me all.'

'In confidence?'

He shook his head.

'Not necessarily, but I must get it off my chest, and I'd like you to know. Can't you guess?'

I did not try, and he went on.

'Mr A. was her father. Eighteen years before he had seduced and left her mother. There's no need to say more. This was Paulina's revenge. She'd nursed it for years – remember her Javanese strain.'

'You mean...?' I gasped, in spite of myself.

'Exactly. She used a native poison... a secret from her ancestors on that side – now dead with her. She planned the whole thing. And to help her attract him and others – myself included – she doped our tea and coffee with a filthy, horrible concoction brewed from – no, I can't even mention that to you.'

The rain was falling again. Gloom once more pervaded the room. My thoughts jumped to the funeral.

'And the baby?' I asked.

'Was Mr A.'s too,' Warwick answered with a return to his ghoulishly journalistic appreciation of a dramatic point. 'Paulina didn't get up early enough, as the saying is, quite to get top-side of him. Just before she'd decided to apply the poison trick through his nails, he'd got her drunk one night and... well, you can guess the rest. That settled the matter of her living with him. Talk of poetic justice... Ye gods! I've never heard of such a case. Him with rotting fingers, dying by inches – there's no cure – the poison's in his blood. Paulina, as good as a murderess, dying in childbed – and her baby stillborn – born with no fingers – nor toes – hardly hands and feet – just red, puffy lumps of flesh, not even webbed.'

He pulled out a cigarette case, lighted a cigarette, and put the case back.

'I'll have another whisky and soda – double,' he said, 'and then I'll toddle along to the dogs…'

# George Fielding Eliot

# *The Copper Bowl*

Yuan Li, the mandarin, leaned back in his rosewood chair.

'It is written,' he said softly, 'that a good servant is a gift of the gods, whilst a bad one…'

The tall, powerfully built man standing humbly before the robed figure in the chair bowed thrice, hastily, submissively.

Fear glinted in his eye, though he was armed, and, moreover, was accounted a brave soldier. He could have broken the little smooth-faced mandarin across his knee, and yet—

'Ten thousand pardons, beneficent one,' he said. 'I have done all – having regard to your honourable order to slay the man not nor do him permanent injury – I have done all that I can. But—'

'But he speaks not!' murmured the mandarin. 'And you come to me with a tale of failure? I do not like failures, Captain Wang!'

The mandarin toyed with a little paper knife on the low table beside him. Wang shuddered.

'Well, no matter for this time,' the mandarin said after a moment, Wang breathed a sigh of most heartfelt relief, and the mandarin smiled softly, fleetingly. 'Still,' he went on, 'our task is yet to be accomplished. We have the man – he has the information we require; surely some way may be found. The servant has failed; now the master must try his hand. Bring the man to me.'

Wang bowed low and departed with considerable haste.

The mandarin sat silent for a moment, looking across the wide, sunlit room at a pair of singing birds in a wicker cage hanging in the farther window. Presently he nodded – one short, satisfied nod – and struck a little silver bell which stood on his beautifully inlaid table.

Instantly a white-robed, silent-footed servant entered, and stood with bowed head awaiting his master's pleasure. To him Yuan Li gave certain swift, incisive orders.

The white-robed one had scarcely departed when Wang, captain of the mandarin's guard, re-entered the spacious apartment.

'The prisoner, benevolent!' he announced.

The mandarin made a slight motion with his slender hand; Wang barked an order, and there entered, between two heavily muscled, half-naked guardsmen, a short, sturdily built man, barefooted, clad only in a tattered shirt and khaki trousers, but with fearless blue eyes looking straight at Yuan Li under the tousled masses of his blond hair.

A white man!

'Ah!' said Yuan Li, in his calm way, speaking faultless French. 'The excellent Lieutenant Fournet! Still obstinate?'

Fournet cursed him earnestly, in French and three different Chinese dialects.

'You'll pay for this, Yuan Li!' he wound up. 'Don't think your filthy brutes can try the knuckle torture and their other devil's tricks on a French officer and get away with it!'

Yuan Li toyed with his paper knife, smiling.

'You threaten me, Lieutenant Fournet,' he answered, 'yet your threats are but as rose petals wafted away on the morning breeze – unless you return to your post to make your report.'

'Why, damn you!' answered the prisoner. 'You needn't try that sort of thing – you know better than to kill me! My commandant is perfectly aware of my movements – he'll be knocking on your door with a company of the Legion at his back if I don't show up by tomorrow at reveille!'

Yuan Li smiled again.

'Doubtless – and yet we still have the better part of the day before us,' he said. "Much may be accomplished in an afternoon and evening.'

Fournet swore again.

'You can torture me and be damned,' he answered. 'I know and you know that you don't dare to kill me or to injure me so that I can't get back to Fort Deschamps. For the rest, do your worst, you yellow-skinned brute!'

'A challenge!' the mandarin exclaimed. 'And I, Lieutenant Fournet, pick up your glove! Look you – what I require from you is the strength and location of your outpost on the Mephong river. So—'

'So that your cursed bandits, whose murders and lootings keep you here in luxury, can rush the outpost some dark night and open the river route for their boats,' Fournet cut in. 'I know you, Yuan Li, and I know your trade – mandarin of thieves! The military governor of Tonkin sent a battalion of the Foreign Legion here to deal with such as you, and to restore peace and order on the frontier, not to yield to childish threats! That is not the Legion's way, and you should know it. The best thing you can do is to send in your submission, or I can assure you that within a fortnight your head will be rotting over the North Gate of Hanoi, as a warning to others who might follow your bad example.'

The mandarin's smile never altered, though well he knew that this was no idle threat. With Tonkinese tirailleurs, even with Colonial infantry, he could make some sort of headway, but these thrice-accursed Legionnaires were devils from the very pit itself. He – Yuan Li, who had ruled as king in the valley of the Mephong, to whom half a Chinese province and many a square mile of French Tonkin had paid tribute humbly – felt his throne of power tottering beneath him. But one hope remained: down the river, beyond the French outposts, were boats filled with men and with the loot of a dozen villages – the most successful raiding party he had ever sent out. Let these boats come through, let him have back his men (and they were his best), get his hands on the loot, and perhaps something might be done. Gold, jewels, jade – and, though the soldiers of France were terrible, there were in Hanoi certain civilian officials not wholly indifferent to these things. But on the banks of the Mephong, as though they knew his hopes, the Foreign Legion had established an outpost – he must know exactly where, he must know exactly how strong; for till this river post was gone the boats could never reach him.

And now Lieutenant Fournet, staff officer to the commandant, had fallen into his hands. All night his torturers had reasoned with the stubborn young Norman, and all morning they had never left him for a minute. They had marked him in no way, nor broken bones, nor so much as cut or bruised the skin – yet there are ways! Fournet shuddered all over at the thought of what he had gone through, that age-long night and morning.

To Fournet, his duty came first: to Yuan Li, it was life or death that Fournet should speak. And he had taken measures which now marched to their fulfilment.

He dared not go to extremes with Fournet; nor yet could French justice connect the Mandarin Yuan Li with the bandits of the Mephong.

They might suspect, but they could not prove; and an outrage such as the killing or maiming of a French officer in his own palace was more than Yuan Li dared essay. He walked on thin ice indeed those summer days, and walked warily.

Yet – he had taken measures.

'My head is still securely on my shoulders,' he replied to Fournet. 'I do not think it will decorate your gate spikes. So you will not speak?'

'Certainly not!'

Lieutenant Fournet's words were as firm as his jaw.

'Ah, but you will. Wang!'

'Magnanimous!'

'Four more guards. Make the prisoner secure.' Wang clapped his hands.

Instantly four additional half-naked men sprang into the room; two, falling on their knees, seized Fournet round the legs; another threw his corded arms round the lieutenant's waist; another stood by, club in hand, as reserve in case of – what?

The two original guards still retained their grip on Fournet's arms.

Now, in the grip of those sinewy hands, he was held immovable, utterly helpless, a living statue.

Yuan Li, the mandarin, smiled again. One who did not know him would have thought his smile held an infinite tenderness, a divine compassion.

He touched the bell at his side.

Instantly, in the farther doorway, appeared two servants, conducting a veiled figure – a woman, shrouded in a dark drapery.

A word from Yuan Li – rough hands tore the veil aside, and there stood drooping between the impassive servants a vision of loveliness, a girl scarce out of her teens, dark-haired, slender, with the great appealing brown eyes of a fawn – eyes which widened suddenly as they rested on Lieutenant Fournet.

'Lily!' exclaimed Fournet, and his five guards had their hands full to hold him as he struggled to be free.

'You fiend!' he spat at Yuan Li. 'If a hair of this girl's head is touched, by the Holy Virgin of Yvetot I will roast you alive in the flames of your own palace! My God, Lily, how—'

'Quite simply, my dear lieutenant,' the mandarin's silky voice interrupted. 'We knew, of course – every house-servant in North Tonkin is a spy of mine – that you had conceived an affection for this woman; and when I heard you were proving obdurate under the little attentions of my men, I thought it well to send for her. Her father's bungalow is far from the post – indeed, it is in Chinese and not French territory, as you know – and the task was not a difficult one. And now—'

'André! André!' the girl was crying, struggling in her turn with the servants. 'Save me, André – these beasts—'

'Have no fear, Lily,' André Fournet replied. 'They dare not harm you, any more than they dare to kill me. They are bluffing—'

'But have you considered well, Lieutenant?' asked the mandarin gently. 'You, of course, are a French officer. The arm of France – and it is a long and unforgiving arm – will be stretched out to seize your murderers. The gods forbid I should set that arm reaching for me and mine. But this girl – ah, that is different!'

'Different? How is it different? The girl is a French citizen—'

'I think not, my good Lieutenant Fournet. She is three-quarters French in blood, true; but her father is half Chinese, and is a Chinese subject; she is a resident of China – I think you will find that French justice will not be prepared to avenge her death quite so readily as your own. At any rate, it is a chance I am prepared to take.'

Fournet's blood seemed to turn to ice in his veins. The smiling devil was right! Lily – his lovely white Lily, whose only mark of Oriental blood was the rather piquant slant of her great eyes – was not entitled to the protection of the tricolour.

God! What a position! Either betray his flag, his regiment, betray his comrades to their deaths – or see his Lily butchered before his eyes!

'So now, Lieutenant Fournet, we understand each other,' Yuan Li continued after a brief pause to let the full horror of the situation grip the other's soul. 'I think you will be able to remember the location and strength of that outpost for me – now?'

Fournet stared at the man in bitter silence, but the words had given the quick-minded Lily a key to the situation, which she had hardly understood at first.

'No, no, André!' she cried. 'Do not tell him. Better that I should die than that you should be a traitor! See – I am ready.'

Fournet threw back his head: his wavering resolution reincarnate.

'The girl shames me!' he said. 'Slay her if you must, Yuan Li – and if France will not avenge her, *I will!* But traitor I will not be!'

'I do not think that is your last word, Lieutenant,' the mandarin purred. 'Were I to strangle the girl, yes – perhaps. But first she must cry to you for help, and when you hear her screaming in agony, the woman you love, perhaps then you will forget these noble heroics!'

Again he clapped his hands, and again silent servants glided into the room. One bore a small brazier of glowing charcoal; a second had a little cage of thick wire mesh, inside of which something moved horribly; a third bore a copper bowl with handles on each side, to which was attached a steel band that glittered in the sunlight.

The hair rose on the back of Fournet's neck. What horror impended now? Deep within him some instinct warned him that what was now to follow would be fiendish beyond the mind of mortal man to conceive. The mandarin's eyes seemed suddenly to glow with infernal fires. Was he in truth man – or demon?

A sharp word in some Yunnan dialect unknown to Fournet – and the servants had flung the girl upon her back on the floor, spread-eagled in pitiful helplessness, upon a magnificent peacock rug.

Another word from the mandarin's thin lips – and roughly they tore the clothing from the upper half of the girl's body. White and silent she lay upon that splendid rug, her eyes still on Fournet's: silent, lest words of hers should impair the resolution of the man she loved.

Fournet struggled furiously with his guards: but they were five strong men, and they held him fast.

'Remember, Yuan Li!' he panted. 'You'll pay! – damn your yellow soul—!'

The mandarin ignored the threat.

'Proceed,' he said to the servants. 'Note carefully, Monsieur le Lieutenant Fournet, what we are doing. First, you will note, the girl's wrists and ankles are lashed to posts and to heavy articles of furniture, suitably placed so that she cannot move. You wonder at the strength of the rope, the number of turns we take to hold so frail a girl? I assure you, they will be required. Under the copper bowl, I have seen a feeble old man tear his wrist free from an iron chain.'

The mandarin paused; the girl was now bound so tightly that she could scarce move a muscle of her body.

Yuan Li regarded the arrangements.

'Well done,' he approved. 'Yet if she tears any limb free, the man who bound that limb shall have an hour under the bamboo rods. Now – the bowl! Let me see it.'

He held out a slender hand. Respectfully a servant handed him the bowl, with its dangling band of flexible steel. Fournet, watching with eyes full of dread, saw that the band was fitted with a lock, adjustable to various positions. It was like a belt, a girdle.

'Very well,' the mandarin nodded, turning the thing over and over in fingers that almost seemed to caress it. 'But I anticipate – perhaps the Lieutenant and the young lady are not familiar with this little device. Let me explain, or, rather, demonstrate. Put the bowl in place, Kan-su. No, no – just the bowl, this time.'

Another servant, who had started forward, stepped back into his corner. The man addressed as Kan-su took the bowl, knelt at the side of the girl, passed the steel band under her body and placed the bowl, bottom up, on her naked abdomen, tugging at the girdle till the rim of the bowl bit into the soft flesh. Then he snapped the lock fast, holding the bowl thus firmly in place by the locked steel belt attached to its two handles and passing round the girl's waist. He rose, stood silent with folded arms.

Fournet felt his flesh crawling with horror – and all this time Lily had said not one word, though the tight girdle, the pressure of the circular rim of the bowl, must have been hurting her cruelly.

But now she spoke, bravely.

'Do not give way, André,' she said. 'I can bear it – it does – it does not hurt!'

'God!' yelled André Fournet, still fighting vainly against those clutching yellow hands.

'It does not hurt!' the mandarin echoed the girl's last words. 'Well, perhaps not. But we will take it off, notwithstanding. We must be merciful.'

At his order the servant removed bowl and girdle. An angry red circle showed on the white skin of the girl's abdomen where the rim had rested.

'And still I do not think you understand, mademoiselle and monsieur,' he went on. 'For presently we must apply the bowl again – and when we do, under it we will put – *this*!'

With a swift movement of his arm he snatched from the servant in the corner the wire cage and held it up to the sunlight.

The eyes of Fournet and Lily fixed themselves upon it in horror. For within, plainly seen now, moved a great grey rat – a whiskered, beady-eyed, restless, scabrous rat, its white chisel-teeth shining through the mesh.

'*Dieu de Dieu!*' breathed Fournet. His mind refused utterly to grasp the full import of the dreadful fate that was to be Lily's; he could only stare at the unquiet rat – stare – stare—

'You understand *now*, I am sure,' purred the mandarin. 'The rat under the bowl – observe the bottom of the bowl, note the little flange. Here we put the hot charcoal – the copper becomes heated – the heat is overpowering – the rat cannot support it – he has but one means of escape: he gnaws his way through the lady's body! And now about that outpost, Lieutenant Fournet?'

'No – *no* – *No!*' cried Lily. 'They will not do it – they are trying to frighten us – they are human; men cannot do a thing like that – be silent, André, be silent, whatever happens; don't let them beat you! Don't let them make a traitor of you! Ah—!'

At a wave from the mandarin the servant with the bowl again approached the half-naked girl. But this time the man with the cage stepped forward also. Deftly he thrust in a hand, avoided the rat's teeth, jerked the struggling vermin out by the scruff of the neck.

The bowl was placed in position. Fournet fought desperately for freedom – if only he could get one arm clear, snatch a weapon of some sort!

Lily gave a sudden little choking cry.

The rat had been thrust under the bowl.

Click! The steel girdle was made fast – and now they were piling the red-hot charcoal on the upturned bottom of the bowl, while Lily writhed in her bonds as she felt the wriggling, pattering horror of the rat on her bare skin, under that bowl of fiends.

One of the servants handed a tiny object to the impassive mandarin.

Yuan Li held it up in one hand.

It was a little key.

'This key, Lieutenant Fournet,' he said, 'unlocks the steel girdle which holds the bowl in place. It is yours – as a reward for the information I require – Will you not be reasonable? Soon it will be too late!'

Fournet looked at Lily. The girl was quiet now, had ceased to struggle; her eyes were open, or he would have thought she had fainted.

The charcoal glowed redly on the bottom of the copper bowl. And beneath its carven surface Fournet could imagine the great grey rat stirring restlessly, turning round and round, seeking escape from the growing heat, at last sinking his teeth in that soft white skin, gnawing, burrowing desperately...

God!

His duty – his flag – his regiment – France! Young Sous-lieutenant Pierre Desjardins – gay young Pierre, and twenty men – to be surprised and massacred, horribly, some saved for the torture, by an overwhelming rush of bandit devils, through his treachery? He knew in his heart that he could not do it.

He must be strong – he must be firm...

If only he might suffer for Lily – gentle, loving little Lily, brave little Lily, who had never harmed a soul...

Loud and clear through the room rang a terrible scream.

André, turning in fascinated horror, saw that Lily's body, straining upwards in an arc from the rug, was all but tearing asunder the bonds which held it. He saw, what he had not before noticed, that a little nick had been broken from one edge of the bowl – and through this nick and across the white surface of the girl's heaving body was running a tiny trickle of blood!

The rat was at work.

Then something snapped in André's brain. He went mad.

With the strength that is given to madmen, he tore loose his right arm from the grip that held it – tore loose, and dashed his fist into the face of the guard. The man with the club sprang forward unwarily; the next moment André had the weapon, and was laying about him with berserk fury. Three guards were down before Wang drew his sword and leaped into the fray.

Wang was a capable and well-trained soldier. It was cut, thrust, and parry for a moment, steel against wood – then Wang, borne back before that terrible rush, had the reward of his strategy.

The two remaining guards, to whom he had signalled, and a couple of servants flung themselves together on Fournet's back and bore him, roaring, to the floor.

The girl screamed again, shattering the coarser sounds of battle.

Fournet heard her – even in his madness he heard her. And as he heard, a knife hilt in a servant's girdle met his hand. He caught at it, thrust upward savagely; a man howled; the weight on Fournet's back grew less; blood gushed over his neck and shoulders. He thrust again, rolled clear of the press, and saw one man sobbing out his life from a ripped-open throat, while another, with both hands clasped over his groin, writhed in silent agony upon the floor.

André Fournet, gathering a knee under him, sprang like a panther straight at the throat of Wang the captain.

Down the two men went, rolling over and over on the floor. Wang's weapons clashed and clattered – a knife rose, dripping blood, and plunged home...

With a shout of triumph André Fournet sprang to his feet, his terrible knife in one hand, Wang's sword in the other.

Screaming, the remaining servants fled before that awful figure.

Alone, Yuan Li the mandarin faced incarnate vengeance.

'The key!'

Hoarsely Fournet spat out his demand; his reeling brain had room for but one thought: 'The key, you yellow demon!'

Yuan Li took a step backwards into the embrasured window, through which the jasmine-scented afternoon breeze still floated sweetly.

The palace was built on the edge of a cliff; below that window ledge, the precipice fell sheer fifty feet down to the rocks and shallows of the upper Mephong.

Yuan Li smiled once more, his calm unruffled.

'You have beaten me, Fournet,' he said, 'yet I have beaten you, too. I wish you joy of your victory. Here is the key.' He held it up in his hand; and as André sprang forward with a shout, Yuan Li turned, took one step to the window ledge, and without another word was gone into space, taking the key with him.

Far below he crashed in red horror on the rocks, and the waters of the turbulent Mephong closed for ever over the key to the copper bowl.

Back sprang André – back to Lily's side. The blood ran no more from under the edge of the bowl; Lily lay very still, very cold…

God! She was dead!

Her heart was silent in her tortured breast.

André tore vainly at the bowl, the steel girdle – tore with bleeding fingers, with broken teeth, madly – in vain.

He could not move them.

And Lily was dead.

Or was she? What was that?

In her side a pulse beat – beat strongly and more strongly…

Was there still hope?

The mad Fournet began chafing her body and arms.

Could he revive her? Surely she was not dead – could not be dead!

The pulse still beat – strange it beat only in one place, on her soft white side, down under her last rib—

He kissed her cold and unresponsive lips.

When he raised his head the pulse had ceased to beat. Where it had been, blood was flowing sluggishly – dark venous blood, flowing in purple horror.

And from the midst of it, out of the girl's side, the grey, pointed head of the rat was thrust, its muzzle dripping gore, its black eyes glittering beadily at the madman who gibbered and frothed above it.

So, an hour later, his comrades found André Fournet and Lily his beloved – the tortured maniac keening over the tortured dead.

But the grey rat they never found.

# Jack Finney

## Contents of the Dead Man's Pocket

At the little living-room desk Tom Benecke rolled two sheets of flimsy and a heavier top sheet, carbon paper sandwiched between them, into his portable. *Inter-office Memo*, the top sheet was headed, and he typed tomorrow's date just below this; then he glanced at a creased yellow sheet, covered with his own handwriting, beside the typewriter. 'Hot in here,' he muttered to himself. Then from the short hallway at his back he heard the muffled clang of wire coat hangers in the bedroom closet, and at this reminder of what his wife was doing he thought: Hot, hell – guilty conscience.

He got up, shoving his hands into the back pockets of his grey wash slacks, stepped to the living-room window beside the desk and stood breathing on the glass, watching the expanding circlet of mist, staring down through the autumn night at Lexington Avenue, eleven storeys below. He was a tall, lean, dark-haired young man in a pullover sweater, who looked as though he had played not football, probably, but basketball in college. Now he placed the heels of his hands against the top edge of the lower window frame and shoved upwards. But as usual the window didn't budge, and he had to lower his hands and then shoot them hard upwards to jolt the window open a few inches. He dusted his hands, muttering.

But still he didn't begin his work. He crossed the room to the hallway entrance and, leaning against the door jamb, hands shoved into his back pockets again, he called, 'Clare?' When his wife answered, he said, 'Sure you don't mind going alone?'

'No.' Her voice was muffled, and he knew her head and shoulders were in the bedroom closet. Then the tap of her high heels sounded on the wood floor, and she appeared at the end of the little hallway, wearing a slip, both hands raised to one ear, clipping on an earring. She smiled at him – a slender, very pretty girl with light brown, almost blonde, hair – her prettiness emphasized by the pleasant nature that showed in her face. 'It's just that I hate you to miss this movie; you wanted to see it, too.'

'Yeah, I know.' He ran his fingers through his hair. 'Got to get this done, though.'

She nodded, accepting this. Then, glancing at the desk across the living room, she said, 'You work too much, though, Tom – and too hard.'

He smiled. 'You won't mind, though, will you, when the money comes rolling in and I'm known as the Boy Wizard of Wholesale Groceries?'

'I guess not.' She smiled and turned back towards the bedroom.

At his desk again, Tom lighted a cigarette; then a few moments later as Clare appeared, dressed and ready to leave, he set it on the rim of the ashtray. 'Just after seven,' she said. 'I can make the beginning of the first feature.'

He walked to the front-door closet to help her on with her coat. He kissed her then and, for an instant, holding her close, smelling the perfume she had used, he was tempted to go with her; it was not actually true that he had to work tonight, though he very much wanted to. This was his own project, unannounced as yet in his office, and it could be postponed. But then they won't see it till Monday, he thought once again, and if I give it to the boss tomorrow he might read it over the weekend... 'Have a good time,' he said aloud. He gave his wife a little swat and opened the door for her, feeling the air from the building hallway, smelling faintly of floor wax, stream gently past his face.

He watched her walk down the hall, flicked a hand in response as she waved, and then he started to close the door, but it resisted for a moment. As the door opening narrowed, the current of warm air from the hallway, channelled through this smaller opening now, suddenly rushed past him with accelerated force. Behind him he heard the slap of the window curtains against the wall and the sound of paper fluttering from his desk, and he had to push to close the door.

Turning, he saw a sheet of white paper drifting to the floor in a series of arcs, and another sheet, yellow, moving towards the window, caught in the dying current flowing through the narrow opening. As he watched, the paper struck the bottom edge of the window and hung there for an instant, plastered against the glass and wood. Then as the moving air stilled completely, the curtains swinging back from the wall to hang free again, he saw the yellow sheet drop to the window ledge and slide over out of sight.

He ran across the room, grasped the bottom of the window and tugged, staring through the glass. He saw the yellow sheet, dimly now in the darkness outside, lying on the ornamental ledge a yard below the window. Even as he watched, it was moving, scraping slowly along the ledge, pushed by the breeze that pressed steadily against the building wall. He heaved on the window with all his strength, and it shot open with a bang, the window weight rattling in the casing. But the paper was past his reach and, leaning out into the night, he watched it scud steadily along the ledge to the south, half plastered against the building wall. Above the muffled sound of the street traffic far below, he could hear the dry scrape of its movement, like a leaf on the pavement.

The living room of the next apartment to the south projected a yard or more farther out towards the street than this one; because of this the Beneckes paid seven and a half dollars less rent than their neighbours. And now the yellow sheet, sliding along the stone ledge, nearly invisible in the night, was stopped by the projecting blank wall of the next apartment. It lay motionless then, in the corner formed by the two walls a good five yards away, pressed firmly against the ornate corner ornament of the ledge by the breeze that moved past Tom Benecke's face.

He knelt at the window and stared at the yellow paper for a full minute or more, waiting for it to move, to slide off the ledge and fall, hoping he could follow its course to the street, and then hurry down in the elevator and retrieve it. But it didn't move, and then he saw that the paper was caught firmly between a projection of the convoluted corner ornament and the ledge. He thought about the poker from the fireplace, then the broom, then the mop – discarding each thought as it occurred to him. There was nothing in the apartment long enough to reach that paper.

It was hard for him to understand that he actually had to abandon it – it was ridiculous – and he began to curse. Of all the papers on his desk, why did it have to be this one in particular! On four long Saturday afternoons he had stood in supermarkets, counting the people who passed certain displays, and the results were scribbled on that yellow sheet. From stacks of trade publications, gone over page by page in snatched half hours at work and during evenings at home, he had copied facts, quotations, and figures on to that sheet. And he had carried it with him to the Public Library on Fifth Avenue, where he'd spent a dozen lunch hours and early evenings adding more. All were needed to support and lend authority to his idea for a new grocery-store display method; without them his idea was a mere opinion. And there they all lay, in his own improvised shorthand – countless hours of work – out there on the ledge.

For many seconds he believed he was going to abandon the yellow sheet, that there was nothing else to do. The work could be duplicated. But it would take two months, and the time to present this idea, damn it, was *now*, for use in the spring displays. He struck his fist on the window ledge. Then he shrugged. Even though his plan was adopted, he told himself, it wouldn't bring him a raise in pay – not immediately, anyway, or as a direct result. It won't bring me a promotion either, he argued – not of itself.

But just the same, and he couldn't escape the thought, this and other independent projects, some already done and others planned for the future, would gradually mark him out from the score of other young men in his company. They were the way to change from a name on the payroll to a name in the minds of the company officials. They were the beginning of the long, long climb to where he was determined to be – at the very top. And he knew he was going out there in the darkness, after the yellow sheet fifteen feet beyond his reach.

By a kind of instinct, he instantly began making his intention acceptable to himself by laughing at it. The mental picture of himself sidling along the ledge outside was absurd – it was actually comical – and he smiled. He imagined himself describing it; it would make a good story at the office and, it occurred to him, would add a special interest and importance to his memorandum, which would do it no harm at all.

To simply go out and get his paper was an easy task – he could be back here with it in less than two minutes – and he knew he wasn't deceiving himself. The ledge, he saw, measuring it with his eye, was about as wide as the length of his shoe, and perfectly flat. And every fifth row of brick in the face of the building, he remembered – leaning out, he verified this – was indented half an inch, enough for the tips of his fingers, enough to maintain balance easily. It occurred to him that if this ledge and wall were only a yard above ground – as he knelt at the window staring out, this thought was the final confirmation of his intention – he could move along the ledge indefinitely.

On a sudden impulse, he got to his feet, walked to the front closet and took out an old tweed jacket; it would be cold outside. He put it on and buttoned it as he crossed the room rapidly towards the open window. In the back of his mind he knew he'd better hurry and get this over with before he thought too much, and at the window he didn't allow himself to hesitate.

He swung a leg over the sill, then felt for and found the ledge a yard below the window with his foot. Gripping the bottom of the window frame very tightly and carefully, he slowly ducked his head under it, feeling on his face the sudden change from the warm air of the room to the chill outside. With infinite care he brought out his other leg, his mind concentrating on what he was doing. Then he slowly stood erect. Most of the putty, dried out and brittle, had dropped off the bottom edging of the window frame, he found, and the flat wooden edging provided a good gripping surface, a half inch or more deep, for the tips of his fingers.

Now, balanced easily and firmly, he stood on the ledge outside in the slight, chill breeze, eleven storeys above the street, staring into his own lighted apartment, odd and different-seeming now.

First his right hand, then his left, he carefully shifted his finger-tip grip from the puttyless window edging to an indented row of bricks directly to his right. It was hard to take the first shuffling sideways step then – to make himself move – and the fear stirred in his stomach, but he did it, again by not allowing himself time to think. And now – with his chest, stomach, and the left side of his face pressed against the rough cold brick – his lighted apartment was suddenly gone, and it was much darker out here than he had thought.

Without pause he continued – right foot, left foot, right foot, left – his shoe soles shuffling and scraping along the rough stone, never lifting from it, fingers sliding along the exposed edging of brick. He moved on the balls of his feet, heels lifted slightly; the ledge was not quite as wide as he'd expected. But leaning slightly inward towards the face of the building and pressed against it, he could feel his balance firm and secure, and moving along the ledge was quite as easy as he had thought it would be. He could hear the buttons of his jacket scraping steadily along the rough bricks and feel them catch momentarily, tugging a little, at each mortared crack. He simply did not permit himself to look down, though the compulsion to do so never left him; nor did he allow himself actually to think. Mechanically – right foot, left foot, over and again – he shuffled along crab wise, watching the projecting wall ahead loom steadily closer...

Then he reached it and, at the corner – he'd decided how he was going to pick up the paper – he lifted his right foot and placed it carefully on the ledge that ran along the projecting wall at a right angle to the ledge on which his other foot rested. And now, facing the building, he stood in the corner formed by the two walls, one foot on the ledging of each, a hand on the shoulder-high indentation of each wall. His forehead was pressed directly into the corner against the cold bricks, and now he carefully lowered first one hand, then the other, perhaps a foot farther down, to the next indentation in the rows of bricks.

Very slowly, sliding his forehead down the trough of the brick corner and bending his knees, he lowered his body towards the paper lying between his outstretched feet. Again he lowered his fingerholds another foot and bent his knees still more, thigh muscles taut, his forehead sliding and bumping down the brick V. Half squatting now, he dropped his left hand to the next indentation and then slowly reached with his right hand towards the paper between his feet.

He couldn't quite touch it, and his knees now were pressed against the wall; he could bend them no farther. But by ducking his head another inch lower, the top of his head now pressed against the bricks, he lowered his right shoulder and his fingers had the paper by a corner, pulling it loose. At the same instant he saw, between his legs and far below, Lexington Avenue stretched out for miles ahead.

He saw, in that instant, the Loew's theatre sign, blocks ahead past Fiftieth Street; the miles of traffic signals, all green now; the lights of cars and street lamps; countless neon signs; and the moving black dots of people. And a violent, instantaneous explosion of absolute terror roared through him. For a motionless instant he saw himself externally – bent practically double, balanced on this narrow ledge, nearly half his body projecting out above the street far below – and he began to tremble violently, panic flaring through his mind and muscles, and he felt the blood rush from the surface of his skin.

In the fractional moment before horror paralysed him, as he stared between his legs at that terrible length of street far beneath him, a fragment of his mind raised his body in a spasmodic jerk to an upright position again, but so violently that his head scraped hard against the wall, bouncing off it, and his body swayed outwards to the knife edge of balance, and he very nearly plunged backwards and fell. Then he was leaning far into the corner again, squeezing and pushing into it, not only his face but his chest and stomach, his back arching; and his finger tips clung with all the pressure of his pulling arms to the shoulder-high half-inch indentation in the bricks.

He was more than trembling now; his whole body was racked with a violent shuddering beyond control, his eyes squeezed so tightly shut it was painful, though he was past awareness of that. His teeth were exposed in a frozen grimace, the strength draining like water from his knees and calves. It was extremely likely, he knew, that he would faint, slump down along the wall, his face scraping, and then drop backwards, a limp weight, out into nothing. And to save his life he concentrated on holding on to consciousness, drawing deliberate deep breaths of cold air into his lungs, fighting to keep his senses aware.

Then he knew that he would not faint, but he could not stop shaking nor open his eyes. He stood where he was, breathing deeply, trying to hold back the terror of the glimpse he had had of what lay below him; and he knew he had made a mistake in not making himself stare down at the street, getting used to it and accepting it, when he had first stepped out on to the ledge.

It was impossible to walk back. He simply could not do it. He couldn't bring himself to make the slightest movement. The strength was gone from his legs; his shivering hands – numb, cold, and desperately rigid – had lost all deftness; his easy ability to move and balance was gone. Within a step or two, if he tried to move, he knew that he would stumble clumsily and fall.

Seconds passed, with the chill faint wind pressing the side of his face, and he could hear the toned-down volume of the street traffic far beneath him. Again and again it slowed and then stopped, almost to silence; then presently, even this high, he would hear the click of the traffic signals and the subdued roar of the cars starting up again. During a lull in the street sounds, he called out. Then he was shouting '*Help!*' so loudly it rasped his throat. But he felt the steady pressure of the wind, moving between his face and the blank wall, snatch up his cries as he uttered them, and he knew they must sound directionless and distant. And he remembered how habitually, here in New York, he himself heard and ignored shouts in the night. If anyone heard him, there was no sign of it, and presently Tom Benecke knew he had to try moving; there was nothing else he could do.

Eyes squeezed shut, he watched scenes in his mind like scraps of motion-picture film – he could not stop them. He saw himself stumbling suddenly sideways as he crept along the ledge and saw his upper body arc outwards, arms flailing. He saw a dangling shoe string caught between the ledge and the sole of his other shoe, saw a foot start to move, to be stopped with a jerk, and felt his balance leaving him. He saw himself falling with a terrible speed as his body revolved in the air, knees clutched tight to his chest, eyes squeezed shut, moaning softly.

Out of utter necessity, knowing that any of these thoughts might be reality in the very next seconds, he was slowly able to shut his mind against every thought but what he now began to do. With fear-soaked slowness, he slid his left foot an inch or two towards his own impossibly distant window. Then he slid the fingers of his shivering left hand a corresponding distance. For a moment he could not bring himself to lift his right foot from one ledge to the other; then he did it, and became aware of the harsh exhalation of air from his throat and realized that he was panting. As his right hand, then, began to slide along the brick edging, he was astonished to feel the yellow paper pressed to the bricks underneath his stiff fingers, and he uttered a terrible, abrupt bark that might have been a laugh or a moan. He opened his mouth and took the paper in his teeth, pulling it out from under his fingers.

By a kind of trick – by concentrating his entire mind on first his left foot, then his left hand, then the other foot, then the other hand – he was able to move, almost imperceptibly, trembling steadily, very nearly without thought. But he could feel the terrible strength of the pent-up horror on just the other side of the flimsy barrier he had erected in his mind; and he knew that if it broke through he would lose this thin, artificial control of his body.

During one slow step he tried keeping his eyes closed; it made him feel safer, shutting him off a little from the fearful reality of where he was. Then a sudden rush of giddiness swept over him, and he had to open his eyes wide, staring sideways at the cold rough brick and angled lines of mortar, his cheek tight against the building. He kept his eyes open then, knowing that if he once let them flick outwards, to stare for an instant at the lighted windows across the street, he would be past help.

He didn't know how many dozens of tiny sidling steps he had taken, his chest, belly, and face pressed to the wall; but he knew the slender hold he was keeping on his mind and body was going to break. He had a sudden mental picture of his apartment on just the other side of this wall – warm, cheerful, incredibly spacious. And he saw himself striding through it, lying down on the floor on his back, arms spread wide, revelling in its unbelievable security. The impossible remoteness of this utter safety, the contrast between it and where he now stood, was more than he could bear. And the barrier broke then, and the fear of the awful height he stood on coursed through his nerves and muscles.

A fraction of his mind knew he was going to fall, and he began taking rapid blind steps with no feeling of what he was doing, sidling with a clumsy, desperate swiftness, fingers scrabbling along the brick, almost hopelessly resigned to the sudden backward pull and swift motion outward and down. Then his moving hand slid on to not brick but sheer emptiness, an impossible gap in the face of the wall, and he stumbled.

His right foot smashed into his left ankle bone; he staggered sideways, began falling, and the claw of his hand cracked against glass and wood, slid down it, and his finger tips were pressed hard on the puttyless edging of his window. His right hand smacked gropingly beside it as he fell to his knees; and, under the full weight and direct downward pull of his sagging body, the open window dropped shudderingly in its frame till it closed and his wrists struck the sill and were jarred off.

For a single moment he knelt, knee bones against stone on the very edge of the ledge, body swaying and touching nowhere else, fighting for balance. Then he lost it, his shoulders plunging backwards, and he flung his arms forward, his hands smashing against the window casing on either side and – his body moving backwards – his fingers clutched the narrow wood stripping of the upper pane.

For an instant he hung suspended between balance and falling, his finger tips pressed on to the quarter-inch wood strips. Then, with utmost delicacy, with a focused concentration of all his senses, he increased even further the strain on his finger tips hooked to these slim edgings of wood. Elbows slowly bending, he began to draw the full weight of his upper body forward, knowing that the instant his fingers slipped off these quarter-inch strips he'd plunge backwards and be falling. Elbows imperceptibly bending, body shaking with the strain, the sweat starting from his forehead in great sudden drops, he pulled, his entire being and thought concentrated in his finger tips. Then, suddenly, the strain slackened and ended, his chest touching the window sill, and he was kneeling on the ledge, his forehead pressed to the glass of the closed window.

Dropping his palms to the sill, he stared into his living room – at the red-brown davenport across the room, and a magazine he had left there; at the pictures on the walls and the grey rug; the entrance to the hallway; and at his papers, typewriter, and desk, not two feet from his nose. A movement from his desk caught his eye, and he saw that it was a thin curl of blue smoke; his cigarette, the ash long, was still burning in the ashtray where he'd left it – this was past all belief – only a few minutes before.

His head moved, and in faint reflection from the glass before him, he saw the yellow paper clenched in his front teeth. Lifting a hand from the sill he took it from his mouth; the moistened corner parted from the paper, and he spat it out.

For a moment, in the light from the living room, he stared wonderingly at the yellow sheet in his hand and then crushed it into the side pocket of his jacket.

He couldn't open the window. It had been pulled not completely closed, but its lower edge was below the level of the outside sill; there was no room to get his fingers underneath it. Between the upper sash and the lower was a gap not wide enough – reaching up, he tried – to get his fingers into; he couldn't push it open. The upper window panel, he knew from long experience, was impossible to move, frozen tight with dried paint.

Very carefully observing his balance, the finger tips of his left hand again hooked to the narrow stripping of the window casing, he drew his right hand, palm facing the glass, and then struck the glass with the heel of his hand.

His arm rebounded from the pane, his body tottering, and he knew he didn't dare strike a harder blow.

But in the security and relief of his new position, he simply smiled; with only a sheet of glass between him and the room just before him, it was not possible that there wasn't a way past it. Eyes narrowing, he thought for a few moments about what to do. Then his eyes widened, for nothing occurred to him. But still he felt calm: the trembling, he realized, had stopped. At the back of his mind there still lay the thought that once he was again in his home, he could give release to his feelings. He actually *would* lie on the floor, rolling, clenching tufts of the rug in his hands. He would literally run across the room, free to move as he liked, jumping on the floor, testing and revelling in its absolute security, letting the relief flood through him, draining the fear from his mind and body. His yearning for this was astonishingly intense, and somehow he understood that he had better keep this feeling at bay.

He took a half dollar from his pocket and struck it against the pane, but without any hope that the glass would break and with very little disappointment when it did not. After a few moments of thought he drew his leg up on to the ledge and picked loose the knot of his shoe lace. He slipped off his shoe and, holding it across the instep, drew back his arm as far as he dared and struck the leather heel against the glass. The pane rattled, but he knew he'd been a long way from breaking it. His foot was cold and he slipped the shoe back on. He shouted again, experimentally, and then once more, but there was no answer.

The realization suddenly struck him that he might have to wait here till Clare came home, and for a moment the thought was funny. He could see Clare opening the front door, withdrawing her key from the lock, closing the door behind her, and then glancing up to see him crouched on the other side of the window. He could see her rush across the room, face astounded and frightened, and hear himself shouting instructions: 'Never mind how I got here! Just open the wind – ' She couldn't open it, he remembered, she'd never been able to; she'd always had to call him. She'd have to get the building superintendent or a neighbour, and he pictured himself smiling and answering their questions as he climbed in. 'I just wanted to get a breath of fresh air, so—'

He couldn't possibly wait here till Clare came home. It was the second feature she'd wanted to see, and she'd left in time to see the first. She'd be another three hours or— He glanced at his watch; Clare had been gone eight minutes. It wasn't possible, but only eight minutes ago he had kissed his wife goodbye. She wasn't even in the theatre yet!

It would be four hours before she could possibly be home, and he tried to picture himself kneeling out here, finger tips hooked to these narrow strippings, while first one movie, preceded by a slow listing of credits, began, developed, reached its climax and then finally ended. There'd be a newsreel next, maybe, and then an animated cartoon, and then interminable scenes from coming pictures. And then, once more, the beginning of a full-length picture – while all the time he hung out here in the night.

He might possibly get to his feet, but he was afraid to try. Already his legs were cramped, his thigh muscles tired; his knees hurt, his feet felt numb, and his hands were stiff. He couldn't possibly stay out here for four hours or anywhere near it. Long before that his legs and arms would give out; he would be forced to try changing his position often – stiffly, clumsily, his co-ordination and strength gone – and he would fall. Quite realistically, he knew that he would fall; no one could stay out here on this ledge for four hours.

A dozen windows in the apartment building across the street were lighted. Looking over his shoulder, he could see the top of a man's head behind the newspaper he was reading; in another window he saw the blue-grey flicker of a television screen. No more than twenty-odd yards from his back were scores of people, and if just one of them would walk idly to his window and glance out... For some moments he stared over his shoulder at the lighted rectangles, waiting. But no one appeared. The man reading his paper turned a page and then continued his reading. A figure passed another of the windows and was immediately gone.

In the inside pocket of his jacket he found a little sheaf of papers, and he pulled one out and looked at it in the light from the living room. It was an old letter, an advertisement of some sort; his name and address, in purple ink, were on a label pasted to the envelope. Gripping one end of the envelope in his teeth, he twisted it into a tight curl. From his shirt pocket he brought out a book of matches. He didn't dare let go the casing with both hands but, with the twist of paper in his teeth, he opened the match book with his free hand; then he bent one of the matches in two without tearing it from the folder, its red-tipped end now touching the striking surface. With his thumb, he rubbed the red tip across the striking area.

He did it again, then again, and still again, pressing harder each time, and the match suddenly flared, burning his thumb. But he kept it alight, cupping the match book in his hand and shielding it with his body. He held the flame to the paper in his mouth till it caught. Then he snuffed out the match flame with his thumb and forefinger, careless of the burn, and replaced the book in his pocket. Taking the paper twist in his hand, he held it flame down, watching the flame crawl up the paper, till it flared bright. Then he held it behind him over the street, moving it from side to side, watching it over his shoulder, the flame flickering and guttering in the wind.

There were three letters in his pocket and he lighted each of them, holding each till the flame touched his hand and then dropping it to the street below. At one point, watching over his shoulder while the last of the letters burned, he saw the man across the street put down his paper and stand – even seeming, to Tom, to glance towards his window. But when he moved, it was only to walk across the room and disappear from sight.

There were a dozen coins in Tom Benecke's pocket and he dropped them, three or four at a time. But if they struck anyone or if anyone noticed their falling, no one connected them with their source, and no one glanced upwards.

His arms had begun to tremble from the steady strain of clinging to this narrow perch, and he did not know what to do now and was terribly frightened. Clinging to the window stripping with one hand, he again searched his pockets. But now – he had left his wallet on his dresser when he'd changed clothes – there was nothing left but the yellow sheet. It occurred to him irrelevantly that his death on the sidewalk below would be an eternal mystery; the window closed – why, how, and from where could he have fallen? No one would be able to identify his body for a time, either – the thought was somehow unbearable and increased his fear. All they'd find in his pockets would be the yellow sheet. *Contents of the dead man's pockets, he thought, one sheet of paper bearing pencilled notations – incomprehensible.*

He understood fully that he might actually be going to die; his arms, maintaining his balance on the ledge, were trembling steadily now. And it occurred to him then with all the force of a revelation that, if he fell, all he was ever going to have out of life he would then, abruptly, have had. Nothing, then, could ever be changed; and nothing more – no least experience or pleasure – could ever be added to his life. He wished, then, that he had not allowed his wife to go off by herself tonight – and on similar nights. He thought of all the evenings he had spent away from her, working; and he regretted them. He thought wonderingly of his fierce ambition and of the direction his life had taken; he thought of the hours he'd spent by himself, filling the yellow sheet that had brought him out here. *Contents of the dead man's pockets*, he thought with sudden fierce anger, a wasted life.

He was simply not going to cling here till he slipped and fell; he told himself that now. There was one last thing he could try; he had been aware of it for some moments, refusing to think about it, but now he faced it. Kneeling here on the ledge, the finger tips of one hand pressed to the narrow strip of wood, he could, he knew, draw his other hand back a yard perhaps, fist clenched tight, doing it very slowly till he sensed the outer limit of balance, then, as hard as he was able from the distance, he could drive his fist forward against the glass. If it broke, his fist smashing through, he was safe; he might cut himself badly, and probably would, but with his arm inside the room, he would be secure. But if the glass did not break, the rebound, flinging his arm back, would topple him off the ledge. He was certain of that.

He tested his plan. The fingers of his left hand claw-like on the little stripping, he drew back his other fist until his body began teetering backwards. But he had no leverage now – he could feel that there would be no force to his swing – and he moved his fist slowly forward till he rocked forward on his knees again and could sense that his swing would carry its greatest force. Glancing down, however, measuring the distance from his fist to the glass, he saw that it was less than two feet.

It occurred to him that he could raise his arm over his head, to bring it down against the glass. But, experimenting in slow motion, he knew it would be an awkward girllike blow without the force of a driving punch, and not nearly enough to break the glass.

Facing the window, he had to drive a blow from the shoulder, he knew now, at a distance of less than two feet; and he did not know whether it would break through the heavy glass. It might; he could picture it happening, he could feel it in the nerves of his arm. And it might not; he could feel that, too – feel his fist striking this glass and being instantaneously flung back by the unbreaking pane, feel the fingers of his other hand breaking loose, nails scraping along the casing as he fell.

He waited, arm drawn back, fist balled, but in no hurry to strike; this pause, he knew, might be an extension of his life. And to live even a few seconds longer, he felt, even out here on this ledge in the night, was infinitely better than to die a moment earlier than he had to. His arm grew tired, and he brought it down and rested it.

Then he knew that it was time to make the attempt. He could not kneel here hesitating indefinitely till he lost all courage to act, waiting till he slipped off the ledge. Again he drew back his arm, knowing this time that he would not bring it down till he struck. His elbow protruding over Lexington Avenue far below, the fingers of his other hand pressed down bloodlessly tight against the narrow stripping, he waited, feeling the sick tenseness and terrible excitement building. It grew and swelled towards the moment of action, his nerves tautening. He thought of Clare – just a wordless, yearning thought – and then drew his arm back just a bit more, fist so tight his fingers pained him, and knowing he was going to do it. Then with full power, with every last scrap of strength he could bring to bear, he shot his arm forward towards the glass, and he said '*Clare!*'

He heard the sound, felt the blow, felt himself falling forward, and his hand closed on the living-room curtains, the shards and fragments of glass showering on to the floor. And then, kneeling there on the ledge, an arm thrust into the room up to the shoulder, he began picking away the protruding slivers and great wedges of glass from the window frame, tossing them in on to the rug. And, as he grasped the edges of the empty frame and climbed into his home, he was grinning in triumph.

He did not lie down on the floor or run through the apartment, as he had promised himself; even in the first few moments it seemed to him natural and normal that he should be where he was. He simply turned to his desk, pulled the crumpled yellow sheet from his pocket and laid it down where it had been, smoothing it out; then he absently laid a pencil across it to weight it down. He shook his head, wonderingly, and turned to walk towards the closet.

There he got out his topcoat and hat and, without waiting to put them on, opened the front door and stepped out, to go and find his wife. He turned to pull the door closed and the warm air from the hall rushed through the narrow opening again. As he saw the yellow paper, the pencil flying, scooped off the desk and, unimpeded by the glassless window, sail out into the night and out of his life, Tom Benecke burst into laughter and then closed the door behind him.

# Peter Fleming

## *The Kill*

In the cold waiting room of a small railway station in the West of England two men were sitting. They had sat there for an hour, and were likely to sit there longer. There was a thick fog outside. Their train was indefinitely delayed.

The waiting room was a barren and unfriendly place. A naked electric bulb lit it with wan, disdainful efficiency. A notice, 'No Smoking', stood on the mantelpiece: when you turned it round, it said 'No Smoking' on the other side, too. Printed regulations relating to an outbreak of swine fever in 1924 were pinned neatly to one wall, almost, but maddeningly not quite, in the centre of it. The stove gave out a hot, thick smell, powerful already but increasing. A pale leprous flush on the black and beaded window showed that a light was burning on the platform outside, in the fog. Somewhere water dripped with infinite reluctance on to corrugated iron.

The two men sat facing each other over the stove on chairs of an unswerving woodenness. Their acquaintance was no older than their vigil. From such talk as they had had, it seemed likely that they were to remain strangers.

The younger of the two resented the lack of contact in their relationship more than the lack of comfort in their surroundings. His attitude towards his fellow beings had but recently undergone a transition from the subjective to the objective. As with many of his class and age, the routine, unrecognized as such, of an expensive education, with the triennial alternative of those delights normal to wealth and gentility, had atrophied many of his curiosities. For the first twenty-odd years of his life he had read humanity in terms of relevance rather than reality, looking on people who held no ordained place in his own existence much as a buck in a park watches visitors walking up the drive: mildly, rather resentfully inquiring – not inquisitive. Now, hot in reaction from this unconscious provincialism, he treated mankind as a museum, gaping conscientiously at each fresh exhibit, hunting for the non-cumulative evidence of man's complexity with indiscriminate zeal. To each magic circle of individuality he saw himself as a kind of freelance tangent. He aspired to be a connoisseur of men.

There was undoubtedly something arresting about the specimen before him. Of less than medium height, the stranger had yet that sort of ranging leanness that lends vicarious inches. He wore a long black overcoat, very shabby, and his shoes were covered with mud. His face had no colour in it, though the impression it produced was not one of pallor; the skin was of a dark sallow, tinged with grey. The nose was pointed, the jaw sharp and narrow. Deep vertical wrinkles, running down towards it from the high cheekbones, sketched the permanent groundwork of a broader smile than the deep-set honey-coloured eyes seemed likely to authorize. The most striking thing about the face was the incongruity of its frame. On the back of his head the stranger wore a bowler hat with a very narrow brim. No word of such casual implications as a tilt did justice to its angle. It was clamped, by something at least as holy as custom, to the back of his skull, and that thin, questing face confronted the world fiercely from under a black halo of nonchalance. The man's whole appearance suggested *difference* rather than aloofness. The unnatural way he wore his hat had the significance of indirect comment, like the antics of a performing animal. It was as if he was part of some older thing, of which *homo sapiens* in a bowler hat was an expurgated edition. He sat with his shoulders hunched and his hands thrust into his overcoat pockets. The hint of discomfort in his attitude seemed due not so much to the fact that his chair was hard as to the fact that it was a chair.

The young man had found him uncommunicative. The most mobile sympathy, launching consecutive attacks on different fronts, had failed to draw him out. The reserved adequacy of his replies conveyed a rebuff more effectively than sheer surliness. Except to answer him, he did not look at the young man. When he did, his eyes were full of an abstracted amusement. Sometimes he smiled, but for no immediate cause.

Looking back down their hour together, the young man saw a field of endeavour on which frustrated banalities lay thick, like the discards of a routed army. But resolution, curiosity, and the need to kill time all clamoured against an admission of defeat.

'If he will not talk,' thought the young man, 'then I will. The sound of my own voice is infinitely preferable to the sound of none. I will tell him what has just happened to me. It is really a most extraordinary story. I will tell it as well as I can, and I shall be very much surprised if its impact on his mind does not shock this man into some form of self-revelation. He is unaccountable without being *outré*, and I am inordinately curious about him.'

Aloud he said, in a brisk and engaging manner: 'I think you said you were a hunting man?'

The other raised his quick, honey-coloured eyes. They gleamed with inaccessible amusement. Without answering, he lowered them again to contemplate the little beads of light thrown through the ironwork of the stove on to the skirts of his overcoat. Then he spoke. He had a husky voice.

'I came here to hunt,' he agreed.

'In that case,' said the young man, 'you will have heard of Lord Fleer's private pack. Their kennels are not far from here.'

'I know them,' replied the other.

'I have just been staying there,' the young man continued. 'Lord Fleer is my uncle.'

The other looked up, smiled, and nodded, with the bland

inconsequence of a foreigner who does not understand what is being said to him. The young man swallowed his impatience.

'Would you,' he continued, using a slightly more peremptory tone than heretofore, 'would you care to hear a new and rather remarkable story about my uncle? Its dénouement is not two days old. It is quite short.'

From the fastness of some hidden joke, those light eyes mocked the necessity of a definite answer. At length: 'Yes,' said the stranger, 'I would.' The impersonality in his voice might have passed for a parade of sophistication, a reluctance to betray interest. But the eyes hinted that interest was alive elsewhere.

'Very well,' said the young man.

Drawing his chair a little closer to the. stove, he began:

As perhaps you know, my uncle, Lord Fleer, leads a retired, though by no means an inactive life. For the last two or three hundred years, the currents of contemporary thought have passed mainly through the hands of men whose gregarious instincts have been constantly awakened and almost invariably indulged. By the standards of the eighteenth century, when Englishmen first became self-conscious about solitude, my uncle would have been considered unsociable. In the early nineteenth century, those not personally acquainted with him would have thought him romantic. Today, his attitude towards the sound and fury of modern life is too negative to excite comment as an oddity; yet even now, were he to be involved in any occurrence which could be called disastrous or interpreted as discreditable, the press would pillory him as a 'Titled Recluse'.

The truth of the matter is, my uncle has discovered the elixir, or, if you prefer it, the opiate, of self-sufficiency. A man of extremely simple tastes, not cursed with overmuch imagination, he sees no reason to cross frontiers of habit which the years have hallowed into rigidity. He lives in his castle (it may be described as commodious rather than comfortable), runs his estate at a slight profit, shoots a little, rides a great deal, and hunts as often as he can. He never sees his neighbours except by accident, thereby leading them to suppose, with sublime but unconscious arrogance, that he must be slightly mad. If he is, he can at least claim to have padded his own cell.

My uncle has never married. As the only son of his only brother, I was brought up in the expectation of being his heir. During the war, however, an unforeseen development occurred.

In this national crisis my uncle, who was of course too old for active service, showed a lack of public spirit which earned him locally a good deal of unpopularity. Briefly, he declined to recognize the war, or, if he did recognize it, gave no sign of having done so. He continued to lead his own vigorous but (in the circumstances) rather irrelevant life. Though he found himself at last obliged to recruit his hunt-servants from men of advanced age and uncertain mettle in any crisis of the chase, he contrived to mount them well, and twice a week during the season himself rode two horses to a standstill after the hill-foxes which, as no doubt you know, provide the best sport the Fleer country has to offer.

When the local gentry came and made representations to him, saying that it was time he did something for his country besides destroying its vermin by the most unreliable and expensive method ever devised, my uncle was very sensible. He now saw, he said, that he had been standing too aloof from a struggle of whose progress (since he never read the paper) he had been only indirectly aware. The next day he wrote to London and ordered *The Times* and a Belgian refugee. It was the least he could do, he said. I think he was right.

The Belgian refugee turned out to be a female, and dumb. Whether one or both of these characteristics had been stipulated for by my uncle, nobody knew. At any rate, she took up her quarters at Fleer: a heavy, unattractive girl of twenty-five, with a shiny face and small black hairs on the backs of her hands. Her life appeared to be modelled on that of the larger ruminants, except, of course, that the greater part of it took place indoors. She ate a great deal, slept with a will, and had a bath every Sunday, remitting this salubrious custom only when the housekeeper, who enforced it, was away on her holiday. Much of her time she spent sitting on a sofa, on the landing outside her bedroom, with Prescott's *Conquest of Mexico* open on her lap. She read either exceptionally slowly or not at all, for to my knowledge she carried the first volume about with her for eleven years. Hers, I think, was the contemplative type of mind.

The curious, and from my point of view the unfortunate, aspect of my uncle's patriotic gesture was the gradually increasing affection with which he came to regard this unlovable creature. Although, or more probably because, he saw her only at meals, when her features were rather more animated than at other times, his attitude towards her passed from the detached to the courteous, and from the courteous to the paternal. At the end of the war there was no question of her return to Belgium, and one day in 1919 I heard with pardonable mortification that my uncle had legally adopted her, and was altering his will in her favour.

Time, however, reconciled me to being disinherited by a being who, between meals, could scarcely be described as sentient. I continued to pay an annual visit to Fleer, and to ride with my uncle after his big-boned Welsh hounds over the sullen, dark-grey hill country in which – since its possession was no longer assured to me – I now began to see a powerful, though elusive, beauty.

I came down here three days ago, intending to stay for a week. I found my uncle, who is a tall, fine-looking man with a beard, in his usual unassailable good health. The Belgian, as always, gave me the impression of being impervious to disease, to emotion, or indeed to anything short of an act of God. She had been putting on weight since she came to live with my uncle, and was now a very considerable figure of a woman, though not, as yet, unwieldy.

It was at dinner, on the evening of my arrival, that I first noticed a certain malaise behind my uncle's brusque, laconic manner. There was evidently something on his mind. After dinner he asked me to come into his study. I detected, in the delivery of the invitation, the first hint of embarrassment I had known him to betray.

The walls of the study were hung with maps and the extremities of foxes. The room was littered with bills, catalogues, old gloves, fossils, rat-traps, cartridges, and feathers which had been used to clean his pipe – a stale diversity of jetsam which somehow managed to produce an impression of relevance and continuity, like the debris in an animal's lair. I had never been in the study before.

'Paul,' said my uncle as soon as I had shut the door, 'I am very much disturbed.'

I assumed an air of sympathetic inquiry.

'Yesterday,' my uncle went on, 'one of my tenants came to see me. He is a decent man, who farms a strip of land outside the park wall to the northward. He said that he had lost two sheep in a manner for which he was wholly unable to account. He said he thought they had been killed by some wild animal.'

My uncle paused. The gravity of his manner was really portentous.

'Dogs?' I suggested, with the slightly patronizing diffidence of one who has probability on his side.

My uncle shook his head judiciously. 'This man had often seen sheep which had been killed by dogs. He said that they were always badly torn – nipped about the legs, driven into a corner, worried to death; it was never a clean piece of work. These two sheep had not been killed like that. I went down to see them for myself. Their throats had been torn out. They were not bitten or nuzzled. They had both died in the open, not in a corner. Whatever did it was an animal more powerful and more cunning than a dog.'

I said, 'It couldn't have been something that had escaped from a travelling menagerie, I suppose?'

'They don't come into this part of the country,' replied my uncle; 'there are no fairs.'

We were both silent for a moment. It was hard not to show more curiosity than sympathy as I waited on some further revelation to stake out my uncle's claim on the latter emotion. I could put no interpretation on those two dead sheep wild enough to account for his evident distress.

He spoke again, but with obvious reluctance.

'Another was killed early this morning,' he said in a low voice, 'on the Home Farm. In the same way.'

For lack of any better comment, I suggested beating the nearby coverts. There might be some...

'We've scoured the woods,' interrupted my uncle brusquely.

'And found nothing?'

'Nothing... Except some tracks.'

'What sort of tracks?'

My uncle's eyes were suddenly evasive. He turned his head away.

'They were a man's tracks,' he said slowly. A log fell over in the fireplace.

Again a silence. The interview appeared to be causing him pain rather than relief. I decided that the situation could lose nothing through the frank expression of my curiosity. Plucking up courage, I asked him roundly what cause he had to be upset? Three sheep, the property of his tenants, had died deaths which, though certainly unusual, were unlikely to remain for long mysterious. Their destroyer, whatever it was, would inevitably be caught, killed, or driven away in the course of the next few days. The loss of another sheep or two was the worst he had to fear.

When I had finished, my uncle gave me an anxious, almost a guilty look. I was suddenly aware that he had a confession to make.

'Sit down,' he said. 'I wish to tell you something.'

This is what he told me:

A quarter of a century ago, my uncle had had occasion to engage a new housekeeper. With the blend of fatalism and sloth which is the foundation of the bachelor's attitude to the servant problem, he took on the first applicant. She was a tall, black, slant-eyed woman from the Welsh border, aged about thirty. My uncle said nothing about her character, but described her as having 'powers'. When she had been at Fleer some months, my uncle began to notice her, instead of taking her for granted. She was not averse to being noticed.

One day she came and told my uncle that she was with child by him. He took it calmly enough till he found that she expected him to marry her, or pretended to expect it. Then he flew into a rage, called her a whore, and told her she must leave the house as soon as the child was born. Instead of breaking down or continuing the scene, she began to croon to herself in Welsh, looking at him sideways with a certain amusement. This frightened him. He forbade her to come near him again, had her things moved into an unused wing of the castle, and engaged another housekeeper.

A child was born, and they came and told my uncle that the woman was going to die; she asked for him continually, they said. As much frightened as distressed, he went through passages long unfamiliar to her room. When the woman saw him, she began to gabble in a preoccupied kind of way, looking at him all the time, as if she were repeating a lesson. Then she stopped, and asked that he should be shown the child.

It was a boy. The midwife, my uncle noticed, handled it with a reluctance almost amounting to disgust.

'That is your heir,' said the dying woman in a harsh, unstable voice. 'I have told him what he is to do. He will be a good son to me, and jealous of his birthright.' And she went off, my uncle said, into a wild yet cogent rigmarole about a curse, embodied in the child, which would fall on any whom he made his heir over the bastard's head. At last her voice trailed away, and she fell back, exhausted and staring.

As my uncle turned to go, the midwife whispered to him to look at the child's hands. Gently unclasping the podgy, futile little fists, she showed him that on each hand the third finger was longer than the second....

Here I interrupted. The story had a certain queer force behind it, perhaps from its obvious effect on the teller. My uncle feared and hated the things he was saying.

'What did that mean,' I asked; 'the third finger longer than the second?'

'It took me a long time to discover,' replied my uncle. 'My own servants, when they saw I did not know, would not tell me. But at last I found out through the doctor, who had it from an old woman in the village. People born with their third finger longer than their second become werewolves. At least' – he made a perfunctory effort at amused indulgence – 'that is what the common people here think.'

'And what does that – what is that supposed to mean?' I, too, found myself throwing rather hasty sops to scepticism. I was growing strangely credulous.

'A werewolf,' said my uncle, dabbling in improbability without self-consciousness, 'is a human being who becomes, at intervals, to all intents and purposes a wolf. The transformation – or the supposed transformation – takes place at night. The werewolf kills men and animals, and is supposed to drink their blood. Its preference is for men. All through the Middle Ages, down to the seventeenth century, there were innumerable cases (especially in France) of men and women being legally tried for offences which they had committed as animals. Like the witches, they were rarely acquitted, but, unlike the witches, they seem seldom to have been unjustly condemned.' My uncle paused. 'I have been reading the old books,' he explained. 'I wrote to a man in London who is interested in these things when I heard what was believed about the child.'

'What became of the child?' I asked.

'The wife of one of my keepers took it in,' said my uncle. 'She was a stolid woman from the North who, I think, welcomed the opportunity to show what little store she set by the local superstitions. The boy lived with them till he was ten. Then he ran away. I had not heard of him since then till' – my uncle glanced at me almost apologetically – 'till yesterday.'

We sat for a moment in silence, looking at the fire. My imagination had betrayed my reason in its full surrender to the story. I had not got it in me to dispel his fears with a parade of sanity. I was a little frightened myself.

'You think it is your son, the werewolf, who is killing the sheep?' I said at length.

'Yes. For a boast: or for a warning: or perhaps out of spite, at a night's hunting wasted.'

'Wasted?'

My uncle looked at me with troubled eyes.

'His business is not with sheep,' he said uneasily.

For the first time I realized the implications of the Welshwoman's curse. The hunt was up. The quarry was the heir to Fleer. I was glad to have been disinherited.

'I have told Germaine not to go out after dusk,' said my uncle, coming in pat on my train of thought.

The Belgian was called Germaine; her other name was Vom.

I confess I spent no very tranquil night. My uncle's story had not wholly worked in me that 'suspension of disbelief' which someone speaks of as being the prime requisite of good drama. But I have a powerful imagination. Neither fatigue nor common sense could quite banish the vision of that metamorphosed malignancy ranging, with design, the black and silver silences outside my window. I found my-self listening for the sound of loping footfalls on a frost-baked crust of beech leaves...

Whether it was in my dream that I heard, once, the sound of howling, I do not know. But the next morning I saw, as I dressed, a man walking quickly up the drive. He looked like a shepherd. There was a dog at his heels, trotting with a noticeable lack of assurance. At breakfast my uncle told me that another sheep had been killed, almost under the noses of the watchers. His voice shook a little. Solicitude sat oddly on his features as he looked at Germaine. She was eating porridge, as if for a wager.

After breakfast we decided on a campaign. I will not weary you with the details of its launching and its failure. All day we quartered the woods with thirty men, mounted and on foot. Near the scene of the kill our dogs picked up a scent which they followed for two miles and more, only to lose it on the railway line. But the ground was too hard for tracks, and the men said it could only have been a fox or a polecat, so surely and readily did the dogs follow it.

The exercise and the occupation were good for our nerves. But late in the afternoon my uncle grew anxious; twilight was closing in swiftly under a sky heavy with clouds, and we were some distance from Fleer. He gave final instructions for the penning of the sheep by night, and we turned our horses' heads for home.

We approached the castle by the back drive, which was little used: a dank, unholy alley, running the gauntlet of a belt of firs and laurels. Beneath our horses' hoofs flints chinked remotely under a thick carpet of moss. Each consecutive cloud from their nostrils hung with an air of permanency, as if bequeathed to the unmoving air.

We were perhaps three hundred yards from the tall gates leading to the stableyard when both horses stopped dead, simultaneously. Their heads were turned towards the trees on our right, beyond which, I knew, the sweep of the main drive converged on ours.

My uncle gave a short, inarticulate cry in which premonition stood aghast at the foreseen. At the same moment something howled on the other side of the trees. There was relish, and a kind of sobbing laughter, in that hateful sound. It rose and fell luxuriously, and rose and fell again, fouling the night. Then it died away, fawning on society in a throaty whimper.

The forces of silence fell unavailingly on its rear; its filthy echoes still went reeling through our heads. We were aware that feet went loping lightly down the iron-hard drive... two feet.

My uncle flung himself off his horse and dashed through the trees. I followed. We scrambled down a bank and out into the open. The only figure in sight was motionless.

Germaine Vom lay doubled up in the drive, a solid, black mark against the shifting values of the dusk. We ran forward...

To me she had always been an improbable cipher rather than a real person. I could not help reflecting that she died, as she had lived, in the livestock tradition. Her throat had been torn out.

The young man leant back in his chair, a little dizzy from talking and from the heat of the stove. The inconvenient realities of the waiting room, forgotten in his narrative, closed in on him again. He sighed, and smiled rather apologetically at the stranger.

'It is a wild and improbable story,' he said. 'I do not expect you to believe the whole of it. For me, perhaps, the reality of its implications has obscured its almost ludicrous lack of verisimilitude. You see, by the death of the Belgian I am heir to Fleer.'

The stranger smiled: a slow, but no longer an abstracted smile. His honey-coloured eyes were bright. Under his long black overcoat his body seemed to be stretching itself in sensual anticipation. He rose silently to his feet.

The other found a sharp, cold fear drilling into his vitals. Something behind those shining eyes threatened him with appalling immediacy, like a sword at his heart. He was sweating. He dared not move.

The stranger's smile was now a grin, a ravening convulsion of the face. His eyes blazed with a hard and purposeful delight. A thread of saliva dangled from the corner of his mouth.

Very slowly he lifted one hand and removed his bowler hat. Of the fingers crooked about its brim, the young man saw that the third was longer than the second.

# C. S. Forester

## *The Physiology of Fear*

Dr Georg Schmidt was not a young man, and perhaps because of that he sometimes found it hard to believe that this was a real, permanent world in which he was moving and living. He had qualified as a doctor in the days of the Kaiser, before 1914. A man who had vivid recollections of the Hohenzollern empire, with all its tradition and appearance of permanence, and who had then seen the Weimar Republic come and go, and who had lived through the inflation and through several revolutions, abortive and otherwise, found it a little difficult to believe in the prospective existence of the Third Reich for a thousand years, which its supporters predicted for it. This was especially the case because Schmidt was of a cynical turn of mind, with his cynicism accentuated by a scientific education. But his cynicism was not of the right type to be of use to him under Hitler and the Nazis, considering the sort of work he was called upon by them to do. For he was appointed a surgeon in the SS, and posted as medical officer to the Rosenberg concentration camp. There he could inspect water supply and sanitary arrangements, he could combat epidemics, and do all the things he had learned to do thoroughly well between 1914 and 1918, but a medical officer in a concentration camp had other duties as well, which were hard to perform; there is no need to enlarge upon them, except to comment that perhaps the easiest duty was to advise upon the issue of rations so that the prisoners had the minimum diet on which life could be sustained.

All the hideous things that Schmidt had to do, he had to do. That was simple. The Party cast a cold eye upon any man who flinched from obeying orders; those orders came down from the Fuehrer himself, and they were not rendered any less sacred by the fact that they were transmitted, interpreted, and expanded by a number of officials before they reached Schmidt. Those officials held their authority from the Fuehrer, and a man who cavilled at doing what he was told by them to do was guilty of treason against the Fuehrer, against the Reich, and no fate could be too bad for him – even though anyone who knew the sort of fate that was meted out (and Schmidt saw it meted out) might have thought it was too bad for anyone. Schmidt knew all about the gallows and the block, the torture cells and the gas chambers, so he did what he was told, moving in a world that was like a bad dream, hoping that what he saw and did was not really happening, hoping that some time soon he would wake up and find it was only a dream after all.

So, when his leave came round in the summer of 1940, he welcomed it with as much gladness as he had done in the old days of 1917. He handed over to the doctor who came to relieve him; he packed his fibre suitcase, saw that his papers were in order, and started off for the railway station and for the city that he called 'home'. He had few relations – his wife was dead – but his brilliant nephew Heinrich had invited him to spend his leave at his house there, and Schmidt was looking forward to that. Young Heinz was a product of the new generation, he knew – because of the exigencies of the service he had seen little of him lately – but Schmidt was quite certain that he was a nephew to be proud of. He had not only qualified in medicine, but he had attained a Doctorate of Science, and even now, with Germany mobilized, he was still a civilian, holding a research fellowship at the university – a sure proof of the esteem in which he was held. Schmidt had read the early papers he had contributed to the university 'Transactions' and had glowed with pride. His nephew was clearly destined to be one of the great physiologists of the world, a man whose name would always be remembered.

Schmidt would have liked to have been a famous research worker himself, and he found a vicarious, almost a parental, pleasure in his nephew's achievements.

Heinz himself opened the door to him when he rang the door bell after a tedious night journey across wartime Germany.

'Welcome, uncle,' he said, relieving him of his suitcase.

Heinz was everything an uncle might wish for, tall and blond and handsome, smartly dressed, vigorous – he had all those advantages as well as being a man of brilliant mind. And his wife, Caecilie, was a desirable niece, too, a very pretty girl in a uniform not too obtrusive. She made Schmidt welcome with the utmost kindness and hospitality.

'You look tired, uncle,' said Caecilie, 'we must try to remedy that while you are with us.'

Schmidt glowed with something like happiness as they showed him his room and saw to his comfort. More than ever at that moment did his duties at the Rosenberg concentration camp appear like a bad dream.

'You and I have an appointment for luncheon, uncle,' said Heinz.

'Indeed?'

'With Standartenfuehrer Kroide. The president himself.'

There was a humorous twinkle in Heinz' eye as he spoke. He could see the incongruity of having a Nazi official as president of a university which dated back to the Middle Ages.

'How is it that I am invited?' asked Schmidt.

'I mentioned to him that I was expecting you,' explained Heinz, 'and that you were my uncle.'

'And he wanted to meet the uncle of the great physiologist?' said Schmidt. 'I have attained fame at last.'

'Turn round, uncle,' said Caecilie, clothes brush in hand. 'I want to brush your shoulders.'

On the way to the university, walking through the streets multi-coloured with uniforms, Schmidt asked his nephew about his work.

'Is it still intercellular osmosis?' he asked.

'No,' said Heinz. 'It's a larger project altogether. Immensely larger, and it may prove to be of great importance to the Reich.'

'Is it a war secret?'

'The results may be, when we see what they are. But there is no need for secrecy at present. I'm working on the physiology of fear.'

'Very interesting.'

'Very interesting indeed. The government is of course assisting the university. I understand that the Fuehrer himself knows about my research. At any rate, it is the government, of course, that is providing me with suitable subjects.'

'That must be a great help,' said Schmidt.

'Oh yes, of course. It would be hard to conduct such a research without a plentiful supply. And the university has been most cooperative. I have a thousand cubic metres of laboratory space for my use. Actually I am using the laboratories once used by Liebig and Hertz – remodelled, of course.'

'That's a compliment in itself,' said Schmidt.

The university had a long and honourable record for scientific research. The world was at least a healthier place, if not a happier, as a result of the labours of the university's scientists.

'I'll take you round and show you after lunch,' said Heinz.

'Thank you. That will be very interesting.'

Schmidt was not quite sure that he wanted to be shown. The physiology of fear could hardly be investigated without causing fear, and he did not specially want to be shown terrified animals; many animals, obviously, with the government undertaking to supply them.

'I suppose rats and guinea pigs are unsuitable for your investigation?' asked Schmidt.

'Of course,' said Heinz, and then the glow of enthusiasm in his face died away as he changed the subject and pointed across the road. 'Here's the president's house.'

Standartenfuehrer Kroide was no scientist, not even a scientist in uniform. As head of the university he represented the Ministry of Enlightenment and Propaganda, naturally. It was his business to see that German youth not only was educated along the lines most useful to the Reich, but also that it was not educated along the lines that were improper.

'We are proud of our young man here,' said Kroide, indicating Heinz. 'A splendid example of the new growth of scientists of the Third Reich. One of our earliest, but with the example he has set he will not be our last.'

Kroide was a man with the same personal charm as the head of his ministry. He could talk charmingly and interestingly, and at luncheon he entertained Schmidt, who sat at his right, with a vivid account of the success of the new system of education, a success demonstrated by the correct thinking of all the new generation, and resulting from consistent methods employed from earliest childhood.

'Your nephew himself was distinguished as a boy in the Hitler Youth,' said Kroide.

'I remember,' answered Schmidt, and that was only true as he said it. He had forgotten about Heinz' early activities, and he thought Heinz probably had forgotten them too. The notion crept into his mind that it might be difficult to retain the ideas of Nazism when one was a true scientist, but he put it hastily aside. Some people would have thought it blasphemous; Schmidt knew it was dangerous.

When lunch was over, Kroide shook Schmidt's hand.

'I have no doubt your nephew is impatient to carry you off,' he said. 'He wants to get back to his experiments as well as to show you his work. I hope when your leave comes round again, you will let me know so that I can again have the pleasure of entertaining you.'

'Thank you, Standartenfuehrer,' said Schmidt.

Walking from the president's house over to the laboratories Heinz began to go into further detail regarding his work.

'Thanks to the Reich and the Fuehrer,' he said, 'I am able to investigate the subject in a way that has not been possible before. There could never be exact measurements of any sort, and I expect that is why fear has never been analysed physiologically until now. All that is known is contained in two paragraphs in any standard textbook of physiology, as I expect you remember, uncle.'

'A line or two about the suprarenals,' agreed Schmidt. 'A little about blood pressure.'

'Exactly. All vague and unscientific. But now we can tackle the subject quantitatively and scientifically. Some of the results I have already obtained are most significant and illuminating.'

Schmidt wondered vaguely how fear could be measured with any exactness, even if intelligent animals, even if monkeys were employed. But now conversation was interrupted, as they were passing through doors guarded by SS sentries, and crossing courtyards similarly patrolled. There were salutes in plenty for the Herr Professor, and it occurred to Schmidt that the government must be anxious to keep the research a secret to provide these guards.

'And here we are,' said Heinz, holding open a door for Schmidt to pass through.

There were guards here as well, in the long well-lit laboratory, guards in black uniforms with death's head insignia; guards carrying whips – it was they whom Schmidt saw first, and the sight puzzled him. There were seated workers and standing workers; the seated workers, each at a separate bench, were covered with scientific instruments of all sorts applied to their naked bodies. Schmidt could guess at the use of most of them; there were instruments for measuring blood pressure, and instruments for measuring the amount of air inspired, for recording respiration and heart beat. Beside each seated worker another, standing, was diligently employed in noting the recordings. The nakedness of the seated workers was surprising. More surprising still was the sight of the apparatus before each one, when Schmidt came to notice it. Each one had a roulette wheel in front of him, and was spinning it and was dropping the little ivory ball into the basin as he spun it. Schmidt could understand nothing of what he saw, and looked at his nephew in complete bewilderment.

'What is happening here?' he asked. 'Where are the animals?'

'Animals?' said Heinz. 'I thought I made it plain to you that I do not use animals. These are my subjects. These.'

He indicated with a sweep of his hand the twelve naked men sitting at the roulette wheels.

'Oh,' said Schmidt weakly.

'With animals,' said Heinz, and something faintly professorial crept into his manner as he spoke, 'it would be quite impossible, as I told you, to obtain quantitative results of any value. For those, intelligence on the part of the subject is necessary. Besides, I have already proved that there is almost no analogy between the physiological effects of fear in animals and in man.'

'But what are they doing?' asked Schmidt.

'It is simple,' explained Heinz, 'as practical ideas usually are. They spin their roulette wheels, as you see. The numbers that turn up are immaterial. It is the red and black that count.'

'Yes?'

'It is explained to each subject when he is brought here that when he spins eight consecutive reds it is the end for him.'

'The end?'

'These subjects are all people who are destined for liquidation, of course. They might as well be usefully employed first. And some of my most valuable data are acquired at the autopsies, as you can understand.'

'Yes.'

'And so these subjects are spinning their roulette wheels, and that is how I get my quantitative results. It is remarkable how exact they can be. A man spins a single red, and he hardly cares. Two, he is not much more concerned either. With the third and the fourth the physiological effects become more marked, and when it reaches seven the graphs show a very steep incline.'

'I suppose so,' said Schmidt.

He told himself that he was in a real world, with these things actually happening in it, and yet he found himself still wishing wildly that he would awake from the nightmare. There was a sharp crack and a cry of pain from the far end of the room, and Schmidt looked in that direction in time to see a guard turn away from one of the subjects after dealing a blow with his whip.

'As the number of consecutive reds increases the subject grows reluctant to go on spinning the wheel,' explained Heinz. 'Compulsion has to be employed with most of them.'

'Naturally,' said Schmidt. He knew perfectly well that if he blazed out in protest he would be proved not to be wholeheartedly for the regime – he might even find himself sitting spinning a roulette wheel.

'And yet the psychology is as interesting as the physiology,' went on Heinz. 'There are some who spin feverishly as if anxious to reach the end. We have even had a few who anticipated it, killing themselves in their cells at night – a nuisance, because it means a premature termination of the results in their case.'

'That must be a nuisance,' said Schmidt.

'The psychological findings are of course being analysed by another department,' said Heinz. 'Old Engel has a team of assistants at work on them. But psychology is by no means as exact a science as physiology – it can hardly be called a science at all, can it?'

'I suppose not.'

'With half these subjects,' explained Heinz, 'it is made clear to them that when they spin their eight reds they will meet their end by the quick SS neck shot, all over in a second. The other half are told that it will be a more painful process, prolonged as far as the SS can manage it. But it is quite surprising how little difference that prospect makes to the physiological results – the subjects really do not look beyond the fact that they will die when they spin their eight consecutive reds. In fact, I am thinking of discontinuing that part of the investigation, for the treatment administered by the SS brings about a serious confusion in the eventual findings at the autopsy. My work is more important than that of the psychologists.'

'Of course,' said Schmidt. He wanted to sit down, but Heinz went on talking, enthusiastic about his subject.

'Most of this apparatus I designed myself,' he said. 'This one here provides a continuous record of the rate of sweat secretion. The curves I am obtaining with it sometimes offer interesting contrasts with the graphs of blood pressure and respiration.'

He bent over to show the apparatus to Schmidt, standing close to the subject, a heavily built and swarthy man, who at that moment uttered a groan of despair.

'Seven, I see,' said Heinz. 'You notice how the blood pressure rises?'

The subject struggled on his stool – it was only then that Schmidt noticed that the subjects were leg ironed and chained in their places. A guard came sidling up, his whip whistling shrilly as he swung it in the air, and at the sound of it the subject subsided.

'Spin,' said the assistant who was taking the recordings, and the subject spun the wheel and dropped in the ivory ball, which bounced clicking against the metal studs.

'Ah, black,' said Heinz. 'Most of his curves will show an abrupt decline at this point.'

Schmidt felt relief that it had been black this time.

'Some of these subjects last literally for weeks,' commented Heinz. 'It takes that long sometimes for them to spin their eight consecutive reds. And yet there is very little flattening of the curves – you would be surprised at the consistency of the results. I'll show you some of my graphs in a moment.'

'That would be very interesting,' said Schmidt.

'One at least of my preconceived notions has been disposed of already,' said Heinz. 'I had formed a theory regarding possible fatigue of the suprarenals, but I've proved myself wrong. It was one more example of the necessity to correlate relevant facts before forming an hypothesis.'

Heinz twinkled at the memory; he did not mind admitting the human weakness.

'Yes, it is very necessary,' agreed Schmidt.

It was in the adjoining smaller laboratory that the graphs were kept. Heinz dilated on them with enthusiasm as he displayed them to his uncle, the saw-backed curves, continuous lines and broken lines, dotted lines and starred lines, lines of different colours, a dozen curves on each sheet for the various physiological measurements of an individual subject, mounting irregularly upwards towards an abrupt end; each sheet told the physiological history of the last days of a man.

'Extremely interesting,' said Schmidt, trying not to think about that part of it.

Back at the house Caecilie was quite indignant with her husband.

'Uncle looks more tired than ever, Heinz,' she said. 'You've worn him out today. I'm sorry, uncle. These scientists never know when to stop when they get started on their hobby. Why don't you have a little rest before the evening meal?'

Schmidt certainly needed a rest, and at dinner fortunately the conversation was not directed towards the physiology of fear. The Luftwaffe was at that time engaged upon the subjugation of England, so there were plenty of other subjects to discuss – the results of the day's air fighting, and the possibility that England might accept the Fuehrer's magnanimous offer of peace without the necessity of submitting to invasion, and the future of a world enlightened by the ideas of Nazidom. It was only at intervals during the rest of Schmidt's stay that Heinz discussed his research work. Once was when Caecilie had displayed some feminine weakness or other.

'Odd,' said Heinz when he was alone with his uncle, 'how inconsistent women can be. Some of the curves I've obtained with women subjects at the laboratory show the most remarkable variations from normal. The psychologists have seized upon them to help prove some of their theories. And I have to admit there's something to be said for them, too.'

And another time, after they had listened to a broadcast speech by Baldur von Schirach, Heinz talked about race in connection with his research.

'Of course,' he said, 'most of my subjects are Poles and Czechs. I expect you noticed that they were all of the Alpine or Mediterranean types. Even the non-Slavs were of these types. Naturally there are Semitics as well in plenty, but to make my research more complete I need Nordic types.'

'Naturally,' said Schmidt.

'And Nordic types are not so readily available. But I have asked the president to make the strongest representations on the point, and he is doing so. A Nordic type may commit a murder, perhaps. Or there is always the chance of a few Norwegians.'

'Of course that's possible.'

'And then I shall get a new set of curves. And the postmortem appearances should be most interesting.'

'Yes.'

It was a great surprise to Schmidt to hear his nephew talking the Nazi nonsense about race, about Nordics and Alpines. It was hard to believe that a scientist, a scientist with a good mind – even though completely heartless in his work – could possibly give any weight at all to those old theories. Schmidt had to remind himself that Heinz had been exposed to that sort of talk since his boyhood, had hardly known a world where Nordic superiority was not assumed as an article of faith – at least publicly – by everyone. That upbringing of his would largely account for the utter heartlessness, too. So that to Schmidt it was hard to decide which was the greater strain, to stay and listen to his nephew talking about his physiological research or to go back to his nightmare duties at the concentration camp. But he had no choice; when his leave was up he had to go back to Rosenberg camp, into the dreadful conditions there, and he had to do the dreadful things he was called upon to do. It was in the winter that he received a letter from Caecilie. He recognized the writing on the envelope, but the postmark was strange.

*They have taken Heinz away* [wrote Caecilie]. *Two SS men came and arrested him at night and of course they did not say why. Uncle, I am very worried and I am writing to you to ask you to help because you are in the SS. I am going to post this letter in another town in case they see me posting it and open it. Uncle, please help me. Please find out where he is and try to help him. He was always a good Nazi, as you know. He has never said anything or thought anything that the SS could say was treason. I pray you to help me, uncle. He would have been an army doctor gladly except that the Ministry decided he would be more useful in research. Please help me.*

The first thing that Schmidt did after reading that letter was to burn it. It was dangerous enough to be related to a man who had been arrested by the SS; to be asked by that man's wife to help was very dangerous indeed. And there was nothing he could do, either. The SS kept its secrets, and no insignificant surgeon could hope to be admitted to them, and if that surgeon began to ask questions it might be – it would certainly be – too bad for him. Schmidt did not even answer Caecilie's letter; her mail would undoubtedly be opened and read, and he could not risk even expressing sympathy for a man whose guilt was obvious because of his arrest. He worried about it, though.

The following summer, after the invasion of Russia had begun, Schmidt attended a selection parade in his official capacity.

'A hundred and twenty,' said the camp commandant to him; from the little office they could hear the shouts of the guards and the kapos as they formed up their party for the parade. 'There will be five hundred present, so you can take one in four. A few more than a hundred and twenty will not matter.'

This was the worst of Schmidt's duties, to select the men and women who were to die in the Rosenberg gas chamber. Those were the times when he almost thought he would rather have the gas chamber for himself – almost. That 'almost' might explain how he had come to be selected as surgeon in the SS and posted to a concentration camp; the SS picked their instruments carefully, and they had noted how fear had forced Schmidt into accepting duties progressively more revolting.

Schmidt drank a glass of schnapps, saw to it that his uniform was correct, and stepped out into the blinding sunshine on the parade ground. Perhaps it was not as bad to select men victims as women. Usually the men made less commotion about it; many of them tried to appear brave, and were ashamed to show emotion before their fellows – some of them, not very many, would try desperately to make a joke when they were selected. And on the other hand they were often so worn down with harsh treatment that they were apathetic. Schmidt hoped that would be the case now.

He walked along the line. Behind him followed the guards to herd away the victims he selected. He had to choose one in four. He might merely have indicated every fourth man, by pure chance, but he dared not do so, lest the anomalies should be too glaring. If he picked those who were still fit and able, and left the old, the sick, and the worn out, it would be noticed. He had to exercise some care in the selection.

He did not look at the faces; he could not. He looked at the bodies. The diseased, the old, the starved; he had to keep his head clear and his mind active so as to keep count and maintain the proportion of roughly one in four. He pointed to those he selected and passed on. Behind him there were groans of despair; sometimes hysterical screams, the sharp sound of blows, sometimes even a shot as some desperate man resisted and was given his end on the spot. Halfway down the line Schmidt heard a sudden whisper from the line; a single word.

'Uncle!'

He looked up from the body to the face. It was Heinz; but if the word had not been spoken he would not have recognized him. The growth of dirty beard alone was a disguise. And Heinz had lost some of his teeth, and his nose was not quite straight now, and his cheeks were hollow, with the cheekbones standing out. Schmidt looked down again at the scars and sores on the body. If he had not looked at the face he might well have selected Heinz for the gas chamber, young and vigorous though he had recently been.

Neither man dared show further sign of recognition. Luckily the SS men were some yards behind and had not heard the whispered word. Luckily the men on either side of Heinz were old and could be picked as victims – luckily Schmidt's mind was clear enough for him to think of that, lest they should talk and should involve him in Heinz' catastrophe. Schmidt passed on and left Heinz standing in the line, unchosen. Schmidt was shaking with the shock, after his moment of clear thinking, and it was all he could do to complete the parade.

As medical officer Schmidt had access to the files in the central office, and after a decent interval he went to examine them. He went through the card index elaborately, looking at many names, so that the corporal on duty there would not guess what was the real object of his search. Heinz' card was there, but – as Schmidt fully expected – it told him nothing of importance. There were only dates and the names of camps. Heinz had been in two bad ones before coming to Rosenberg, which accounted for the scars and the sores. But there was no indication of what his offence had been – that was only given on the cards of prisoners who were guilty of crimes in the old sense. The SS kept its secrets; Schmidt came away from his examination of the files knowing no more than he had done before. Nor was he going to make any further inquiries. No one ever inquired about an SS prisoner; nobody wanted to be thought interested in an SS prisoner's fate.

He was due to have leave soon again, and it called for an effort to decide what he was to do then. He had heard from Caecilie that she had been conscripted into factory work, but her house was still open to him, of course. There was almost nowhere else that he could go, and he went, eventually, and Caecilie made him welcome as always. The house was by no means entirely hers now, as a number of technical workers had been billeted in it – to Schmidt that was something of a relief, because it restricted conversation about Heinz. Caecilie could only speak about him when they were quite alone, and then no louder than a whisper. Schmidt was sympathetic but non-committal; he had decided after prolonged thought not to tell her about his encounter with Heinz. It would do her no good, and it might do her a great deal of harm. She would want to know all about him, how his health was and how he looked, and Schmidt neither wanted to tell her nor could he trust himself to lie convincingly. And, moreover, Caecilie would expect him to do something to alleviate Heinz' fate, and Schmidt knew that to be downright impossible. He could not bear having to tell her that.

And there was the question of his oaths; at the time of his induction into the SS he had sworn to keep the secrets of the organization, and he had sworn a further oath never to reveal to the outside world anything about what went on in concentration camps; secrecy made the SS more dreaded than ever, and it was even possible that the SS did not feel happy at the thought that the outside world should know about the nature of the punishments it inflicted. Schmidt had no scruples about the oaths he had taken, but he did not want to violate them by telling Caecilie what he knew. Caecilie might at any time be arrested, and under questioning by the SS she would certainly reveal (Schmidt knew about that questioning) anything Schmidt had told her. It was best not to tell her anything.

But because of the prickings of his conscience in the matter he decided in the end to do what he had had in the back of his mind for some time. There was a risk about it, but it was the best he could do. He sent a polite note to Standartenfuehrer Kroide at the university, telling him of his presence in the city on leave, and – he had not really expected it but only hoped for it – received in return an invitation to luncheon.

It was the usual large party, and Kroide was his usual charming self, the perfect host. It occurred to Schmidt as he listened to the conversation that these parties were one tiny strand in a vast spider's web spread all over the country, in the centre of which was the spider, Dr Goebbels himself, attentive to all the vibrations that passed along the strands. There was wine, there was the freest of conversation, and after such a party Kroide would be able to pass along a good deal of information regarding the attitude of the local intellectuals.

Today there was no lack of a subject to talk about. The army was pressing far and fast into Russia, and the communiques were blaring victory. There could be no doubt that the Russian colossus would soon be beaten to the ground. No army could long endure the defeats the Fuehrer was inflicting on the Russians. They would collapse, and that would be the end of Germany's last rival save for England, impotent across the sea and fast being strangled by the U-boat campaign. There were some quite amusing jokes about what the Fuehrer would do with Stalin when he fell into his hands. Standartenfuehrer Kroide sat beaming as he listened to the talk, and he let it be understood, by his significant reticences, that he could, if security did not forbid, add much to the conversation, and that, as a high official of the Ministry of Propaganda, he was cognisant of many secrets regarding the further surprises the Fuehrer had up his sleeve for the enemies of the Reich. He beamed and he drank wine, mellowed by alcohol and victory. It was after lunch was over, as the guests still stood chatting, that he addressed himself to Schmidt.

'Too bad about that young nephew of yours,' he said.

'My nephew Heinrich?' asked Schmidt, without committing himself.

'Yes. I once had great hopes of him. I thought he was a talented scientist and a fervent friend of the Reich, but to my disappointment I found he was neither.'

'I am sorry about that, Standartenfuehrer,' said Schmidt. It was safe to be sorry about Kroide's hurt feelings, even if it was not safe to be sorry about Heinz' fate.

'The silly young fool,' said Kroide. 'Not only was he completely wrong-headed, but he wanted to proclaim the fact publicly.'

'How very extraordinary!' said Schmidt.

'Yes, indeed. He told me he had completed the piece of physiological research on which he was engaged – you remember – and I was quite delighted. I encouraged him all the time he was writing his paper regarding his results, and I looked forward to the time when it should be completed.'

'And did he complete it, Standartenfuehrer?'

'Yes. Of course I did not read it; it was far too technical for me. I forwarded it, just as it was, graphs, statistics, and all, to Dr Goebbels' office, as was my duty, of course.'

'Yes?' Schmidt hoped he was not displaying too much interest. Despite the wine which made his head swim he tried to put exactly the right intonation into what he said.

'I was really only concerned with security – I thought it was possible, or even likely, that the paper might contain material that our enemies could find useful as well as us. It was a routine step, to decide whether it would be desirable to publish the paper in the university Transactions'.'

Kroide took off his spectacles and polished them, and blinked short-sightedly at Schmidt.

'It was a great shock to me,' went on Kroide, 'when the teletype message came in ordering me to suppress everything to do with your nephew's paper. The SS, of course, had already arrested him by the time the message reached me.'

'How shocking!' said Schmidt. He still did not dare to ask the obvious question, but he waited hopefully and his hope was not disappointed.

'Yes,' said Kroide, almost with regret. 'The SS had no choice but to arrest him and put him where his ridiculous theories could do no harm. Do you know what the madman had written?'

'I simply cannot guess,' said Schmidt.

Kroide leaned forward confidentially and tapped Schmidt on the chest with his spectacles.

'He had it all wrong. I even think he might have had insane delusions. He thought he had proved that fear had exactly the same physiological results with Nordics as with the lesser races! Can you imagine anything more insane or more treasonable?'

'No,' said Schmidt.

# L. P. Hartley

## *W. S.*

The first postcard came from Forfar. *I thought you might like a picture of Forfar, it began. You have always been so interested in Scotland, and that is one reason why I am interested in you. I have enjoyed all your books, but do you really get to grips with people? I doubt it. Try to think of this as a handshake from your devoted admirer. — W. S.*

Like other novelists, Walter Streeter was used to getting communications from strangers. Usually they were friendly but sometimes they were critical. In either case he always answered them, for he was conscientious. But answering them took up the time and energy he needed for his writing, so that he was rather relieved that W. S. had given no address. The photograph of Forfar was uninteresting and he tore it up. His anonymous correspondent's criticism, however, lingered in his mind. Did he really fail to come to grips with his characters? Perhaps he did. He was aware that in most cases they were either projections of his own personality or, in different forms, the antitheses of it. The Me and the Not Me. Perhaps W. S. had spotted this. Not for the first time Walter made a vow to be more objective.

About ten days later arrived another postcard, this time from Berwick-on-Tweed. *What do you think of Berwick-on-Tweed? it said. Like you, it's on the Border. I hope this doesn't sound rude. I don't mean that you are a borderline case! You know how much I admire your stories. Some people call them other-worldly. I think you should plump for one world or the other. Another warm handshake from. – W. S.*

Walter Streeter pondered over this and began to wonder about the sender. Was his correspondent a man or a woman? It looked like a man's handwriting – commercial, un-selfconscious, and the criticism was like a man's. On the other hand, it was like a woman to probe – to want to make him feel at the same time flattered and unsure of himself. He felt the faint stirrings of curiosity but soon dismissed them; he was not a man to experiment with acquaintances. Still, it was odd to think of this unknown person speculating about him, sizing him up. Other-worldly, indeed! He reread the last two chapters he had written. Perhaps they didn't have their feet firm on the ground. Perhaps he was too ready to escape, as other novelists were nowadays, into an ambiguous world, a world where the conscious mind did not have things too much its own way. But did that matter? He threw the picture of Berwick-on-Tweed into his November fire and tried to write; but the words came haltingly, as though contending with an extra-strong barrier of self-criticism. And as the days passed, he became uncomfortably aware of self-division, as though someone had taken hold of his personality and was pulling it apart. His work was no longer homogeneous; there were two strains in it, unreconciled and opposing, and it went much slower as he tried to resolve the discord. Never mind, he thought: perhaps I was getting into a groove. These difficulties may be growing pains; I may have tapped a new source of supply. If only I could correlate the two and make their conflict fruitful, as many artists have!

The third postcard showed a picture of York Minster. *I know you are interested in cathedrals,* it said. *I'm sure this isn't a sign of megalomania in your case, but smaller churches are sometimes more rewarding. I'm seeking a good many churches on my way south. Are you busy writing or are you looking round for ideas? Another hearty handshake from your friend. – W. S.*

It was true that Walter Streeter was interested in cathedrals. Lincoln Cathedral had been the subject of one of his youthful fantasies and he had written about it in a travel book. And it was also true that he admired mere size and was inclined to undervalue parish churches. But how could W. S. have known that? And was it really a sign of megalomania? And who was W. S., anyhow?

For the first time it struck him that the initials were his own. No, not for the first time. He had noticed it before, but they were such commonplace initials; they were Gilbert's, they were Maugham's, they were Shakespeare's – a common possession. Anyone might have them. Yet now it seemed to him an odd coincidence; and the idea came into his mind – suppose I have been writing postcards to myself? People did such things, especially people with split personalities. Not that he was one of them, of course. And yet there were these unexplained developments – the dichotomy in his writing, which had now extended from his thought to his style, making one paragraph languorous with semicolons and subordinate clauses, and another sharp and incisive with main verbs and fullstops.

He looked at the handwriting again. It had seemed the perfection of ordinariness – anybody's hand – so ordinary as perhaps to be disguised. Now he fancied he saw in it resemblances to his own. He was just going to pitch the postcard in the fire when suddenly he decided not to. I'll show it to somebody, he thought.

His friend said, 'My dear fellow, it's all quite plain. The woman's a lunatic. I'm sure it's a woman. She has probably fallen in love with you and wants to make you interested in her. I should pay no attention whatsoever. People in the public eye are always getting letters from lunatics. If they worry you, destroy them without reading them. That sort of person is often a little psychic, and if she senses that she's getting a rise out of you, she'll go on.'

For a moment Walter Streeter felt reassured. A woman, a little mouse-like creature, who had somehow taken a fancy to him! What was there to feel uneasy about in that? Then his subconscious mind, searching for something to torment him with, and assuming the authority of logic, said: Supposing those postcards are a lunatic's, and you are writing them to yourself; doesn't it follow that you must be a lunatic too?

He tried to put the thought away from him; he tried to destroy the postcard as he had the others. But something in him wanted to preserve it. It had become a piece of him, he felt. Yielding to an irresistible compulsion, which he dreaded, he found himself putting it behind the clock on the chimney piece. He couldn't see it, but he knew that it was there.

He now had to admit to himself that the postcard business had become a leading factor in his life. It had created a new area of thoughts and feelings, and they were most unhelpful. His being was strung up in expectation of the next postcard.

Yet when it came it took him completely by surprise. He could not bring himself to look at the picture. *I am coming nearer,* the postcard said; *I have got as near as Warwick Castle. Perhaps we shall come to grips after all. I advised you to come to grips with your characters, didn't I? Have I given you any new ideas? If I have, you ought to thank me, for they are what novelists want, I understand. I have been re-reading your novels, living in them, I might say. Je vous serre la main. As always. – W. S.*

A wave of panic surged up in Walter Streeter. How was it that he had never noticed, all this time, the most significant fact about the postcards – that each one came from a place geographically closer to him than the last? *I am coming nearer.* Had his mind, unconsciously self-protective, worn blinkers? If it had, he wished he could put them back. He took an atlas and idly traced out W. S.'s itinerary. An interval of eighty miles or so seemed to separate the stopping places. Walter lived in a large West Country town about eighty miles from Warwick.

Should he show the postcards to an alienist? But what could an alienist tell him? He would not know, what Walter wanted to know, whether he had anything to fear from W. S.

Better go to the police. The police were used to dealing with poison pens. If they laughed at him, so much the better.

They did not laugh, however. They said they thought the postcards were a hoax and that W. S. would never show up in the flesh. Then they asked if there was anyone who had a grudge against him. 'No one that I know of,' Walter said. They, too, took the view that the writer was probably a woman. They told him not to worry, but to let them know if further postcards came.

A little comforted, Walter went home. The talk with the police had done him good. He thought it over. It was quite true what he had told them – that he had no enemies. He was not a man of strong personal feelings; such feelings as he had went into his books. In his books he had drawn some pretty nasty characters. Not of recent years, however. Of recent years he had felt a reluctance to draw a very bad man or woman: he thought it morally irresponsible and artistically unconvincing, too. There was good in everyone: Iagos were a myth. Latterly – but he had to admit that it was several weeks since he laid pen to paper, so much had this ridiculous business of the postcards weighed upon his mind – if he had to draw a really wicked person he represented him as a Communist or a Nazi – someone who had deliberately put off his human characteristics. But in the past, when he was younger and more inclined to see things as black or white, he had let himself go once or twice. He did not remember his old books very well, but there was a character in one, *The Pariah*, into whom he had really got his knife. He had written about him with extreme vindictiveness, just as if he was a real person whom he was trying to show up. He had experienced a curious pleasure in attributing every kind of wickedness to this man. He never gave him the benefit of the doubt. He never felt a twinge of pity for him, even when he paid the penalty for his misdeeds on the gallows. He had so worked himself up that the idea of this dark creature, creeping about brimful of malevolence, had almost frightened him.

Odd that he couldn't remember the man's name. He took the book down from the shelf and turned the pages – even now they affected him uncomfortably. Yes, here it was, William… William… he would have to look back to find the surname. William Stainsforth.

His own initials.

He did not think the coincidence meant anything, but it coloured his mind and weakened its resistance to his obsession. So uneasy was he that when the next postcard came, it came as a relief.

*I am quite close now,* he read, and involuntarily turned the postcard over. The splendid central tower of Gloucester Cathedral met his eyes. He stared at it as if it could tell him something, then with an effort went on reading. *My movements, as you may have guessed, are not quite under my control, but all being well, I look forward to seeing you some time this weekend. Then we can really come to grips. I wonder if you'll recognize me! It won't be the first time you have given me hospitality. Ti serro lo mano. As always. – W. S.*

Walter took the postcard straight to the police station, and asked if he could have police protection over the weekend. The officer in charge smiled at him and said he was quite sure it was a hoax; but he would send someone to keep an eye on the place.

'You still have no idea who it would be?' he asked.

Walter shook his head.

It was Tuesday; Walter Streeter had plenty of time to think about the weekend. At first he felt he would not be able to live through the interval but, strange to say, his confidence increased instead of waning. He set himself to work as though he could work, and presently he found he could – differently from before and, he thought, better. It was as though the nervous strain he had been living under had, like an acid, dissolved a layer of nonconductive thought that came between him and his subject; he was nearer to it now, and instead of responding only too readily to his stage directions, his characters responded wholeheartedly and with all their beings to the tests he put them to. So passed the days, and the dawn of Friday seemed like any other day until something jerked him out of his self-induced trance and suddenly he asked himself, 'When does a weekend begin?'

A long weekend begins on Friday. At that his panic returned. He went to the street door and looked out. It was a suburban, unfrequented street of detached Regency houses like his own. They had tall square gateposts, some crowned with semicircular iron brackets holding lanterns. Most of these were out of repair: only two or three were ever lit. A car went slowly down the street; some people crossed it; everything was normal.

Several times that day he went to look and saw nothing suspicious, and when Saturday came, bringing no postcard, his panic had almost subsided. He nearly rang up the police to tell them not to bother to send anyone after all.

They were as good as their word: they did send someone. Between tea and dinner, the time when weekend guests most commonly arrive, Walter went to the door and there, between two unlit gateposts, he saw a policeman standing – the first policeman he had ever seen in Charlotte Street. At the sight and the relief it brought him, he realized how anxious he had been. Now he felt safer than he had ever felt in his life, and also a little ashamed at having given extra trouble to a hard-worked body of men. Should he go and speak to his unknown guardian, offer him a cup of tea and a drink? It would be nice to hear him laugh at Walter's fancies. But no – somehow he felt his security the greater when its source was impersonal and anonymous. 'PC Smith' was somehow less impressive than 'police protection'.

Several times from an upper window (he didn't like to open the door and stare) he made sure that his guardian was still there; and once, for added proof, he asked his housekeeper to verify the strange phenomenon. Disappointingly, she came back saying she had seen no policeman; but she was not very good at seeing things, and when Walter went a few minutes later, he saw him plain enough. The man must walk about, of course; perhaps he had been taking a stroll when Mrs Kendal looked.

It was contrary to his routine to work after dinner but tonight he did – he felt so much in the vein. Indeed, a sort of exaltation possessed him; the words ran off his pen; it would be foolish to check the creative impulse for the sake of a little extra sleep. On, on. They were right who said the small hours were the time to work. When his housekeeper came in to say goodnight, he scarcely raised his eyes.

In the warm, snug little room the silence purred around him like a kettle. He did not even hear the doorbell till it had been ringing for some time.

A visitor at this hour?

His knees trembling, he went to the door, scarcely knowing what he expected to find; so what was his relief, on opening it, to see the doorway filled by the tall figure of a policeman. Without waiting for the man to speak,

'Come in, come in, my dear fellow,' he exclaimed. He held his hand out, but the policeman did not take it. 'You must have been very cold standing out there. I didn't know that it was snowing, though,' he added, seeing the snowflakes on the policeman's cape and helmet. 'Come in and warm yourself.'

'Thanks,' said the policeman. 'I don't mind if I do.'

Walter knew enough of the phrases used by men of the policeman's stamp not to mistake this for a grudging acceptance. 'This way,' he prattled on. 'I was writing in my study. By Jove, it is cold, I'll turn the gas on more. Now, won't you take your traps off and make yourself at home?'

'I can't stay long,' the policeman said, 'I've got a job to do, as *you* know.'

'Oh yes,' said Walter, 'such a silly job, a sinecure.' He stopped, wondering if the policeman would know what a sinecure was. 'I suppose you know what it's about – the postcards?'

The policeman nodded.

'But nothing can happen to me as long as you are here,' said Walter. 'I shall be as safe... as safe as houses. Stay as long as you can, and have a drink.'

'I never drink on duty,' said the policeman. Still in his cape and helmet, he looked round. 'So this is where you work?' he said.

'Yes, I was writing when you rang.'

'Some poor chap's for it, I expect,' the policeman said.

'Oh, why?' Walter was hurt by his unfriendly tone, and noticed how hard his eyes were.

'I'll tell you in a minute,' said the policeman, and then the telephone bell rang. Walter excused himself and hurried from the room.

'This is the police station,' said a voice. 'Is that Mr Streeter?'

Walter said it was.

'Well, Mr Streeter, how is everything at your place? All right, I hope? I'll tell you why I ask. I'm sorry to say we quite forgot about that little job we were going to do for you. Bad co-ordination, I'm afraid.'

'But,' said Walter, 'you did send someone.'

'No, Mr Streeter, I'm afraid we didn't.'

'But there's a policeman here, here in this very house.'

There was a pause, then his interlocutor said, in a less casual voice,

'He can't be one of our chaps. Did you see his number by any chance?'

'No.'

Another pause and the voice said,

'Would you like us to send somebody now?'

'Yes p–please.'

'All right, then; we'll be with you in a jiffy.'

Walter put back the receiver. 'What now?' he asked himself. Should he barricade the door? Should he run out into the street? While he was debating, the door opened and his guest came in.

'No room's private when the street door's once passed,' he said. 'Had you forgotten I was a policeman?'

'Was?' said Walter, edging away from him. 'You *are* a policeman.'

'I have been other things as well,' the policeman said. 'Thief, pimp, blackmailer, not to mention murderer. *You* should know.'

The policeman, if such he was, seemed to be moving towards him, and Walter suddenly became alive to the importance of small distances – from the sideboard to the table, from one chair to another.

'I don't know what you mean,' he said. 'Why do you speak like that? I've never done you any harm. I've never set eyes on you before.'

'Oh, haven't you?' the man said. 'But you've thought about me, and' – his voice rose – 'and you've written about me. You got some fun out of me, didn't you? Now I'm going to get some fun out of you. You made me just as nasty as you could. Wasn't that doing me harm? You didn't think what it would be like to be me, did you? You didn't put yourself in my place, did you? You hadn't any pity for me, had you? Well, I'm not going to have any pity for you.'

'But I tell you,' cried Walter, fingering the table's edge, 'I don't know you!'

'And now you say you don't know me! You did all that to me and then forget me!' His voice became a whine, charged with self-pity. 'You forgot William Stainsforth.'

'William Stainsforth!'

'Yes. I was your scapegoat, wasn't I? You unloaded all your self-dislike on me. You felt pretty good while you were writing about me. Now, as one W. S. to another, what shall I do, if I behave in character?'

'I – I don't know,' muttered Walter.

'You don't know?' Stainsforth sneered. 'You ought to know, you fathered me. What would William Stainsforth do if he met his old dad in a quiet place, his kind old dad who made him swing?'

Walter could only stare at him.

'You know what he'd do as well as I,' said Stainsforth. Then his face changed and he said abruptly, 'No you don't, because you never really understood me. I'm not so black as you painted me.' He paused and a flame of hope flickered in Walter's breast. 'You never gave me a chance, did you? Well, I'm going to give you one. That shows you never understood me, doesn't it?'

Walter nodded.

'And there's another thing you have forgotten.'

'What is that?'

'I was a kid once,' the ex-policeman said.

Walter said nothing.

'You admit that?' said William Stainsforth grimly. 'Well, if you can tell me of one virtue you ever credited me with – just one kind thought – just one redeeming feature –'

'Yes,' said Walter, trembling.

'Well, then I'll let you off.'

'And if I can't?' whispered Walter.

'Well, then, that's just too bad. We'll have to come to grips, and you know what that means. You took off one of my arms but I've still got the other. "Stainsforth of the iron arm", you called me.'

Walter began to pant.

'I'll give you two minutes to remember,' Stainsforth said.

They both looked at the clock. At first the stealthy movement of the hand paralysed Walter's thoughts. He stared at William Stainsforth's face, his cruel and crafty face, which seemed to be always in shadow, as if it was something the light could not touch. Desperately he searched his memory for the one fact that would save him; but his memory, clenched like a fist, would give up nothing.

'I must invent something,' he thought, and suddenly his mind relaxed and he saw, printed on it like a photograph, the last page of the book. Then, with the speed and magic of a dream, each page appeared before him in perfect clarity until the first was reached, and he realized with overwhelming force that what he looked for was not there. In all that evil there was not one hint of good. And he felt, compulsively and with a kind of exaltation, that unless he testified to this, the cause of goodness everywhere would be betrayed.

'There's nothing to be said for you!' he shouted. 'Of all your dirty tricks this is the dirtiest! The very snow-flakes on you are turning black! How dare you ask me for a character? I've given you one already! God forbid that I should ever say a good word for you! I'd rather die!'

Stainsforth's one arm shot out. 'Then die!' he said.

The police found Walter Streeter slumped across the dining-table. In view of what had happened previously, they did not exclude the possibility of foul play. But the pathologist could not state with certainty the cause of death. There was a clue, but it led nowhere. On the table and on the victim's clothes were flakes of melting snow. It had run down his neck, soaking his underclothes. It had even, in some way, got into his stomach and might have killed him for, on analysis, it was found to be poisonous. Perhaps he had taken his own life. But what the substance was, and where it came from, remained a mystery, for no snow was reported from any district on the day he died.

# Hazel Heald

# *The Horror in the Museum*

It was languid curiosity which first brought Stephen Jones to Rogers's Museum. Someone had told him about the queer underground place in Southwark Street across the river, where waxen things so much more horrible than the worst effigies at Madame Tussaud's were shown, and he had strolled in one April day to see how disappointing he would find it. Oddly, he was not disappointed. There was something different and distinctive here, after all. Of course, the usual gory commonplaces were present – Landru, Doctor Crippen, Madame Demers, Rizzio, Lady Jane Grey, endless maimed victims of war and revolution, and monsters like Gilles de Rais and Marquis de Sade – but there were other things which had made him breathe faster and stay till the ringing of the closing bell. The man who had fashioned this collection could be no ordinary mountebank. There was imagination – even a kind of diseased genius – in some of this stuff.

Later he had learned about George Rogers. The man had been on the Tussaud staff, but some trouble had developed which led to his discharge. There were aspersions on his sanity and tales of his crazy forms of secret worship – though latterly his success with his own basement museum had dulled the edge of some criticisms while sharpening the insidious point of others. Teratology and the iconography of nightmare were his hobbies, and even he had had the prudence to screen off some of his worst effigies in a special alcove for adults only. It was this alcove which had fascinated Jones so much. There were lumpish hybrid things which only fantasy could spawn, moulded with devilish skill, and coloured in a horribly lifelike fashion.

Some were the figures of well-known myths – gorgons, chimeras, dragons, cyclops, and all their shuddersome congeners. Others were drawn from darker and more furtively whispered cycles of subterranean legend – black, formless Tsathoggua, many tentacled Cthulhu, proboscidian Chaugnar Faugn, and other rumoured blasphemies from forbidden books like the *Necronomicon*, the *Book of Eibon*, or the *Unaussprechlichen Kulten* of von Junzt. But the worst were wholly original with Rogers, and represented shapes which no tale of antiquity had ever dared to suggest. Several were hideous parodies on forms of organic life we know, while others seemed taken from feverish dreams of other planets and other galaxies. The wilder paintings of Clark Ashton Smith might suggest a few – but nothing could suggest the effect of poignant, loathsome terror created by their great size and fiendishly cunning workmanship, and by the diabolically clever lighting conditions under which they were exhibited.

Stephen Jones, as a leisurely connoisseur of the bizarre in art, had sought out Rogers himself in the dingy office and workroom behind the vaulted museum chamber – an evil-looking crypt lighted dimly by dusty windows set slitlike and horizontal in the brick wall on a level with the ancient cobblestones of a hidden courtyard. It was here that the images were repaired – here, too, where some of them had been made. Waxen arms, legs, heads, and torsos lay in grotesque array on various benches, while on high tiers of shelves matted wigs, ravenous-looking teeth, and glassy, staring eyes were indiscriminately scattered. Costumes of all sorts hung from hooks, and in one alcove were great piles of flesh-coloured wax cakes and shelves filled with paint cans and brushes of every description. In the centre of the room was a large melting furnace used to prepare the wax for moulding, its firebox topped by a huge iron container on hinges, with a spout which permitted the pouring of melted wax with the merest touch of a finger.

Other things in the dismal crypt were less describable – isolated parts of problematical entities whose assembled forms were the phantoms of delirium. At one end was a door of heavy plank, fastened by an unusually large padlock and with a very peculiar symbol painted over it. Jones, who had once had access to the dreaded Necronomicon, shivered involuntarily as he recognized that symbol. This showman, he reflected, must indeed be a person of disconcertingly wide scholarship in dark and dubious fields.

Nor did the conversation of Rogers disappoint him. The man was tall, lean, and rather unkempt, with large black eyes which gazed combustively from a pallid and unusually stubble-covered face. He did not resent Jones's intrusion, but seemed to welcome the chance of unburdening himself to an interested person. His voice was of singular depth and resonance, and harboured a sort of repressed intensity bordering on the feverish. Jones did not wonder that many had thought him mad.

With every successive call – and such calls became a habit as the weeks went by – Jones had found Rogers more communicative and confidential. From the first there had been hints of strange faiths and practices on the showman's part, and later on these hints expanded into tales – despite a few odd corroborative photographs – whose extravagance was almost comic. It was some time in June, on a night when Jones had brought a bottle of good whisky and plied his host somewhat freely, that the really demented talk first appeared. Before that there had been wild enough stories – accounts of mysterious trips to Tibet, the African interior, the Arabian desert, the Amazon valley, Alaska, and certain little-known islands of the South Pacific, plus claims of having read such monstrous and half-fabulous books as the prehistoric Poakotic fragments and the Dhol chants attributed to malign and non-human Leng – but nothing in all this had been so unmistakably insane as what had cropped out that June evening under the spell of the whisky.

To be plain, Rogers began making vague boasts of having found certain things in nature that no one had found before, and of having brought back tangible evidences of such discoveries. According to his bibulous harangue, he had gone farther than anyone else in interpreting the obscure and primal books he studied, and had been directed by them to certain remote places where strange survivals are hidden – survivals of eons and life cycles earlier than mankind, and in some cases connected with other dimensions and other worlds, communication with which was frequent in the forgotten pre-human days. Jones marvelled at the fancy which could conjure up such notions, and wondered just what Rogers's mental history had been. Had his work amidst the morbid grotesqueries of Madame Tussaud's been the start of his imaginative flights, or was the tendency innate, so that his choice of an occupation was merely one of its manifestations? At any rate, the man's work was merely very closely linked with his notions. Even now there was no mistaking the trend of his blackest hints about the nightmare monstrosities in the screened-off 'Adults only' alcove. Heedless of ridicule, he was trying to imply that not all of these demoniac abnormalities were artificial.

It was Jones's frank scepticism and amusement at these irresponsible claims which broke up the growing cordiality. Rogers, it was clear, took himself very seriously; for fie now became morose and resentful, continuing to tolerate Jones only through a dogged urge to break down his will of urbane and complacent incredulity. Wild tales and suggestions of rites and sacrifices to nameless elder gods continued, and now and then Rogers would lead his guest to one of the hideous blasphemies in the screened-off alcove and point out features difficult to reconcile with even the finest human craftsmanship. Jones continued his visits through sheer fascination, though he knew he had forfeited his host's regard. At times he would try to humour Rogers with pretended assent to some mad hint or assertion, but the gaunt showman was seldom to be deceived by such tactics.

The tension came to a head later in September. Jones had casually dropped into the museum one afternoon, and was wandering through the dim corridors whose horrors were now so familiar, when he heard a very peculiar sound from the general direction of Rogers's workroom. Others heard it, too, and started nervously as the echoes reverberated through the great vaulted basement. The three attendants exchanged odd glances; and one of them, a dark, taciturn, foreign-looking fellow who always served Rogers as a repairer and assistant designer, smiled in a way which seemed to puzzle his colleagues and which grated very harshly on some facet of Jones's sensibilities. It was the yelp or scream of a dog, and was such a sound as could be made only under conditions of the utmost fright and agony combined. Its stark, anguished frenzy was appalling to hear, and in this setting of grotesque abnormality it held a double hideousness. Jones remembered that no dogs were allowed in the museum.

He was about to go to the door leading into the workroom, when the dark attendant stopped him with a word and a gesture. Mr Rogers, the man said in a soft, somewhat accented voice, at once apologetic and vaguely sardonic, was out, and there were standing orders to admit no one to the workroom during his absence. As for that yelp, it was undoubtedly something out in the courtyard behind the museum. This neighbourhood was full of stray mongrels, and their fights were sometimes shockingly noisy. There were no dogs in any part of the museum. But if Mr Jones wished to see Mr Rogers he might find him just before closing-time.

After this Jones had climbed the old stone steps to the street outside and examined the squalid neighbourhood curiously. The leaning, decrepit buildings – once dwellings but now largely shops and warehouses – were very ancient indeed. Some of them were of a gabled type seeming to go back to Tudor times, and a faint miasmatic stench hung subtly about the whole region. Beside the dingy house whose basement held the museum was a low archway pierced by a dark, cobbled alley, and this Jones entered in a vague wish to find the courtyard behind the workroom and settle the affair of the dog more comfortably in his mind. The courtyard was dim in the late-afternoon light, hemmed in by rear walls even uglier and more intangibly menacing than the crumbling street façades of the evil old houses. Not a dog was in sight, and Jones wondered how the aftermath of such a frantic turmoil could have completely vanished so soon.

Despite the assistant's statement that no dog had been in the museum, Jones glanced nervously at the three small windows of the basement workroom – narrow, horizontal rectangles close to the grass-grown pavement, with grimy panes that stared repulsively and incuriously like the eyes of dead fish. To their left a worn flight of steps led to an opaque and heavily bolted door. Some impulse urged him to crouch low on the damp, broken cobblestones and peer in, on the chance that the thick green shades, worked by long cords that hung down to a reachable level, might not be drawn. The outer surfaces were thick with dirt, but as he rubbed them with his handkerchief he saw that there were no obscuring curtains in the way of his vision.

So shadowed was the cellar from the inside that not much could be made out, but the grotesque working paraphernalia now and then loomed up spectrally as Jones tried each of the windows in turn. It seemed evident at first that no one was within; yet when he peered through the extreme right-hand window – the one nearest the entrance alley – he saw a glow of light at the farther end of the apartment which made him pause in bewilderment. These was no reason why any light should be there. It was an inner side of the room, and he could not recall any gas or electric fixture near that point. Another look defined the glow as a large vertical rectangle, and a thought occurred to him. It was in that direction that he had always noticed the heavy plank door with the abnormally large padlock – the door which was never opened, and above which was crudely smeared that hideous, cryptic symbol from the fragmentary records of forbidden elder magic. It must be open now – and there was a light inside. All his former speculations as to where that door led, and as to what lay beyond it, were now renewed with trebly disquieting force.

Jones wandered aimlessly around the dismal locality till close to six o'clock, when he returned to the museum to make a call on Rogers. He could hardly tell why he wished so especially to see the man just then, but there must have been some subconscious misgivings about that terribly un-placeable canine scream of the afternoon, and about the glow of light in that disturbing and usually unopened inner doorway with the heavy padlock. The attendants were leaving as he arrived, and he thought that Orabona – the dark, foreign-looking assistant – eyed him with something like sly, repressed amusement. He did not relish that look – even though he had seen the fellow turn it on his employer many times.

The vaulted exhibition room was ghoulish in its desertion, but he strode quickly through it and rapped at the door of the office and workroom. Response was slow in coming, though there were footsteps inside. Finally, in response to a second knock, the lock rattled, and the ancient six-panelled portal creaked reluctantly open to reveal the slouching, feverish-eyed form of George Rogers. From the first it was clear that the showman was in an unusual mood. There was a curious mixture of reluctance and actual gloating in his welcome, and his talk at once veered to extravagances of the most hideous and incredible sort.

Surviving elder gods – nameless sacrifices – the other than artificial nature of some of the alcove horrors – all the usual boasts, but uttered in a tone of peculiarly increasing confidence. Obviously, Jones reflected, the poor fellow's madness was gaining on him. From time to time Rogers would send furtive glances towards the heavy padlocked inner door at the end of the room, or towards a piece of coarse burlap on the floor not far from it, beneath which some small object appeared to be lying. Jones grew more nervous as the moments passed, and began to feel as hesitant about mentioning the afternoon's oddities as he had formerly been anxious to do so.

Rogers's sepulchrally resonant bass almost cracked under the excitement of his fevered rambling.

'Do you remember,' he shouted, 'what I told you about that

ruined city in Indo-China where the Tcho-Tchos lived? You had to admit I'd been there when you saw the photographs, even if you did think I made that oblong swimmer in darkness out of wax. If you'd seen it writhing in the underground pools as I did...

'Well, this is bigger still. I never told you about this, because I wanted to work out the later parts before making any claim. When you see the snapshots you'll know the geography couldn't have been faked, and I fancy I have another way of proving that *It* isn't any waxed concoction of mine. You've never seen it, for the experiments wouldn't let me keep It on exhibition.'

The showman glanced queerly at the padlocked door.

'It all comes from that long ritual in the eighth Puahotic fragment. When I got it figured out I saw it could have only one meaning. There were things in the north before the land of Lomar – before mankind existed – and this was one of them. It took us all the way to Alaska, and up the Nootak from Fort Morton, but the thing was there, as we knew it would be. Great cyclopean ruins, acres of them. There was less left than we had hoped for, but after three million years what could one expect? And weren't the Eskimo legends all in the right direction? We couldn't get one of the beggars to go with us, and had to sledge all the way back to Nome for Americans. Orabona was no good up in that climate – it made him sullen and hateful.

'I'll tell you later how we found It. When we got the ice blasted out of the pylons of the central ruin the stairway was just as we knew it would be. Some carvings still there, and it was no trouble keeping the Yankees from following us in. Orabona shivered like a leaf – you'd never think it from the damned insolent way he struts around here. He knew enough of the Elder Lore to be properly afraid. The eternal light was gone, but our torches showed enough. We saw the bones of others who had been before us – aeons ago, when the climate was warm. Some of these bones were of things you couldn't even imagine. At the third level down we found the ivory throne the fragments said so much about – and I may as well tell you it wasn't empty.

'The thing on that throne didn't move – and we knew then that

It needed the nourishment of sacrifice. But we didn't want to wake It then. Better to get It to London first. Orabona and I went to the surface for the big box, but when we had packed it we couldn't get It up the three flights of steps. These steps weren't made for human beings, and their size bothered us. Anyway, It was devilish heavy. We had to have the Americans down to get It out. They weren't anxious to go into the place, but of course the worst thing was safely inside the box. We told them it was a batch of ivory carvings – archaeological stuff; and after seeing the carved throne they probably believed us. It's a wonder they didn't suspect hidden treasure and demand a share. They must have told queer tales around Nome later on; though I doubt if they ever went back to those ruins, even for the ivory throne.'

Rogers paused, felt around in his desk, and produced an envelope of good-sized photographic prints. Extracting one and laying it face down before him, he handed the rest to Jones. The setting was certainly an odd one; ice-clad hills, dog sledges, men in furs, and vast, tumbled ruins against a background of snow – ruins whose bizarre outlines and enormous stone blocks could hardly be accounted for. One flashlight view showed an incredible interior chamber with wild carvings and a curious throne whose proportion could not have been designed for a human occupant. The carvings on the gigantic masonry – high walls and peculiar vaulting overhead – were mainly symbolic, and involved both wholly unknown designs and certain hieroglyphs darkly cited in obscene legends. Over the throne loomed the same dreadful symbol which was now painted on the workroom wall above the padlocked plank door. Jones darted a nervous glance at the closed portal. Assuredly, Rogers had been to strange places and had seen strange things. Yet this mad interior picture might easily be a fraud – taken from a very clever stage setting. One must not be too credulous. But Rogers was continuing:

'Well, we shipped the box from Nome and got to London without any trouble. That was the first time we'd ever brought back anything that had a chance of coming alive. I didn't put It on display, because there were more important things to do for It. It needed the nourishment of sacrifice, for It was a god. Of course, I couldn't get It the sort of sacrifices which It used to have in Its day, for such things don't exist now. But there were other things which might do. The blood is the life, you know. Even the lemurs and elementals that are older than the earth will come when the blood of men or beasts is offered under the right conditions.'

The expression on the narrator's face was growing very alarming and repulsive, so that Jones fidgeted involuntarily in his chair. Rogers seemed to notice his guest's nervousness, and continued with a distinctly evil smile.

'It was last year that I got It, and ever since then I've been trying rites and sacrifices. Orabona hasn't been much help, for he was always against the idea of waking It. He hates It – probably because he's afraid of what It will come to mean. He carries a pistol all the time to protect himself – fool, as if there were human protection against It! If I ever see him draw that pistol, I'll strangle him. He wanted me to kill It and make an effigy of It. But I've stuck by my plans, and I'm coming out on top in spite of all the cowards like Orabona and damned sniggering sceptics like you, Jones! I've chanted the rites and made certain sacrifices, *and last week the transition came.* The sacrifice was – received and enjoyed!'

Rogers actually licked his lips, while Jones held himself uneasily rigid. The showman paused and rose, crossing the room to the piece of burlap at which he had glanced so often. Bending down, he took hold of one corner as he spoke again.

'You've laughed enough at my work – now it's time for you to get some facts. Orabona tells me you heard a dog screaming around here this afternoon. *Do you know what that meant?'*

Jones started. For all his curiosity, he would have been glad to get out without further light on the point which had so puzzled him. But Rogers was inexorable, and began to lift the square of burlap. Beneath it lay a crushed, almost shapeless mass which Jones was slow to classify. Was it a once-living thing which some agency had flattened, sucked dry of blood, punctured in a thousand places, and wrung into a limp, broken-boned heap of grotesqueness? After a moment Jones realized what it must be. It was what was left of a dog – a dog perhaps of considerable size, and whitish colour. Its breed was past recognition, for distortion had come in nameless and hideous ways. Most of the hair was burned off as by some pungent acid, and the exposed, bloodless skin was riddled by innumerable circular wounds or incisions. The form of torture necessary to cause such results was past imagining.

Electrified with a pure loathing, which conquered his mounting disgust, Jones sprang up with a cry.

'You damned sadist – you madman – you do a thing like this and dare to speak to a decent man!'

Rogers dropped the burlap with a malignant sneer and faced his oncoming guest. His words held an unnatural calm.

'Why, you fool, do you think *I* did this? Let us admit that the results are unbeautiful from our limited human standpoint. What of it? It is not human, and does not pretend to be. To sacrifice is merely to offer. I gave the dog to It. What happened is Its work, not mine. It needed the nourishment of the offering, and took it in Its own way. But let me show you what It looks like.'

As Jones stood hesitating, the speaker returned to his desk and took up the photograph he had laid face down without showing. Now he extended it with a curious look. Jones took it and glanced at it in an almost mechanical way. After a moment the visitor's glance became sharper and more absorbed, for the utterly satanic force of the object depicted had an almost hypnotic effect. Certainly Rogers had outdone himself in modelling the eldritch nightmare which the camera had caught. The thing was a work of sheer, infernal genius, and Jones wondered how the public would react when it was placed on exhibition. So hideous a thing had no right to exist; probably the mere contemplation of it, after it was done, had completed the unhinging of its maker's mind and led him to worship it with brutal sacrifices. Only a stout sanity could resist the insidious suggestion that the blasphemy was – or had once been – some morbid and exotic form of actual life.

The thing in the picture squatted or was balanced on what appeared to be a clever reproduction of the monstrously carved throne in the other curious photograph. To describe it with any ordinary vocabulary would be impossible, for nothing even roughly corresponding to it has ever come within the imagination of sane mankind. It represented something meant perhaps to be roughly connected with the vertebrates of this planet – though one could not be too sure of that. Its bulk was cyclopean, for, even squatted, it towered to almost twice the height of Orabona, who was shown beside it. Looking sharply, one might trace its approximations towards the bodily features of the higher vertebrates.

There was an almost globular torso, with six long sinuous limbs terminating in crab-like claws. From the upper end a subsidiary globe bulged forward bubble-like; its triangle of three staring, fishy eyes, its foot-long and evidently flexible proboscis, and a distended lateral system analogous to gills, suggesting that it was a head. Most of the body was covered with what at first appeared to be fur, but which on closer examination proved to be a dense growth of dark, slender tentacles or sucking filaments, each tipped with a mouth suggesting the head of an asp. On the head and below the proboscis the tentacles tended to be longer and thicker, and marked with spiral stripes – suggesting the traditional serpent-locks of Medusa. To say that such a thing could have an expression seems paradoxical; yet Jones felt that that triangle of bulging fish-eyes and that obliquely poised proboscis all bespoke a blend of hate, greed, and sheer cruelty incomprehensible to mankind because mixed with other emotions not of the world or this solar system. Into this bestial abnormality, he reflected, Rogers must have poured at once all his malignant insanity and all his uncanny sculptural genius. The thing was incredible – and yet the photograph proved that it existed.

Rogers interrupted his reveries.

'Well – what do you think of It? Now do you wonder what crushed the dog and sucked it dry with a million mouths? It needed nourishment – and It will need more. It is a god, and I am the first priest of Its latter-day hierarchy. Iä! Shub-Niggurath! The Goat with a Thousand Young!'

Jones lowered the photograph in disgust and pity.

'See here, Rogers, this won't do. There are limits, you know. It's a great piece of work, and all that, but it isn't good for you. Better not see it any more – let Orabona break it up, and try to forget about it. And let me tear this beastly picture up too.'

With a snarl Rogers snatched the photograph and returned it to the desk.

'Idiot – you – and you still think It's all a fraud! You still think I made It, and you still think my figures are nothing but lifeless wax! Why, damn you, you're a worse clod than a wax image yourself! But I've got proof this time, and you're going to know! Not just now, for It is resting after the sacrifice – but later. Oh yes – you will not doubt the power of It then.'

As Rogers glanced towards the padlocked inner door, Jones retrieved his hat and stick from a nearby bench.

'Very well, Rogers, let it be later. I must be going now, but I'll call around tomorrow afternoon. Think my advice over and see if it doesn't sound sensible. Ask Orabona what he thinks, too.'

Rogers actually bared his teeth in wild-beast fashion.

'Must be going now, eh? Afraid after all! Afraid, for all your bold talk! You say the effigies are only wax, and yet you run away when I begin to prove that they aren't. You're like the fellows who take my standing bet that they daren't spend the night in the museum – they come boldly enough, but after an hour they shriek and hammer to get out! Want me to ask Orabona, eh? You two – always against me! You want to break down the coming earthly reign of It!'

Jones preserved his calm.

'No, Rogers – there's nobody against you. And I'm not afraid of your figures, either, much as I admire your skill. But we're both a bit nervous tonight, and I fancy some rest will do us good.'

Again Rogers checked his guest's departure.

'Not afraid, eh? Then why are you so anxious to go? Look

here – do you or don't you dare to stay alone here in the dark? What's your hurry if you don't believe in It?'

Some new idea seemed to have struck Rogers, and Jones eyed him closely.

'Why, I've no special hurry – but what would be gained by my staying here alone? What would it prove? My only objection is that it isn't very comfortable for sleeping. What good would it do either of us?'

This time it was Jones who was struck with an idea. He continued in a tone of conciliation.

'See here, Rogers – I've just asked you what it would prove if I stayed, when we both know. It would prove that your effigies are just effigies, and that you oughtn't to let your imagination go the way it's been going lately. Suppose I do stay. If I stick it out till morning, will you agree to take a new view of things – go on a vacation for three months or so, and let Orabona destroy that new thing of yours? Come, now – isn't that fair?'

The expression on the showman's face was hard to read. It was obvious that he was thinking quickly, and that, of sundry conflicting emotions, malign triumph was getting the upper hand. His voice held a choking quality as he replied:

'Fair enough! *If you do stick it out,* I'll take your advice. But stick you must. We'll go out to dinner and come back. I'll lock you in the display room and go home. In the morning I'll come down ahead of Orabona – he comes half an hour before the rest – and see how you are. But don't try it unless you are very sure of your scepticism. Others have backed out – you have that chance. And I suppose a pounding on the outer door would always bring a constable. You may not like it so well after a while – you'll be in the same building, though not in the same room with It.'

As they left the rear door into the dingy courtyard, Rogers took with him the piece of burlap – weighted with a gruesome burden. Near the centre of the court was a manhole, whose cover the showman lifted quietly and with a shuddersome suggestion of familiarity.

Burlap and all, the burden went down to the oblivion of a cloacal labyrinth. Jones shuddered, and almost shrank from the gaunt figure at his side as they emerged into the street.

By unspoken mutual consent, they did not dine together, but agreed to meet in front of the museum at eleven.

Jones hailed a cab, and breathed more freely when he had crossed Waterloo Bridge and was approaching the brilliantly lighted Strand. He dined at a quiet cafe, and subsequently went to his home in Portland Place to bath and get a few things. Idly he wondered what Rogers was doing. He had heard that the man had a vast, dismal house in the Walworth Road, full of obscure and forbidden books, occult paraphernalia, and wax images which he did not choose to place on exhibition. Orabona, he understood, lived in separate quarters in the same house.

At eleven Jones found Rogers waiting by the basement door in Southwark Street. Their words were few, but each seemed taut with a menacing tension. They agreed that the vaulted exhibition room alone should form the scene of the vigil, and Rogers did not insist that the watcher sit in the special adult alcove of supreme horrors. The showman, having extinguished all the lights with switches in the workroom, locked the door of that crypt with one of the keys on his crowded ring. Without shaking hands, he passed out of the street door, locked it after him, and stamped up the worn steps to the pavement outside. As his tread receded, Jones realized that the long, tedious vigil had commenced.

## II

Later, in the utter blackness of the great arched cellar, Jones cursed the childish naivete which had brought him there. For the first half hour he had kept flashing on his pocket light at intervals, but now, just sitting in the dark on one of the visitors' benches had become a more nerve-racking thing. Every time the beam shot out it lighted up some morbid, grotesque object – a guillotine, a nameless hybrid monster, a pasty bearded face crafty with evil, a body with red torrents streaming from a severed throat. Jones knew that no sinister reality was attached to these things, but after that first half hour he preferred not to see them.

Why he had bothered to humour that madman he could scarcely imagine. It would have been much simpler merely to have let him alone, or to have called in a mental specialist. Probably, he reflected, it was the fellow feeling of one artist for another. There was so much genius in Rogers that he deserved every possible chance to be helped quietly out of his growing mania. Any man who could imagine and construct the incredibly lifelike things that he had produced was surely not far from actual greatness. He had the fancy of a Sime or a Doré joined to the minute, scientific craftsmanship of a Blatschka. Indeed, he had done for the world of nightmare what the Blatschkas with their marvellously accurate plant models of finely wrought and coloured glass had done for the world of botany.

At midnight the strokes of a distant clock filtered through the darkness, and Jones felt cheered by the message from a still-surviving outside world. The vaulted museum chamber was like a tomb – ghastly in its utter solitude. Even a mouse would be cheering company; yet Rogers had once boasted that – for 'certain reasons', as he said – no mice or even insects ever came near the place. That was very curious, yet it seemed to be true. The deadness and silence were virtually complete. If only something would make a sound! He shuffled his feet, and the echoes came spectrally out of the absolute stillness. He coughed, but there was something mocking in the staccato reverberations. He could not, he vowed, begin talking to himself. That meant nervous disintegration. Time seemed to pass with abnormal and disconcerting slowness. He could have sworn that hours had elapsed since he last flashed the light on his watch, yet here was only the stroke of midnight.

He wished that his senses were not so preternaturally keen. Something in the darkness and stillness seemed to have sharpened them, so that they responded to faint intimations hardly strong enough to be called true impressions. His ears seemed at times to catch a faint, elusive susurration which could not *quite* be identified with the nocturnal hum of the squalid streets outside, and he thought of vague, irrelevant things like the music of the spheres and the unknown, inaccessible life of alien dimensions pressing on our own. Rogers often speculated about such things.

The floating specks of light in his blackness-drowned eyes seemed inclined to take on curious symmetries of pattern and motion. He had often wondered about those strange rays from the unplumbed abyss which scintillate before us in the absence of all earthly illumination, but he had never known any that behaved just as these were behaving. They lacked the restful aimlessness of ordinary light specks – suggesting some will and purpose remote from any terrestrial conception.

Then there was that suggestion of odd stirrings. Nothing was open, yet in spite of the general draughtlessness Jones felt that the air was not uniformly quiet. There were intangible variations in pressure – not quite decided enough to suggest the loathsome pawings of unseen elementals. It was abnormally chilly, too. He did not like any of this. The air tasted salty, as if it were mixed with the brine of dark subterrene waters, and there was a bare hint of some odour of ineffable mustiness. In the daytime he had never noticed that the waxen figures had an odour. Even now the half-received hint was not the way wax figures ought to smell. It was more like the faint smell of specimens in a natural-history museum. Curious, in view of Rogers's claims that his figures were not all artificial – indeed, it was probably that claim which made one's imagination conjure up the olfactory suspicion. One must guard against excesses of the imagination – had not such things driven poor Rogers mad?

But the utter loneliness of this place was frightful. Even the distant chimes seemed to come from across cosmic gulfs. It made Jones think of that insane picture which Rogers had shown him – the wildly carved chamber with the cryptic throne which the fellow had claimed was part of a three-million-year-old ruin in the shunned and inaccessible solitudes of the Arctic. Perhaps Rogers had been to Alaska, but that picture was certainly nothing but stage scenery. It couldn't normally be otherwise, with all that carving and those terrible symbols. And that monstrous shape supposed to have been found on that throne – what a flight of diseased fancy! Jones wondered just how far he actually was from the insane masterpiece in wax – probably it was kept behind that heavy, padlocked plank door leading somewhere out of the workroom. But it would never do to brood about a waxen image. Was not the present room full of such things, some of them scarcely less horrible than the dreadful 'IT'? And beyond a thin canvas screen on the left was the 'Adults only' alcove with its nameless phantoms of delirium.

The proximity of the numberless waxen shapes began to get on Jones's nerves more and more as the quarter-hours wore on. He knew the museum so well that he could not get rid of their usual images even in the total darkness. Indeed, the darkness had the effect of adding to the remembered images certain very disturbing imaginative overtones. The guillotine seemed to creak, and the bearded face of Landru, slayer of his fifty wives, twisted itself into expressions of monstrous menace. From the severed throat of Madame Demers a hideous bubbling sound seemed to emanate, while the headless, legless victim of a trunk murder tried to edge closer and closer on its gory stumps. Jones began shutting his eyes to see if that would dim the images, but found it was useless. Besides, when he shut his eyes the strange, purposeful patterns of light specks became more disturbingly pronounced.

Then suddenly he began trying to keep the hideous images he had formerly been trying to banish. He tried to keep them because they were giving place to still more hideous ones. In spite of himself, his memory began reconstructing the utterly non-human blasphemies that lurked in the obscurer corners, and these lumpish hybrid growths oozed and wriggled towards him as though hunting him down in a circle. Black Tsathoggua moulded itself from a toad-like gargoyle to a long, sinuous line with hundreds of rudimentary feet, and a lean, rubbery night-gaunt spread its wings as if to advance and smother the watcher. Jones braced himself to keep from screaming. He knew he was reverting to the traditional terrors of his childhood, and resolved to use his adult reason to keep the phantoms at bay. It helped a bit, he found, to flash the light again. Frightful as were the images it showed, these were not as bad as what his fancy called out of the utter blackness.

But there were drawbacks. Even in the light of his torch he could not help suspecting a slight, furtive trembling on the part of the canvas partition screening off the terrible 'Adults only' alcove. He knew what lay beyond, and shivered. Imagination called up the shocking form of fabulous Yog-Sothoth – only a congeries of iridescent globes, yet stupendous in its malign suggestiveness. What was this accursed mass slowly floating towards him and bumping on the partition that stood in the way? A small bulge in the canvas far to the right suggested the sharp horn of Gnoph-keh, the hairy myth-thing of the Greenland ice that walked sometimes on two legs, sometimes on four, and sometimes on six. To get this stuff out of his head Jones walked boldly towards the hellish alcove with torch burning steadily. Of course, none of his fears was true. Yet were not the long, facial tentacles of great Cthulhu actually swaying, slowly and insidiously? He knew they were flexible, but he had not realized that the draught caused by his advance was enough to set them in motion.

Returning to his former seat outside the alcove, he shut his eyes and let the symmetrical light specks do their worst. The distant clock boomed a single stroke. Could it be only one? He flashed the light on his watch and saw that it was precisely that hour. It would be hard indeed waiting for morning. Rogers would be down at about eight o'clock, ahead of even Orabona. It would be light outside in the main basement long before that, but none of it could penetrate here. All the windows in this basement had been bricked up but the three small ones facing the court. A pretty bad wait, all told.

His ears were getting most of the hallucinations now – for he could swear he heard stealthy, plodding footsteps in the workroom beyond the closed and locked door. He had no business thinking of that unexhibited horror which Rogers called 'It'. The thing was a contamination – it had driven its maker mad, and now even its picture was calling up imaginative terrors. It could not be in the workroom – it was very obviously beyond that padlocked door of heavy planking. Those steps were certainly pure imagination.

Then he thought he heard the key turn in the workroom door. Flashing on his torch, he saw nothing but the ancient six-panelled portal in its proper position. Again he tried darkness and closed eyes, but there followed a harrowing illusion of creaking – not the guillotine this time, but the slow, furtive opening of the workroom door. He would not scream. Once he screamed, he would be lost. There was a sort of padding or shuffling audible now, and it was slowly advancing towards him. He must retain command of himself. Had he not done so when the nameless brainshapes tried to close in on him? The shuffling crept nearer, and his resolution failed. He did not scream, but merely gulped out a challenge.

'Who goes there? Who are you? What do you want?'

There was no answer, but the shuffling kept on. Jones did not know which he feared most to do – turn on his flashlight or stay in the dark while the thing crept upon him. This thing was different, he felt profoundly, from the other terrors of the evening. His fingers and throat worked spasmodically. Silence was impossible, and the suspense of utter blackness was beginning to be the most intolerable of all conditions. Again he cried out hysterically: 'Halt! Who goes there?' as he switched on the revealing beams of his torch. Then, paralysed by what he saw, he dropped the flashlight and screamed – not once, but many times.

Shuffling towards him in the darkness was the gigantic, blasphemous form of a black thing not wholly ape and not wholly insect. Its hide hung loosely upon its frame, and its rugose, dead-eyed rudiment of a head swayed drunkenly from side to side. Its forepaws were extended, with talons spread wide, and its whole body was taut with murderous malignity despite its utter lack of facial expression. After the screams and the final coming of darkness, it leaped, and in a moment had Jones pinned to the floor. There was no struggle, for the watcher had fainted.

Jones's fainting-spell could not have lasted more than a moment, for the nameless thing was apishly dragging him through the darkness when he began recovering consciousness. What started him fully awake were the sounds which the thing was making – or rather the voice with which it was making them. That voice was human, and it was familiar. Only one living being could be behind the hoarse, feverish accents which were chanting to an unknown horror.

'Iä! Iä!' it was howling. 'I am coming, O Rhan-Tegoth, coming with the nourishment. You have waited long and fed ill, but now you shall have what was promised. That and more, for instead of Orabona it will be one of high degree who had doubted you. You shall crush and drain him, with all his doubts, and grow strong thereby. And ever after among men he shall be shown as a monument to your glory. Rhan-Tegoth, infinite and invincible, I am your slave and high-priest. You are hungry, and I provide. I read the sign and have led you forth. I shall feed you with blood, and you shall feed me with power. Iä! Shub-Nig-gurath! The Goat with a Thousand Young!'

In an instant all the terrors of the night dropped from Jones like a discarded cloak. He was again master of his mind, for he knew the very earthly and material peril he had to deal with. This was no monster of fable, but a dangerous madman. It was Rogers, dressed in some nightmare covering of his own insane designing, and about to make a frightful sacrifice to the devil-god he had fashioned out of wax. Clearly, he must have entered the workroom from the rear courtyard, donned his disguise, and then advanced to seize his neatly trapped and fear-broken victim. His strength was prodigious, and if he were to be thwarted one must act quickly. Counting on the madman's confidence in his unconsciousness, he determined to take him by surprise while his grasp was relatively lax. The feel of a threshold told him he was crossing into the pitch-black workroom.

With the strength of mortal fear Jones made a sudden spring from the half-recumbent posture in which he was being dragged. For an instant he was free of the astonished maniac's hands, and in another instant a lucky lunge in the dark had put his own hands at his captor's weirdly concealed throat. Simultaneously Rogers gripped him again, and without further preliminaries the two were locked in a desperate struggle of life and death. Jones's athletic training, without doubt, was his sole salvation, for his mad assailant, freed from every inhibition of fair play, decency, or even self-preservation, was an engine of savage destruction as formidable as a wolf or panther.

Guttural cries sometimes punctured the hideous tussle in the dark. Blood spurted, clothing ripped, and Jones at last felt the actual throat of the maniac shorn of its spectral mask. He spoke not a word, but put every ounce of energy into the defence of his life. Rogers kicked, gouged, butted, bit, clawed, and spat – yet found strength to yelp out actual sentences at times. Most of his speech was in a ritualistic jargon full of references to 'It' or 'Rhan-Tegoth', and to Jones's overwrought nerves it seemed as if the cries echoed from an infinite distance of demoniac snortings and bayings. Towards the last they were rolling on the floor, overturning benches or striking against the walls and the brick foundations of the central melting-furnace. Up to the very end Jones could not be certain of saving himself, but chance finally intervened in his favour. A jab of his knee against Rogers's chest produced a general relaxation, and a moment later he knew he had won.

Though hardly able to hold himself up, Jones rose and stumbled about the walls, seeking the light switch – for his flashlight was gone, together with most of his clothing. As he lurched along he dragged his limp opponent with him, fearing a sudden attack when the madman came to. Finding the switch box, he fumbled till he had the right handle. Then, as the wildly disordered workroom burst into sudden radiance, he set about binding Rogers with such cords and belts as he could easily find. The fellow's disguise – or what was left of it – seemed to be made of a puzzlingly queer sort of leather. For some reason it made Jones's flesh crawl to touch it, and there seemed to be an alien, rusty odour about it. In the normal clothes beneath it was Rogers's key ring, and this the exhausted victor seized as his final passport to freedom. The shades at the small, slit-like windows were all securely drawn, and he let them remain so.

Washing off the blood of battle at a convenient sink, Jones donned the most ordinary-looking and least ill-fitting clothes he could find on the costume hooks. Testing the door to the courtyard, he found it fastened with a spring lock which did not require a key from the inside. He kept the key ring, however, to admit him on his return with aid – for plainly the thing to do was to call in an alienist. There was no telephone in the museum, but it would not take long to find an all-night restaurant or chemist's shop where one could be had. He had almost opened the door to go when a torrent of hideous abuse from across the room told him that Rogers – whose visible injuries were confined to a long, deep scratch down the left cheek – had regained consciousness.

'Fool! Spawn of Noth-Yidik and effluvium of K'thun! Son of the dogs that howl in the maelstrom of Azathoth! You would have been sacred and immortal, and now you are betraying It and Its priest! Beware – for It is hungry! It would have been Orabona – that damned treacherous dog ready to turn against me and It – but I gave you the first honour instead. Now you must both beware, for It is not gentle without Its priest.

'Iä! Iä! Vengeance is at hand! Do you know how you would have been immortal? Look at the furnace! There is a fire ready to light, and there is wax in the kettle. I would have done with you as I have done with other once-living forms. Hei! You, who have vowed all my effigies are waxen, would have become a waxen effigy yourself! The furnace was all ready! When It had had Its fill, and you were like that dog I showed you, I would have made your flattened, punctured fragments immortal! Wax would have done it. Haven't you said I'm a great artist? Wax in every pore – wax over every square inch of you – Iä! Iä! And ever after the world would have looked at your mangled carcass and wondered how I ever imagined and made such a thing! Hei! And Orabona would have come next, and others after him – and thus would my waxen family have grown!

'Dog – do you still think I *made* all my effigies? Why not say *preserved*? You know by this time the strange places I've been to, and the strange things I've brought back. Coward – you could never face the dimensional shambler whose hide I put on to scare you – the mere sight of it alive, or even the full-fledged thought of it, would kill you instantly with fright! Iä! Iä! It waits hungry for the blood that is the life!'

Rogers, propped against the wall, swayed to and fro in his bonds.

'See here, Jones – if I let you go, will you let me go? It must be taken care of by Its high priest. Orabona will be enough to keep It alive – and when he is finished I will make his fragments immortal in wax for the world to see. It could have been you, but you have rejected the honour. I won't bother you again. Let me go, and I will share with you the power that It will bring me. Iä! Iä! Great is Rhan-Tegoth! Let me go! Let me go! It is starving down there beyond that door, and if It dies the Old Ones can never come back. Hei! Hei! Let me go!'

Jones merely shook his head, though the hideousness of the showman's imaginings revolted him. Rogers, now staring wildly at the padlocked plank door, thumped his head again and again against the brick wall and kicked with his tightly bound ankles. Jones was afraid he would injure himself, and advanced to bind him more firmly to some stationary object. Writhing, Rogers edged away from him and set up a series of phrenetic ululations whose utter, monstrous unhumanness was appalling, and whose sheer volume was almost incredible. It seemed impossible that any human throat could produce noises so loud and piercing, and Jones felt that if this continued there would be no need to telephone for aid. It could not be long before a constable would investigate, even granting that there were no listening neighbours in this deserted warehouse district.

'*Wza-y'ei! Wza-y'ei!*' howled the madman. '*Y'kaa baa bho – ii, Rhan-Tegoth – Cthulhu fthagn – Ei! Ei! Ei! Ei! – Rhan-Tegoth, Rhan-Tegoth, Rhan-Tegoth!*'

The tautly trussed creature, who had started squirming his way across the littered floor, now reached the padlocked plank door and commenced knocking his head thunderously against it. Jones dreaded the task of binding him further and wished he were not so exhausted from the previous struggle. This violent aftermath was getting hideously on his nerves, and he began to feel a return of the nameless qualms he had felt in the dark. Everything about Rogers and his museum was so hellishly morbid and suggestive of black vistas beyond life! It was loathsome to think of the waxen masterpiece of abnormal genius which must at this very moment be lurking close at hand in the blackness beyond the heavy padlocked door.

And now something happened which sent an additional chill down Jones's spine, and caused every hair – even the tiny growth on the backs of his hands – to bristle with a vague fright beyond classification. Rogers had suddenly stopped screaming and beating his head against the stout plank door and was straining up to a sitting posture, head cocked on one side as if listening intently for something. All at once a smile of devilish triumph overspread his face, and he began speaking intelligibly again – this time in a hoarse whisper contrasting oddly with his former stentorian howling.

'Listen, fool! Listen hard! *It* has heard me and is coming. Can't you hear It splashing out of Its tank down there at the end of the runway? I dug it deep, because there was nothing too good for It. It is amphibious, you know – you saw the gills in the picture. It came to the earth from lead-grey Yuggoth, where the cities are under the warm, deep sea. It can't stand up in there – too tall – has to sit or crouch. Let me get my keys – we must let It out and kneel down before It. Then we will go out and find a dog or cat – or perhaps a drunken man – to give It the nourishment It needs.'

It was not what the madman said, but the way he said it, that disorganized Jones so badly. The utter, insane confidence and sincerity in that crazed whisper were damnably contagious. Imagination with such a stimulus could find an active menace in the devilish wax figure that lurked unseen just beyond the heavy planking. Eyeing the door in unholy fascination, Jones noticed that it bore several distinct cracks, though no marks of violent treatment were visible on this side. He wondered how large a room or closet lay behind it, and how the waxen figure was arranged. The maniac's idea of a tank and runway was as clever as all his other imaginings.

Then, in one terrible instant, Jones completely lost the power to draw a breath. The leather belt he had seized for Rogers's further strapping fell from his limp hands, and a spasm of shivering convulsed him from head to foot. He might have known the place would drive him mad as it had driven Rogers – and now he *was* mad. He was mad, for he now harboured hallucinations more weird than any which had assailed him earlier that night. The madman was bidding him hear the splashing of a mythical monster in a tank beyond the door – and now, God help him, *he did hear it!*

Rogers saw the spasm of horror reach Jones's face and transform it to a staring mask of fear. He cackled.

'At last, fool, you believe! At last you know! You hear It and It comes! Get me my keys, fool – we must do homage and serve It!'

But Jones was past paying attention to any human words, mad or sane. Phobic paralysis held him immobile and half conscious with wild images racing phantasmagorically through his helpless imagination. There *was* a splashing. There was a padding or shuffling, as of great wet paws on a solid surface. Something *was* approaching. Into his nostrils, from the cracks in that nightmare plank door, poured a noisome animal stench like and yet unlike that of the mammal cages at the Zoological Gardens in Regent's Park.

He did not know now whether Rogers was talking or not. Everything real had faded away, and he was a statue obsessed with dreams and hallucinations so unnatural that they became almost objective and remote from him. He thought he heard a sniffing or snorting from the unknown gulf beyond the door, and when a sudden baying, trumpeting noise assailed his ears he could not feel sure that it came from the tightly bound maniac whose image swam uncertainly in his shaken vision. The photograph of that accursed unseen wax thing persisted in floating through his consciousness. Such a thing had no right to exist. Had it not driven him mad?

Even as he reflected, a fresh evidence of madness beset him. Something, he thought, was fumbling with the latch of the heavy padlocked door. It was patting and pawing and pushing at the planks. There was a thudding on the stout wood, which grew louder and louder. The stench was horrible. And now the assault on that door from the inside was a malign, determined pounding like the strokes of a battering-ram. There was an ominous cracking – a splintering – a welling fetor – a falling plank – *a black paw ending in a crab-like claw....*

'Help! Help! God help me!... Aaaaaaa!...'

With intense effort Jones is today able to recall a sudden bursting of his fear paralysis into the liberation of frenzied automatic flight. What he evidently did must have paralleled curiously the wild, plunging flights of maddest nightmares; for he seems to have leaped across the disordered crypt at almost a single bound, yanked open the outside door, which closed and locked itself after him with a clatter, sprung up the worn stone steps three at a time, and raced frantically and aimlessly out of that dank cobblestoned court and through the squalid streets of Southwark.

Here the memory ends. Jones does not know how he got home, and there is no evidence of his having hired a cab. Probably he raced all the way by blind instinct – over Waterloo Bridge, along the Strand and Charing Cross, and up Haymarket and Regent Street to his own neighbourhood. He still had on the queer *mélange* of museum costumes when he grew conscious enough to call the doctor.

A week later the nerve specialist allowed him to leave his bed and walk in the open air.

But he had not told the specialists much. Over his whole experience hung a pall of madness and nightmare, and he felt that silence was the only course. When he was up, he scanned intently all the papers which had accumulated since that hideous night, but found no reference to anything queer at the museum. How much, after all, had been reality? Where did reality end and morbid dream begin? Had his mind gone wholly to pieces in that dark exhibition chamber, and had the whole fight with Rogers been a phantasm of fever? It would help to put him on his feet if he could settle some of these maddening points. He must have seen that damnable photograph of the wax image called 'It', for no brain but Rogers's could ever have conceived such a blasphemy.

It was a fortnight before he dared to enter Southwark Street again. He went in the middle of the morning, when there was the greatest amount of sane, wholesome activity around the ancient, crumbling shops and warehouses. The museum's sign was still there, and as he approached he saw that the place was open. The gateman nodded in pleasant recognition as he summoned up the courage to enter, and in the vaulted chamber below an attendant touched his cap cheerfully. Perhaps everything had been a dream. Would he dare to knock at the door of the workroom and look for Rogers?

Then Orabona advanced to greet him. His dark, sleek face was a trifle sardonic, but Jones felt that he was not unfriendly. He spoke with a trace of accent.

'Good morning, Mr Jones. It is some time since we have seen you here. Did you wish Mr Rogers? I'm sorry, but he is away. He had word of business in America, and had to go. Yes, it was very sudden. I am in charge now – here, and at the house. I try to maintain Mr Rogers's high standard – till he is back.'

The foreigner smiled – perhaps from affability alone. Jones scarcely knew how to reply, but managed to mumble out a few inquiries about the day after his last visit. Orabona seemed greatly amused by the questions, and took considerable care in framing his replies.

'Oh yes, Mr Jones – the twenty-eighth of last month. I remember it for many reasons. In the morning – before Mr Rogers got here, you understand – I found the workroom in quite a mess. There was a great deal of – cleaning up – to do. There had been – late work, you see. Important new specimen given its secondary baking process. I took complete charge when I came.

'It was a hard specimen to prepare – but, of course, Mr Rogers has taught me a great deal. He is, as you know, a very great artist. When he came he helped me complete the specimen – helped very materially, I assure you – but he left soon without even greeting the men. As I tell you, he was called away suddenly. There were important chemical reactions involved. They made loud noises – in fact, some lorry drivers in that court outside fancy they heard several pistol shots – very amusing idea!

'As for the new specimen – that matter is very unfortunate. It is a great masterpiece – designed and made, you understand, by Mr Rogers. He will see about it when he gets back.'

Again Orabona smiled.

'The police, you know. We put it on display a week ago, and there were two or three faintings. One poor fellow had an epileptic fit in front of it. You see, it is a trifle – stronger – than the rest. Larger, for one thing. Of course, it was in the adult alcove. The next day a couple of men from Scotland Yard looked it over and said it was too morbid to be shown. Said we'd have to remove it. It was a tremendous shame – such a masterpiece of art – but I didn't feel justified in appealing to the courts in Mr Rogers's absence. He would not like so much publicity with the police now – but when he gets back – when he gets back....'

For some reason or other Jones felt a mounting tide of uneasiness and repulsion. But Orabona was continuing.

'You are a connoisseur, Mr Jones. I am sure I violate no law in offering you a private view. It may be – subject, of course, to Mr Rogers's wishes – that we shall destroy the specimen some day – but that would be a crime.'

Jones had a powerful impulse to refuse the sight and flee precipitately, but Orabona was leading him forward by the arm with an artist's enthusiasm. The adult alcove, crowded with nameless horrors, held no visitors. In the farther corner a large niche had been curtained off, and to this the smiling assistant advanced.

'You must know, Mr Jones, that the title of this specimen is "The Sacrifice to Rhan-Tegoth".'

Jones started violently, but Orabona appeared not to notice.

'The shapeless, colossal god is a feature in certain obscure legends which Mr Rogers has studied. All nonsense, of course, as you've so often assured Mr Rogers. It is supposed to have come from outer space, and to have lived in the Arctic three million years ago. It treated its sacrifices rather peculiarly and horribly, as you shall see. Mr Rogers had made it fiendishly lifelike – even to the face of the victim.'

Now trembling violently, Jones clung to the brass railing in front of the curtained niche. He almost reached out to stop Orabona when he saw the curtain beginning to swing aside, but some conflicting impulse held him back. The foreigner smiled triumphantly.

'Behold!'

Jones reeled in spite of his grip on the railing.

'Good – great heavens!'

Fully ten feet high, despite a shambling, crouching attitude expressive of infinite cosmic malignancy, a monstrosity of unbelievable horror was shown starting forward from a cyclopean ivory throne covered with grotesque carvings. In the central pair of its six legs it bore a crushed, flattened, distorted, bloodless thing, riddled with a million punctures, and in places seared as with some pungent acid. Only the mangled head of the victim, lolling upside-down at one side, revealed that it represented something once human.

The monster itself needed no title for one who had seen a certain hellish photograph. That damnable print had been all too faithful; yet it could not carry the full horror which lay in the gigantic actuality. The globular torso – the bubble-like suggestion of a head – the three fishy eyes — the foot-long proboscis — the bulging gills — the monstrous capillation of asp-like suckers — the six sinuous limbs with their black paws and crab-like claws — Ah!... The familiarity of that black paw ending in a crab-like claw!..

Orabona's smile was utterly damnable. Jones choked, and stared at the hideous exhibit with a mounting fascination which perplexed and disturbed him. What half-revealed horror was holding and forcing him to look longer and search out details? This had driven Rogers mad... Rogers, supreme artist... said they weren't artificial...

Then he localized the thing that held him. It was the crushed waxen victim's lolling head, and something that it implied. This head was not entirely devoid of a face, and that face was familiar. It was like the mad face of poor Rogers. Jones peered closer, hardly knowing why he was driven to do so. Wasn't it natural for a mad egoist to mould his own features into his masterpiece? Was there anything more that subconscious vision had seized on and suppressed in sheer terror?

The wax of the mangled face had been handled with boundless dexterity. Those punctures — how perfectly they reproduced the myriad wounds somehow inflicted on that poor dog! But there was something more. On the left cheek one could trace an irregularity which seemed outside the general scheme — as if the sculptor had sought to cover up a defect of his first modelling. The more Jones looked at it, the more mysteriously it horrified him — and then suddenly he remembered a circumstance which brought his horror to a head. That night of hideousness — the tussle — the bound madman — *and the long, deep scratch down the left cheek of the actual living Rogers...*

Jones, releasing his desperate clutch on the railing, sank in a total faint.

Orabona continued to smile.

# Hester Holland

## *The Library*

The drive was punctuated at intervals by lodges and gates. These were opened by shadowy figures who emerged from their doors at the sound of the motor horn. Then they drove on through endless woods and pasture land. All very lovely in the daytime, thought Margaret, but on this winter night she only wanted to see a fire and a cup of tea. Margaret was essentially practical. Life had meant very little to her from an early age – finding jobs and trying to keep them in the face of ill health. It had always been a struggle to give people the value for their money and keep fit enough to do it.

After Dick had left her, things had seemed harder than ever. There had been the hope that some day they would get married. He had loved her once, and she still loved him. But that was all over, he would never come back any more. After six months of trying to forget him and typing in an underground office, she had broken down. The doctor whom she saw advised a complete rest. 'Go home,' he said, 'and loaf round.' Margaret laughed; she had no relations and nobody cared a button whether she died or not.

'Well,' he said, 'if you have got to work, get some work in the country. Be out of doors all day.'

That was why she answered Lady Farrell's advertisement. Her ladyship wanted a capable young lady to take charge of her country house whilst she was away. Margaret could hardly believe her good luck when she was engaged. Here was a chance to get out of town, so full of memories of Dick, and recuperate. It might even mean a permanent job.

Her ladyship explained that Witcombe Court was lonely. Though there was a full staff always there whether she was away or not. The house must not be neglected. She was very particular about Margaret's family. Had she many relatives? Would they mind her going to a lonely place? When the girl said she had no relatives and was alone in the world, it seemed to please the old lady.

'Poor child!' she exclaimed, jumping up and taking the girl's hand. 'I'm sure you'll suit me. I'm sure we shall like each other.'

She explained the reason of her visits abroad.

'I have to be away half the year for my health. And I must have a lady to look after things for me. The servants are all excellent, but of course a lady at the head of things makes so much difference. One thing I must insist upon, though it does not apply in your case, my dear. I do object to strangers being asked to the house in my absence.'

Lady Farrell was very old, with an ancestry which dated back to Saxon times and earlier. Dressed in a fashion which had been new in the Seventies, she created a sensation in London whenever she appeared. Witcombe Court with its hundreds of acres had been guarded by her with the tenderness of a mother. She was the last of her race and the estate would be sold at her death. There had been reckless gambling by members of the family, who had sold parts of the estate to pay their debts. One of her forebears had despoiled the library of its collection of rare books and sold some historical furniture. There was a legend that the stone wolves mounting guard on the terrace howled when the treasures were taken away. Lady Farrell, incongruous in a West End hotel, spoke of these things as if someone had ill-treated a child.

'My ancestors behaved shamefully. They robbed the house which was defenceless against them. And to think I must die and leave it to be sold to someone who does not understand it. The thought is torture to me. That is why I go for treatment abroad. I must live as long as I can to protect it.'

Margaret's duties would evidently be those of a watchdog. Yet Lady Farrell spoke of her large and efficient staff of servants which were kept on during her absence and seemed an adequate bodyguard. The house must have constant service and constant attention. Margaret must see that there was no jarring note. The girl promised to be vigilant. She had a strong historical sense, though it had been thwarted in London offices. It would be pleasant to wander through rooms which had no recollections of Dick to haunt her; there were sure to be relics, swords, and flags of warriors who had fought against Norman and Yorkist and Roundhead. From earliest times Witcombe Court had been a regular buffer state for invading forces. And always there had been blood spilt in its name. The house expected sacrifices. Lives had been given for it. Margaret decided to read up all its history. It would be wonderful to live so near the past. But with the question of reading came the first disappointment. Lady Farrell was strict about certain things.

'Not yet, my dear,' she said, patting Margaret's hand affectionately. 'I quite realize how eager you will be to go into the library, but we must be ready.'

'Ready for what?' thought the girl. It must be that Lady Farrell did not trust her alone with the rare books. After all, she was a stranger. Great care must be taken to fall in with her employer's ways. She wondered how the other secretaries had fared. There seemed to have been a lot of going and coming as far as they were concerned; perhaps they had got fed up with the country. Well, Witcombe Court might be lonely, but it was better than town, with those imaginary Dicks in every street. On the night of her arrival a silent-footed butler showed her into an immense drawing room. Here she found Lady Farrell sunk on a wide settee in front of a virile fire; the lavish tea and glowing heat of burning wood soon cheered Margaret. She began to feel happy. A tenderness woke in her heart for the fragile old lady who seemed lost in the vastness of her abode. The house was enormous, and was a quaint mixture of early and late architecture. The great hall was hung with flags and battered armour. The wide rooms adjoining were a museum of pathetic relics, telling of the struggle to keep invading foes at bay.

Oddly enough, though it gave the sensation of vastness, there was no atmosphere of peace. The girl noticed this at once. Entering the dark, lofty hall, she had been met by a breath of hostility which conveyed itself forcibly to her sensitive nature. It was as if the house did not want her. Resented the entrance of strangers. The walls which rose darkly around her held no friendliness. As she entered the hall she was conscious of an extraordinary sensation. It was like entering some enormous clock. There was a steady beat coming from a distance, like a pulse, far away certainly, but plain enough to hear. Margaret supposed some engine used for procuring light or water. She got used to this noise as one gets used to the beat of a pendulum, and for a while thought no more of it. But the feeling of hostility remained. This had been enhanced by the first glimpse of the house as the car turned into the drive. There had been no lights in the upper windows. The only illumination came from the porch. It gave the impression of two slit-like eyes. Red eyes gazing out at the night-bound park.

The effect was sinister. The heap of building crouched lumpily against the sky – a dark bulk waiting to spring. Her heart had given a queer, frightened start. It was like entering a living thing to go through that dim doorway. After a few days she put the feeling down to strangeness. She was not accustomed to such vast rooms. Neither was she used to such harmony. It was like a ritual. A competent, perfectly trained staff of servants vied with each other to make the house beautiful. They were obsessed by it. Margaret could see no work for a secretary. She spent the time with her employer making catalogues of portraits which could easily have been done by one of the footmen. It almost seemed as if Lady Farrell made work for her. There were tapestries shaken from obscure boxes, and laces washed and put away again. She had no time to explore alone. Her employer showed her everything herself. The old lady displayed a reverent pride in her possessions; not for her pleasure, but for the house itself, the work went on. Flowers were heaped in the rooms. The servants walked softly so as not to disturb it.

A few days after Margaret's arrival and the day before Lady Farrell was to leave, the girl was in the billiard room. With notebook and pencil she was busy cataloguing the portraits. Sir Walter Raleigh between the windows. Lady Catherine Grey over the fireplace. It was disagreeable being in the room alone. Somehow none of the picture faces seemed friendly. Her footsteps, as she crossed the parquet floor, sounded unnaturally loud. She had the sensation of being the undigested contents of a maw. An alien Thing waiting to be identified with the whole. That was what made her feel remote. The servants and Lady Farrell were in sympathy with the house. A body moving in accord. She alone was strange to it. Was this why she felt herself hated? But how could bricks and mortar hate her? She stood staring at the wall. The room was one of the few unpanelled in the house, and was painted the colour of elephant's hide.

Suddenly, as if a wind had scudded in, a ripple ran along its surface. It was like the clipped skin of a horse trying to get rid of a fly. Again and again it quivered from floor to ceiling. With a scream Margaret stumbled from the room. All she wanted to do was to get away. The house was alive. She knew it now. Waking in the early morning she fancied she heard it stirring, like a great beast, stretching and preparing to rise. Long before the servants were about, Margaret would lie and listen to that pulse which sounded through the rooms. A dull thud, thud, like a heart's beat. She wanted to go, but her wish was greeted with tears.

'What, go and leave me now, just when I have got someone whom I can trust? I could not go away and leave no one in charge of the house. Stay, stay at least till I return.'

Margaret promised to do this, and the old lady was pathetically grateful.

'And you shall go to the library,' she whined. 'You shall go to the library as soon as it is ready for you.'

After her departure the girl tried to engross herself in work.

There was very little to do, and what she did seemed futile. The daily round of service which the house received was not in her province. Its requirements were carried out by a competent staff of priests and priestesses who ministered at its shrine. There was no cessation of this ministration now that the Pontiff had gone. Everything went like clockwork. The Catechumens and Acolytes, whom Margaret secretly called the between-maids and under-maids, showed the same zeal as their superiors. Day after day rooms were cleaned and polished. Beds aired, linen sorted, and silver burnished. Labour was sucked up as a plant takes in moisture. What was it all for? There was no one but herself to appreciate this neatness of the linen cupboard or the shine on the brasses. But the house rejected her as a worker. There was nothing to do. One day she discovered that Lady Farrell had left the key of the library with her.

'That's the library key, miss,' the cook had said, when she had asked where it belonged.

'Oh, of course, Lady Farrell must have left it on the bunch by mistake.'

'Her ladyship always leaves the library key with the secretary,' said the cook, and watched Margaret out of the kitchen with a smile.

What trust, thought the girl. Had all the other secretaries kept faith as she intended to do, or had they just peeped. She had a longing to go into that library. It was as if someone was calling from there. The heart of the house, Lady Farrell had called it. Surely in its heart she would find the root of this animosity to herself. As the days passed, she found it easier to consider the house in the light of an idol, for directly she did this everything fell into place.

The labour was no longer futile if it kept the god alive. It was an idol that must be worshipped and ministered to. A very old god that had grown silent and vindictive with the years, watching with an increasingly jealous eye its hive of priests lest one of them should slacken in zeal. But it was her duty to propitiate it. She sought about for a position among its ministries that was not yet appropriated. With not much knowledge of an idol's requirements, it was difficult to create the perfect circle of service necessary to its well-being. Exorcists, those were the cleaners, and I don't clean – Acolytes, but I don't wait on the butler. Lady Farrell was the High Priestess. Margaret was in the woods overlooking the house. It stood, a grey shape against the hill, its windows dull with sleep, a thin turret of smoke rising from each of its many chimneys. Today, by some mischance, she had unearthed a tie which she had once bought for Dick. She had not given it to him because people in torment don't give away ties. It was just at the time of her discovery that he didn't care any more. The woods had seemed the best place to try and forget in. And then she realized it was that loving she still kept in her heart which put her out of harmony with the house. She was not one with it. Had the other secretaries refused to merge themselves, and was that why they had left? Suddenly Margaret held out her arms.

'House,' she said aloud, 'try not to hate me. Tell me what you would like me to be.'

With dropped arms she waited, fixing anxious eyes on the mountain of stone in front. A voice in her brain whispered:

'Sacrifice.'

A sacrifice, why had she not thought of that? The life of a normal idol was incomplete without it. All the endless tending of altar fires and the prayers, vain. And the victim must come from without. They did not offer up the priests. Did the house want her? Was it angry because she held away from it, fought against its demand for her? Did it want to crush her and make her its own, as those thirsty gods of the old days? But the surrender must come from her. The house was waiting. Margaret shivered. She felt afraid to go back through those heavy doors, or feel again that animosity, like a shield against her.

There was a step among the leaves. The gardeners had a tiresome way of creeping about with wheelbarrows disturbing the solitude. An old man was standing among the trees behind her. He was dressed in a black cassock-like garment, and his small, wrinkled face had the yellow texture of ivory. He raised a round black hat and showed a completely bald head. Margaret stood staring at him.

'Excuse me,' he said, 'but could I come to the house and rest a little? I am so very tired.'

'Lady Farrell is away.'

'I know, but I am a great friend of hers. In fact, I am her chaplain. I am sure she would not mind.'

Well, if he was the chaplain, Lady Farrell could not object. It would be nice to have a chat with someone, she was so lonely.

'Come in,' she said, 'I'll ask them to give you some tea.'

'You are very kind, but I just wanted to rest; you see, I have been on my feet all day, on parish rounds. I thought I would look in here on my way home.'

'Yes, of course. I'm the secretary.'

'Lady Farrell told me you were coming. My name is Father Collard.'

They walked up the drive and on to the terrace. Father Collard stopped to admire the stone wolves which crouched each side of the steps.

'You know the legend about them?' He laid a thin yellow paw on one of the moss-grown heads.

'Oh yes, but there are a lot of legends about the house I should like to know.'

'You should read about them. Lady Farrell has a wonderful library.'

'I thought it was sold.'

'It was sold, but her ladyship bought nearly all the books back. She took the greatest trouble to advertise, and had to pay far more than the books were sold for originally.'

'She is devoted to the house.'

'We must all love what has been in our family for generations. There is no sacrifice we should not make for our own.' The old man spoke with the ardour of fanaticism.

Margaret looked at him. She had a sudden doubt as to his sanity. They were in the lofty hall now, and she saw his pale eyes glitter with excitement as he looked round.

'The house has a lot of disciples.' She could not resist saying that. After all, it was only she and the other secretaries who had not fallen under its spell. He turned to her with a smile on his wizened little face.

'I can understand you not feeling the same as we do. You have only been here a short time. You have not felt its influence yet.'

'Oh, but I have,' began Margaret. Then she stopped. What would be the use of telling him about her fears and fancies? 'I should like to know more about its history, but Lady Farrell does not wish strangers to go into her library.'

'I am sure she would not mind your looking at one or two books. I should so like to show them to you.'

'Well, if you really think it will be all right, and you know their names.' Margaret subsided on one of the wide chairs in the drawing room; suddenly she felt extraordinarily tired. Her companion sat opposite. Without his hat he looked like a small black bottle with a round ivory stopper. She felt inclined to laugh, and wondered whether James the footman, who had come in to draw the curtains, noticed how odd the old priest was. The drawing room was not used in Lady Farrell's absence, as Margaret preferred the smaller and sunnier breakfast room. However, with unabated service given to the house, the blinds were drawn up every morning, a fire laid and lighted.

She asked James to bring tea. The old man was still talking of the books.

'There is one full of legends I should like to show you.'

'What sort of legends?'

But she knew it was not the stories she wanted to hear. They were an excuse to go into the library, and any excuse was enough. The fact that Lady Farrell had forbidden it did not matter any more. Something stronger than her will was compelling her. She did not know whether it was the old man's voice or her brain which droned on about an oubliette in the upper regions which no one had ever found. A legend of a Royalist hidden in a secret room in Cromwell's time.

'His pursuers murdered those who had the secret. He was not found till long after.'

'How horrible,' said Margaret.

There came a chuckle from the chair opposite. A pair of little bony hands were spread out in front of her face in a motion of supplication.

'Do go and fetch the books from the library.'

She wondered vaguely why he didn't wear a proper clergyman's collar and why he had never called before. Why, no one ever called at the house.

'All right,' she said, 'I'll get them.'

He told her their titles and exactly where they stood on the shelves. He seemed to know the room extraordinarily well. She was not sure whether the little black figure with the bald head had really asked her to go, or whether it was a voice in her brain.

The library was in the left wing of the house. At the end of a long stone passage. There were no other rooms near it. It was evident that the perpetual cleaning which went on all day stopped when this part of the house was reached. There was dust on the floor, and a litter of dead leaves had blown in from the garden. A low stone arch over the library door was festooned with cobwebs. The key moved smoothly and she turned the handle to face darkness. There were no windows. She relocked the door and went in search of a candle. James was carrying the tea tray across the hall, and she asked him to tell Father Collard she would join him in a moment.

'Very well, miss.'

He seemed anxious to be gone with his tray, so she took a silver candlestick from the hall table and went slowly back to the library. She stood just inside the door and looked round expectantly. What would she find besides books? As she stood there the door behind her clicked to, as if someone had pulled it from the outside, and Margaret turned quickly. She saw the door was made of shelves and that there was no trace of a handle on the inside wall. There was no way of getting out unless she discovered some spring.

'But I can knock on the door and they will let me out.'

Again she turned and faced the room, and the swaying light of the candle showed her something. It was a small room lined with books from floor to ceiling and furnished only with a few musty-looking chairs. In the centre of it was a table on which for some reason had been heaped a quantity of dead flowers. The slightest breath stirs dead leaves, and these moved continually. What was it which moved them? The girl became aware of a vibration, a beating in the room. The pulsing of a heart which she had heard for so long and not understood. Here was the house's heart. She had entered its shrine, its inner life, its holy of holies. Beat, beat, beat. Her shadow, cast by the feeble light of the candle, trembled along the floor. Thin and long, it was sucked away into the room. It was filled with the smell of hay, and the breath of dying flowers and of incense, and another smell. The terrible smell of decaying flesh. She was not alone. Against the wall, huddled in different positions of abandoned agony and death, were several figures. Figures of women in modern clothes, jerseys, hats, boots. Four in all. Sacrifices. The other secretaries left here to die. Imprisoned sacrifices to the house, whose heart-beats shook the dried flowers on the table. With a scream, Margaret flung herself against the lines of books which formed the door. Wildly, with clenched hands, she struck it. 'Let me out – let me out!' But no one ever came to let her out.

They wrote to Lady Farrell and she returned at once. Father Collard was in the hall to meet her, and all the servants, even down to the kitchen-maid.

A service was held in the chapel, and Lady Farrell cried a little as she knelt before the altar.

'I never can bear to be here at the time,' she said weakly to her chaplain. 'I know it has to be, but it upsets me so. The thought of those dear girls –'

'But, Lady Farrell – if the house requires them, you would not stint it – you would not stint it of sacrifice?'

'No!' exclaimed her ladyship, rising from her knees. 'I don't stint it. So long as I am alive we will give it life. I shall not fail it so long as I am alive.'

'You have given it lives,' whispered Father Collard, 'and it is alive.'

Lady Farrell clasped her hands in worship.

'I will try to procure another secretary,' she murmured.

Fielden Hughes

# *The Mistake*

When I was the Medical Superintendent at the Applesett Private Mental Hospital, there was one patient who had been there so long that he was, in that respect as well as in one other, something of an institution. He was a silent man, and gave so little trouble that he was in a class apart. He was there, so his record showed, at his own request and at his own expense. He was without near relations, and nobody ever visited him or showed the faintest interest in him, except for many doctors, pathologists, and psychologists to whom he was of vast clinical interest. Before he entered our hospital, he had been an obscure parson in some West Country village, unknown to any but his few parishioners. After he came to us, unaware of it though he was, he achieved a wide fame in medical circles. For the simple fact about him was that he never slept. Every night for a considerable time he used to retire and read for a while. Then he would put out his light, go to sleep quite naturally, and five minutes later would wake up as if he had been asleep for hours. After a time he gave up all idea of going to bed, and treated the night as the day.

There was no point in trying to impede him in the habit of twenty-four hours of complete wakefulness, and so a room was placed at his disposal, a room – at his urgent request – without a bed. Usually he spent the night reading or writing, and the sheets of paper he covered he allowed no one to see. Occasionally he would escape from the house during the night, after showing noticeable restlessness for a period. These escapes were always at the same time of the year – in mid-October; and always he was found in the same place – the churchyard in Applesett village. This fact we attributed to some connection in his mind with his former profession. But this became clear when he died, which he did prematurely, for the phenomenon of total insomnia, interesting though it was to us as doctors, was inevitably the cause of quicker wear of his bodily tissues; and this though he was one of the biggest, most powerful men I have ever seen. In youth, he must have been a tremendously strong man. I was always thankful that so muscular a fellow was a quiet inmate. I used to wonder how the attendants would have been able to handle him if he had become violent. But he never did, and we were all truly sorry when he died in his fortieth year. Among his effects, brought to my office after the removal of his body, was a large envelope containing many sheets of paper. It was addressed to me, and marked 'Not to be opened till after my death'. I opened the packet, took out the scribbled sheets and read what follows here:

When I was the Vicar of St Alpha's Church in the village of Smeritone, I was happy enough. I could have said I was completely happy except for one man in the village. That man was my warden, Admiral Sir Anthony Vilpert. It was one of those strange cases of complete natural antipathy. We hated one another for no reason that either of us could have given. I hated his very appearance. He was a very thin man with white moustache and beard, the latter thin like himself and pointed. I privately called him the 'White Goat', for he was pale, with light blue eyes. His voice, so unlike the voice of a sea-going man, was a bleat, and how odious its sound became to me. We bickered and differed about every parish matter, and I found that he was in the wicked habit of talking about me to my detriment behind my back, making mischief and doing all he could to poison people's minds against me, especially newcomers, before I had time to correct by visitation the vile impressions he constantly gave them.

My hatred of the 'White Goat' became an obsession. I found

myself thinking about him with loathing. His image would come before my mind in the silence of my study, and I had to avert my eyes from him when I was taking services in church. He filled me with fear as well as hatred, for the expression in those pale eyes told me that there was no evil turn he would not do me if he had the opportunity. I fell into mortal sin, for I murdered him in my heart many a time, so that I could hardly read certain passages of Scripture without feeling condemned in the face of the congregation; and then I would imagine that he could read my heart, and that thin face would seem to smile bitterly at me and defy me.

One day a message came to the vicarage that he was dangerously ill. I could not repress a terrible hope. However, I set out to his house, but, by the mercy of Heaven, he was dead before I could reach his bedside. And I was overjoyed. To my horror, I was happier than I had ever been.

The day of his funeral arrived, and I met the cortege at the lych gate. As I slowly walked before the coffin to the church door, I heard a tapping sound. My blood chilled as the certainty came to my mind that the tapping came from within the coffin. I dismissed the idea and walked on. It could not be. It was my imagination. It was some weird echo of my hatred of the man. As we moved solemnly up the aisle, I heard the faint sound again. Tap tap. Then three more. Tap tap tap. There was no doubt. I waited for the bearers to act. They must have heard those dreadful sounds even as I had done. One of them would cry out. They would put down the coffin. They would open it, there in the church. But nothing happened, except that I heard the sounds once more, like a muffled, distant drum. I felt faint and had to force my legs to bear me up and on. The dreadful truth was clear. He was not dead. And only I had heard his frantic signals to return to the world.

I cannot tell, even here, of the tumult of my feelings. A terrible sense of his being in my power, there in his coffin, seized me, a glorious power. The thought rushed through my mind like a swift flame that I was a murderer who could never be detected. I who had killed him so often in my thoughts was able now to kill him with a sort of horrible innocence. He was the prisoner of my ears, alone and helpless, dependent for his delivery from the most gruesome bondage upon my silent tongue. The injuries he had done me, the calumnies he had spoken of me, the hatred he had shown to me, all hung upon my lips like locks and bars against my speaking. I seemed to see him lying there, his pale eyes wide open with fear, imploring me to mercy and the release of forgiveness. I saw him as if the coffin lid were made of glass. And with hatred in my heart, I refused his dumb appeal, condemning him to the cruellest of all deaths, a living entombment, a joining of him with the dead before his time, an inescapable, inexorable darkness. Then a kind of healing sanity returned to me. If none other there present had heard the tapping, the quiet frenzy of imprisonment, it must be my imagination.

Calmly and coldly I went on with my duties. I saw him lowered into his grave. The cold damp afternoon lay silent round us – us living upon whose brows the wisps of autumn mist were like the exhalations of death. The fragments of soil fell on the coffin thudding, as if we were knocking his outer door in response to his inner tapping. Perhaps he heard them, and hailed them with a momentary thin hope, like a miner entombed in the dark caverns of his mine. And then I heard it again, fainter this time, and lost amongst the sounds of the soil falling on the coffin.

I turned away and left the group of mourners at the graveside. As I sat in my comfortable study by the fire, the afternoon closed in and the shadows of night gathered. I drew the curtains over my windows, and as I did so, I glanced towards the darkening churchyard. My thoughts seemed suspended. I was living but numb. I had tea, and wrote a number of letters, as if I were not myself but somebody else. I felt as if a spring were tightly coiled inside me. When I retired, about ten o'clock, the vicarage was very silent. My housekeeper was away overnight, and I locked the doors and went upstairs. I read till half past ten, and then fell asleep. Suddenly I was wide awake, as if I had slept for many hours. I looked at my watch. The time was twenty minutes to eleven. I was wholly refreshed and knew I should sleep no more. The spring had uncoiled inside me. I lay awake in the darkness, as if waiting for something or someone. The church clock struck the quarter, and as if an order had been given me, I knew what I had to do. I rose and dressed. What I had to do, I must do alone. I could not seek any earthly aid. I must know the truth, and there was nobody to help me.

I went downstairs, unlocked the back door, and stepped out into the damp air. The night was still and pitch black. I went to the hut where the sexton kept his tools. I lit his lantern and took his shovel with me to the newly filled in grave under the trees. I was young and exceptionally strong then, and I had the night before me. The only sound in the black churchyard was the occasional drip of water from the branches of trees. I could hardly see the bulk of the church against the black sky. I stood the lamp on the ground and taking off my coat, I began to reopen the grave where the 'White Goat' lay. If I had been mistaken about the sounds from the coffin, I must know it, for the peace of the rest of my life. If I had been right, then I must do what I could to redress the wrong I had done. I must find him, and restore him, even though the two enemies should meet alone in the black night of the churchyard, the one in his premature shroud, the other in his costume of grave digger.

Chilly though the night, the sweat poured from my body, and I took off shirt and vest. The clock chimed the night along, shocking me each time it made its solemn sound, as if it were watching me at my horrid work. The earth piled up on the sides of the grave, and I sank slowly down into the pit I was digging. At length, my spade struck the coffin lid. I cleared away the soil as far as I could, and there I made myself a recess where I could brace myself to tear away the lid. The night closed around me and above as if it were itself a tomb. I had not realized the impossibility of raising the coffin alone, nor the great difficulty of pulling away the lid. Somehow, by taking out the screws and using my spade as a lever, I forced the top to one side. I reached up for my lantern and stared at what lay within. There was my enemy, the man I had hated. The faint beams of my lantern fell upon him. The most terrible feeling gripped me. I knew in that moment what death is: dark, silent, mysterious; yes, but appallingly silly. I began to shake with laughter. I could not let it out in peals in his presence. I scrambled out of the grave and began feverishly filling it in with the earth I had piled around. I had never worked so hard or so fast. A kind of deathly rhythm fell upon my strokes... cover it up... fill it in... hide it away... and all the time I laughed till I ached. What a mistake it all was.

I had seen for myself. The 'White Goat' was dead. *But he was lying on his side.*

# Nigel Kneale

## *Oh, Mirror, Mirror*

'The Old Queen possessed a wonderful mirror and when she stepped before it and said:

> *"Oh, mirror, mirror on the wall,*
> *Who is the fairest one of all?"*

it replied:

> *"Thou art the fairest, Lady Queen."*

Then she was pleased.'

'Snow White and the Seven Dwarfs', *Grimm's Fairy Tales*

There's no call to start so, Judith. It's only your auntie. Lie back in the bed now. Let me pull the covers round you against the draught. And a sip of water: your forehead's hot.

No, you're wrong, dearest. It's hot, not normal. So often that way; I don't like it. Oh! You mustn't listen when I say such things, talking to myself. I'm such a silly; I meant nothing. Really – nothing. Yes, I know it feels cool to you, but then – never mind! Poor little Judy!

I'm going to sit with you for a while. There! What jolly cane chairs you have in your room, haven't you? I think they are two of the cosiest in the whole house. Age doesn't matter with really good articles, you know that. Don't you? And fumbling repairs sometimes spoil things we've grown used to and fond of.

Now, I want you to lie quite still and restful. I'm going to talk to you, dear.

Yes, it's about what happened yesterday afternoon.

Won't you tell me why you did it, Judith? You may as well. Because I know, anyway; more than you do.

No! No!

Don't hide your face like that! Oh, it hurts your auntie more than you can tell when her little girl won't speak to her.

Yesterday I was arranging her tea and wondering what would please her most. I had found a bright, clean napkin for her tray, and I was cutting bread thin as thin, and cornerwise, because that is how she likes it. And then I looked out of the window.

What I saw upset me very much. It was my little girl running, wasn't it? Running far down the garden to where the wall joins the big door. And peeping behind her to see if I watched. But I was behind the curtains.

Then I felt something inside me. Here. A tight, cold feeling all round my heart.

Because of two things. One was that she should go so terribly against my wishes. So many times I have said, since she was quite tiny, 'You mustn't go outside the garden, Judith,' and 'You ought never to run.' But there she was, in spite of all I had said and done for her. It made your auntie extremely unhappy, Judith.

But the second reason was sadder still. As I ran out on to the lawn, I was saying to myself, 'Now she will have to be told everything, and it may break her heart. Something wicked has made her do this, and she must know, so that she can resist it.' That's what I said to myself as I was running down the path. 'She will have to be told,' I said.

You weren't able to go very fast, were you, dear? You are so young, and I am your old aunt, and yet I caught up with you among the pear trees. Was it really that you slipped upon the path? Or was it perhaps, something else?

Now I want you to take another sip of water – there! Are you quite comfortable? You must be very brave. Give me your hand, dear. Such a frail little hand, tight in mine.

Very brave indeed, Judith. I'll have to tell you something that will be a very great shock. I'm going to be as gentle as I can, but it will still be a shock.

Let me see. You remember that fairy tale from when you were very small – 'The Ugly Duckling'? It looked so odd and different that the other ducks and everybody drove it away. And then it changed and grew into a beautiful swan. Do you know what 'beautiful' is, Judy? You liked that story very much, though.

Now, just think, dear. Supposing – just supposing that the duckling hadn't changed at all. Supposing it became a still uglier one? That wouldn't have made a happy ending, would it?

Hold your auntie's hand very tightly, my love, and try to be ever such a brave girl. You see, Judith, I'm afraid you're that kind of duckling.

There, there!

Ever since you came here as a tiny tot with no mother and daddy, I've known some day I'd have to tell you that you were – different from other people.

Now you're understanding. Why nobody comes here. Why I have to have a high, safe wall round the garden – that you never go outside. And why your auntie takes such care of you, every minute of the day.

I suppose you've often wondered why it was like that, haven't you? But you've always been so good and done as auntie bid, and auntie loves you so very much.

It would have been the same if your – parents had lived. Your lovely mamma would have done what I did; we understood each other so well, as sisters do. I knew everything she should have, every single thing that was best for her. And then she married your father – she had no right...

We – we'll not talk about that. It's only what I said before. He wasn't really for her. Not for her. That's it, he wasn't – good enough.

And so, they've both gone a long time, and poor old auntie's minding this little girl instead.

And the little girl wants to know why she cannot go out and see the world at last. Because she's grown to fifteen years old.

Well now, just wait a minute.

Here's the mirror, down from its hook. I can rest it against the foot of the bed. Carefully does it when the frame is loose.

Can you see into it, Judith? Raise yourself a little, dear. There. See the precious duckling clearly?

This is the part that is going to hurt, even with her auntie's arm tight round her.

I want you to look at that shape in the mirror, Judy. Such a slender, curvy body, isn't it? So soft and pale. Those swollen little breasts.

Did you think that was right? Did you?

Now look at me, dear. I'm not like that at all. See how strong and solid I am, straight everywhere, in every line? That's the way people are, Judith. People outside.

That little face of yours, Judy. Pale, nearly like the bed-sheets, except for two pinky cheeks and red lips. Eyes as blue as – copper rot. Mine are dark brown, and my skin is dark and tough. And hair – look in the mirror, dear; see that thin, soft, shiny yellow, like fading grass? Not thick and black, like other people's.

My little Judy – crying! Oh, what sobs!

You just didn't know how – different you were. I've always kept it from you. That is why there are no pictures of people in the rooms. I didn't want you to be hurt.

Brown skinned and hard, they are, with strong black hair. I'm one of them.

So I can go out and talk among them. And they don't know about you, these dark people. Only I think of my little girl at home that's different.

Now, Judy, do you know what would have happened if your old auntie hadn't cared for you yesterday, and run to stop you and guide you back to this house? Do you know what would have happened if you had gone past the pear trees and the green water tank, and up to the big door? And if it hadn't been locked – but it always is – and you had opened and walked outside?

Something very horrible, Judith.

You would have seen people like me – all like me, Judy – only not smiling, I'm afraid.

You would have seen them halt in the distance, and point, and murmur to each other in their dry, grey roads; and move softly in the shadows. And presently, as you walked, you would hear tiny shufflings and mutterings. And you would glimpse a head of a person on the other side of a wall, keeping pace with you, or a grey hand signalling in a doorway. And then things would come quietly through the hot dust. They would be people. And they would be following you. Because you were different.

Remember how all the animals were unkind to the Ugly Duckling? People can be far crueller.

You might speak to one of them, but your voice would be tiny with fright. His head would turn away, with eyes remaining on you, and he would talk loudly and hard. Not to you – to the others. You would feel the whisper run through, sealing them against you, and teeth and eyes would shine out from the whole band of them. Then they would be thrustling, jostling, screaming, and all the roads clattering with laughter. 'Look at their eyes!' they would shout. 'See it! How it cries! There it is, running!' And the shouts would become the echo of your own feet beating along the middle of the lanes, and the stones ringing under them. Running until you couldn't go any longer! And behind, they would be coming, closing on you!

Like one of those dreams auntie calls nightmares, but this time it would be true, Judy. Perhaps in your dreams, you know.

It's terrible to be different.

But your auntie's here. She understands. And there's a high wall, and nothing to be afraid of, if they don't see inside.

And when you make that singing, or sit watching the clouds and wondering, or tremble at the thunder, there's only auntie to know that you're doing what no one else does. Isn't there? And auntie's your friend who understands.

My Judith is brave, and she won't cry any more now, will she? Just one last look in the mirror at that strange little face, so that she'll know finally what her auntie meant.

Oh, my poor girl! Can't she bear to look? Can't she, then?

Don't hide in the bedclothes, dear. You're never strange to me, you know.

Take the mirror away? Wait, Judith.

I've something for you. I knew what a horrible shock it would be, and I got what may help my little girl to bear it.

There. Right in her little hand. Do you know what it is, dear? A bottle of stain – quite harmless brown stain. It smells rather sweet.

If she wants, she can add a little to her washing water. To darken those hands and those pink and white cheeks. And when she looks in the mirror, she won't seem so different after all. She can pretend to be like me, can't she?

And after that we must simply be patient and auntie loving, because we haven't so very long in this world, have we? And if we're not ordinary...

Now, if the little girl stops crying and lies quietly and still, she shall have a plate of bread and butter cut just as she likes it. And some little secret treat. Her auntie will sit with her in this beautiful cosy room, and we shall have a game of ludo.

For I understand. And she's my very own. For always. Poor little Judy.

# Noel Langley

## *Serenade for Baboons*

The doctor was a chubby, benign little man who had taken his degree in Edinburgh, married, become old-fashioned, and come to South Africa because he had been told that the practices were not overcrowded as they were in Glasgow, and patients were less inclined to demand newfangled gadgets and fancy remedies for ordinary ailments.

'I am a practical, down-to-earth doctor,' he chose to say, 'and I don't believe in anything that isn't practical and down-to-earth. A stomachache is a stomachache, and the gripes is the gripes: and imagination is the enemy of man.'

He said this to a fellow traveller on the Union Castle boat on his way to Cape Town, and the fellow traveller had answered: 'Then I hope you're wise in going to South Africa.'

'I hope so!' said the Doctor, with feeling, who had spent his last capital on his tickets. 'I was told there was plenty of room for a competent man!'

'That I wouldn't deny,' agreed the fellow traveller. 'It's the imagination that may give you trouble. The rural folks are superstitious, you know.'

'I'm sure I can cure them of *that!*' said the Doctor in mild relief. 'May it be the least of my problems.'

It proved to be the greatest, however; for when he eventually bought a country practice in a village of tin shanties at the foot of the

Drakensberg Mountains, he found his patients hard to woo. They were rugged and taciturn and still resentful of an English accent. When they came to him with the stomachache, expecting to have it called a romantic ailment and to be made much of, his airy pooh pooh and his casual prescriptions of sodium bicarbonate, instead of reassuring them, sent them away discontented.

One day the Doctor learned that an ancient Hottentot witch-doctor called M'Pini was doing better business with the local farmers than he was, and it struck his professional pride in a vulnerable spot. He tried to register a complaint with the Mounted Police when they made their rounds of the district, and he tried to enlist the moral support of Mr Coetze, the local minister; but in both cases he met with polite evasion. He complained indignantly to his wife, a discreet and reserved Scotch woman who kept her place. 'They believe in witchcraft!' he said. 'That shrivelled little savage gives them the entrails of animals and burns feathers! I shall fight this out, Agnes, on principle rather than as competition!'

'I was talking with Mrs Naude,' said his wife, referring to the wife of the storekeeper. 'She said you'd do well to tolerate the local feeling a wee bitty more than you do. It'd be quicker, she was saying, for you to come round to their way of thinking than to wait for them to come round to yours.'

'I would sooner,' decreed the Doctor from the bottom of his heart, 'become a savage myself.'

But it did not help to pay his bills, and when their income was almost gone, she spoke to him again about it.

'A little deception,' said the good woman, 'need hurt nobody's conscience when it's in the cause of good. Just a little mumbo-jumbo with their cough medicine is all they want, and pretty names on the labels; and you'd put that Hottentot out of business; and come now, Jamie, how could it hurt you?'

'I'll make no concessions to superstitious folk who should know better,' he said doggedly. 'They'll come round to my way of thinking, or we'll stay as we are.'

'I'm having to borrow from the storekeeper,' his wife pointed out.

'I cured him of the toothache,' said her husband, 'long before the witchdoctor rubbed hippopotamus fat on his silly head; we owe him nothing.'

'I'd like to convince him,' said his wife sadly.

By now the hostility between the Doctor and the witchdoctor M'Pini was openly recognized. If they passed each other on the dirt roads, it was all the Doctor could do to control himself, but he knew there was nothing to gain by antagonizing the locals further, so he held his peace; though by now he believed fanatically that he stood for the principles of enlightenment and was prepared to die for them.

That he would have is certain, for he still had to eat; but in his hour of need, Fate sent him a client who hated witchdoctors as much as he did. He was a farmer from the wilds of the mountains, called Hoareb, and despite his unprepossessing shape, the Doctor could have wept with joy when he came to his house to have a wound in his arm dressed, and paid his money, and went away again without more than ten words being exchanged between them.

'There goes a patient after my own heart,' said the Doctor, even though there wasn't a man in the village who didn't hate the sight of Hoareb and give him a wide berth when they saw him coming; slouching along with his huge shoulders stooped forward, and his cold beady eyes sunk so far back into his head that his eyebrows seemed to hang over black pits, and his tight-shut mouth that looked like a badly healed scar across his face. He never stayed longer in the village than necessity kept him, and never came in from his farm up in the mountains more often than he could help.

Some of them put his age at sixty, others at forty, and one or two insisted that he had been up in his farm on the mountains since the Lord put the mountains there, and there he would always be, with his slouching shoulders and snake's eyes, until the Lord sent the mountains to dust on Judgement Day, and plunged Hoareb into everlasting fire.

The Doctor, however, thought of him with pride and satisfaction.

He had had to make no concessions to him and he had gone away satisfied with the Doctor's work. He was the model patient, and the exoneration of the doctor's rigid principles.

A few days later, as if in substantiation of this, Hoareb came back. He rode unhurriedly through the village, reined his horse up in front of the Doctor's cottage, and banged at the door until he broke the brass knocker the Doctor's wife had brought all the way from Edinburgh. The Doctor was in his bath, but climbed out, sopping wet, and hurried down in his towel to save the door from bursting off its hinges, while his wife hid herself in the kitchen. He unlatched the door and Hoareb nearly threw him on his back by thrusting his way into the hall without waiting invitation. 'My friend is ill,' he said without preamble. 'I think perhaps dying. You had better come. Now.'

'As soon as I can,' the Doctor assured him.

'Now,' repeated Hoareb.

'I'll have to dress,' the Doctor pointed out, 'I'll be ready in ten minutes.' He left Hoareb in the hall and scuttled back upstairs to dress, delighted beyond words, and stiff with pride and assurance. He was into his clothes and had his bag packed, back into the hall, in just under ten minutes. Hoareb was standing where he left him, staring into nothing.

'My horse. Won't take me a minute,' said the Doctor, and ran round to the stable. He had two horses so that one was always saddled in readiness. He strapped his bag to the saddle, and cantered back to the high street.

Hoareb was mounted, waiting.

As soon as the Doctor appeared he swung his horse round and set off on the forty-seven miles without a word, and the Doctor fell behind obediently. The village watched them go, and speculation ran high.

The whole of the journey was conducted in silence. After twenty miles the Doctor's elation abated a little, for as they left the flat veld and began climbing the pass up into the Drakensberg, a strong sense of loneliness came over him and Hoareb's back seemed to grow larger and more ominous. A hundred and one stories of Hoareb's rages, his insane attacks on his natives, his utter secrecy in all he did, came flooding back, though he cast them sternly from his mind, concentrating on the duties of his profession, and thought of the friend – 'perhaps dying', Hoareb had said.

They entered the bush growing round the foothills, and when the sunlight was shut out by the squat trees, his nerves began to show the first signs of strain. The path was steep and slippery with moss. Loose pebbles broke away under the horses' feet and made them stumble. Branches whipped him across the face and flicked his ears painfully. Occasionally animals, frightened by their noise, rustled away under the bushes with a suddenness that brought his heart into his mouth, but Hoareb continued on his way stolidly, never once turning in his saddle to see whether the Doctor was still following.

Africa at her wildest lay round them. They passed a small waterfall and a pool where evil little arrow-heads cut the water, and larger snakes lay curled beside its edge. Farther on they came to a headless waterbuck at the side of the path, and here Hoareb reined up and pointed to it with a twisted finger.

'Baboons done it,' he said, and his face twisted with anger. 'Baboons.' It came through his teeth with vitriolic intensity. 'Baboons done it. Cursed of God!' His eyes were pinpoints of fanatical hatred. 'I tear their heads off, like they done that, you hear? Like they tear that head off, I tear theirs! Cursed of God! Cursed of God!' His gaze met the Doctor's, and the Doctor looked away, discomfited. 'You think I'm afraid of them, maybe? Me, afraid of baboons, the spawn of Satan? They think I'm afraid of them, too, but every one I shall kill, by tearing off the head, like that buck, you hear? I not afraid!' He suddenly stood up in his stirrups and shouted at the top of his terrific voice: 'Do you hear? Cursed of God! I not afraid! I not afraid! Do you hear?'

The echoes came thundering back from all round them, and

when they had died away he waited for a few seconds, straining for something he didn't want to hear.

The Doctor held his breath, and felt that the whole of the wildness about them hung in silent suspense, waiting with them. The seconds trickled by, and then Hoareb suddenly threw his head back and bellowed with laughter, a hoarse laughter more removed from humour than anything the Doctor had ever heard. His horse shied sideways with fear and he held it to the path with difficulty. Hoareb laughed again, stopped suddenly, spat at the dead waterbuck, and brought his heels down into his horse's ribs with a vicious kick, then continued along the path, sinking back into morose silence, and gazing in front of him.

Another hour's riding through the gloom of the bush brought them into a clearing where the outbuildings of the farm stood. They were ordinary wattle and tin sheds, daubed with mud and well kept, reassuringly conventional in layout, and yet looking slyly wrong in every line and corner. A few hens were scratching at the rubbish heap, and from somewhere came the sound of a dog howling, but there was no sign of a human being anywhere in sight.

They rode past the sheds and, turning a clump of wild mimosa, came upon the farmhouse, still and deserted. The howling of the dog grew clearer, it rose mournfully in the stillness, wavered, and sank into a low whine, and then rose again more insistently than before.

Hoareb brought his horse up to the steps of the verandah, let the reins drag, and waited for the Doctor to dismount without speaking, a leather whip thumping against his leg. The Doctor swung off his horse, undid his bag, and came up to the steps. Hoareb jerked his head over his shoulder.

'Hear dog?' he said. 'Maybe you come too late.'

'Where is she?' the Doctor asked.

Hoareb turned and went into the house, and he followed unhappily. There was a dank stuffy smell of animals in the dark room, but not of animals the Doctor knew or recognized. As his eyes grew used to the gloom he found himself in a poorly furnished dining room with the remains of a meal still on the table. One of the chairs had been broken and the pieces lay scattered across the floor. In a corner something moved, and he turned with defensive speed to face it. Two children were crouching against the wall, their eyes wide with fear, and as he looked at them, a strange feeling of uncertainty crept over him. There was something more than imbecility in the eyes gazing into his. His mind flew back to animals again, and he remembered a sick Gibbon monkey he had once tried to save from dying. It had cried like a human being. The children were about twelve or fourteen, a boy and a girl, dark skinned. He made a movement towards them, and they shrank farther back against the wall. An almost inaudible whimper of terror came from the girl, and he drew back in distress. Hoareb from the other end of the room broke the silence.

'Baboons!' he said. 'A fine couple, do you hear?' He came across and stood towering over them, then uncurled the whip and flicked it lightly. The girl began a poor sickly scream that quavered into nothing, and he laughed. 'Baboons; do you hear? Look how they fear me! I have only to raise my foot and they squeal. Do you see how they fear me? And you think I am afraid of baboons!' He laughed again, and the whip cracked. 'Out! Out of here! Cursed of God!' he shouted with sudden rage. 'Back to your filth!'

The two children fled, stumbling in their panic, and he followed them to the door. The boy missed his footing and fell to the ground, cutting his head on the stones. The girl paused, gasping with fright, and helped him scramble to his feet with the blood pouring from his face, and together they disappeared behind the mimosa trees.

The dog, which had been silent for a while, raised its voice again in a long-drawn howl that brought the hair up on the Doctor's neck. Hoareb shouted thickly, and it stopped. He coiled the whip and came back into the room.

'There,' he said, and opened a door that had been hidden by a curtain of sacking. 'Had an accident. I think perhaps she will die.'

The Doctor entered first, and stood stockstill for a moment. On a bed by the window lay a middle-aged Zulu woman, covered by a blanket. He crossed the room swiftly and bent over her. Her lower jaw had been crushed and hung at an ugly angle. The blanket was soaked in blood. He moved it slightly and uncovered a gash across her shoulder. He turned his head and saw Hoareb still standing in the door, watching expressionlessly.

'What do you expect me to do?' the Doctor asked with an effort. 'This woman's dying.'

Hoareb nodded. 'Accident,' he said.

The Doctor remembered the broken chair. 'It's a case for the police and the coroner,' he said, 'not a doctor.'

Hoareb moved slowly across to the bed.

'The police not come here,' he said heavily. 'If she dies, I bury her.'

'You can't do that,' the Doctor said briskly, though it took courage; and then heard a faint scratching behind him, and turned.

There was a fourth person in the room.

He sat squatting over in a corner; a little wizened, dark shape; older than time, watching them intently.

The Doctor started back, instinctively afraid.

'Who's that?' he asked nervously.

Hoareb followed his glance, and when he saw the little man, he went suddenly mad. He swung his whip in the air with a roar and lunged forward. The Doctor managed to catch his arm in time, and while the whip was still quivering in mid-air, the corner was suddenly empty.

Hoareb stood breathing unevenly, stooped forward and trembling, and then blundered wildly about the room, slashing out at the shadows.

The Doctor had drawn back, for in that moment he had recognized the little witchdoctor, M'Pini, and his rage was as ungovernable as Hoareb's, shuddering through him and making him weak.

The woman on the bed opened her eyes and lay watching them

dispassionately, the glaze of death upon her. Hoareb suddenly paused in his crazy search and turned on her wildly.

'You brought him here!' he said thickly. 'You brought witchdoctors into my house!'

The whip fell across her body, and the Doctor's mind cleared itself of its momentary fury. He caught Hoareb's arm before the whip fell again, and wrenched it out of his hand.

'Are you mad?' he shouted breathlessly. 'Get out of here and leave her to die in peace!'

For a moment he thought Hoareb was going to fall upon him barehanded; but instead, he backed slowly to the door, his eyes shrunk to insane pin-points.

'She brought witchdoctors into my house,' he mumbled dully. 'Cursed of God!' He leant against the doorpost, struggling with his breath. 'Because I beat her, she brought witchdoctors to kill me!'

'Get out of here!' said the Doctor steadily, realizing that the man was insane with fright and not anger, and handed him back the whip.

Hoareb stood a second undecided, then with a heavy shambling gait he disappeared through the door, and the Doctor heard him cross the dining room and go down the steps of the verandah, swearing incoherently.

The woman on the bed stirred, and he came back to her. She was looking up at him and trying to speak. He shook his head gently, but the torn muscles about her jaw still quivered, and he bent closer.

'They come. They come,' she whispered, and pointed weakly towards the window, 'look!'

He raised his head and, hearing nothing, slowly moved to the window; and then he stood frozen, unable to take in what he saw outside. The dark had fallen, but he could see, in the centre of the clearing, the motionless figure of Hoareb; his eyes straining out of his head and bright with horror.

Round him in a still, shadowy half circle; between him and the undergrowth; sat fifty or sixty baboons, sitting as the little man had sat, watching him intently.

No one – no thing – moved.

How long the Doctor stood watching, he did not know. It seemed endless waiting, while outside nothing moved nor made a sound. They could all have been stuffed figures in a ghoulish charade; Hoareb standing there staring; the baboons in their half circle watching him. Even the air was still, even the earth about them seemed to be locked in a moment of time.

A trickle of foam ran down Hoareb's chin. He raised his hand automatically and wiped it away. Then he began to look round him, slowly, as if he were counting them.

But he never moved, and the baboons sat watching him as if they were carved from stone.

The Doctor could hear his own watch ticking like a muffled sledgehammer in his waistcoat pocket.

Then the chant began – a thin, shining trail of sound that came from nowhere and everywhere; too faint to catch, too loud to shut out of the brain; with no rhythm or beat, no tune, no words. It was the noise of the innocent crying for revenge against the wicked, and Hoareb knew it for that, for he made a blind, groping step towards the house. He had not moved a foot when, as if by magic, the half circle completed itself.

The baboons came from nowhere.

One moment there was a clear track back to the house; the next he was surrounded by them, and stood with his body sagging, glaring at them. They sat squatting in the dust, watching him intently; and still the chant went on, without pause, like the drone of flies against a window or water through dry reeds.

He was shuddering now, and his breath was beginning to come in jerky sobs that shook his body. For a second his frantic gaze met the Doctor's and the Doctor's spine crawled; but he stood where he was, unable to help.

Then the chant changed; subtly and inexplicably; and with one liquid movement the baboons closed in until they were half as near again.

Hoareb began to gibber, but still he stood, transfixed, while the circle of baboons sat motionless; watching him still, and the chant continued on and on monotonously. Then he began to laugh.

He began to laugh, low at first, a queer broken chuckle, then it grew to a discordant clatter of hysteria, rolling and echoing back in distorted keys.

The Doctor stood watching, paralysed, until a noise from the bed made him turn his head. The woman had raised her arm above her head. As she did so, the chant gathered strength; becoming shriller and more insistent. He glanced back out of the window, and saw they were still as they were, save that the baboons seemed to be crouching to spring, rather than squatting; awaiting an order. And then he heard the woman's arm drop and swing lifeless over the side of the bed, and on that second, with one movement, they sprang, and Hoareb's scream was cut short in his throat.

When the Doctor uncovered his eyes and looked through the window again, the clearing was empty save for the leather whip, which lay where it had fallen.

As the Doctor looked, the little witchdoctor came from behind the mimosa trees and picked it up.

Then he advanced to below the window and raised his hand respectfully. 'Perhaps the Master should return home,' he suggested politely in Zulu. 'There is little left for him to do here.'

'I will,' said the Doctor limply, and fainted flat on his face.

It was midnight by the time he had made his report to the police and reached his house, and his wife was still waiting supper. When she saw his face, however, she gave a wail of anxiety and hurried towards him.

'Jamie!' she cried. 'Are you ill? Indeed you are! What shall I get you for it?'

He shook his head weakly.

'There's nothing I need, Agnes,' he said with an unfamiliar meekness. 'I've just seen a doctor.'

# Hamilton Macallister

# *The Lady Who Didn't Waste Words*

She had legs that stuck down from her dress as if they ought to have had castors on them, and under each ear was a thick glass ball. They were the only two passengers in the whole of the last carriage. They'd sat there in silence, until he said, 'Excuse me, d'you mind?' He held his pipe in his hand.

She just smiled. One front tooth was missing and one was as black as soot.

'D'you mind if I smoke?'

She continued to smile: he took in her various oddities. 'I said,' he said, 'd'you mind if I smoke?'

'Words,' she said to him, 'that aren't in the praise of God are wasted words.'

'I'm sorry.' He put it back in his pocket, and fixed his eye on a picture of Barnard Castle. After a bit he gave her a quick look: she was smiling full at him. He looked away and prepared to sleep.

He opened his eyes in a tunnel that was so dark he couldn't even see the walls of the compartment. No lights went on: an old, decrepit carriage, without corridors, peeling and dirty. He kept his eyes open in the close, dusty blackness, and out of it came the lady's smile, facing him. She had moved.

He produced a small smile that got itself twisted, and closed his eyes again.

But he didn't sleep. He drowsed, and returned sharply to consciousness with the dark over his retina again. He opened his eyes in the complete blackness. He wondered if she were still smiling. But when the light returned, she was there no longer. Then he saw that she had moved on to his seat, and was two or three feet away, by his side.

It was becoming annoying. He gave her a deliberate, angry look. She was still smiling at him, face half turned; she looked quite stupid, obviously was. He turned his attention to the hedges, opening and closing past the window. They were getting into the mountains.

They were in another tunnel soon. The four sharp cries of the wheels became dull. And now he began to feel an intense discomfort and irritation. He moved his right hand up and down the wood in his preoccupation. He met the line of the communication cord, just within reach, which he caressed with one finger. He was furious with himself. He dropped his hand and managed to pull himself together just before they left the tunnel.

She'd moved again. She'd edged along the seat till she was about two feet from him; he could see this out of the corner of his eye. He opened his mouth to say something angry, and she said, smiling and waggishly shaking her head, 'It's no good pulling the communication cord in a tunnel. Trains never stop in tunnels.'

After that they sat together in silence till they entered the next tunnel.

In the darkness he couldn't hear the slightest movement, but he felt her smile on him, all the time. Gradually he began to have an extraordinary feeling that she was crawling past his legs, still smiling up at him as she crawled. His legs tingled all over, but he felt he couldn't move them an inch. He nodded his head violently up and down and pressed into the seat with his fists, and this helped him slightly. Suddenly the light came back.

The lady was on the other side again, so she had moved past him. Furious, he looked straight at her to tell her to damn well stay where she was, but as he encountered the impact of her silly smile, the words dried in his mouth.

In the daylight it was absurd. Physically, she was intensively repulsive. He could feel sorry for her, out of the tunnels; she was an obvious mental, half his size. When he saw the next tunnel coming up – and it was going to be the main one, by the look of the mountain that was folding over them – he'd made up his mind that he wasn't going to bother with her; she could prowl about where she wanted. For a minute or two he sat still, relaxed.

Very cautiously he put out his left hand an inch or two. After another minute of tunnel he raised it to shoulder level, and did the same. The third time he touched something, soft and cold like the horn of a snail, so yielding as to be almost unfelt. Like a snail's horn, it withdrew. Then it came again. Then it stayed. He felt its length: oval, and underneath it hung a round glass ball. It moved closer.

He pulled the communication cord.

The train pulled clear of the tunnel before it stopped. There was a peculiar sort of silence, after which he heard the guard coming down the track.

The lady sat by his side. He looked at her, and found her smiling away. 'What's the idea?' he said.

She put her hand to her mouth and said, 'Sh!'

'What d'you mean?' He could hear the guard coming nearer, looking in at the carriages as he passed.

'Words – ' she said, smiling.

'Oh to hell!' he said. He felt indescribably foolish. He was a heavy man, fat and powerful, and she was dumpy – a sticky-looking woman. He grabbed his suitcase and opened the door on the other side from the approaching guard. There was a rail track and a steep drop over the embankment. He looked back at the lady; she had stopped smiling at last, and was looking shocked now. Then he jumped, in front of an express train.

The guard opened the carriage door and said, 'Yes, lady?' He could see that this was the one.

But she just sat very still, looking shocked.

'Did you pull the cord?' he said. But her eyes, in dumb horror, indicated the swinging door. He crossed the carriage and looked out: the express had gone by with a roar and a flicker of windows. 'Good – God!' he said. 'Well, I've served the railways for fifteen years and this is IT.' He went back and took the lady's hand, very sympathetically. 'Did 'e do anything to you afore 'e jumped out?' The poor old thing was trembling. She wouldn't say anything. 'Maybe 'e got what 'e deserved,' he said. 'Are you all right then, lady?'

He beckoned to a doctor whom he had picked up on his way down. 'Just look aht the other side,' he whispered. The doctor looked, and told the guard there was nothing left to do. Sightseers had begun to collect, looking into the carriage and at the remains of the man, with a blank, reserved look on their faces, like people suddenly asked to give money. They were sent back to their carriages, and the doctor stayed with the lady.

He was a neat, dark man. He wore rimless glasses, and had a quiet, scientific righteousness. He said to her, 'Now what is your name please, madam?'

But she said nothing. She sat very still, looking shaken.

'I take it you're not – related?' He indicated the other door.

'We're all brothers in the sight of Him.'

'Oh yes.'

The train clanked into motion again, and the doctor sat down by her. He said, 'I'm a doctor, and I'm used to these things, you know. Now the coroner will want to know just what he did. You know that, don't you? Don't worry, you'll be all right now.'

She smiled at him.

The doctor smiled back. 'Can I have your name and address?'

'Words that aren't to the praise of the Lord are wasted,' she said.

'Yes.' He flicked his notebook. 'Bit of a shock, eh?'

She said nothing.

'Must have been a bit of a shock.'

He looked at her intently. Something about him seemed to

reassure her, and she leaned right up to his face and whispered, 'I looked at him!'

'Yes?' He opened his notebook again.

'He said, "To hell!" '

'Yes?'

'And the Lord – struck!' Then she closed her mouth tight, and looked at the doctor with big, shocked eyes.

He put away his notebook and withdrew an inch or two from her. 'I see,' he said. She followed him along the seat, and opened her mouth to say something else, then thought the better of it. She broke out into smiles again. They sat in silence, very close together, till they reached the next station. When the train stopped, the doctor got up and asked briskly, 'Now before I go, won't you give me your name and address?'

For an answer she took him by the lapels of his coat and pulled his face right down to hers. She was looking very pleased with herself, as if she had made a discovery. 'I'm an angel of the Lord,' she whispered.

'I see,' the doctor said again, disengaging himself. He left the carriage.

It was now quite dark. For the rest of the journey she was on her own again. Each time the train stopped, the guard, as he walked past with his flag, looked in. She smiled at him, and he said, 'All right? Wouldn't you like to come and sit in the van then?' he said at the last stop. She smiled in answer. 'No?' he said. 'It'd be company now!'

'Sh!' she said.

'Ah yes,' he said. The doctor was with him. They went down the platform, talking, and the train moved on.

Suddenly there was a low boom of thunder. Black clouds, which had hurried the night on, were bringing a storm. The night became charged with electricity. The thunder and flashes grew swiftly stronger and closer together; it was coming right at them. As it folded over the train like a mountain, a flash lit up the compartment, and there was a terrific clap. She stood up and opened the carriage door. Her eyes glittered with excitement; she stood half in and half out of the door, waiting for something to happen. Lightning lit her up and thunder followed, crashing up and down the sky. But nothing happened.

The storm had rushed to its climax and was speeding away. The apocalypse passed into wet black normality. The lightning lost its jagged edge, and after a while a long low sweeping noise indicated rain.

She hung on, and each rumble of thunder sounded as if it would be the last. The rumbling now sounded infinitely far away, like the troubles of another planet, and seemed to be fading more quickly, like the expanding galaxies, as it moved farther away. Eventually she let go her hold, while the thunder was still just audible, leaving the door swinging open behind her in the beating rain. The sky cleared; the rain stopped, and the train slowed into the terminus.

When it had pulled to a stop, the guard came to the window again. He jumped in. 'She's hopped it!' he called, and noticed the far door open again. 'She's jumped out like the other one,' he said.

The doctor pushed past behind him. 'It's my fault,' he cried, looking out; he'd turned bright red with embarrassment and annoyance.

'She's gone,' said the guard, 'gone from our ken.'

'That's nonsense, man, go and ring down the line again.'

'She's gone the way she came.'

'Don't be *absurd*,' cried the doctor.

They both began talking at once, until the stationmaster, who had come in behind them, was abruptly revealed to them by the electric light which now unexpectedly came on.

They stood and listened to the rain, as if they expected to hear the lady come pattering down the track after them. The guard said to the stationmaster, 'She said she was an angel of the Lord!'

He was a hard-bitten old man with a black skin, and he took this without surprise. After a minute or two of silence, he said slowly and contemptuously, 'Now there'll be an inquiry.'

He went to the far side of the compartment, and slowly pushed one finger four inches down the wall, making a path in the dust. Then he held his finger in front of the guard: 'Look at this.'

The guard became immediately damped. 'Aye; it's shocking.'

'Right,' said the stationmaster, and the two of them left the compartment together, like two animals of the same breed, leaving the fretting doctor to follow. With its electric light on, the carriage began to lurch and grind towards the siding.

# Chris Massie

## *A Fragment of Fact*

Starting from my home in Whitby, with the fanatical enthusiasm of youth I had traced out a cycling itinerary which would keep me in touch with the sea round the walls of England until I reached Blackpool, and from there I proposed to cut through the hills back home to Yorkshire.

Embarking on this ambitious programme, I found myself one evening, between the hours of ten and eleven, cycling through the flat country of the sea reaches at the mouth of the Thames. While it was yet light, I had had fully communicated to me the melancholy desolation of that bog-held situation, heightened by the weird cries of some marsh bird I did not recognize.

The day had become sticky with heat: a sullen, breathless atmosphere which made cycling a conscious effort. Sweat oozed from my hair down my forehead, and past my ears, to trickle down the open neck of my cricket shirt. The journey was uncomfortable and uninteresting and, having taken a long bypath route, there was nothing much on the way to engage my attention.

When night fell, I had hoped for cooler conditions, being so near the sea and the river; but as is not unusual following such days, the night air became closer and more menacing. The air was so dense it seemed I was cutting through a solid surface; and indeed the conditions were something like this, for a low, clinging mist had come up from the marshland, and I could not see more than a few yards away by the light of my lamp.

I might have made the journey without considerable discomfort had I not become intolerably thirsty; but it was too late for an inn to be open, had I encountered one, which did not seem likely on this inhospitable bypath.

Growing weary of pedalling and feeling the need of sleep as well as drink, I got off my bike and made my progression on foot. On either side of me stretched miles of dangerous bogland and, though closed in by the mist, I was fully aware of the treacherous, naked countryside through which I was passing.

Now I was on foot travelling slowly; the sticky, warm mist seemed to impede my path by definite resistance. I was tired, thirsty, sleepy, and uncertain of my whereabouts. It was a source of considerable irritation to me that I was almost in touch with the most populous city in the world where every comfort might be obtained at any hour, and yet, for the predicament I was in, I might have been lost in the Sahara.

I plodded on feeling very stupid, regretting the foolhardy presumption which had turned night into day, and overtaxed my endurance. I reflected irritably on the folly of taking bypaths in a fantastically situated country like England. For the first time I deplored my solitude. I had made similar tours with one or more companions, but had found that, however amiable company might be, two ideas were not better than one on the road. Arguing at cross roads had a mean and spoiling effect on a cycling holiday. But the situation was getting on my nerves. I am one of those peculiar people who are not comfortable in wide, flat, open spaces; and though at this hour I could not see the dreary prospect, being closed in by the mist, I could feel it in every nerve of my body.

'I don't suppose there's a house round here for miles,' I was thinking, when to my great relief I could see through the mist a bright patch to the right of the road which indicated, high up, the window of a lighted room.

I pushed on anxiously in the direction, and was soon aware that the light came from a house standing some distance back off the bypath which was approached by a wooden gate which I opened and against which I rested my bicycle.

The way up to the house was hedged on either side by some tall evergreen. It was perhaps fifty yards to the main door, and such is the peculiarity of the abominable torture set up by thirst, that now I was within sight of quenching it, my sufferings from that cause were inconceivably intensified. What if I should fail to get a drink after all? On that short journey I dwelt on pints, quarts, gallons of ice-cold water from a deep well, and in imagination I was quaffing greedily.

As I drew near, I saw the head and shoulders of a man, enormously magnified, pass across the window blind. The shadow had a downward projection, as if he had made a sudden sweeping movement to the floor. I rang a queer, old-fashioned bell which had to be pulled out and let go. A swift peal clattered through the house, which subsided with the lessening vibration to one or two isolated sounds before it ceased altogether.

I stood there, self-conscious, foolish; remembering having made a similar request for water when a child, and how graciously I had been received by a good woman, and accommodated with two juicy apples to follow my refreshing swill. But I was a young man now and the hour was late.

There was no stir in response to my ringing. Impatient and desperate with my need, I rang again, and listened once more for those last, halting reverberations. This time I had succeeded. A foot was on the stair. A moment later the door opened, and a voice out of the darkness, for there was no light in the hall, asked, 'What do you want?'

'I have been held up in the mist,' I replied. 'I am very thirsty and would be glad of a drink of water.'

The man stood for a moment as if in deep thought. It was then I noticed his enormous proportions, not only in height but girth and shoulder span. He was well over six feet tall even in the attitude in which he stood, with head bowed and shoulders humped. His long arms hung in dragging, helpless fashion at his sides, like an ape's.

'Come in,' he said. 'Come into the light.'

I followed him, and he touched a door and said, 'Go and wait for me in there. I will be back again soon with what you want.'

The room I walked into was only feebly lit, giving a twilight effect. It was a large room, but very barely furnished. Though it was obviously a dining or sitting room, a deal table took the centre of the room, and there were three Windsor chairs in various positions. There were no pictures, and nothing of comfort and pleasure in the apartment. I thought by this evidence that the house was unoccupied and that the man I had seen was the caretaker.

He returned in a few moments holding a heavy bowl in both hands, and as I was still standing in the middle of the room, he brought it straight forward and placed it in my hands, so that now I was holding it in precisely the manner he had done a moment before. It was an enormous drinking vessel despite the thirst which oppressed me. I looked down into the water, and saw round the edges at the bottom a dark stain that might have been a sediment of mud.

At that moment I looked up at him in my vexation, and in the dim light I saw his face. The huge size of the man suggested the lineaments of a gorilla, and I expected to be revolted by his appearance; but he was not like that at all. He wore a beard which to the worst of faces adds a venerable sort of dignity. His brows were heavy and overhanging, so that his eyes were invisible in these cavernous projections. His nose was long, with a melancholy downward depression, and his mouth hidden beneath a drooping moustache.

'This must have been a mistake,' I said, indicating the water.

At once he reached out with his immense hands and took the bowl away from me. Without a word of explanation he left the room, and I could hear him descending stairs.

I was alarmed, and inclined to make my escape from the house in his absence, for I had noticed, as the bowl swung round in his hands, the word DOG on its glazed earthenware surface.

In the state of thirst which tortured me, I was appalled that this unmannered giant should be so lacking in all human consideration as to offer me a dog's trough from which to drink. And not a clean one. But he had returned before I could come to a decision, and this time he was bearing a jug and a half pint tumbler.

He set them on the table in front of me, and invited me to sit down. When I had done so, he sat down opposite me on the other side of the table. He looked across at me in the dim light and made this extraordinary statement: 'Between your first ringing at the bell and your second my wife died. I was attending to her upstairs. That will explain my delay in coming down to you.'

The words were uttered simply, as a matter of course, in a deep but gentle voice with unexpected culture in its phrasing.

For the moment I had nothing to reply. Between the first ringing and the second I had been thinking of that good woman who, when I was a child, had supplemented a cooling drink with two juicy apples; and precisely at that moment a woman had died. This, for some unknown reason, seemed to invest the information with a special horror. I felt myself a most insolent intruder.

'I humbly beg your pardon,' I said, getting up. 'That is most terrible news. I ought not to have blundered into the house in this fashion. I will be going now, and thank you for your hospitality.'

He stood up when I did, and with a quick movement preceded me to the door, lifting his hand in a manner which suggested I should be seated again.

'Don't go,' he said. 'I am glad of your company. There is no one else in the house. And I'm not used to this kind of thing. Perhaps it is a trifle unusual in a man of my age, but this is the first time I have seen death happen to... to a human being.... It so happens that her dog died only this morning.'

'And your wife has died almost immediately after the dog?' I asked for no particular reason.

'Yes,' he replied. 'My wife was very fond of it; indeed, she idolized it.'

'Was your wife's death sudden? I mean, were you expecting it?' I asked.

'Yes, I was expecting it. Both my wife and the dog were very ill.' He hesitated a moment then continued, 'When I say I expected it, I was not expecting it at that moment although she was so ill. I had been intent on her condition, trying to make her position in the bed more comfortable, when I heard your first ring. My mind wandered at the psychological moment. It's often so. At the psychological moment we are not there; our minds are floating about in time. That is life's illusion; so much of it is lost in ranging back over the past or trying to explore the future. Then we look at death, and it is all over.'

His remarks were too metaphysical and self-conscious for me to answer. I merely nodded and sat down again. It was ridiculous to stand in the middle of the room and listen to such conversation. He also returned to his chair.

'Between your first ring and your second, she died,' he went on. 'I had been nursing both of them. I mean I was attending the sick dog up to the moment when it died.'

'What sort of dog was it?' I asked.

'A sheepdog,' he replied. 'One of those grey-black, shaggy fellows with the peculiar white-ringed eyes that seem blind, but are far from being so.'

'Oh yes,' I replied casually, but I was suddenly oppressed by a breathtaking sensation of unreality.

He sat before me in idle helplessness, observing me occasionally, and then turning a glance towards the door.

'When the dog died, it was impossible to deceive her about it,' he went on. 'At all times of the day she asked where it was, and implored me to bring it to her. It's lying there now, at the foot of the bed.'

'Do you mean that your wife is dead, and lying at her feet is a dead dog?' I asked. He had just said that, but the picture it brought to my mind was horrifying in the extreme.

'She made me place it there,' he said. 'Her wish was that they should be placed in the same coffin.'

'But no undertaker on earth – ' I began.

'I know,' he replied. 'I know. But it was her last wish, and I cannot bring myself to bury the dog. I cannot sum up sufficient courage to take it away from her feet.'

'Don't you think,' I asked, for the situation was worrying me, 'don't you think you ought to be upstairs with her instead of here, if only to make sure she's dead?... And really I must go; I have an appointment.'

Another thing had occurred to me.

'You ought to go for a doctor,' I told him. 'Shall I call on the first doctor I come across on my way? What's the name of this house?'

He made no reply at once, then he said, 'I must think the matter over carefully. You have no idea what it is like to live in this lonely situation. It was no more than a bond to keep them together until they died. Why should I go upstairs again? I have done my part. I shall be going to the village tomorrow as I have always gone, to get the meat and vegetables, and I may call on a doctor then.'

'May!' I almost screamed. 'You simply must!'

'Must, then,' he concurred.

'I'm sorry,' I said. The words seemed particularly futile, utterly absurd.

He did not reply. He was resting his head on his hands, with his elbows on the table.

'I must be going now,' I said. 'Thank you for the drink.'

Again he did not reply or even look up. I passed out of the room into the dark passage, and very quietly opened the front door and closed it after me. I dashed down through the dark evergreens, and jumped on my bicycle. As I was getting up speed, I heard the pad of feet and a snarling behind me. The next moment the heavy bulk of a big animal caught me broadside on and nearly unseated me. As the handles swung, my lamp was brought round to the creature's face, and I saw a pair of savage eyes. It was a sheepdog.

He came at me again, and lifting my foot from the pedal, I jabbed at his nose with my heel; but it was a push rather than a kick, and he was not hurt. He bared his teeth and leapt at my handlebars, and the lamp, coming off its fittings, dropped in the road and went out; but he had fallen without getting a grip of me. Before he had completely recovered, I rode on, and for a mile I heard him pattering behind.

'That must have been another sheepdog,' I reflected.

An involuntary shudder shook me so that I swerved on my bicycle; but this was not an account of my affray with the dog, but because that strange man with the unkempt hair and beard looked so much like a sheepdog himself.

I did not tell my story to anyone until I reached home. It has remained with me ever since, and from time to time I turn it over in my mind in an effort to clarify and rationalize it; but it remains insoluble.

# Seabury Quinn

# *The House of Horror*

'Morbleau, friend Trowbridge, have a care,' Jules de Grandin warned as my lurching motor car almost ran into the brimming ditch beside the rain-soaked road.

I wrenched the steering wheel viciously and swore softly under my breath as I leaned forward, striving vainly to pierce the curtains of rain which shut us in.

'No use, old fellow,' I confessed, turning to my companion, 'we're lost; that's all there is to it.'

'Ha,' he laughed shortly, 'do you just begin to discover that fact, my friend? *Parbleu*, I have known it this last half hour.'

Throttling my engine down, I crept along the concrete roadway, peering through my streaming windscreen and storm curtains for some familiar landmark, but nothing but blackness, wet and impenetrable, met my eyes.

Two hours before, answering an insistent phone call, de Grandin and I had left the security of my warm office to administer a dose of toxin antitoxin to an Italian labourer's child who lay choking with diphtheria in a hut at the workmen's settlement where the new branch of the railway was being put through. The cold, driving rain and the Stygian darkness of the night had misled me when I made the detour round the railway cut, and for the past hour and a half I had been feeling my way over unfamiliar roads as futilely as a lost child wandering in the woods.

'*Grâce à Dieu*,' de Grandin exclaimed, seizing my arm with both his small, strong hands, 'a light! See, there it shines in the night. Come, let us go to it. Even the meanest hovel is preferable to this so villainous rain.'

I peeped through a joint in the curtains and saw a faint, intermittent light flickering through the driving rain some two hundred yards away.

'All right,' I acquiesced, climbing from the car; 'we've lost so much time already we probably couldn't do anything for the Vivianti child, and maybe these people can put us on the right road, anyway.'

Plunging through puddles like miniature lakes, soaked by the wind-driven rain, barking our shins again and again on invisible obstacles, we made for the light, finally drawing up to a large, square house of red brick fronted by an imposing white-pillared porch. Light streamed out through the fan-light over the white door and from the two tall windows flanking the portal.

'*Parbleu*, a house of circumstance, this,' de Grandin commented, mounting the porch and banging lustily at the polished brass knocker.

I wrinkled my forehead in thought while he rattled the knocker a second time. 'Strange, I can't remember this place,' I muttered. 'I thought I knew every building within thirty miles, but this is a new one – '

'Ah, bah!' de Grandin interrupted. 'Always you must be casting a wet blanket on the parade, Friend Trowbridge. First you insist on losing us in the midst of a *sacré* rainstorm, then when I, Jules de Grandin, find us a shelter from the weather, you must needs waste time in wondering why it is you know not the place. *Morbleu*, you will refuse shelter because you have never been presented to the master of the house, if I do not watch you, I fear.'

'But I ought to know the place, de Grandin,' I protested. 'It's certainly imposing enough to – '

My defence was cut short by the sharp click of a lock, and the wide, white door swung inwards before us.

We strode over the threshold, removing our dripping hats as we did so, and turned to address the person who had opened the door.

'Why – ' I began, and stared about me in open-mouthed surprise.

'Name of a little blue man!' said Jules de Grandin, and added his incredulous stare to mine.

As far as we could see, we were alone in the mansion's imposing hall. Straight before us, perhaps for forty feet, ran a corridor of parquetry flooring, covered here and there by rich-hued Oriental rugs. White-panelled walls, adorned with oil paintings of imposing-looking individuals, rose for eighteen feet or so to a beautifully frescoed ceiling, and a graceful, curving staircase swept upwards from the farther end of the room. Candles in cut-glass sconces lighted the high-ceiled apartment, the hospitable glow from a log fire burning under the high white marble mantel lent an air of homely cosiness to the place, but of anything living, human or animal, there was no faintest trace or sign.

*Click!* Behind us the heavy outer door swung to silently on well-oiled hinges and the automatic lock latched firmly.

'Death of my life!' de Grandin murmured, reaching for the door's silver-plated knob and giving it a vigorous twist. '*Par la moustache du diable*, Friend Trowbridge, it is locked! Truly, perhaps it had been better if we had remained outside in the rain!'

'Not at all, I assure you, my dear sir,' a rich, mellow voice answered him from the curve of the stairs. 'Your arrival was nothing less than providential, gentlemen.'

Coming towards us, walking heavily with the aid of a stout cane, was an unusually handsome man attired in pyjamas and dressing gown, a sort of nightcap of flowered silk on his white head, slippers of softest Morocco on his feet.

'You are a physician, sir?' he asked, glancing inquiringly at the medicine case in my hand.

'Yes,' I answered. 'I am Dr Samuel Trowbridge, from Harrisonville, and this is Dr Jules de Grandin, of Paris, who is my guest.'

'Ah,' replied our host, 'I am very, very glad to welcome you to

Marston Hall, gentlemen. It so happens that one – er – my daughter, is quite ill, and I have been unable to obtain medical aid for her on account of my infirmities and the lack of a telephone. If I may trespass on your charity to attend my poor child, I shall be delighted to have you as my guests for the night. If you will lay aside your coats…' He paused expectantly. 'Ah, thank you' – as we hung our dripping garments over a chair. 'You will come this way, please?'

We followed him up the broad stairs and down an upper corridor to a tastefully furnished chamber, where a young girl – fifteen years of age, perhaps – lay propped up with a pile of diminutive pillows.

'Anabel, Anabel, my love, here are two doctors to see you,' the old gentleman called softly.

The girl moved her fair head with a weary, peevish motion and whimpered softly in her sleep, but gave no further recognition of our presence.

'And what have been her symptoms, if you please, monsieur?' de Grandin asked, as he rolled back the cuffs of his jacket and prepared to make an examination.

'Sleep,' replied our host; 'just sleep. Some time ago she suffered from influenza; lately she has been given to fits of protracted slumber from which I cannot waken her. I fear she may have contracted sleeping sickness, sir. I am told it sometimes follows influenza.'

'H'm.' De Grandin passed his small, pliable hands rapidly over the girl's cheeks in the region of the ears, felt rapidly along her neck over the jugular vein, then raised a puzzled glance to me. 'Have you some laudanum and aconite in your bag, Friend Trowbridge?' he asked.

'There's some morphine,' I answered, 'and aconite; but no laudanum.'

'No matter.' He waved his hand impatiently, bustling over to the medicine case and extracting two small phials from it. 'No matter – this will do as well. Some water, if you please, monsieur' – he turned to the father, a medicine bottle in each hand.

'But, de Grandin –' I began, when a sudden kick from one of his slender, heavily shod feet nearly broke my shin.

'De Grandin, do you think that's the proper medication?' I finished lamely.

'Oh, *mais oui*, undoubtedly,' he replied. 'Nothing else would do in this case. Water, if you please, monsieur,' he repeated, again addressing the father.

I stared at him in ill-disguised amazement as he extracted a pellet from each of the bottles and quickly ground them to powder while the old gentleman filled a tumbler with water from the porcelain pitcher which stood on the chintz-draped washstand in the corner of the chamber. He was as familiar with the arrangement of my medicine case as I was, I knew, and knew that my phials were arranged by numbers instead of being labelled. Deliberately, I saw, he had passed over the morphine and aconite, and had chosen two bottles of plain, unmedicated sugar-of-milk pills. What his object was I had no idea, but I watched him measure out four teaspoonsful of water, dissolve the powder in it, and pour the sham medication down the unconscious girl's throat.

'Good,' he proclaimed, as he washed the glass with meticulous care. 'She will rest easily until the morning, monsieur. When daylight comes we shall decide on further treatment. Will you now permit that we retire?' He bowed politely to the master of the house, who returned his courtesy and led us to a comfortably furnished room farther down the corridor.

'See here, de Grandin,' I demanded, when our host had wished us a pleasant good night and closed the door upon us, 'what was your idea in giving that child an impotent dose like that – ?'

'S-s-sh!' he cut me short with a fierce whisper. 'That young girl, *mon ami*, is no more suffering from encephalitis than you and I. There is no characteristic swelling of the face or neck, no diagnostic hardening of the jugular vein. Her temperature was a bit subnormal, it is true – but upon her breath I detected the odour of chloral hydrate. For some reason – good, I hope, but bad I fear – she is drugged, and I thought it best to play the fool and pretend I believed the man's statements. *Pardieu*, the fool who knows himself no fool has an immense advantage over the fool who believes him one, my friend.'

'But – '

'But me no buts, Friend Trowbridge; remember how the door of this house opened with none to touch it; recall how it closed behind us in the same way, and observe this, if you will.' Stepping softly, he crossed the room, pulled aside the chintz curtains at the window, and tapped lightly on the frame which held the thick plate-glass panes. '*Regardez vous,*' he ordered, tapping the frame a second time.

Like every other window I had seen in the house, this one was of the casement type, small panes of heavy glass being sunk into lattice-like frames. Under de Grandin's directions I tapped the latter, and found them not painted wood, as I had supposed, but stoutly welded and bolted metal. Also to my surprise, I found the turn buckles for opening the casement were only dummies, the metal frames being actually securely bolted to the stone sills. To all intents, we were as firmly incarcerated as though serving a sentence in the state penitentiary.

'The door – ' I began, but he shook his head.

Obeying his gesture, I crossed the room and turned the handle lightly. It twisted under the pressure of my fingers, but, though we had heard no warning click of lock or bolt, the door itself was as firmly fastened as though nailed shut.

'Wh – why,' I asked stupidly, 'what's it all mean, de Grandin?'

'*Je ne sais quoi,*' he answered with a shrug; 'but one thing I know: I like not this house, Friend Trowbridge. I –

Above the hissing of the rain against the windows and the howl of the sea-wind about the gables there suddenly rose a scream, wire-edged with inarticulate terror, freighted with utter, transcendental anguish of body and soul.

'*Cordieu!*' He threw up his head like a hound hearing the call of the pack from far away. 'Did you hear it, too, Friend Trowbridge?'

'Of course,' I answered, every nerve in my body trembling in horripilation with the echo of the hopeless wail.

'*Pardieu,*' he repeated, 'I like this house less than ever now. Come, let us move this dresser before our door. It is safer that we sleep behind barricades this night, I think.'

We blocked the door, and I was soon sound asleep.

'Trowbridge, Trowbridge, my friend' – de Grandin drove a sharp elbow into my ribs – 'wake up, I beseech you. Name of a green goat, you lie like one dead, save for your so abominable snoring!'

'Eh?' I answered sleepily, thrusting myself deeper beneath the voluminous bedclothes. Despite the unusual occurrences of the night, I was tired to the point of exhaustion, and fairly drunk with sleep.

'Up; arise, my friend,' he ordered, shaking me excitedly. 'The coast is clear, I think, and it is high time we did some exploring.'

'Rats!' I scoffed, disinclined to leave my comfortable couch. 'What's the use of wandering about a strange house to gratify a few unfounded suspicions? The girl might have been given a dose of chloral hydrate, but the chances are her father thought he was helping her when he gave it. As for these trick devices for opening and locking doors, the old man apparently lives here alone and has installed these mechanical aids to lessen his work. He has to hobble around with a cane, you know.'

'Ah!' my companion assented sarcastically. 'And that scream we heard, did he install that as an aid to his infirmities, also?'

'Perhaps the girl woke up with a nightmare,' I hazarded, but he made an impatient gesture.

'Perhaps the moon is composed of green cheese also,' he replied. 'Up, up and dress, my friend. This house should be investigated while yet there is time. Attend me: but five minutes ago, through this very window, I did observe monsieur our host, attired in a raincoat, depart from his own front door, and without his cane. *Parbleu*, he did skip as agilely as any boy, I assure you. Even now he is almost at the spot where we abandoned your automobile. What he intends doing there, I know not. What I intend doing I know full well. Do you accompany me or not?'

'Oh, I suppose so,' I agreed, crawling from the bed and slipping into my clothes. 'How are you going to get past that locked door?'

He flashed me one of his sudden smiles, shooting the points of his little blond moustache upwards like the horns of an inverted crescent. 'Observe,' he ordered, displaying a short length of thin wire. 'In the days when woman's hair was still her crowning glory, what mighty deeds a lady could encompass with a hairpin! *Pardieu*, there was one little *grisette* in Paris who showed me some tricks in the days before the war! Regard me, if you please.'

Deftly he thrust the pliable loop of wire into the keyhole, twisting it tentatively back and forth, at length pulling it out and regarding it carefully. '*Très bien*,' he muttered, as he reached into an inside pocket, bringing out a heavier bit of wire.

'See' – he displayed the finer wire – 'with this I take an impression of that lock's tumblers, now' – quickly he bent the heavier wire to conform to the waved outline of the lighter loop – '*voilà*, I have a key!'

And he had. The lock gave readily to the pressure of his improvised key, and we stood in the long, dark hall, staring about us half curiously, half fearfully.

'This way, if you please,' de Grandin ordered; 'first we will look in upon *la jeunesse*, to see how it goes with her.'

We walked on tiptoe down the corridor, entered the chamber where the girl lay, and approached the bed.

She was lying with her hands folded upon her breast in the manner of those composed for their final rest, her wide, periwinkle-blue eyes staring sightlessly before her, the short, tightly curled ringlets of her blonde, bobbed hair surrounding her drawn, pallid face like a golden nimbus encircling the ivory features of a saint in some carved icon.

My companion approached the bed softly, placing one hand on the girl's wrist with professional precision. 'Temperature low, pulse weak,' he murmured, checking off her symptoms. 'Complexion pale to the point of lividity – ha, now for the eyes; sleeping, her pupils should have been contracted, while they should now be dilate – *Dieu de Dieu!* Trowbridge, my friend, come here.'

'Look!' he commanded, pointing to the apathetic girl's face. 'Those eyes – *grand Dieu*, those eyes! It is sacrilege, nothing less.'

I looked into the girl's face, then started back with a half suppressed cry of horror. Asleep, as she had been when we first saw her, the child had been pretty to the point of loveliness. Her features were small and regular, clean-cut as those of a face in a cameo, the tendrils of her light-yellow hair had lent her a dainty, ethereal charm comparable to that of a Dresden-china shepherdess. It had needed but the raising of her delicate, long-lashed eyelids to give her face the animation of some laughing sprite playing truant from fairyland.

Her lids were raised now, but the eyes they unveiled were no clear, joyous windows of a tranquil soul. Rather they were the peepholes of a spirit in torment. The irises were a lovely shade of blue, it is true, but the optics themselves were things of horror. Rolling grotesquely to right and left, they peered futilely in opposite directions, lending to her sweet, pale face the half ludicrous, wholly hideous expression of a bloating frog.

'Good heavens!' I exclaimed, turning from the deformed girl with a feeling of disgust akin to nausea. 'What a terrible affliction!'

De Grandin made no reply, but bent over the girl's still form, gazing intently at her malformed eyes. 'It is not natural,' he announced. 'The muscles have been tampered with, and tampered with by someone who is a master hand at surgery. Will you get me your syringe and some strychnine, Friend Trowbridge? This poor one is still unconscious.'

I hastened to our bedroom and returned with the hypodermic and stimulant, then stood beside him, watching eagerly, as he administered a strong injection.

The girl's narrow chest fluttered as the powerful drug took effect, and the pale lids dropped for a second over her repulsive eyes. Then, with a sob which was half moan, she attempted to raise herself on her elbow, fell back again, and, with apparent effort, gasped, 'The mirror, let me have the mirror! Oh, tell me it isn't true; tell me it was a trick of some sort. Oh, the horrible thing I saw in the glass couldn't have been I. Was it?'

'*Tiens, ma petite,*' de Grandin replied; 'but you speak in riddles. What is it you would know?'

'He – he,' the girl faltered weakly, forcing her trembling lips to frame the words – 'that horrible old man showed me a mirror a little while ago and said the face in it was mine. Oh, it was horrible, horrible!'

'Eh? What is this?' de Grandin demanded on a rising note. ' 'He'? 'Horrible old man'? Are you not his daughter? Is he not your father?'

'No,' the girl gasped, so low her denial was scarcely audible. 'I was driving home from Mackettsdale last – oh, I forget when it was, but it was at night – and my tyres punctured. I – I think there must have been glass on the road, for the shoes were cut to ribbons. I saw the light in this house and came to ask for help. An old man – oh, I thought he was so nice and kind! – let me in and said he was all alone here and about to eat dinner, and asked me to join him. I ate some – some – oh, I don't remember what it was – and the next thing I knew he was standing by my bed, holding a mirror up to me and telling me it was my face I saw in the glass. Oh, please, *please* tell me it was some terrible trick he played on me. I'm not truly hideous, am I?'

'*Morbleu!*' de Grandin muttered softly, tugging at the ends of his moustache. 'What is all this?'

To the girl he said: 'But of course not. You are like a flower, mademoiselle. A little flower that dances in the wind. You – '

'And my eyes, they aren't – they aren't' – she interrupted with piteous eagerness – 'please tell me they aren't – '

'*Mais non, ma chère*' he assured her. 'Your eyes are like the *pervenche* that mirrors the sky in springtime. They are – '

'Let – let me see the mirror, please,' she interrupted in an anxious whisper. 'I'd like to see for myself, if you – oh, I feel all weak inside – ' She lapsed back against the pillow, her lids mercifully veiling the hideously distorted eyes and restoring her face to tranquil beauty.

'*Cordieu!*' de Grandin breathed. 'The chloral reasserted itself none too soon for Jules de Grandin's comfort, Friend Trowbridge. Sooner would I have gone to the rack than have shown that pitiful child her face in a mirror.'

'But what's it all mean?' I asked. 'She says she came here, and –'

'And the rest remains for us to find out, I think,' he replied evenly. 'Come, we lose time, and to lose time is to be caught, my friend.'

De Grandin led the way down the hall, peering eagerly into each door we passed in search of the owner's chamber, but before his quest was satisfied he stopped abruptly at the head of the stairs. 'Observe, Friend Trowbridge,' he ordered, pointing a carefully manicured forefinger to a pair of buttons, one white, one black, set in the wall. 'Unless I am more mistaken than I think I am, we have here the key to the situation – or at least to the front door.'

He pushed vigorously at the white button, then ran to the curve of the stairs to note the result.

Sure enough, the heavy door swung open on its hinges of cast bronze, letting gusts of rain drive into the lower hall.

'*Pardieu,*' he ejaculated, 'we have here the open sesame; let us see if we possess the closing secret as well! Press the black button, Trowbridge, my friend, while I watch.'

I did his bidding, and a delighted exclamation told me the door had closed.

'Now what?' I asked, joining him on the staircase.

'U'm' – he pulled first one end, then the other, of his diminutive moustache meditatively – 'the house possesses its attractions, Friend Trowbridge, but I believe it would be well if we went out to observe what our friend, *le vieillard horrible,* does. I like not to have one who shows young girls their disfigured faces in mirrors near our conveyance.'

Slipping into our raincoats, we opened the door, taking care to place a wad of paper on the sill to prevent its closing tightly enough to latch, and scurried out into the storm.

As we left the shelter of the porch a shaft of indistinct light shone through the rain, as my car was swung from the highway and headed towards a depression to the left of the house.

'*Parbleu*, he is a thief, this one!' de Grandin exclaimed excitedly. '*Hola, monsieur!*' He ran forward swinging his arms like a pair of semaphores. 'What sort of business is it you make with our auto?'

The wailing of the storm tore the words from his lips and hurled them away, but the little Frenchman was not to be thwarted. '*Pardieu*,' he gasped, bending his head against the wind-driven rain, 'I will stop the scoundrel if – *nom d'un coq*, he has done it!'

Even as he spoke the old man flung open the car's forward door and leaped, allowing the machine to go crashing down a steep embankment into a lake of slimy swamp-mud.

For a moment the vandal stood contemplating his work, then burst into a peal of wild laughter more malignant than any profanity.

'*Parbleu*, robber! *Apache!* You shall laugh from the other side of your mouth!' de Grandin promised, as he made for the old man.

But the other seemed oblivious of our presence. Still chuckling at his work, he turned towards the house, stopped short as a sudden heavy gust of wind shook the trees along the roadway, then started forward with a yell of terror as a great branch, torn bodily from a towering oak-tree, came crashing towards the earth.

He might as well have attempted to dodge a meteorite. Like an arrow from the bow of divine justice the great timber hurtled down, pinning his frail body to the ground like a worm beneath a labourer's brogan.

'Trowbridge, my friend,' de Grandin announced matter-of-factly, 'observe the evil effects of stealing motor cars.'

We lifted the heavy bough from the prostrate man and turned him over on his back. De Grandin on one side, I on the other, we made a hasty examination, arriving at the same finding simultaneously. His spinal column was snapped like a pipe stem.

'You have some last statement to make, monsieur?' de Grandin asked curtly. 'If so, you had best be about it, your time is short.'

'Y – yes,' the stricken man replied weakly. 'I – I meant to kill you, for you might have hit upon my secret. As it is, you may publish it to the world, that all may know what it meant to offend a Marston. In my room you will find the documents. My – my pets – are – in – the – cellar. She – was – to – have – been – one – of – them.' The pauses between his words became longer and longer, his voice grew weaker with each laboured syllable. As he whispered the last sentence painfully there was a gurgling sound, and a tiny stream of blood welled up at the corner of his mouth. His narrow chest rose and fell once with a convulsive movement, then his jaw dropped limply. He was dead.

'Oh-ho,' de Grandin remarked, 'it is a haemorrhage which finished him. A broken rib piercing his lung. U'm? I should have guessed it. Come, my friend, let us carry him to the house, then see what it was he meant by that talk of documents and pets. A pest upon the fellow for dying with his riddle half explained! Did he not know that Jules de Grandin cannot resist the challenge of a riddle? *Parbleu*, we will solve this mystery, *Monsieur le Mort*, if we have to hold an autopsy to do so!'

'Oh, for heaven's sake, hush, de Grandin!' I besought, shocked at his heartlessness. 'The man is dead.'

'Ah, bah!' he returned scornfully. 'Dead or not, did he not steal your motor car?'

We laid our gruesome burden on the hall couch and mounted the stairs to the second floor. With de Grandin in the lead we found the dead man's room and began a systematic search for the papers he had mentioned, almost with his last breath. After some time my companion unearthed a thick, leather-bound portfolio from the lower drawer of a beautiful old mahogany highboy, and spread its wide leaves open on the white-counterpaned bed.

'Ah' – he drew forth several papers and held them to the light – 'we begin to make the progress, Friend Trowbridge. What is this?'

He held out a newspaper-clipping cracked from long folding and yellowed with age. It read:

### Actress Jilts Surgeon's Crippled Son on Eve of Wedding

Declaring she could not stand the sight of his deformity, and that she had engaged herself to him only in a moment of thoughtless pity, Dora Lee, well-known variety actress, last night repudiated her promise to marry John Biersfield Marston, Jr., hopelessly crippled son of Dr John Biersfield Marston, the well-known surgeon and expert osteologist. Neither the abandoned bridegroom nor his father could be seen by reporters from the *Planet* last night.

'Very good,' de Grandin nodded, 'we need go no farther with that account. A young woman, it would seem, once broke her promise to marry a cripple, and, judging from this paper's date, that was in 1896. Here is another; what do you make of it?'

The clipping he handed me read as follows:

### Surgeon's Son a Suicide

Still sitting in the wheel chair, from which he has not moved during his waking hours since he was hopelessly crippled while playing polo in England ten years ago, John Biers-field Marston, son of the famous surgeon of the same name, was found in his bedroom this morning by his valet. A rubber hose was connected with a gas jet, the other end being held in the young man's mouth.

Young Marston was jilted by Dora Lee, well-known vaudeville actress, on the day before the date set for their wedding, one month ago. He is reported to have been extremely low-spirited since his desertion by his fiancée.

Dr Marston, the bereaved father, when seen by reporters from the *Planet* this morning, declared the actress was responsible for his son's death, and announced his intention of holding her accountable. When asked if legal proceedings were contemplated, he declined further information.

'So?' de Grandin nodded shortly. 'Now this one, if you please.'
The third clipping was brief to the point of curtness:

WELL-KNOWN SURGEON RETIRES

Dr John Biersfield Marston, widely known throughout this section of the country as an expert in operations concerning the bones, has announced his intention of retiring from practice. His house has been sold, and he will move from the city.

'The record is clear so far,' de Grandin asserted, studying the first clipping with raised eyebrows, 'but – *morbleu*, my friend, look – look at this picture. This Dora Lee, of whom does she remind you? Eh?'

I took the clipping again and looked intently at the illustration of the article announcing young Marston's broken engagement. The woman in the picture was young and inclined to be overdressed in the voluminous, fluffy mode of the days before the Spanish-American War.

'U'm, no one whom I know – ' I began, but halted abruptly as a sudden likeness struck me. Despite the towering pompadour arrangement of her blonde hair, and the unbecoming straw sailor hat above the coiffure, the woman in the picture bore a certain resemblance to the disfigured girl we had seen a half hour before.

The Frenchman saw recognition dawn in my face, and nodded agreement. 'But of course,' he said. 'Now, the question is, is this young girl whose eyes are so out of alignment a relative of this Dora Lee, or is the resemblance a coincidence, and, if so, what lies behind it? *Hein?*'

'I don't know,' I admitted, 'but there must be some connection – '

'Connection? Of course there is a connection,' de Grandin affirmed, rummaging deeper in the portfolio. 'A-a-ah! What is this? *Nom d'un nom*, Friend Trowbridge, I think I smell the daylight! Look!'

He held a full-page story from one of the sensational New York dailies before him, his eyes glued to the flowing type and crude, coarse-screen half-tones of half a dozen young women which composed the article.

'WHAT HAS BECOME OF THE MISSING GIRLS?'

I read in bold-faced type across the top of the page.

'Are sinister, unseen hands reaching out from the darkness to seize our girls from palace and hovel, shop, stage, and office?' the article asked rhetorically. 'Where are Ellen Munro and Dorothy Sawyer and Phyllis Bouchet and three other lovely light-haired girls who have walked into oblivion during the past year?'

I read to the end the sensational account of the girls' disappearances. The cases seemed fairly similar; each of the vanished young women had failed to return to her home and had never been accounted for in any manner, and in no instance, according to the newspaper, had there been any assignable reason for voluntary departure.

'*Parbleu*, but he was stupid, even for a journalist!' de Grandin asserted as I completed my inspection of the story. 'Why, I wager even my good Friend Trowbridge has already noticed one important fact which this writer has treated as though it were as commonplace as the nose on his face.'

'Sorry to disappoint you, old chap,' I answered, 'but it looks to me as though the reporter had covered the case from every possible angle.'

'Ah? So?' he replied sarcastically. '*Morbleu*, we shall have to consult the oculist in your behalf when we return home, my friend. Look, look, I beseech you, upon the pictures of these so totally absent and unaccounted-for young women, *cher ami*, and tell me if you do not observe a certain likeness among them; not only a resemblance to each other, but to that Mademoiselle Lee who jilted the son of Dr Marston? Can you see it, now I have pointed it out?'

'No – wh – why, yes – yes, of course!' I responded, running my eye over the pictures accompanying the story. 'By the Lord Harry, de Grandin, you're right; you might almost say there is a family resemblance between these girls! You've put your finger on it, I do believe.'

'*Hélas*, no!' he answered with a shrug. 'I have put my finger on nothing as yet, my friend. I reach, I grope, I feel about me like a blind man tormented by a crowd of naughty little boys, but nothing do the poor fingers of my mind encounter. Pah! Jules de Grandin, you are one great fool! Think, think, stupid one!'

He sat on the edge of the bed, cupping his face in his hands and leaning forward till his elbows rested on his knees.

Suddenly he sprang erect, one of his elfish smiles passing across his small, regular features. '*Nom d'un chat rouge*, my friend, I have it — I have it!' he announced. 'The pets — the pets that old stealer of motor cars spoke of! They are in the basement! *Pardieu*, we will see those pets, *cher* Trowbridge; with our four collective eyes we will see them. Did not that so execrable stealer declare she was to have been one of them? Now, in the name of Satan and brimstone, whom could he have meant by "she" if not that unfortunate child with eyes like *la grenouille*? Eh?'

'Why — ' I began, but he waved me forward.

'Come, come; let us go,' he urged. 'I am impatient, I am restless, I am not to be restrained. We shall investigate and see for ourselves what sort of pets are kept by one who shows young girls their deformed faces in mirrors and — *parbleu!* — steals motor cars from my friends.'

Hurrying down the main staircase, we hunted about for the cellar entrance, finally located the door, and, holding above our heads a pair of candles from the hall, began descending a flight of rickety steps into a pitch-black basement, rock walled and, judging by its damp, mouldy odour, unfloored save by the bare, moist earth beneath the house.

'*Parbleu*, the dungeons of the chateau at Carcassonne are more cheerful than this,' de Grandin commented as he paused at the stairs' foot, holding his candle aloft to make a better inspection of the dismal place.

I suppressed a shudder of mingled chill and apprehension as I stared at the blank stone walls, unpierced by windows or other openings of any sort, and made ready to retrace my steps. 'Nothing here,' I announced. 'You can see that with half an eye. The place is as empty as – '

'Perhaps, Friend Trowbridge,' he agreed, 'but Jules de Grandin does not look with half an eye. He uses both eyes, and uses them more than once if his first glance does not prove sufficient. Behold that bit of wood on the earth yonder. What do you make of it?'

'U'm – a piece of flooring, maybe,' I hazarded.

'Maybe yes, maybe no,' he answered. 'Let us see.'

Crossing the cellar, he bent above the planks, then turned to me with a satisfied smile. 'Flooring does not ordinarily have ring bolts in it, my friend,' he remarked, bending to seize the iron ring which was made fast to the boards by a stout staple.

'Ha!' As he heaved upwards the planks came away from the black earth, disclosing a board-lined well about three feet square and of uncertain depth. An almost vertical ladder of two-by-four timbers led downward from the trapdoor to the well's impenetrable blackness.

'*Allons*, we descend,' he commented, turning about and setting his foot on the topmost rung of the ladder.

'Don't be a fool,' I advised. 'You don't know what's down there.'

'True' – his head was level with the floor as he answered – 'but I shall know, with luck, in a few moments. Do you come?'

I sighed with vexation as I prepared to follow him.

At the ladder's foot he paused, raising his candle and looking about inquiringly. Directly before us was a passageway through the earth, ceiled with heavy planks and shored up with timbers like the lateral workings of a primitive mine.

'Ah, the plot shows complications,' he murmured, stepping briskly into the dark tunnel. 'Do you come, Friend Trowbridge?'

I followed, wondering what manner of thing might be at the end of the black, musty passage, but nothing but fungus-grown timbers and walls of moist, black earth met my questing gaze.

De Grandin preceded me by some paces, and I suppose we had gone fifteen feet through the passage when a gasp of mingled surprise and horror from my companion brought me beside him in two long strides. Fastened with nails to the timbers at each side of the tunnel were a number of white, glistening objects – objects which, because of their very familiarity, denied their identity to my wondering eyes. There was no mistaking the things; even a layman could not have failed to recognize them for what they were. I, as a physician, knew them even better. To the right of the passage hung fourteen perfectly articulated skeletons of human legs, complete from foot to ilium, gleaming white and ghostly in the flickering light of the candles.

'Good heavens!' I exclaimed.

'*Sang du diable!*' Jules de Grandin commented. 'Behold what is there, my friend.' He pointed to the opposite wall. Fourteen bony arms, complete from hand to shoulder joint, hung pendulously from the tunnel's upright timbers.

'*Pardieu,*' de Grandin muttered, 'I have known men who collected stuffed birds and dried insects; I have known those who stored away Egyptian mummies – even the skulls of men long dead – but never before have I seen a collection of arms and legs! *Parbleu*, he was *caduo* – mad as a hatter, this one, or I am much mistaken!'

'So these were his pets,' I answered. 'Yes, the man was undoubtedly mad to keep such a collection, and in a place like this. Poor fellow – '

'*Nom d'un canon!*' de Grandin broke in; 'what was that?'

From the darkness before us there came a queer, inarticulate sound such as a man might make attempting to speak with a mouth half filled with food, and, as though the noise had wakened an echo slumbering in the cavern, the sound was repeated, multiplied again and again till it resembled the babbling of half a dozen overgrown infants – or an equal number of full-grown imbeciles.

'Onward!' Responding to the challenge of the unknown like a warrior obeying the trumpet's call to charge, de Grandin dashed towards the strange noise, swung about, flashing his candle this side and that, then:

'*Nom de Dieu de nom de Dieu!*' he almost shrieked. 'Look, Friend Trowbridge – look and say that you see what I see, or have I, too, gone mad?'

Lined up against the wall was a series of seven small wooden boxes, each with a door composed of upright slats before it, similar in construction to the coops in which country-folk pen brooding hens – and no larger. In each of the hutches huddled an object the like of which I had never before seen, even in the terrors of nightmare.

The things had the torsos of human beings, though hideously shrunken from starvation and incrusted with scales of filth, but there all resemblance to mankind ceased. From shoulders and waist there twisted flaccid tentacles of unsupported flesh, the upper ones terminating in flat, paddle-like flippers which had some remote resemblance to hands, the lower ones ending in almost shapeless stubs which resembled feet only in that each had a fringe of five shrivelled, unsupported protuberances of withered flesh.

On scrawny necks were balanced caricatures of faces, flat, noseless, chinless countenances with horrible crossed or divergent eyes, mouths widened almost beyond resemblance to buccal orifices, and – horror of horrors! – elongated, *split* tongues protruding several inches from the lips and wagging impotently in vain efforts to form words.

'Satan, thou art outdone!' de Grandin cried, as he held his candle before a scrap of paper decorating one of the cages after the manner of a sign before an animal's den at the Zoo. 'Observe!' he ordered, pointing a shaking finger at the notice.

I looked, then recoiled, sick with horror. The paper bore the picture and name of Ellen Munro, one of the girls mentioned as missing in the newspaper article we had found in the dead man's bedroom.

Beneath the photograph was scribbled in an irregular hand: *Paid 12-5-97.*

Sick at heart, we walked down the line of pens. Each was labelled with the picture of a young and pretty girl with the notation, 'Paid', followed by a date. Every girl named as missing in the newspaper was represented in the cages.

Last of all, in a coop somewhat smaller than the rest, we found a body more terribly mutilated than any. This was marked with the photograph and name of Dora Lee. Beneath her name was the date of her 'payment', written in bold red figures.

'*Parbleu*, what are we to do, my friend?' de Grandin asked in an hysterical whisper. 'We cannot return these poor ones to the world; that would be the worst form of cruelty; yet – yet I shrink from the act of mercy I know they would ask me to perform if they could speak.'

'Let's go up,' I begged. 'We must think this thing over, de Grandin, and if I stay here any longer I shall faint.'

'*Bien*,' he agreed, and turned to follow me from the cavern of horrors.

'It is to consider,' he began as we reached the upper hall once more. 'If we give those so pitiful ones the stroke of mercy we are murderers before the law, yet what service could we render them by bringing them once more into the world? Our choice is a hard one, my friend.'

I nodded.

'*Morbleu*, but he was clever, that one,' the Frenchman continued, half to me, half to himself. 'What a surgeon! Fourteen instances of Wyeth's amputation of the hip and as many more of the shoulder – and every patient lived, lived to suffer the tortures of that hell-hole down there! But it is marvellous! None but a madman could have done it.

'Bethink you, Friend Trowbridge. Think how the mighty man of medicine brooded over the suicide of his crippled son, meditating hatred and vengeance for the heartless woman who had jilted him. Then – snap, went his great mentality, and from hating one woman he fell to hating all, to plotting vengeance against the many for the sin of the one. And, *cordieu*, what a vengeance! How he must have laid his plans to secure his victims; how he must have worked to prepare that hell-under-the-earth to house those poor, broken bodies which were his handiwork, and how he must have drawn upon the great surgical skill which was his, even in his madness, to transform those once lovely ones into the visions of horror we have just beheld! Horror of horrors! To remove the bones and let the girls still live!'

He rose, pacing impatiently across the hall. 'What to do? What to do?' he demanded, striking his open hands against his forehead.

I followed his nervous steps with my eyes, but my brain was too numbed by the hideous things I had just seen to be able to respond to his question.

I looked hopelessly past him at the angle of the wall by the great fireplace, rubbed my eyes, and looked again. Slowly, but surely, the wall was declining from the perpendicular.

'De Grandin,' I shouted, glad of some new phenomenon to command my thoughts, 'the wall – the wall's leaning!'

'Eh, the wall?' he queried. '*Pardieu*, yes! It is the rain; the foundations are undermined. Quick, quick, my friend! To the cellars, or those unfortunate ones are undone!'

We scrambled down the stairs leading to the basement, but already the earth floor was sopping with water. The well leading to the madman's sub-cellar was more than half full of bubbling, earthy ooze.

'Mary, have pity!' de Grandin exclaimed. 'Like rats in a trap, they did die. God rest their tired souls' – he shrugged his shoulders as he turned to retrace his steps – 'it is better so. Now, Friend Trowbridge, do you hasten aloft and bring down that young girl from the room above. We must run for it if we do not wish to be crushed under the falling timbers of this house of abominations!'

The storm had spent itself, and a red, springtime sun was peeping over the horizon as de Grandin and I trudged up my front steps with the mutilated girl stumbling wearily between us.

'Put her to bed, my excellent one,' de Grandin ordered Nora, my housekeeper, who came to meet us enveloped in righteous indignation and an outsize flannel nightgown. '*Parbleu*, she has had many troubles!'

In the study, a glass of steaming whisky and hot water in one hand, a vile-smelling French cigarette in the other, he faced me across the desk. 'How was it you knew not that house, my friend?' he demanded.

I grinned sheepishly. 'I took the wrong turning at the detour,' I explained, 'and got on the Yerbyshire Road. It's just recently been hard-surfaced, and I haven't used it for years because it was always impassable. Thinking we were on the Andover Pike all the while, I never connected the place with the old Olmsted Mansion I'd seen hundreds of times from the road.'

'Ah yes,' he agreed, nodding thoughtfully, 'a little turn from the right way, and – pouf – what a distance we have to retrace!'

'Now, about the girl upstairs…' I began; but he waved the question aside.

'The mad one had but begun his devil's work on her,' he replied. 'I, Jules de Grandin, will operate on her eyes and make them as straight as before, nor will I accept one penny for my work. Meantime, we must find her kindred and notify them she is safe and in good hands.

'And now' – he handed me his empty tumbler – 'a little more whisky, if you please, Friend Trowbridge.'

# Flavia Richardson

## *Behind the Yellow Door*

The house was plain – stucco to the height of the first storey and brick for the remaining two. The bricks had recently been pointed; the whole building looked well kept and as if it were inhabited by well-to-do and intelligent people. Only the door was an eyesore. Yellow – not cheerful orange or even a clear lemon or saffron, but a blatant shade that could not be described by any known hue – crude chrome, perhaps, was the closest analogy.

Marcia Miles, standing on the doorstep, felt a little shiver run through her as she waited for the bell to be answered. Never given to 'feelings' or premonitions, she was at a loss to account for the cold goose-flesh sensation that attacked her ankles in spite of the warm July sun.

Then the door was opened, and she stepped into the most ordinary hall: walls papered with lincrusta for three feet from the floor and then distempered cream... staircase turning at the half-landing with a large bowl of carnations on an oak chest in the window... thick brown carpet, blue curtains, making a background for the pink flower-heads... nothing could have been more sane, more conventional. And yet in her innermost heart she felt a desire to turn and run... but why, she could not say. But companion-secretaries who have been out of work for three months, and whose qualifications are far more those of companions than of secretaries, do not run on their first day in new positions.

The maid led her upstairs to the back drawing room, which had been converted into a study. And there Mrs Merrill came to her.

Mrs Merrill was tall, slender, and good looking. Her clever, capable hands had the strength of a surgeon's. Marcia, secretly surveying her, realized why this woman had made a name as a consultant physician. She had personality... almost hypnotic persuasion. Not a woman it would be easy to withstand.

'My correspondence is not very heavy,' she explained. 'The maid who brought you up attends to my professional appointments. She keeps the book, and you need only consult it in order to prevent my social engagements clashing.'

Marcia heaved a sigh of relief. She had been afraid, even though it had been expressly stipulated that the secretarial duties would be light. She was only too well aware of her own shortcomings from a professional point of view.

'What I really need you for,' the cool, clearly modulated tone went on, 'is as a companion for my daughter. She needs someone to be with from time to time...'

She broke off. Marcia longed to ask the age of the daughter, but she did not like to do so. Time enough when she saw the girl. Covertly surveying Mrs Merrill, Marcia placed her as a well-preserved forty-three. Her daughter might easily be nearly grown-up – in the betwixt and between stage, probably.

The morning passed without anything of note. Marcia took down the answers to a number of letters, answered the telephone twice, and made notes of various engagements.

But all the time she was conscious of a queer undercurrent. Mrs Merrill looked at her every now and then as it were in an appraising way. Marcia fidgeted once under the scrutiny, and was aware that it was instantly withdrawn... but she felt uncomfortable, all the same. The parlourmaid came in with a message... and Marcia sensed that she too was looking at her more intently than was usual, even with old and valued servants. She did not like the maid. There was an opaqueness, a steeliness about the grey eyes that was almost frightening... as though the woman's mind were always turned inwards. She looked like a woman with a mission.

Marcia tried to scold herself for her imagination. It was no business of hers. Her job was to do her work so well that Mrs Merrill would keep her as her employee for a long time to come.

Luncheon was served in a small dining room under the study, but there was no sign of the daughter. Marcia supposed she was out, but a chance remark about the tray for upstairs between Mrs Merrill and the maid made her suspect that the girl was indisposed.

More letters and odds and ends followed during the afternoon, and at last, about five o'clock, Mrs Merrill said:

'If you have finished those cards, we will go upstairs and you can meet my daughter. She will be expecting us now.'

Marcia hurried through the cards. There was a hint of something unusual in Mrs Merrill's voice that made her wonder what was to come next. Was the daughter an invalid? Had she got to amuse a fretful adolescent? She wondered anxiously how her voice would hold out if she were expected to do much reading aloud.

Mrs Merrill put aside her book, took off the tortoise-shell glasses she habitually wore for reading, and rose to her feet.

Marcia followed her docilely, but with a throb of expectation.

They went up another flight of stairs, past two doors, and then up a further flight that curled unexpectedly. Marcia realized that they were going to the attics. At the top of the stairs was a heavy door, shrouded in baize and rubber-sheathed... and sound-proofed effectively if not in the newest manner. The sight of it seemed menacing... Marcia hesitated involuntarily as she followed Mrs Merrill... What lay on the other side?... What could she not hear?

Mrs Merrill went on without a word and pushed the door open. It gave on to a small entrance lobby, dark except for the light that came in through the opened door. From it another door led. As Marcia stepped into the lobby the door behind her swung noiselessly to on its hinges. With a little gasp she realized as they stood in the dark that it had shut. Instinctively she put out a hand and pushed against it. It remained firm.

The sensation of horror deepened. In a second of time she appreciated the fact that she was shut up on the top floor of this strange house with a woman whom she did not know... a woman who was reputed to be a brilliant pathologist, but about whom strange stories were already being whispered.

'Come in and see my daughter.' Mrs Merrill's voice was so ordinary that it almost took Marcia by surprise. She realized that she had been waiting almost rudely in the lobby, and at the same time realized that scarcely ten seconds had gone since the door had swung to at her back. Time had seemed to stand still. She pulled herself together with an effort.

'Of course,' she said, then, summoning her courage, 'Is she – is she an invalid?'

For a moment it seemed as if Mrs Merrill paused. 'Not an invalid,' she said at length, with a harsh note in her voice; 'no, not an invalid. Come in, please.'

She opened the door, and Marcia automatically followed her into the big attic. The room ran the entire length of the house, and was gay with cretonne. The floor was covered with a big straw mat, curtains hung straight in the airless July day, the canary in his cage in the window was too sleepy to sing.

For a moment Marcia glanced round . . . Then it was a child, a nursery. The furniture was all on the small scale. There was a tiny chair, a table, cupboards, and wardrobe. The bed was small and beautifully carved. On it, under the lightest of summer rugs, lay a child, her face exquisitely beautiful in the Greuze style.

'Olivette,' said Mrs Merrill softly. The child stirred, flung one arm up to shield her opening eyes from the sun, and then got down from the bed.

And Marcia found herself clenching her hands till the nails began to pierce the skin of the palms in her effort to keep from crying out. For the lovely child, Olivette, beautifully made to the waist, had no semblance of beauty below. Her thighs, her legs, and ankles were barely a foot long all told. Her feet were little larger than doll's feet, and she tottered on them as she came to her mother. The beauty of the torso was made more terrible by the horror that stretched below.

'My daughter,' said Mrs Merrill, and there was a trace of defiance in her voice as she bent down to caress the child who barely reached her own waist.

Marcia held her horror in check. Leaning down to shake hands, she looked more closely at the face below, and realized that in years Olivette was no child. The features, expression, hair, the very development of the breast, betrayed the fact that she was coming to full maturity. In spite of herself, a shudder ran through her as she felt the touch of the dwarf. Noticing it, Olivette's deep-blue eyes flashed fury – her lips parted in a bitter curve.

Suddenly Marcia felt that she could stand the situation no longer. She felt faint... she turned... Mrs Merrill looked at her in surprise.

'Forgive me... the heat,' gasped Marcia, as she moved to the door.

The high-pitched laughter of Olivette warned her that she was not to escape so easily. Again the foreboding swept over her like a cloud... What would happen? Something terrible was hovering in the room... She clutched the door handle dizzily, turned it... It did not respond. And then she realized that she had been trapped.

Trapped for what purpose she did not know. But that she was in the hands of Mrs Merrill and the dwarf for no good purpose she was firmly convinced. She could have cried at the lack of heed she had paid earlier to the warnings of her sixth sense, yet how could she, the sane and unemotional, be expected to trouble about unknown fears and premonitions?... For a moment she thought she would faint.

Mrs Merrill's voice brought her to herself. It was so cold, so calm, that for the moment Marcia did not take in the full purport of the words. Gradually the sense penetrated to her dulled mind.

'My daughter, Olivette... As you see, she has never had a chance.

An accident shortly before her birth... My lovely child condemned to a life of horror and regret. I had to wait for her to come to maturity. I had to lay my plans. Now they are ready and you came in answer to my advertisement. You will do well. You are approximately the same age as Olivette. You are the size to which she ought to have grown – to which she shall grow...'

Mrs Merrill paused. Marcia drew a deep breath. What did she mean? What was all this preamble? What were they going to do?

She gazed into the hypnotic eyes of the woman facing her and felt her strength waning. She was still conscious of her own individuality, but she was paralysed, as a rabbit before a snake.

She did not hear the door open behind her. Her whole being was concentrated on the woman who stood in front – fighting to retain awareness. So deep was her absorption that the gentle touch of silk on her wrists almost passed unnoticed. When she realized it was too late. The hard-faced parlourmaid, now in a white nurse's overall, had bound her wrists tightly behind her back.

Marcia opened her mouth to scream, but a hand was laid over her mouth and at the same time the prick of a hypodermic needle in her arm started the lapsing of her consciousness.

'She didn't give much trouble,' said the parlourmaid, as they laid the inert form on the bed. 'I didn't think she would give in so easily. And she's just what you wanted, isn't she?'

Mrs Merrill nodded. 'Just what I wanted,' she said, and her hand went out to Olivette. 'Only a little while longer, my darling, and you shall be like other girls.'

'Shall you tell her...?' The maid nodded at Marcia.

Mrs Merrill's eyebrows went up. 'Tell her? Of course,' she responded. 'She is to form part of a stupendous scientific experiment. Of course I shall tell her. Now help me carry her down.'

Marcia came slowly to her senses and could not for the moment realize where she was. She was lying flat on something very hard and even, not painful but definitely uncomfortable. She tried to raise her hand, but found it impossible. Then she realized that not only could she not move her head but that she could scarcely move at all. Her arms were bound tightly to her sides and her ankles were tied together. Over her chest and legs straps were passed that fastened under the table on which she was lying. Her head was held in place by a further band that passed round her neck and again under the table. If she made any effort to sit up, she felt the preliminary symptoms of strangulation.

The room was nearly dark. She must have lost consciousness for some time. The sun had sunk below the houses, and the summer twilight blurred the outlines of the furniture. Marcia tried to call out, but her voice seemed weak and distant.

The sound, however, carried further than she thought. A strong electric light was switched on at once and Mrs Merrill came into Marcia's line of vision. Marcia stared at her, first blankly, then with growing horror. She was wearing a surgeon's overall and in her hand was a case of instruments.

'What... what...' Marcia began feebly.

Mrs Merrill came over to the table and felt the straps. Then she nodded. 'That'll do,' she said, half to herself. Then she turned to Marcia. 'You are going to see one of the most interesting and stupendous operations that has ever been attempted in modern surgery,' she said, and there was a detached, professional note in her voice that was more alarming than any emotion. 'You and my daughter are to change lower parts of your bodies. I have been waiting for a long time to get everything ready. In a few moments I shall begin to operate. You will know nothing about it until afterwards. Then, assuming that the operation is successful, as it must be, you will find Olivette's deformed legs grafted on to your body, while Olivette will be at last able to enjoy her life as a normal human being. She has waited nearly twenty years. You have had twenty years. It is her turn.'

Marcia screamed... just once. Then a gag was slipped into her mouth and she found she could do nothing but gurgle helplessly. Her whole body shook with terror.

'Dorcas,' Mrs Merrill called, and the former parlourmaid came from another part of the room where she had been waiting.

'Bring Olivette in, please.'

Dorcas reappeared, and Marcia, out of the tail of her eye, could see her lay Olivette, already under an anaesthetic, on an operating table similar to the one on which she was strapped. Mrs Merrill busied herself with preparations. Then she stood up and turned to Dorcas.

'If everything is ready in the sterilizer, we'll begin,' she announced. 'Are you ready with the anaesthetic?'

Marcia struggled feebly against her bonds. Helpless, unable to cry out, fully aware that every effort was useless, she still made a frantic appeal with her eyes. But no attention was paid. She realized that she was dealing with a mad woman, a woman with so deep an obsession about her daughter that nothing else mattered – and that Dorcas had no other idea than to serve her mistress.

With a refinement of cruelty, Mrs Merrill continued her preparations within Marcia's line of vision. Try as she would, Marcia could not keep her eyes closed. She must know... must see how near she was coming to the fatal moment. Death or deformity?... She did not know if the experiment were possible... but, if it were a success, would not death be more kind?

And all the time she was making ready Mrs Merrill talked. 'Think what a fortunate woman you are to be the subject of such an amazing experiment,' she said, laying out one deadly instrument after another. 'And we shan't ask you to endure it without ether. I don't want you to die – dead limbs would be no good to Olivette. After all, you will be able to walk – just as she can; it is not as if we were proposing to stop with the grafting on of your limbs to her body... I will finish the operation properly...'

Involuntarily, Marcia tried to scream, but only the merest sound came from her white lips. She strained again at the straps, and fell back, choking.

'Don't be silly,' admonished Mrs Merrill. 'You will only hurt yourself, and you won't be able to stand the strain of the operation.'

'Everything is ready, madam,' said Dorcas, coming again into the line of vision.

Marcia thought wildly: 'They'll surely take the gag out before they give me the ether... I can give one scream. This is a big street. Someone must be passing.' She lay still and tried to relax, saving her strength. Spots danced before her eyes; her lips, strained by the gag, were dry and colourless.

'Now!' Mrs Merrill approached, a surgeon's mask over her face. Only the bright eyes gleamed, brighter against the white gauze.

Suddenly the cone was dropped over Marcia's nostrils, and with the realization of despair she knew that they were not going to give her even that one poor little chance.

Hours later, Mrs Merrill lifted her face, a face so haggard that the lines and pallor could be seen even under the mask.

'Both gone?' she whispered.

Dorcas, standing between the tables, nodded. 'Both madam.'

'Failed!'

'You did your best, madam,' comforted the maid. 'Miss Olivette didn't suffer, and it was better she should die than live like – like she was. As for the other one – '

Mrs Merrill scarcely glanced at the dismembered body on the table under her hand.

'Secretaries are plentiful,' was all she said.

# Muriel Spark

## *The Portobello Road*

One day in my young youth at high summer, lolling with my lovely companions upon a haystack, I found a needle. Already and privately for some years I had been guessing that I was set apart from the common run, but this of the needle attested the fact to my whole public, George, Kathleen, and Skinny. I sucked my thumb, for when I had thrust my idle hand deep into the hay, the thumb was where the needle had stuck.

When everyone had recovered George said, 'She put in her thumb and pulled out a plum.' Then away we were into our merciless hacking-hecking laughter again.

The needle had gone fairly deep into the thumb cushion, and a small red river flowed and spread from the tiny puncture. So that nothing of our joy should lag, George put in quickly:

'Mind your bloody thumb on my shirt.'

Then hac-hec-hoo, we shrieked into the hot Borderland afternoon. Really I should not care to be so young of heart again. That is my thought every time I turn over my old papers and come across the photograph. Skinny, Kathleen, and myself are in the photo atop the haystack. Skinny had just finished analysing the inwards of my find.

'It couldn't have been done by brains. You haven't much brains, but you're a lucky wee thing.'

Everyone agreed that the needle betokened extraordinary luck. As it was becoming a serious conversation, George said:

'I'll take a photo.'

I wrapped my hanky round my thumb and got myself organized. George pointed up from his camera and shouted:

'Look, there's a mouse!'

Kathleen screamed and I screamed, although I think we knew there was no mouse. But this gave us an extra session of squalling hee-hoos. Finally, we three composed ourselves for George's picture. We look lovely, and it was a great day at the time, but I would not care for it all over again. From that day I was known as Needle.

One Saturday in recent years I was mooching down the Portobello Road from the Ladbroke Grove end, threading among the crowds of marketers on the narrow pavement, when I saw a woman. She had a haggard, careworn, wealthy look, thin but for the breasts forced-up high like a pigeon's. I had not seen her for nearly five years. How changed she was! But I recognized Kathleen my friend; her features had already begun to sink and protrude in the way that mouths and noses do in people destined always to be old for their years. When I had last seen her, nearly five years ago, Kathleen, barely thirty, had said:

'I've lost all my looks; it's in the family. All the woman are handsome as girls, but we go off early, we go brown and nosey.'

I stood silently among the people, watching. As you will see, I wasn't in a position to speak to Kathleen. I saw her shoving in her avid manner from stall to stall. She was always fond of antique jewellery and of bargains. I wondered that I had not seen her before in the Portobello Road on my Saturday morning ambles. Her long stiff-crooked fingers pounced to select a jade ring from amongst the jumble of brooches and pendants, onyx, moonstone, and gold, set out on the stall.

'What d'you think of this?' she said.

I saw then who was with her. I had been half conscious of the huge man following several paces behind her, and now I noticed him.

'It looks all right,' he said. 'How much is it?'

'How much is it?' Kathleen asked the vendor.

I took a good look at this man accompanying Kathleen. It was her husband. The beard was unfamiliar, but I recognized beneath it his enormous mouth, the bright, sensuous lips, the large brown eyes for ever brimming with pathos.

It was not for me to speak to Kathleen, but I had a sudden inspiration which caused me to say quietly:

'Hallo, George.'

The giant of a man turned round to face the direction of my voice. There were so many people – but at length he saw me.

'Hallo, George,' I said again.

Kathleen had started to haggle with the stall owner, in her old way, over the price of the jade ring. George continued to stare at me, his big mouth slightly parted so that I could see a wide slit of red lips and white teeth between the fair grassy growths of beard and moustache.

'My God!' he said.

'What's the matter?' said Kathleen.

'Hallo, George!' I said again, quite loud this time and cheerfully.

'Look!' said George. 'Look who's there, over beside the fruit stall.'

Kathleen looked but didn't see.

'Who is it?' she said impatiently.

'It's Needle,' he said. 'She said "Hallo George".'

'*Needle*,' said Kathleen. 'Who do you mean? You don't mean our old friend *Needle* who – '

'Yes. There she is. My God!'

He looked very ill, although when I had said 'Hallo George', I had spoken friendly enough.

'I don't see anyone faintly resembling poor Needle,' said Kathleen, looking at him. She was worried.

George pointed straight at me. 'Look *there*. I tell you that is Needle.'

'You're ill, George. Heavens, you must be seeing things. Come on home. Needle isn't there. You know as well as I do, Needle is dead.'

I must explain that I departed this life nearly five years ago. But I did not altogether depart this world. There were those odd things still to be done which one's executors can never do properly. Papers to be looked over, even after the executors have torn them up. Lots of business except of course on Sundays and Holidays of Obligation, plenty to take an interest in for the time being. I take my recreation on Saturday mornings. If it is a wet Saturday, I wander up and down the substantial lanes of Woolworths as I did when I was young and visible. There is a pleasurable spread of objects on the counters which I now perceive and exploit with a certain detachment, since it suits with my condition of life. Creams, toothpastes, combs and hankies, cotton gloves, flimsy flowering scarves, writing paper and crayons, ice-cream cones and orangeade, screwdrivers, boxes of tacks, tins of paint, of glue, marmalade; I always liked them, but far more now that I have no need of any. When Saturdays are fine I go instead to the Portobello Road, where formerly I would jaunt with Kathleen in our grown-up days. The barrow loads do not change much, of apples and rayon vests in common blues and low-taste mauve, of silver plate, trays, and teapots long since changed hands from the bygone citizens to dealers, from shops to the new flats and breakable homes, and then over to the barrow stalls and the dealers again: Georgian spoons, rings, earrings of turquoise and opal set in the butterfly pattern or true-lovers' knot, patch boxes with miniature paintings of ladies on ivory, snuff boxes of silver with Scotch pebbles inset.

Sometimes as occasion arises on a Saturday morning, my friend Kathleen who is a Catholic has a Mass said for my soul, and then I am in attendance as it were at the church. But most Saturdays I take my delight among the solemn crowds with their aimless purposes, their eternal life not far away, who push past the counters and stalls, who handle, buy, steal, touch, desire and ogle the merchandise. I hear the tinkling tills, I hear the jangle of loose change and tongues and children wanting to hold and have.

That is how I came to be in the Portobello Road that Saturday morning when I saw George and Kathleen. I would not have spoken had I not been inspired to it. Indeed, it is one of the things I can't do now – to speak out, unless inspired. And most extraordinary, on that morning as I spoke a degree of visibility set in. I suppose from poor George's point of view it was like seeing a ghost when he saw me standing by the fruit barrow repeating in so friendly a manner, 'Hallo, George!'

We were bound for the south. When our education, what we could get of it from the north, was thought to be finished, one by one we were sent or sent for to London. John Skinner, whom we called Skinny, went to study more archaeology; George to join his uncle's tobacco firm; Kathleen to stay with her rich connections and to potter intermittently in the Mayfair hat shop which one of them owned. A little later I also went to London to see life, for it was my ambition to write about life, which first I had to see.

'We four must stick together,' George said very often in that yearning way of his. He was always desperately afraid of neglect. We four looked likely to shift off in different directions and George did not trust the other three of us not to forget all about him. More and more as the time came for him to depart for his uncle's tobacco farm in Africa he said:

'We four must keep in touch.'

And before he left he told each of us anxiously:

'I'll write regularly, once a month. We must keep together for the sake of the old times.' He had three prints taken from the negative of that photo on the haystack, wrote on the back of them, 'George took this the day that Needle found the needle', and gave us a copy each. I think we all wished he could become a bit more callous.

During my lifetime I was a drifter, nothing organized. It was difficult for my friends to follow the logic of my life. By the normal reckonings I should have come to starvation and ruin, which I never did. Of course I did not live to write about life as I wanted to do.

Possibly that is why I am inspired to do so now in these peculiar circumstances.

I taught in a private school in Kensington for almost three months, very small children. I didn't know what to do with them, but I was kept fairly busy escorting incontinent little boys to the lavatory and telling the little girls to use their handkerchiefs. After that I lived a winter holiday in London on my small capital, and when that had run out I found a diamond bracelet in a cinema for which I received a reward of fifty pounds. When it was used up, I got a job with a publicity man, writing speeches for absorbed industrialists, in which the dictionary of quotations came in very useful. So it went on. I got engaged to Skinny, but shortly after that I was left a small legacy, enough to keep me for six months. This somehow decided me that I didn't love Skinny, so I gave him back the ring.

But it was through Skinny that I went to Africa. He was engaged with a party of researchers to investigate King Solomon's mines, that series of ancient workings ranging from the ancient port of Ophir, now called Beira, across Portuguese East Africa and Southern Rhodesia to the mighty jungle-city of Zimbabwe, whose temple walls still stand by the approach to an ancient and sacred mountain, where the rubble of that civilization scatters itself over the surrounding Rhodesian waste. I accompanied the party as a sort of secretary. Skinny vouched for me, he paid my fare, he sympathized by his action with my inconsequential life although when he spoke of it he disapproved. A life like mine annoys most people; they go to their jobs every day, attend to things, give orders, pummel typewriters, and get two or three weeks off every year, and it vexes them to see someone else not bothering to do these things and yet getting away with it, not starving, being lucky as they call it. Skinny, when I had broken off our engagement, lectured me about this, but still he took me to Africa knowing I should probably leave his unit within a few months.

We were there a few weeks before we began inquiring for

George, who was farming about four hundred miles away to the north. We had not told him of our plans.

'If we tell George to expect us in his part of the world, he'll come rushing to pester us the first week. After all, we're going on business,' Skinny had said.

Before we left, Kathleen told us, 'Give George my love, and tell him not to send frantic cables every time I don't answer his letters right away. Tell him I'm busy in the hat shop and being presented. You would think he hadn't another friend in the world the way he carries on.'

We had settled first at Fort Victoria, our nearest place of access to the Zimbabwe ruins. There we made inquiries about George. It was clear he hadn't many friends. The older settlers were the most tolerant about the half-caste woman he was living with, as we learned, but they were furious about his methods of raising tobacco, which we learned were most unprofessional and in some mysterious way disloyal to the whites. We could never discover how it was that George's style of tobacco farming gave the blacks opinions about themselves, but that's what the older settlers claimed. The newer immigrants thought he was unsociable, and of course his living with that nig made visiting impossible.

I must say I was myself a bit offput by this news about the brown woman. I was brought up in a university town where there were Indian, African, and Asiatic students abounding in a variety of tints and hues. I was brought up to avoid them for reasons connected with local reputation and God's ordinances. You cannot easily go against what you were brought up to do unless you are a rebel by nature.

Anyhow, we visited George eventually, taking advantage of the offer of transport from some people bound north in search of game. He had heard of our arrival in Rhodesia, and though he was glad, almost relieved, to see us, he pursued a policy of sullenness for the first hour.

'We wanted to give you a surprise, George.'

'How were we to know that you'd get to hear of our arrival, George? News here must travel faster than light, George.'

'We did hope to give you a surprise, George.'

We flattered and 'Georged' him until at last he said, 'Well, I must say it's good to see you. All we need now is Kathleen. We four simply must stick together. You find when you're in a place like this, there's nothing like old friends.'

He showed us his drying sheds. He showed us a paddock where he was experimenting with a horse and a zebra mare, attempting to mate them. They were frolicking happily, but not together. They passed each other in their private play time and again, but without acknowledgment and without resentment.

'It's been done before,' George said. 'It makes a fine, strong beast, more intelligent than a mule and sturdier than a horse. But I'm not having any success with this pair; they won't look at each other.'

After a while he said, 'Come in for a drink and meet Matilda.'

She was dark brown, with a subservient hollow chest and round shoulders, a gawky woman, very snappy with the houseboys. We said pleasant things as we drank on the stoep before dinner, but we found George difficult. For some reason he began to rail me for breaking off my engagement to Skinny, saying what a dirty trick it was after all those good times in the old days. I diverted attention to Matilda. I supposed, I said, she knew this part of the country well?

'No,' said she, 'I been a-shellitered my life. I not put out to working. Me nothing to go from place to place is allowed like dirty girls does.' In her speech she gave every syllable equal stress.

George explained. 'Her father was a white magistrate in Natal. She had a sheltered upbringing, different from the other coloureds, you realize.'

'Man, me no black-eyed Susan,' said Matilda, 'no, no.'

On the whole, George treated her as a servant. She was about four months advanced in pregnancy, but he made her get up and fetch for him many times. Soap: that was one of the things Matilda had to fetch. George made his own bath soap, showed it proudly, gave us the recipe which I did not trouble to remember; I was fond of nice soaps during my lifetime, and George's smelt of brilliantine and looked likely to soil one's skin.

'D'you brahn?' Matilda asked me.

George said, 'She is asking if you go brown in the sun.'

'No, I go freckled.'

'I got sister-in-law go freckles.'

She never spoke another word to Skinny nor to me, and we never saw her again.

Some months later I said to Skinny.

'I'm fed up with being a camp follower.'

He was not surprised that I was leaving his unit, but he hated my way of expressing it. He gave me a Presbyterian look.

'Don't talk like that. Are you going back to England or staying?'

'Staying for a while.'

'Well, don't wander too far off.'

I was able to live on the fee I got for writing a gossip column in a local weekly, which wasn't my idea of writing about life, of course. I made friends, more than I could cope with, after I left Skinny's exclusive little band of archaeologists. I had the attractions of being newly out from England and of wanting to see life. Of the countless young men and go-ahead families who purred me along the Rhodesian roads hundred after hundred miles, I only kept up with one family when I returned to my native land. I think that was because they were the most representative, they stood for all the rest; people in those parts are very typical of each other, as one group of standing stones in that wilderness is like the next.

I met George once more in an hotel in Bulawayo. We drank highballs and spoke of war. Skinny's party were just then deciding whether to remain in the country or return home. They had reached an exciting part of their research, and whenever I got a chance to visit Zimbabwe he would take me for a moonlight walk in the ruined temple, and try to make me see phantom Phoenicians flitting ahead of us or along the walls. I had half a mind to marry Skinny; perhaps, I thought, when his studies were finished. The impending war was in our bones; so I remarked to George as we sat drinking highballs on the hotel stoep in the hard, bright, sunny July winter of that year.

George was inquisitive about my relations with Skinny. He tried to pump me for about half an hour, and when at last I said, 'You are becoming aggressive, George,' he stopped. He became quite pathetic. He said, 'War or no war, I'm clearing out of this.'

'It's the heat does it,' I said.

'I'm clearing out, in any case. I've lost a fortune in tobacco. My uncle is making a fuss. It's the other bloody planters; once you get the wrong side of them you're finished in this wide land.'

'What about Matilda?' I asked.

He said, 'She'll be all right. She's got hundreds of relatives.'

I had already heard about the baby girl. Coal black, by repute, with George's features. And another on the way, they said.

'What about the child?'

He didn't say anything to that. He ordered more highballs, and when they arrived he swizzled his for a long time with a stick. 'Why didn't you ask me to your twenty-first?' he said then.

'I didn't have anything special, no party, George. We had a quiet drink among ourselves, George, just Skinny and the old professors and two of the wives and me, George.'

'You didn't ask me to your twenty-first,' he said. 'Kathleen writes to me regularly.'

This wasn't true. Kathleen sent me letters fairly often in which she said, 'Don't tell George I wrote to you, as he will be expecting word from me and I can't be bothered actually.'

'But you,' said George, 'don't seem to have any sense of old friendships, you and Skinny.'

'Oh, George!' I said.

'Remember the times we had,' George said. 'We used to have times.' His large brown eyes began to water.

'I'll have to be getting along,' I said.

'Please don't go. Don't leave me just yet. I've something to tell you.'

'Something nice?' I laid on an eager smile. All responses to George had to be overdone.

'You don't know how lucky you are,' George said.

'How?' I said. Sometimes I got tired of being called lucky by everybody. There were times when, privately practising my writings about life, I knew the bitter side of my fortune. When I failed again and again to reproduce life in some satisfactory and perfect form, I was the more imprisoned, for all my carefree living, within my craving for this satisfaction. Sometimes, in my impotence and need I secreted a venom which infected all my life for days on end, and which spurted out indiscriminately on Skinny or on anyone who crossed my path.

'You aren't bound by anyone,' George said. 'You come and go as you please. Something always turns up for you. You're free, and you don't know your luck.'

'You're a damn sight more free than I am,' I said sharply. 'You've got your rich uncle.'

'He's losing interest in me,' George said. 'He's had enough.'

'Oh well, you're young yet. What was it you wanted to tell me?'

'A secret,' George said. 'Remember we used to have those secrets!'

'Oh yes, we did.'

'Did you ever tell any of mine?'

'Oh no, George.' In reality, I couldn't remember any particular secret out of the dozens we must have exchanged from our schooldays onwards.

'Well, this is a secret, mind. Promise not to tell.'

'Promise.'

'I'm married.'

'Married, George! Oh, who to?'

'Matilda.'

'How dreadful!' I spoke before I could think, but he agreed with me.

'Yes, it's awful, but what could I do?'

'You might have asked my advice,' I said pompously.

'I'm two years older than you are. I don't ask advice from you, Needle, little beast.'

'Don't ask for sympathy, then.'

'A nice friend you are,' he said, 'I must say, after all these years.'

'Poor George,' I said.

'There are three white men to one white woman in this country,' said George. 'An isolated planter doesn't see a white woman, and if he sees one she doesn't see him. What could I do? I needed the woman.'

I was nearly sick. One, because of my Scottish upbringing. Two, because of my horror of corny phrases like 'I needed the woman', which George repeated twice again.

'And Matilda got tough,' said George, 'after you and Skinny came to visit us. She had some friends at the Mission, and she packed up and went to them.'

'You should have let her go,' I said.

'I went after her,' George said. 'She insisted on being married, so I married her.'

'That's not a proper secret, then,' I said. 'The news of a mixed marriage soon gets about.'

'I took care of that,' George said. 'Crazy as I was, I took her to the Congo and married her there. She promised to keep quiet about it.'

'Well, you can't clear off and leave her now, surely,' I said.

'I'm going to get out of this place. I can't stand the woman, and I can't stand the country. I didn't realize what it would be like. Two years of the country and three months of my wife has been enough.'

'Will you get a divorce?'

'No, Matilda's Catholic. She won't divorce.'

George was fairly getting through the highballs, and I wasn't far behind him. His brown eyes floated shiny and liquid as he told me how he had written to tell his uncle of his plight. 'Except of course, I didn't say we were married, that would have been too much for him. He's a prejudiced, hardened old colonial. I only said I'd had a child by a coloured woman and was expecting another, and he perfectly understood. He came at once by plane a few weeks ago. He's made a settlement on her, providing she keeps her mouth shut about her association with me.'

'Will she do that?'

'Oh yes, or she won't get the money.'

'But as your wife she has a claim on you, in any case.'

'If she claimed as my wife, she'd get far less. Matilda knows what she's doing, greedy bitch she is. She'll keep her mouth shut.'

'Only, you won't be able to marry again, will you George?'

'Not unless she dies,' he said. 'And she's as strong as a trek ox.'

'Well, I'm sorry, George,' I said.

'Good of you to say so,' he said. 'But I can see by your chin that you disapprove of me. Even my old uncle understood.'

'Oh, George, I quite understand. You were lonely, I suppose.'

'You didn't even ask me to your twenty-first. If you and Skinny had been nicer to me, I would never have lost my head and married the woman, never.'

'You didn't ask me to your wedding,' I said.

'You're a catty bissom, Needle; not like what you were in the old times when you used to tell us your wee stories.'

'I'll have to be getting along,' I said.

'Mind you keep the secret,' George said.

'Can't I tell Skinny? He would be very sorry for you, George.'

'You mustn't tell anyone. Keep it a secret. Promise.'

'Promise,' I said. I understood that he wished to enforce some sort of bond between us with this secret, and I thought, 'Oh well, I suppose he's lonely. Keeping his secret won't do any harm.'

I returned to England with Skinny's party just before the war.

I did not see George again till just before my death, five years ago.

After the war Skinny returned to his studies. He had two more exams, over a period of eighteen months, and I thought I might marry him when the exams were over.

'You might do worse than Skinny,' Kathleen used to say to me on our Saturday morning excursions to the antique shops and the junk stalls.

She, too, was getting on in years. The remainder of our families in Scotland were hinting that it was time we settled down with husbands. Kathleen was a little younger than me, but looked much older. She knew her chances were diminishing, but at that time I did not think she cared very much. As for myself, the main attraction of marrying Skinny was his prospective expeditions in Mesopotamia. My desire to marry him had to be stimulated by the continual reading of books about Babylon and Assyria; perhaps Skinny felt this, because he supplied the books, and even started instructing me in the art of deciphering cuneiform tables.

Kathleen was more interested in marriage than I thought. Like me she had racketed around a good deal during the war; she had actually been engaged to an officer in the US navy, who was killed. Now she kept an antique shop near Lambeth, was doing very nicely, lived in a Chelsea square, but for all that she must have wanted to be married and have children. She would stop and look into all the prams which the mothers had left outside shops or area gates.

'The poet Swinburne used to do that,' I told her once.

'Really? Did he want children of his own?'

'I shouldn't think so. He simply liked babies.'

Before Skinny's final exam, he fell ill and was sent to a sanatorium in Switzerland.

'You're fortunate, after all, not to be married to him,' Kathleen said. 'You might have caught TB.'

I was fortunate, I was lucky... so everyone kept telling me on different occasions. Although it annoyed me to hear, I knew they were right, but in a way that was different from what they meant. It took me very small effort to make a living; book reviews, odd jobs for Kathleen, a few months with the publicity man again, still getting up speeches about literature, art, and life for industrial tycoons. I was waiting to write about life, and it seemed to me that the good fortune lay in this whenever it should be. And until then I was assured of my charmed life, the necessities of existence always coming my way, and I with far more leisure than anyone else. I thought of my type of luck after I became a Catholic and was being confirmed. The bishop touches the candidate on the cheek, a symbolic reminder of the sufferings a Christian is supposed to undertake. I thought, how lucky, what a feathery symbol to stand for the hellish violence of its true meaning.

I visited Skinny twice in the two years that he was in the sanatorium. He was almost cured, and expected to be home within a few months. I told Kathleen after my last visit.

'Maybe I'll marry Skinny when he's well again.'

'Make it definite, Needle, and not so much of the maybe. You don't know when you're well off,' she said.

This was five years ago, in the last year of my life. Kathleen and I had become very close friends. We met several times each week, and after our Saturday morning excursions in the Portobello Road very often I would accompany Kathleen to her aunt's house in Kent for a long weekend.

One day in the June of that year I met Kathleen specially for lunch because she had phoned me to say she had news.

'Guess who came into the shop this afternoon,' she said.

'Who?'

'George.'

We had half imagined George was dead. We had received no letters in the past ten years. Early in the war we had heard rumours of his keeping a night club in Durban, but nothing after that. We could have made inquiries if we had felt moved to do so.

At one time, when we discussed him, Kathleen had said:

'I ought to get in touch with poor George. But, then, I think he would write back. He would demand a regular correspondence again.'

'We four must stick together,' I mimicked.

'I can visualize his reproachful limpid orbs,' Kathleen said.

Skinny said, 'He's probably gone native. With his coffee concubine and a dozen mahogany kids.'

'Perhaps he's dead,' Kathleen said.

I did not speak of George's marriage, nor any of his confidences in the hotel at Bulawayo. As the years passed, we ceased to mention him except in passing, as someone more or less dead so far as we were concerned.

Kathleen was excited about George's turning up. She had forgotten her impatience with him in former days; she said:

'It was so wonderful to see old George. He seems to need a friend, feels neglected, out of touch with things.'

'He needs mothering, I suppose.'

Kathleen didn't notice the malice. She declared, 'That's exactly the case with George. It always has been. I can see it now.'

She seemed ready to come to any rapid new and happy conclusion about George. In the course of the morning he had told her of his wartime night club in Durban, his game-shooting expeditions since. It was clear he had not mentioned Matilda. He had put on weight, Kathleen told me, but he could carry it.

I was curious to see this version of George, but I was leaving for Scotland next day and did not see him till September of that year just before my death.

While I was in Scotland I gathered from Kathleen's letters that she was seeing George very frequently, finding enjoyable company in him, looking after him. 'You'll be surprised to see how he has developed.' Apparently he would hang round Kathleen in her shop most days – 'it makes him feel useful' as she maternally expressed it. He had an old relative in Kent whom he visited at weekends; this old lady lived a few miles from Kathleen's aunt, which made it easy for them to travel down together on Saturdays and go for long country walks.

'You'll see such a difference in George,' Kathleen said on my return to London in September. I was to meet him that night, a

Saturday. Kathleen's aunt was abroad, the maid on holiday, and I was to keep Kathleen company in the empty house.

George had left London for Kent a few days earlier. 'He's actually helping with the harvest down there!' Kathleen told me lovingly.

Kathleen and I had planned to travel down together, but on that Saturday she was unexpectedly delayed in London on some business. It was arranged that I should go ahead of her in the early afternoon to see to the provisions for our party; Kathleen had invited George to dinner at her aunt's house that night.

'I should be with you by seven,' she said. 'Sure you won't mind the empty house? I hate arriving at empty houses myself.'

I said no, I liked an empty house.

So I did, when I got there. I had never found the house more likeable. A large Georgian vicarage in about eight acres, most of the rooms shut and sheeted, there being only one servant. I discovered that I wouldn't need to go shopping, Kathleen's aunt had left many and delicate supplies with notes attached to them: *Eat this up please do, see also fridge,* and *A treat for three hungry people, see also 2 bttles beaune for yr party on back kn table.* It was like a treasure hunt as I followed clue after clue through the cool, silent domestic quarters. A house in which there are no people – but with all the signs of tenancy – can be a most tranquil, good place. People take up space in a house out of proportion to their size. On my previous visits I had seen the rooms overflowing as it seemed, with Kathleen, her aunt, and the little fat maidservant; they were always on the move. As I wandered through that part of the house which was in use, opening windows to let in the pale yellow air of September, I was not conscious that I, Needle, was taking up any space at all, I might have been a ghost.

The only thing to be fetched was the milk. I waited till after four when the milking should be done, then set off for the farm which lay across two fields at the back of the orchard. There, when the byreman was handing me the bottle, I saw George.

'Hallo, George,' I said.

'Needle! What are you doing here?' he said.

'Fetching milk,' I said.

'So am I. Well, it's good to see you, I must say.'

As we paid the farmhand, George said, 'I'll walk back with you part of the way. But I mustn't stop, my old cousin's without any milk for her tea. How's Kathleen?'

'She was kept in London. She's coming on later, about seven, she expects.'

We had reached the end of the first field. George's way led to the left and on to the main road.

'We'll see you tonight, then?' I said.

'Yes, and talk about old times.'

'Grand,' I said.

But George got over the stile with me.

'Look here,' he said. 'I'd like to talk to you, Needle.'

'We'll talk tonight, George. Better not keep your cousin waiting for the milk.' I found myself speaking to him almost as if he were a child.

'No, I want to talk to you alone. This is a good opportunity.'

We began to cross the second field. I had been hoping to have the house to myself for a couple more hours, and I was rather petulant.

'See,' he said suddenly, 'that haystack.'

'Yes,' I said absently.

'Let's sit there and talk. I'd like to see you up on a haystack again. I still keep that photo. Remember that time when – '

'I found the needle,' I said very quickly, to get it over.

But I was glad to rest. The stack had been broken up, but we managed to find a nest in it. I buried my bottle of milk in the hay for coolness. George placed his carefully at the foot of the stack.

'My old cousin is terribly vague, poor soul. A bit hazy in her head. She hasn't the least sense of time. If I tell her I've only been gone ten minutes, she'll believe it.'

I giggled and looked at him. His face had grown much larger, his lips full, wide, and with a ripe colour that is strange in a man. His brown eyes were abounding as before with some inarticulate plea.

'So you're going to marry Skinny after all these years?'

'I really don't know, George.'

'You played him up properly.'

'It isn't for you to judge. I have my own reasons for what I do.'

'Don't get sharp,' he said, 'I was only funning.' To prove it, he lifted a tuft of hay and brushed my face with it.

'D'you know,' he said next, 'I didn't think you and Skinny treated me very decently in Rhodesia.'

'Well, we were busy, George. And we were younger then; we had a lot to do and see. After all, we could see you any other time, George.'

'A touch of selfishness,' he said.

'I'll have to be getting along, George.' I made to get down from the stack.

He pulled me back. 'Wait, I've got something to tell you.'

'OK, George, tell me.'

'First promise not to tell Kathleen. She wants it kept a secret so that she can tell you herself.'

'All right. Promise.'

'I'm going to marry Kathleen.'

'But you're already married.'

Sometimes I heard news of Matilda from the one Rhodesian family with whom I still kept up. They referred to her as 'George's Dark Lady', and of course they did not know he was married to her. She had apparently made a good thing out of George, they said, for she minced around all tarted up, never did a stroke of work, and was always unsettling the respectable coloured girls in their neighbourhood. According to accounts, she was a living example of the folly of behaving as George did.

'I married Matilda in the Congo,' George was saying.

'It would still be bigamy,' I said.

He was furious when I used that word bigamy. He lifted a handful of hay as if he would throw it in my face, but controlling himself meanwhile, he fanned it at me playfully.

'I'm not sure that the Congo marriage was valid,' he continued. 'Anyway, as far as I'm concerned, it isn't.'

'You can't do a thing like that,' I said.

'I need Kathleen. She's been decent to me. I think we were always meant for each other, me and Kathleen.'

'I'll have to be going,' I said.

But he put his knee over my ankles so that I couldn't move. I sat still and gazed into space.

He tickled my face with a wisp of hay.

'Smile up, Needle,' he said; 'let's talk like old times.'

'Well?'

'No one knows about my marriage to Matilda except you and me.'

'And Matilda,' I said.

'She'll hold her tongue so long as she gets her payments. My uncle left an annuity for the purpose; his lawyers see to it.'

'Let me go, George.'

'You promised to keep it a secret,' he said, 'you promised.'

'Yes, I promised.'

'And now that you're going to marry Skinny, we'll be properly coupled off as we should have been years ago. We should have been, but youth – our youth – got in the way, didn't it?'

'Life got in the way,' I said.

'But everything's going to be all right now. You'll keep my secret, won't you? You promised.' He had released my feet. I edged a little farther from him.

I said, 'If Kathleen intends to marry you, I shall tell her that you're already married.'

'You wouldn't do a dirty trick like that, Needle? You're going to be happy with Skinny, you wouldn't stand in the way of my – '

'I must, Kathleen's my best friend,' I said swiftly.

He looked as if he would murder me, and he did; he stuffed hay into my mouth until it could hold no more, kneeling on my body to keep it prone, holding both my wrists tight in his huge left hand. I saw the red full lines of his mouth, and the white slit of his teeth last thing on earth. Not another soul passed by as he pressed my body into the stack, as he made a deep nest for me, tearing up the hay to make a groove the length of my corpse, and finally pulling the warm dry stuff in a mound over this concealment, so natural looking in a broken haystack. Then George climbed down, took up his bottle of milk and went his way. I suppose that was why he looked so unwell when I stood, nearly five years later, by the barrow in the Portobello Road and said in easy tones, 'Hallo, George!'

The Haystack Murder was one of the notorious crimes of that year.

My friends said, 'A girl who had everything to live for.'

After a search that lasted twenty hours, when my body was found, the evening papers said, ' "Needle" is found: in haystack!'

Kathleen, speaking from that Catholic point of view which takes some getting used to said, 'She was at Confession only the day before she died – wasn't she lucky?'

The poor byrehand who sold us the milk was grilled for hour after hour by the local police, and later by Scotland Yard. So was George. He admitted walking as far as the haystack with me, but he denied lingering there.

'You hadn't seen your friend for ten years?' the inspector asked him.

'That's right,' said George.

'And you didn't stop to have a chat?'

'No. We'd arranged to meet later at dinner. My cousin was waiting for the milk, I couldn't stop.'

The old soul, his cousin, swore that he hadn't been gone more than ten minutes in all, and she believed it to the day of her death a few months later. There was the microscopic evidence of hay on George's jacket, of course, but the same evidence was on every man's jacket in the district that fine harvest year. Unfortunately, the byreman's hands were even brawnier and mightier than George's. The marks on my wrists had been done by such hands, so the laboratory charts indicated when my postmortem was all completed.

But the wristmarks weren't enough to pin down the crime to either man. If I hadn't been wearing my long-sleeved cardigan, it was said, the bruises might have matched up properly with someone's fingers.

Kathleen, to prove that George had absolutely no motive, told the police that she was engaged to him. George thought this a little foolish. They checked up on his life in Africa, right back to his living with Matilda. But the marriage didn't come out – who would think of looking up registers in the Congo? Not that this would have proved any motive for murder. All the same, George was relieved when the inquiries were over without the marriage to Matilda being disclosed. He was able to have his nervous breakdown at the same time as Kathleen had hers, and they recovered together and got married, long after the police had shifted their inquiries to an Air Force camp five miles from Kathleen's aunt's home. Only a lot of excitement and drinks came of those investigations. The Haystack Murder was one of the unsolved crimes that year.

Shortly afterwards the byrehand emigrated to Canada to start afresh, with the help of Skinny who felt sorry for him.

After seeing George taken away home by Kathleen that Saturday in the Portobello Road, I thought that perhaps I might be seeing more of him in similar circumstances. The next Saturday I looked out for him, and at last there he was, without Kathleen, half worried, half hopeful.

I dashed his hopes, I said, 'Hallo, George!'

He looked in my direction, rooted in the midst of the flowing market mongers in that convivial street. I thought to myself, 'He looks as if he had a mouthful of hay.' It was the new bristly maize-coloured beard and moustache surrounding his great mouth suggested the thought, gay and lyrical as life.

'Hallo, George!' I said again.

I might have been inspired to say more on that agreeable morning, but he didn't wait. He was away down a side street and along another street and down one more, zigzag, as far and as devious as he could take himself from the Portobello Road.

Nevertheless, he was back again next week. Poor Kathleen had brought him in her car. She left it at the top of the street, and got out with him, holding him tight by the arm. It grieved me to see Kathleen ignoring the spread of scintillations on the stalls. I had myself seen a charming Battersea box quite to her taste, also a pair of enamelled silver earrings. But she took no notice of these wares, clinging close to George, and, poor Kathleen – I hate to say how she looked.

And George was haggard. His eyes seemed to have got smaller as if he had been recently in pain. He advanced up the road with Kathleen on his arm, letting himself lurch from side to side with his wife bobbing beside him, as the crowds asserted their rights of way.

'Oh, George!' I said. 'You don't look at all well, George.'

'Look!' said George. 'Over there by the hardwear barrow. That's Needle.'

Kathleen was crying. 'Come back home, dear,' she said.

'Oh, you don't look well, George!' I said.

They took him to a nursing home. He was fairly quiet, except on Saturday mornings when they had a hard time of it to keep him indoors and away from the Portobello Road.

But a couple of months later he did escape. It was a Monday.

They searched for him in the Portobello Road, but actually he had gone off to Kent to the village near the scene of the Haystack Murder. There he went to the police and gave himself up, but they could tell from the way he was talking that there was something wrong with the man.

'I saw Needle in the Portobello Road three Saturdays running,' he explained, 'and they put me in a private ward, but I got away while the nurses were seeing to the new patient. You remember the murder of Needle – well, I did it. Now you know the truth, and that will keep bloody Needle's mouth shut.'

Dozens of poor mad fellows confess to every murder. The police obtained an ambulance to take him back to the nursing home. He wasn't there long. Kathleen gave up her shop, and devoted herself to looking after him at home. But she found that the Saturday mornings were a strain. He insisted on going to see me in the Portobello Road, and would come back to insist that he'd murdered Needle. Once he tried to tell her something about Matilda, but Kathleen was so kind and solicitous, I don't think he had the courage to remember what he had to say.

Skinny had always been rather reserved with George since the murder. But he was kind to Kathleen. It was he who persuaded them to emigrate to Canada so that George should be well out of reach of the Portobello Road.

George has recovered somewhat in Canada, but of course he will never be the old George again, as Kathleen writes to Skinny. 'That Haystack tragedy did for George,' she writes. 'I feel sorrier for George sometimes than I am for poor Needle. But I do often have Masses said for Needle's soul.'

I doubt if George will ever see me again in the Portobello Road. He broods much over the crumpled snapshot he took of us on the haystack. Kathleen does not like the photograph. I don't wonder. For my part, I consider it quite a jolly snap, but I don't think we were any of us so lovely as we look in it, gazing blatantly over the ripe cornfields – Skinny with his humorous expression, I secure in my difference from the rest, Kathleen with her head prettily perched on her hand, each reflecting fearlessly in the face of George's camera the glory of the world, as if it would never pass.

# Bram Stoker

# *The Squaw*

Nurnberg at the time was not so much exploited as it has been since then. Irving had not been playing *Faust*, and the very name of the old town was hardly known to the great bulk of the travelling public. My wife and I being in the second week of our honeymoon, naturally wanted someone else to join our party, so that when the cheery stranger, Elias P. Hutcheson, hailing from Isthmian City, Bleeding Gulch, Maple Tree County, Neb., turned up at the station at Frankfort, and casually remarked that he was going on to see the most all-fired old Methuselah of a town in Yurrup, and that he guessed that so much travelling alone was enough to send an intelligent, active citizen into the melancholy ward of a dafthouse, we took the pretty broad hint and suggested that we should join forces. We found, on comparing notes afterwards, that we had each intended to speak with some diffidence or hesitation so as not to appear too eager, such not being a good compliment to the success of our married life; but the effect was entirely marred by our both beginning to speak at the same instant – stopping simultaneously and then going on together again. Anyhow, no matter how, it was done; and Elias P. Hutcheson became one of our party. Straightway Amelia and I found the pleasant benefit; instead of quarrelling, as we had been doing, we found that the restraining influence of a third party was such that we now took every opportunity of spooning in odd corners. Amelia declares that ever since she has, as the result of that experience, advised all her friends to take a friend on the honeymoon. Well, we 'did' Nurnberg together, and much enjoyed the racy remarks of our transatlantic friend, who, from his quaint speech and his wonderful stock of adventures, might have stepped out of a novel. We kept for the last object of interest in the city to be visited the Burg, and on the day appointed for the visit strolled round the outer wall of the city by the eastern side.

The Burg is seated on a rock dominating the town, and an immensely deep fosse guards it on the northern side. Nurnberg has been happy in that it was never sacked; had it been it would certainly not be so spick-and-span perfect as it is at present. The ditch has not been used for centuries, and now its base is spread with tea gardens and orchards, of which some of the trees are of quite respectable growth. As we wandered round the wall, dawdling in the hot July sunshine, we often paused to admire the views spread before us, and in especial the great plain covered with towns and villages and bounded with a blue line of hills, like a landscape of Claude Lorraine. From this we always turned with new delight to the city itself, with its myriad of quaint old gables and acre-wide red roofs dotted with dormer windows, tier upon tier. A little to our right rose the towers of the Burg, and nearer still, standing grim, the Torture Tower, which was, and is, perhaps, the most interesting place in the city. For centuries the tradition of the Iron Virgin of Nurnberg has been handed down as an instance of the horrors of cruelty of which man is capable; we had long looked forward to seeing it; and here at last was its home.

In one of our pauses we leaned over the wall of the moat and looked down. The garden seemed quite fifty or sixty feet below us, and the sun pouring into it with an intense, moveless heat like that of an oven. Beyond rose the grey, grim wall seemingly of endless height, and losing itself right and left in the angles of bastion and counterscarp. Trees and bushes crowned the wall, and above again towered the lofty houses on whose massive beauty Time has only set the hand of approval. The sun was hot and we were lazy; time was our own, and we lingered, leaning on the wall. Just below us was a pretty sight – a great black cat lying stretched in the sun, whilst round her gambolled prettily a tiny black kitten. The mother would wave her tail for the kitten to play with, or would raise her feet and push away the little one as an encouragement to further play. They were just at the foot of the wall, and Elias P. Hutcheson, in order to help the play, stooped and took from the walk a moderate-sized pebble.

'See!' he said. 'I will drop it near the kitten, and they will both wonder where it came from.'

'Oh, be careful,' said my wife; 'you might hit the dear little thing!'

'Not me, ma'am,' said Elias P. 'Why, I'm as tender as a Maine cherry tree. Lor, bless ye, I wouldn't hurt the poor pooty little critter more'n I'd scalp a baby. An' you may bet your variegated socks on that! See, I'll drop it fur away on the outside so's not to go near her!' Thus saying, he leaned over and held his arm out at full length and dropped the stone. It may be that there is some attractive force which draws lesser matters to greater; or more probably that the wall was not plumb but sloped to its base – we not noticing the inclination from above; but the stone fell with a sickening thud that came up to us through the hot air, right on the kitten's head, and shattered out its little brains then and there. The black cat cast a swift upward glance, and we saw her eyes like green fire fixed an instant on Elias P. Hutcheson; and then her attention was given to the kitten, which lay still with just a quiver of her tiny limbs, whilst a thin red stream trickled from a gaping wound. With a muffled cry, such as a human being might give, she bent over the kitten licking its wound and moaning. Suddenly she seemed to realize that it was dead, and again threw her eyes up at us. I shall never forget the sight, for she looked the perfect incarnation of hate. Her green eyes blazed with lurid fire, and the white, sharp teeth seemed to almost shine through the blood which dabbled her mouth and whiskers. She gnashed her teeth, and her claws stood out stark and at full length on every paw. Then she made a wild rush up the wall as if to reach us, but when the momentum ended fell back, and further added to her horrible appearance for she fell on the kitten, and rose with her black fur smeared with its brains and blood. Amelia turned quite faint, and I had to lift her back from the wall. There was a seat close by in shade of a spreading plane tree, and here I placed her whilst she composed herself. Then I went back to Hutcheson, who stood without moving, looking down on the angry cat below.

As I joined him, he said:

'Wall, I guess that air the savagest beast I ever see – 'cept once when an Apache squaw had an edge on a half breed what they nicknamed "Splinters" 'cos of the way he fixed up her papoose which he stole on a raid just to show that he appreciated the way they had given his mother the fire torture. She got that kinder look so set on her face that it jest seemed to grow there. She followed Splinters more'n three year till at last the braves got him and handed him over to her. They did say that no man, white or Injun, had ever been so long a-dying under the tortures of the Apaches. The only time I ever see her smile was when I wiped her out. I kem on the camp just in time to see Splinters pass in his checks, and he wasn't sorry to go either. He was a hard citizen, and though I never could shake with him after that papoose business – for it was bitter bad, and he should have been a white man, for he looked like one – I see he had got paid out in full. Durn me, but I took a piece of his hide from one of his skinnin' posts an' had it made into a pocket book. It's here now!' and he slapped the breast pocket of his coat.

Whilst he was speaking the cat was continuing her frantic efforts to get up the wall. She would take a run back and then charge up, sometimes reaching an incredible height. She did not seem to mind the heavy fall which she got each time, but started with renewed vigour; and at every tumble her appearance became more horrible. Hutcheson was a kind-hearted man – my wife and I had both noticed little acts of kindness to animals as well as to persons – and he seemed concerned at the state of fury to which the cat had wrought herself.

'Wall, now!' he said, 'I du declare that that poor critter seems quite desperate. There! there! poor thing, it was all an accident – though that won't bring back your little one to you. Say! I wouldn't have had such a thing happen for a thousand! Just shows what a clumsy fool of a man can do when he tries to play! Seems I'm too darned slipper-handed to even play with a cat. Say, Colonel!' – it was a pleasant way he had to bestow titles freely – 'I hope your wife don't hold no grudge against me on account of this unpleasantness? Why, I wouldn't have had it occur on no account.'

He came over to Amelia and apologized profusely, and she with her usual kindness of heart hastened to assure him that she quite understood that it was an accident. Then we all went again to the wall and looked over.

The cat missing Hutcheson's face had drawn back across the moat, and was sitting on her haunches as though ready to spring. Indeed, the very instant she saw him she did spring, and with a blind, unreasoning fury, which would have been grotesque, only that it was so frightfully real. She did not try to run up the wall, but simply launched herself at him as though hate and fury could lend her wings to pass straight through the great distance between them. Amelia, womanlike, got quite concerned, and said to Elias P. in a warning voice:

'Oh! you must be very careful. That animal would try to kill you if she were here; her eyes look like positive murder.'

He laughed out jovially. 'Excuse me, ma'am,' he said, 'but I can't help laughin'. Fancy a man that has fought grizzlies an' Injuns bein' careful of bein' murdered by a cat!'

When the cat heard him laugh, her whole demeanour seemed to change. She no longer tried to jump or run up the wall, but went quietly over and, sitting again beside the dead kitten, began to lick and fondle it as though it were alive.

'See!' said I, 'the effect of a really strong man. Even that animal in the midst of her fury recognizes the voice of a master, and bows to him!'

'Like a squaw!' was the only comment of Elias P. Hutcheson, as we moved on our way round the city fosse. Every now and then we looked over the wall and each time saw the cat following us. At first she had kept going back to the dead kitten, and then as the distance grew greater took it in her mouth and so followed. After a while, however, she abandoned this, for we saw her following all alone; she had evidently hidden the body somewhere. Amelia's alarm grew at the cat's persistence, and more than once she repeated her warning; but the American always laughed with amusement, till finally, seeing that she was beginning to be worried, he said:

'I say, ma'am, you needn't be skeered over that cat. I go heeled, I du!' Here he slapped his pistol pocket at the back of his lumbar region. 'Why, sooner'n have you worried, I'll shoot the critter, right here, an' risk the police interferin' with a citizen of the United States for carryin' arms contrairy to reg'lations!' As he spoke he looked over the wall, but the cat, on seeing him, retreated, with a growl, into a bed of tall flowers, and was hidden. He went on: 'Blest if that ar critter ain't got more sense of what's good for her than most Christians. I guess we've seen the last of her! You bet, she'll go back now to that busted kitten and have a private funeral of it, all to herself!'

Amelia did not like to say more, lest he might, in mistaken kindness to her, fulfil his threat of shooting the cat; and so we went on and crossed the little wooden bridge leading to the gateway whence ran the steep paved roadway between the Burg and the pentagonal Torture Tower. As we crossed the bridge we saw the cat again down below us. When she saw us her fury seemed to return, and she made frantic efforts to get up the steep wall. Hutcheson laughed as he looked down at her, and said:

'Goodbye, old girl. Sorry I injured your feelin's, but you'll get over it in time! So long!' And then we passed through the long, dim archway and came to the gate of the Burg.

When we came out again after our survey of this most beautiful old place which not even the well-intentioned efforts of the Gothic restorers of forty years ago have been able to spoil – though their restoration was then glaring white – we seemed to have quite forgotten the unpleasant episode of the morning. The old lime tree with its great trunk gnarled with the passing of nearly nine centuries, the deep well cut through the heart of the rock by those captives of old, and the lovely view from the city wall whence we heard, spread over almost a full quarter of an hour, the multitudinous chimes of the city, had all helped to wipe out from our minds the incident of the slain kitten.

We were the only visitors who had entered the Torture Tower that morning – so at least said the old custodian – and as we had the place all to ourselves were able to make a minute and more satisfactory survey than would have otherwise been possible. The custodian, looking to us as the sole source of his gains for the day, was willing to meet our wishes in any way. The Torture Tower is truly a grim place, even now when many thousands of visitors have sent a stream of life, and the joy that follows life, into the place; but at the time I mention it wore its grimmest and most gruesome aspect. The dust of ages seemed to have settled on it, and the darkness and the horror of its memories seem to have become sentient in a way that would have satisfied the Pantheistic souls of Philo or Spinoza. The lower chamber where we entered was seemingly, in its normal state, filled with incarnate darkness; even the hot sunlight streaming in through the door seemed to be lost in the vast thickness of the walls, and only showed the masonry rough as when the builder's scaffolding had come down, but coated with dust and marked here and there with patches of dark stain which, if walls could speak, could have given their own dread memories of fear and pain. We were glad to pass up the dusty wooden staircase, the custodian leaving the outer door open to light us somewhat on our way; for to our eyes the one long-wick'd, evil-smelling candle stuck in a sconce on the wall gave an inadequate light. When we came up through the open trap in the corner of the chamber overhead, Amelia held on to me so tightly that I could actually feel her heart beat. I must say for my own part that I was not surprised at her fear, for this room was even more gruesome than that below. Here there was certainly more light, but only just sufficient to realize the horrible surroundings of the place. The builders of the tower had evidently intended that only they who should gain the top should have any of the joys of light and prospect. There, as we had noticed from below, were ranges of windows, albeit of medieval smallness, but elsewhere in the tower were only a very few narrow slits such as were habitual in places of medieval defence. A few of these only lit the chamber, and these so high up in the wall that from no part could the sky be seen through the thickness of the walls. In racks, and leaning in disorder against the walls, were a number of headsmen's swords, great double-handed weapons with broad blade and keen edge. Hard by were several blocks whereon the necks of the victims had lain, with here and there deep notches where the steel had bitten through the guard of flesh and shored into the wood. Round the chamber, placed in all sorts of irregular ways, were many implements of torture which made one's heart ache to see – chairs full of spikes which gave instant and excruciating pain; chairs and couches with dull knobs whose torture was seemingly less, but which, though slower, were equally efficacious – racks, belts, boots, gloves, collars, all made for compressing at will; steel baskets in which the head could be slowly crushed into a pulp if necessary; watchmen's hooks with long handle and knife that cut at resistance – this a specialty of the old Nurnberg police system; and many, many other devices for man's injury to man. Amelia grew quite pale with the horror of the things, but fortunately did not faint, for being a little overcome she sat down on a torture chair, but jumped up again with a shriek, all tendency to faint gone. We both pretended that it was the injury done to her dress by the dust of the chair and the rusty spikes which had upset her, and Mr Hutcheson acquiesced in accepting the explanation with a kind-hearted laugh.

But the central object in the whole of this chamber of horrors was the engine known as the Iron Virgin, which stood near the centre of the room. It was a rudely shaped figure of a woman, something of the bell order, or, to make a closer comparison, of the figure of Mrs Noah in the children's Ark, but without that slimness of waist and perfect *rondeur* of hip which marks the aesthetic type of the Noah family. One would hardly have recognized it as intended for a human figure at all had not the founder shaped on the forehead a rude semblance of a woman's face. This machine was coated with rust without and covered with dust; a rope was fastened to a ring in the front of the figure, about where the waist should have been, and was drawn through a pulley, fastened on the wooden pillar which sustained the flooring above. The custodian pulling this rope showed that a section of the front was hinged like a door at one side; we then saw that the engine was of considerable thickness, leaving just room enough inside for a man to be placed. The door was of equal thickness and of great weight, for it took the custodian all his strength, aided though he was by the contrivance of the pulley, to open it. This weight was partly due to the fact that the door was of manifest purpose hung so as to throw its weight downwards, so that it might shut of its own accord when the strain was released. The inside was honeycombed with rust – nay more, the rust alone that comes through time would hardly have eaten so deep into the iron walls; the rust of the cruel stains was deep indeed! It was only, however, when we came to look at the inside of the door that the diabolical intention was manifest to the full. Here were several long spikes, square and massive, broad at the base and sharp at the points, placed in such a position that when the door should close the upper ones would pierce the eyes of the victim, and the lower ones his heart and vitals. The sight was too much for poor Amelia, and this time she fainted dead off, and I had to carry her down the stairs and place her on a bench outside till she recovered. That she felt it to the quick was afterwards shown by the fact that my eldest son bears to this day a rude birthmark on his breast, which has, by family consent, been accepted as representing the Nurnberg Virgin.

When we got back to the chamber we found Hutcheson still opposite the Iron Virgin; he had been evidently philosophizing, and now gave us the benefits of this thought in the shape of a sort of exordium.

'Wall, I guess I've been learnin' somethin' here while madam has been gettin' over her faint. 'Pears to me that we're a long way behind the times on our side of the big drink. We uster think out on the plains that the Injun could give us points in tryin' to make a man oncomfortable; but I guess your old medieval law-and-order party could raise him every time. Splinters was pretty good in his bluff on the squaw, but this here young miss held a straight flush all high on him. The points of them spikes air sharp enough still, though even the edges air eaten out by what uster be on them. It'd be a good thing for our Indian section to get some specimens of this here play-toy to send round to the Reservations jest to knock the stuffin' out of the bucks, and the squaws too, by showing them as how old civilization lays over them at their best. Guess but I'll get in that box a minute jest to see how it feels!'

'Oh no! no!' said Amelia. 'It is too terrible!'

'Guess, ma'am, nothin's too terrible to the explorin' mind. I've been in some queer places in my time. Spent a night inside a dead horse while a prairie fire swept over me in Montana Territory – an' another time slept inside a dead buffler when the Comanches was on the warpath an' I didn't keer to leave my kyard on them. I've been two days in a caved-in tunnel in the Billy Broncho gold mine in New Mexico, an' was one of the four shut up for three parts of a day in the caisson what slid over on her side when we was settin' the foundations of the Buffalo Bridge.

I've not funked an odd experience yet, an' I don't propose to begin now!'

We saw that he was set on the experiment, so I said: 'Well, hurry up, old man, and get through it quick.'

'All right, General,' said he, 'but I calculate we ain't quite ready yet. The gentlemen, my predecessors, what stood in that thar canister, didn't volunteer for the office – not much! And I guess there was some ornamental tyin' up before the big stroke was made. I want to go into this thing fair and square, so I must get fixed up proper first. I dare say this old galoot can rise some string and tie me up accordin' to sample?'

This was said interrogatively to the old custodian, but the latter, who understood the drift of his speech, though perhaps not appreciating to the full the niceties of dialect and imagery, shook his head. His protest was, however, only formal and made to be overcome. The American thrust a gold piece into his hand, saying, 'Take it, pard! it's your pot; and don't be skeer'd. This ain't no necktie party that you're asked to assist in!' He produced some thin frayed rope and proceeded to bind our companion with sufficient strictness for the purpose. When the upper part of his body was bound, Hutcheson said:

'Hold on a moment, Judge. Guess I'm too heavy for you to tote into the canister. You jest let me walk in, and then you can wash up regardin' my legs!'

Whilst speaking he had backed himself into the opening which was just enough to hold him. It was a close fit and no mistake. Amelia looked on with fear in her eyes, but she evidently did not like to say anything. Then the custodian completed his task by tying the American's feet together so that he was now absolutely helpless and fixed in his voluntary prison. He seemed to really enjoy it, and the incipient smile which was habitual to his face blossomed into actuality as he said:

'Guess this here Eve was made out of the rib of a dwarf! There ain't much room for a full-grown citizen of the United States to hustle. We uster make our coffins more roomier in Idaho territory. Now, Judge, you jest begin to let this door down, slow, on to me. I want to feel the same pleasure as the other jays had when those spikes began to move toward their eyes!'

'Oh no! no! no!' broke in Amelia hysterically. 'It is too terrible! I can't bear to see it! I can't! I can't!'

But the American was obdurate. 'Say, Colonel,' said he, 'why not take Madame for a little promenade? I wouldn't hurt her feelin's for the world; but now that I am here, havin' kem eight thousand miles, wouldn't it be too hard to give up the very experience I've been pinin' an' pantin' fur? A man can't get to feel like canned goods every time! Me and the Judge here'll fix up this thing in no time, an' then you'll come back, an' we'll all laugh together!'

Once more the resolution that is born of curiosity triumphed, and Amelia stayed holding tight to my arm and shivering whilst the custodian began to slacken slowly inch by inch the rope that held back the iron door. Hutcheson's face was positively radiant as his eyes followed the first movement of the spikes.

'Wall!' he said, 'I guess I've not had enjoyment like this since I left Noo York. Bar a scrap with a French sailor at Wapping – an' that warn't much of a picnic neither – I've not had a show fur real pleasure in this dod-rotted Continent, where there ain't no b'ars nor no Injuns, an' wheer nary man goes heeled. Slow there, Judge! Don't you rush this business! I want a show for my money this game – I du!'

The custodian must have had in him some of the blood of his predecessors in that ghastly tower, for he worked the engine with a deliberate and excruciating slowness which after five minutes, in which the outer edge of the door had not moved half as many inches, began to overcome Amelia. I saw her lips whiten and felt her hold upon my arm relax. I looked around an instant for a place whereon to lay her, and when I looked at her again found that her eye had become fixed on the side of the Virgin. Following its direction I saw the black cat crouching out of sight. Her green eyes shone like danger lamps in the gloom of the place, and their colour was heightened by the blood which still smeared her coat and reddened her mouth. I cried out:

'The cat! Look out for the cat!' for even then she sprang out before the engine. At this moment she looked like a triumphant demon. Her eyes blazed with ferocity, her hair bristled out till she seemed twice her normal size, and her tail lashed about as does a tiger's when the quarry is before it. Elias P. Hutcheson when he saw her was amused, and his eyes positively sparkled with fun as he said:

'Darned if the squaw hain't got on all her war paint! Jest give her a shove off if she comes any of her tricks on me, for I'm so fixed everlastingly by the boss, that durn my skin if I can keep my eyes from her if she wants them! Easy there, Judge! Don't you slack that ar rope or I'm euchered!'

At this moment Amelia completed her faint, and I had to clutch hold of her round the waist or she would have fallen to the floor. Whilst attending to her I saw the black cat crouching for a spring, and jumped up to turn the creature out.

But at that instant, with a sort of hellish scream, she hurled herself, not as we expected at Hutcheson, but straight at the face of the custodian. Her claws seemed to be tearing wildly as one sees in the Chinese drawings of the dragon rampant, and as I looked I saw one of them light on the poor man's eye, and actually tear through it and down his cheek, leaving a wide band of red where the blood seemed to spurt from every vein.

With a yell of sheer terror which came quicker than even his sense of pain, the man leaped back, dropping as he did so the rope which held back the iron door. I jumped for it, but was too late, for the cord ran like lightning through the pulley block, and the heavy mass fell forward from its own weight.

As the door closed I caught a glimpse of our poor companion's face. He seemed frozen with terror. His eyes stared with a horrible anguish, as if dazed, and no sound came from his lips.

And then the spikes did their work. Happily the end was quick, for when I wrenched open the door they had pierced so deep that they had locked in the bones of the skull through which they had crushed, and actually tore him – it – out of his own prison till, bound as he was, he fell at full length with a sickly thud upon the floor, the face turning upwards as he fell.

I rushed to my wife, lifted her up and carried her out, for I feared for her very reason if she should wake from her faint to such a scene. I laid her on the bench outside and ran back. Leaning against the wooden column was the custodian, moaning in pain while he held his reddening handkerchief to his eyes. And sitting on the head of the poor American was the cat, purring loudly as she licked the blood which trickled through the gashed socket of his eyes.

I think no one will call me cruel because I seized one of the old executioner's swords and shore her in two as she sat.

# Anthony Vercoe

# *Flies*

Here is the story as I got it from the tramp himself, an ex-university don, I believe, who had come down in the world through some misadventure, and who now lay close to death's door in the workhouse infirmary.

It was sickening weather – a typical English summer. All day long the rain had pattered on the rooftops and poured in a gurgling stream into the street gutters of the City. The dome of St Paul's lay enveloped in a great black cloud, and the whole sky to the westward was angry and dark with foreboding.

Towards the dusk the rain ceased for a while, and I crept out from the crude shelter of an arch to find some more tempting spot in which to spend the night.

Not that it was cold – far from it! The atmosphere was almost tropically oppressive, and grew worse as still the thunder held off; but I was sick and faint from want of food, and longed with all the fever of despair for a clean soft bed and palatable fare before I finally handed in my checks.

It was while I dragged myself painfully in the direction of High Holborn that I first saw – the house! Would that I had been mercifully obliterated at that moment by some passing lorry rather than live to repeat this tale!

It was a little old-fashioned dwelling, like many that are to be seen in that district – relics of Elizabethan times. It smirked at my misery through its diamond-paned windows, challenging me. A notice was plastered across a signboard protruding above the portal, bearing the heaven-sent words 'To Let'. The hour was late, the street practically deserted, and my head seemed to reel under the weight of the unexploded storm. As if to aid me in making up my mind, a large splash of rain as big as a penny fell with a soft plop on to my forehead. It was warm and sticky, like the night outside, and I hesitated no longer. Within that smirking, self-satisfied, wise old house lay refuge from the deluge which threatened.

Cautiously I approached the door. It was locked, of course. I examined the window fastenings of the ground-floor window and cursed my usual bad luck. Then a weakness in the lead round one of the diamonds caught my attention. I glanced quickly to right and left. The policeman at the corner had his back to me. Two couples hurried by. Another quick look; I was unobserved; a tinkle of breaking glass, a thrust of the arm, a turn of the wrist – and the window was open.

Open – and beckoning.

I scrabbled with my hands on the window ledge and painfully drew myself up. The effort cost me what little strength I had left; but at last I lay exhausted, though triumphant – inside.

I don't know how long I remained there gasping on the floor, my heart hammering in my breast, my temples knocking. It may have been an hour or only a few moments. Perhaps I fainted. Remember, I had had no food for three days! But at last I rose, closed the window again to avoid suspicion, and felt in my pockets for an odd match.

I struck it. Then at what its light revealed I nearly dropped it.

The room was furnished – splendidly furnished in a style three centuries old! A sevenfold candelabra gleamed metallic on the mantel, and I hurriedly applied my wavering match to it that I might see better.

I held my hand over the flame, thinking that my weakness was playing tricks with me – but no. It was true! I, a hungry, homeless vagabond, had found sanctuary in a home beyond my wildest dreams. An antiquary's paradise!

Carrying my candelabra, I advanced to the door, then on the threshold I halted. A sudden fear had shaken me. The house I had seen from the outside had looked bare and empty, and there had been that 'To Let' sign to confirm its appearance. This house, on the contrary, was comfortably, even sumptuously, furnished, and it had the feel of a house that is lived in! Suppose I had made a mistake!

Suppose in my feeble and overwrought state I had broken into the wrong house? I could expect little mercy at the hands of the occupants. There was a policeman at the corner, and I was virtually a burglar – I realized how tame my excuses would sound as he hauled me off with him to the station.

Prison? Yes, there was always shelter there, but my old pride had always forbidden me to avail myself of it. Pride? I laughed a little mirthlessly, remembering my condition – and then I first heard it.

It seemed to come from within my brain – a low-pitched buzzing – and I began to wonder what new trick my failing strength was playing me. The sound droned on, sometimes increasing, sometimes decreasing, in volume, but never finally abating – like the noise of a distant aeroplane performing gyrations over the house. I shook my head stupidly as I stood by the door, hoping thereby to stop it as one stops the sound of singing in one's ears – but to no avail. The clamour persisted until I felt as though my head was resting against a hive of busy bees.

Then, as this simile occurred to me, I became conscious that the room was growing warmer. I swayed a little and stretched out my hand to the door. It opened easily, and a moment later I stood in the hall. Almost immediately I realized that the buzzing had stopped.

By the light of my candles I marked a little door in the passage which presumably led to the kitchen and staggered towards it – there might food lie! The long flight of oak stairs, trending upwards, I disregarded for fear of waking the householder.

Cautiously I pushed open the little door and stepped through.

I was in a kind of parlour, and beyond, through another door, I could see the kitchen.

I lifted my candelabra and gazed about me. To my right a second door showed me where the housekeeper slept. I looked to my left and nearly cried out with excitement at what I saw!

Spread on a small oak table was the most delicious repast I could have hoped for. I stumbled towards it, and setting down my light began to eat ravenously. All moral scruples vanished at the sight of food – I was a man, I was starving – surely none would deny me the means to stay those gnawing pangs?

And then it came again – a low, continuous buzzing. But not in my head this time – my head was clear. I set down my glass which I had filled from a beaker with some sweet wine and listened.

The sound seemed to come from the housekeeper's room. I filled my mouth, and, approaching the door, bent my head to the crack.

Buzz – zz – zzz!

Yes, unmistakably it came from within. I put my eye to the keyhole, but the room was in darkness. A queer temptation came to me to trace this sound to its source, and at risk of waking anyone who might be sleeping inside I placed my hand on the knob and cautiously turned it.

Almost immediately the sound of buzzing stopped. Slowly, very slowly, I opened the door and peeped inside. Then I think my heart froze!

Supported across two chairs was a long wooden box whose shape filled me with an unnameable dread. Two three-branch candelabra stood with their fuel guttered out upon the floor, and in a corner of the room was a four-poster bed with tumbled clothes. The lid of the coffin was off.

At first, by my candlelight, I thought that the occupant of the coffin was a negro. Then, as I peered, horror-stricken by my gruesome discovery, the ghastly buzzing recommenced.

It seemed as though a veil was plucked simultaneously from the corpse's face, leaving what had been mercifully hidden bare in all its festering corruption to my revolted gaze. I stifled a cry and stepped backwards to the door, shutting my eyes to the white baldness of that putrefying thing in the coffin, while I held my breath to withstand the stench that arose from it. Something got in the way of my foot and I stumbled. The door knob flew out of my hand, and I heard the door slam behind me, then the next instant I was battling frenziedly with the monstrous droning, buzzing cloud of blowflies which had been feasting on the corpse!

Madly I beat at them with my fists, but with little impression. The whole room seemed alive with little hairy legs, with tiny, sticky feet, trying to settle on my skin. And all the time they kept up that hideous buzzing sound as they beat furiously with their wings on the fetid atmosphere. One, larger than the rest, to judge by its weight, settled on my lip and sought to insert its leprous body into my mouth. The thought of the thing it had just been feeding off flashed into my mind, nauseating me, and as I struck savagely at it with my bare hand I felt its huge, fat body squelch on my cheek and drop.

Somehow I gained the door and opened it. I had dropped my candelabra in my panic, and now, panting and sweating with fear, I half crawled, half rolled into the parlour. As I heard the door of the bedroom slam to after me I breathed a prayer of relief for my escape. There had been something unnatural in the behaviour of those flies, something almost wickedly intelligent in the way they had attacked me. Their assault had had the appearance of being carefully organized by a superior brain – by the mind of some great leader or general.

Deprived my light, I groped in the darkness for the little door which led into the hall. My fingers closed on the knob and turned it. Round and round it went, meeting with no resistance from the lock, while all the time a chill fear crept up my spine paralysing my very thoughts. Something had happened to the catch – the knob was useless. I was locked in!

Madly I shook and rattled at the door knob. Time and again I flung the pitiful weight of my wasted body against the sturdy oak of that small, relentless door, exhausting my newly gained strength in useless effort. Then, when all hope had nearly left me, with a flash of illumination I remembered the kitchen.

'Fool!' I cursed my stupidity as stumblingly I fumbled across the pitch-dark parlour to the kitchen door. Here, surely, would be a way of escape! I turned and shook my fist in the direction of those half human flies buzzing maddeningly behind that shut door – that other door – the door of death!

It was my body they wanted – to drink live blood and taste live flesh! I had felt it – known it – there in that room while I had fought them. But I would cheat them yet!

I laughed hysterically as I staggered across the threshold into the kitchen and made my way to the back door. A big window yawned to the right of it, flooding the place with a queer white moonlight. I tried the latch – O Blessed Virgin! it turned, and then – I ceased to laugh. Not a fraction of an inch would the door move either way! I strained and tugged and pulled. At last I felt round the edges of the door, and the mystery stood revealed. Sharp points of nails placed at regular intervals touched my fingers – my exit had been nailed up from the outside!

But why?

Even as I wondered I heard the clanging of a bell somewhere in the street. I peered through the window. Queer how different London looks by moonlight!

I realized I was gazing at a part of the City I had not dreamed existed. The houses opposite seemed almost to invade those on my side of the road, so narrow was the thoroughfare between. Decorative, too, they were – their black beams ornamented here and there with fantastic designs, while their gables lowered menacingly above my head, leaving but a strip of sky.

Clang-a-clang! Clang-a-clang!

Again that bell – nearer this time – and with it I could fancy I heard the scrape and bump of heavy wheels over cobbles. A voice was calling something – a hoarse, melancholy voice, but the words eluded me.

Who could be selling things in Holborn at this time of night? But at least he might render me assistance if only I could attract his attention. I clambered on to a table which stood by the window and looked down. Here the street was on a lower level than at the front of the house – to jump would be difficult, even dangerous.

The cart – for cart it was – rolled into view, drawn by a great black horse. A man was leading it, ringing a bell and occasionally shouting his melancholy cry, while behind him on the cart itself another man was sitting, queerly silent, his whole attitude indicative of the deepest despair.

There was a lantern on the table beside me, and, finding another match, I lit it, moving it slowly from side to side in front of the window. Soon they would see it – would stop their cart below me – and let me jump to the clean comfort of the open street. Anything rather than stay another moment in the evil silence of this uncanny house.

Ah! He had seen me and was looking up at the window. What was that he was calling? I smiled and nodded, beckoning him nearer.

Now his words came clearer. Was I mad? I knew nothing of the corpse in the other room, yet why did he point up at me like that, why chant that unearthly cry of his: 'Bring out your dead! Bring out your dead!'

He pointed to the back of his great, ponderous cart. It was full – heaped high with – with what? Shuddering, I saw that the tortuous tangled mass in the back of the cart was human freight, and as a shaft of moonlight fell for an instant across them – that some were not dead – yet!

Scarce understanding even then what it meant, I looked across at the darkened doorways of the houses opposite – and gasped. Each door was marked with a large cross – the cross of despair, the cross of humanity, *the cross of the plague!*

The cart rumbled on and I let it go. I was dazed with the meaning of it all. Had I stepped back through three hundred years when

I broke through the window of the house in Holborn? Had I died outside when I lay under that arch in the pouring rain, and could this be my hell? And even while I clasped my tortured head in my hands I heard again that dread buzzing of the flies.

Fearfully I tiptoed to the kitchen door and held my lantern aloft. The droning from the death chamber swelled louder than a swarm of bees. They were angry at being baulked of their prey – the living prey that was so much rarer than the dead!

The atmosphere in the parlour was stifling, and I longed for something to drink. I thought of the wine and food on the table in the corner, then, seeing it, recoiled. Had I really eaten that writhing mass of great white worms? Or had the food putrefied during the few minutes I had been out of the room?

Something hummed triumphantly round my head and out of reach. I turned and stared, hypnotized at what I saw.

Watching me from its perch on a piece of rotten meat on the table was an enormous fat blowfly. There seemed to be something malevolent about its very immovability. As I looked it was joined by another and yet another, and now the buzzing became apparent within the parlour itself.

I turned my head and stared at the bedroom door – and then I screamed my fear. From under a crack in the bottom of the door came an endless wriggling stream of fat, black bodies as big as nutmegs. One by one they spread their wings and hummed clumsily up on to the table, where they settled and fixed me – a motionless dark mass behind the three leaders.

The noise of the buzzing filled the thick atmosphere of the room – and into it crept a new note – a note almost of exultation – of fiendish delight at the way they had outwitted me. They formed up in companies awaiting the signal to charge, while I could only stare – held spellbound by their uncanny discipline.

For a moment there was a complete stillness as the last of them joined the watching army – then in a mass they rose, and the room echoed to the shrill, savage beating of their wings.

With a wild yell I dropped the lantern and fled into the kitchen, while all about me the disease-carrying vermin buzzed and whirred, settling on my face, my neck, my ears. I fought them off blindly and leaped on to the table by the window. It was a sixteen-foot drop at least down to the street, but I did not hesitate. The plague was in the house – the flies carried the plague, the food I had eaten had been infected – I could feel a lump under my arm and a curious feeling of nausea overcame me.

With my bare arm I smashed the glass of the window, tearing and beating down the leads between the panes like a maniac. Though I had the dread scourge I'd cheat the buzzing pest. They might feast on my carcass, but never whilst I drew breath.

'Bring out your dead!' I cried. 'Bring out your dead!'

Then I crashed headlong down into the street below!

Here the tramp left off, and the doctor added his portion to the tale when I met him outside the ward and walked with him to the infirmary door.

'He was picked up in a street off Holborn – run over by a lorry – broken legs. Nearly dead with starvation, poor fellow, and naturally light-headed. Can't get that nonsense he's just told you out of his head!'

But that night at home I found myself wondering if it was 'nonsense'. There was no sign of a house such as he had described in that particular corner of Holborn which the ambulance driver pointed out to me was the spot where the tramp was found – but a well-known authority informed me that the road there crosses the site of one of the many plague pits which harbour the bodies of the victims who died as a result of the Great Plague!

# Angus Wilson

## *Raspberry Jam*

'How are your funny friends at Potter's Farm, Johnnie?' asked his aunt from London. 'Very well, thank you, Aunt Eva,' said the little boy in the window in a high prim voice. He had been drawing faces on his bare knee and now put down the indelible pencil. The moment that he had been dreading all day had arrived. Now they would probe and probe with their silly questions, and the whole story of that dreadful tea party with his old friends would come tumbling out. There would be scenes and abuse and the old ladies would be made to suffer further. This he could not bear, for although he never wanted to see them again and had come, in brooding over the afternoon's events, almost to hate them, to bring them further misery, to be the means of their disgrace would be worse than any of the horrible things that had already happened. Apart from his fear of what might follow he did not intend to pursue the conversation himself, for he disliked his aunt's bright patronizing tone. He knew that she felt ill at ease with children and would soon lapse into that embarrassing 'leg-pulling' manner which some grown-ups used. For himself, he did not mind this, but if she made silly jokes about the old ladies at Potter's Farm he would get angry and then Mummy would say all that about his having to learn to take a joke and about his being highly strung and where could he have got it from, not from her.

But he need not have feared. For though the grown-ups

continued to speak of the old ladies as 'Johnnie's friends', the topic soon became a general one. Many of the things the others said made the little boy bite his lip, but he was able to go on drawing on his knee with the feigned abstraction of a child among adults.

'My dear,' said Johnnie's mother to her sister, 'you really must meet them. They're the *most* wonderful pair of freaks. They live in a great barn of a farmhouse. The inside's like a museum, full of old junk mixed up with some really lovely things all mouldering to pieces. The family's been there for hundreds of years, and they're madly proud of it. They won't let anyone do a single thing for them, although they're both well over sixty, and of course the result is that the place is in the most *frightful* mess. It's really rather ghastly and one oughtn't to laugh, but if you could *see* them, my dear. The elder one, Marian, wears a long tweed skirt almost to the ankles, she had a terrible hunting accident or something, and a school blazer. The younger one's said to have been a beauty, but she's really rather sinister now, inches thick in enamel and rouge, and dressed in all colours of the rainbow, with dyed red hair which is constantly falling down. Of course, Johnnie's made tremendous friends with them and I must say they've been immensely kind to him, but what Harry will say when he comes back from Germany, I can't think. As it is, he's always complaining that the child is too much with women and has no friends of his own age.'

'I don't honestly think you need worry about that, Grace,' said her brother Jim, assuming the attitude of the sole male in the company, for of the masculinity of old Mr Codrington their guest he instinctively made little. 'Harry ought to be very pleased with the way old Miss Marian's encouraged Johnnie's cricket and riding; it's pretty uphill work, too. Johnnie's not exactly a Don Bradman or a Gordon Richards, are you, old man? I like the old girl, personally. She's got a bee in her bonnet about the Bolsheviks, but she's stood up to those damned council people about the drainage like a good 'un; she does no end for the village people as well and says very little about it.'

'I don't like the sound of "doing good to the village" very much,' said Eva, 'it usually means patronage and disappointed old maids meddling in other people's affairs. It's only in villages like this that people can go on serving out sermons with gifts of soup.'

'Curiously enough, Eva old dear,' Jim said, for he believed in being rude to his progressive sister, 'in this particular case, you happen to be wrong. Miss Swindale is extremely broadminded. You remember, Grace,' he said, addressing his other sister, 'what she said about giving money to old Cooper, when the rector protested it would only go on drink – "You have a perfect right to consign us all to hell, rector, but you must allow us the choice of how we get there." Serve him damn well right for interfering too.'

'Well, Jim darling,' said Grace, 'I must say she could hardly have the nerve to object to drink – the poor old thing has the most dreadful bouts herself. Sometimes when I can't get gin from the grocer's it makes me absolutely livid to think of all that secret drinking, and they say it only makes her more and more gloomy. All the same, I suppose I should drink if I had a sister like Dolly. It must be horrifying when one is family proud like she is to have such a skeleton in the cupboard. I'm sure there's going to be the most awful trouble in the village about Dolly before she's finished. You've heard the squalid story about young Tony Calkett, haven't you? My dear, he went round there to fix the lights, and apparently Dolly invited him up to her bedroom to have a cherry brandy of all things and made the *most* unfortunate proposals. Of course I know she's been very lonely and it's all a ghastly tragedy really, but Mrs Calkett's a terribly silly little woman and a very jealous mother and she won't see it that way at all. The awful thing is that both the Miss Swindales give me the creeps rather. I have a dreadful feeling when I'm with them that I don't know who's the keeper and who's the lunatic. In fact, Eva my dear, they're both really rather horrors, and I suppose I ought never to let Johnnie go near them.'

'I think you have no cause for alarm, Mrs Allingham,' put in old Mr Codrington in a purring voice. He had been waiting for some time to take the floor, and now that he had got it he did not intend to relinquish it. Had it not been for the small range of village society he would not have been a visitor at Mrs Allingham's, for, as he frequently remarked, if there was one thing he deplored more than her vulgarity it was her loquacity. 'No one delights in scandal more than I do, but it is always a little distorted, a trifle *exageré*, indeed where would be its charm if it were not so! No doubt Miss Marian has her solaces, but she remains a noble-hearted woman. No doubt Miss Dolly is often a trifle naughty' – he dwelt on this word caressingly – 'but she really only uses the privilege of one, who has been that rare thing, a beautiful woman. As for Tony Calkett, it is really time that that young man ceased to be so unnecessarily virginal. If my calculations are correct and I have every reason to think they are, he must be twenty-two, an age at which modesty should have been put behind one long since. No, dear Mrs Allingham, you should rejoice that Johnnie has been given the friendship of two women who can still, in this vulgar age, be honoured with a name that, for all that it has been cheapened and degraded, one is still proud to bestow – the name of a lady.' Mr Codrington threw his head back and stared round the room as though defying anyone to deny him his own right to this name. 'Miss Marian will encourage him in the manlier virtues, Miss Dolly in the arts. Her own water-colours, though perhaps lacking in strength, are not to be despised. She has a fine sense of colour, though I could wish that she was a little less bold with it in her costume. Nevertheless, with that red gold hair there is something splendid about her appearance, something especially wistful to an old man like myself. Those peacock blue linen gowns take me back through Conder's fans and Whistler's rooms to Rossetti's "Mona Vanna". Unfortunately as she gets older, the linen is not overclean. We are given a "Mona Vanna" with the collected dust of age, but surely,' he added with a little cackle, 'it is dirt that lends patina to a picture. It is interesting that you should say you are uncertain which of the two sisters is a trifle peculiar, because, in point of fact, both have been away, as they used to phrase it in the servants' hall of my youth. Strange,' he mused, 'that one's knowledge of the servants' hall should always belong to the period of one's infancy, be, as it were, eternally outmoded. I have no conception of how they may speak of an asylum in the servants' hall of today. No doubt Johnnie could tell us. But, of course, I forget that social progress has removed the servants' hall from the ken of all but the most privileged children. I wonder now whether that is a loss or a blessing in disguise.'

'A blessing without any doubt at all,' said Aunt Eva, irrepressible in the cause of Advance. 'Think of all the appalling inhibitions we acquired from servants' chatter. I had an old nurse who was always talking about ghosts and dead bodies and curses on the family in a way that must have set up terrible phobias in me. I still have those ugly, morbid nightmares about spiders,' she said, turning to Grace.

'I refuse,' said Mr Codrington in a voice of great contempt, for he was greatly displeased at the interruption, 'to believe that any dream of yours could be ugly; morbid, perhaps, but with a sense of drama and artistry that would befit the dreamer. I confess that if I have inhibitions, and I trust I have many, I cling to them. I should not wish to give way unreservedly to what is so unattractively called the libido, it suggests a state of affairs in which beach pyjamas are worn and jitterbugging is compulsory. No, let us retain the fantasies, the imaginative games of childhood, even at the expense of a little fear, for they are the true magnificence of the springtime of life.'

'Darling Mr Codrington,' cried Grace, 'I do pray and hope you're right. It's exactly what I keep on telling myself about Johnnie, but I really don't know. Johnnie, darling, run upstairs and fetch mummy's bag.' But his mother need not have been so solicitous about Johnnie's overhearing what she had to say, for the child had already left the room. 'There you are, Eva,' she said, 'he's the strangest child. He slips away without so much as a word. I must say he's very good at amusing himself, but I very much wonder if all the funny games he plays aren't very bad for him. He's certainly been very peculiar lately, strange silences and sudden tears, and, my dear, the awful nightmares he has! About a fortnight ago, after he'd been at tea with the Miss Swindales, I don't know whether it was something he'd eaten there, but he made the most awful sobbing noise in the night. Sometimes I think it's just temper, like Harry. The other day at tea I only offered him some jam, my best home-made raspberry too, and he just screamed at me.'

'You should take him to a child psychologist,' said her sister.

'Well, darling, I expect you're right. It's so difficult to know whether they're frauds, everyone recommends somebody different. I'm sure Harry would disapprove, too, and then think of the expense... You know how desperately poor we are, although I think I manage as well as anyone could.' At this point Mr Codrington took a deep breath and sat back, for on the merits of her household management Grace Allingham was at her most boring and could by no possible stratagem be restrained.

Upstairs, in the room which had been known as the nursery until his eleventh birthday but was now called his bedroom, Johnnie was playing with his farm animals. The ritual involved in the game was very complicated and had a long history. It was on his ninth birthday that he had been given the farm set by his father. 'Something a bit less babyish than those woolly animals of yours,' he had said, and Johnnie had accepted them, since they made in fact no difference whatever to the games he played; games at which could Major Allingham have guessed he would have been distinctly puzzled. The little ducks, pigs, and cows of lead no more remained themselves in Johnnie's games than had the pink woollen sheep and green cloth horses of his early childhood. Johnnie's world was a strange compound of the adult world in which he had always lived and a book world composed from Grimm, the Arabian Nights, Alice's adventures, natural history books, and more recently the novels of Dickens and Jane Austen. His imagination was taken by anything odd – strange faces, strange names, strange animals, strange voices, and catchphrases – all these appeared in his games. The black pig and the white duck were keeping an hotel; the black pig was called that funny name of Granny's friend – Mrs Gudgeon-Rogers. She was always holding her skirt tight round the knees and warming her bottom over the fire – like Mrs Coates, and whenever anyone in the hotel asked for anything she would reply 'Darling, I can't stop now. I've simply got to fly,' like Aunt Sophie, and then she would fly out of the window. The duck was an Echidna, or Spiny Ant-eater who wore a picture hat and a fish train like in the picture of Aunt Eleanor; she used to weep a lot, because, like Granny, when she described her games of bridge, she was 'vulnerable', and she would yawn at the hotel guests and say 'Lord, I am tired' like Lydia Bennet. The two collie dogs had 'been asked to leave', like in the story of Mummy's friend Gertie who 'got tight' at the Hunt Ball, they were going to be divorced and were consequently wearing 'corespondent shoes'. The lady collie who was called Minnie Mongelheim kept on saying 'That chap's got a proud stomach. Let him eat chaff' like Mr F's Aunt in *Little Dorrit*. The sheep, who always played the part of a bore, kept on and on talking like Daddy about 'leg cuts and fine shots to cover'; sometimes when the rest of the animal guests got too bored, the sheep would change into Grandfather Graham and tell a funny story about a Scotsman so that they were bored in a different way. Finally the cat, who was a grand vizier and worked by magic, would say, 'All the ways round here belong to me', like the Red Queen and he would have all the guests torn in pieces and flayed alive until Johnnie felt so sorry for them that the game would come to an end. Mummy was already saying that he was getting too old for the farm animals: one always seemed to be getting too old for something. In fact, the animals were no longer necessary to Johnnie's games, for most of the time now he liked to read and when he wanted to play games he could do so in his head without the aid of any toys, but he hated the idea of throwing things away because they were no longer needed. Mummy and Daddy were always throwing things away and never thinking of their feelings. When he had been much younger, Mummy had given him an old petticoat to put in the dustbin, but Johnnie had taken it to his room and hugged it and cried over it, because it was no longer wanted. Daddy had been very upset. Daddy was always being upset at what Johnnie did. Only the last time that he was home there had been an awful row, because Johnnie had tried to make up like old Mrs Langdon and could not wash the blue paint off his eyes. Daddy had beaten him and looked very hurt all day, and said to Mummy that he'd 'rather see him dead than grow up a cissie'. No, it was better not to do imitations oneself, but to leave it to the animals.

This afternoon, however, Johnnie was not attending seriously to his game, he was sitting and thinking of what the grown-ups had been saying and of how he would never see his friends, the old ladies, again, and of how he never, never wanted to. This irrevocable separation lay like a black cloud over his mind, a constant darkness which was lit up momentarily by forks of hysterical horror, as he remembered the nature of their last meeting.

The loss of this friendship was a very serious one to the little boy. It had met so completely the needs and loneliness which are always great in a child isolated from other children and surrounded by unimaginative adults. In a totally unself-conscious way, half crazy as they were and half crazy even though the child sensed them to be, the Misses Swindale possessed just those qualities of which Johnnie felt most in need. To begin with they were odd and fantastic and highly coloured, and more important still they believed that such peculiarities were nothing to be ashamed of, indeed were often a matter for pride. 'How delightfully odd,' Miss Dolly would say in her drawling voice, when Johnnie told her how the duckbilled platypus had chosen spangled tights when Queen Alexandra had ordered her to be shot from a cannon at Brighton Pavilion. 'What a delightfully extravagant creature that duckbilled platypus is, Caro Gabriele,' for Miss Dolly had brought back a touch of Italian here and there from her years in Florence, whilst in Johnnie she fancied a likeness to the angel Gabriel. In describing her own dresses, too, which she would do for hours on end, extravagance was her chief commendation—'As for that gold and silver brocade ball dress,' she would say and her voice would sink to an awed whisper, 'it was richly fantastic.' To Miss Marian, with her more brusque, masculine nature, Johnnie's imaginative powers were a matter of far greater wonder than to her sister and she treated them with even greater respect. In her bluff, simple way like some old-fashioned religious army officer or overgrown but solemn schoolboy, she too admired the eccentric and unusual. 'What a lark!' she would say, when Johnnie told her how the Crown Prince had slipped in some polar bears dressed in pink ballet skirts to sing 'Ta Ra Ra Boomdeay' in the middle of a boring school concert which his royal duties had forced him to attend. 'What a nice chap he must be to know.' In talking of her late father, the general, whose memory she worshipped and of whom she had a never-ending flow of anecdotes, she would give an instance of his warm-hearted but distinctly eccentric behaviour, and say in her gruff voice, 'Wasn't it rum? That's the bit I like best.' But in neither of the sisters was there the least trace of that self-conscious whimsicality which Johnnie had met and hated in so many grown-ups. They were the first people he had met who liked what he liked and as he liked it.

Their love of lost causes and their defence of the broken, the worn out, and the forgotten met a deep demand in his nature, which had grown almost sickly sentimental in the dead, practical world of his home. He loved the disorder of the old eighteenth-century farmhouse, the collection of miscellaneous objects of all kinds that littered the rooms, and thoroughly sympathized with the sisters' magpie propensity to collect dress ends, feathers, string, old whistles, and broken cups. He grew excited with them in their fights to prevent drunken old men being taken to workhouses and cancerous old women to hospitals, though he sensed something crazy in their constant fear of intruders, Bolsheviks, and prying doctors. He would often try to change the conversation when Miss Marion became excited about spies in the village or told him of how torches had been flashing all night in the garden, and of how the vicar was slandering her father's memory in a whispering campaign. He felt deeply embarrassed when Miss Dolly insisted on looking into all the cupboards and behind the curtains to see, as she said, 'if there were any eyes or ears where they were not wanted. For, Caro Gabriele, those who hate beauty are many and strong, those who love it are few.'

It was, above all, their kindness and their deep affection which held the love-starved child. His friendship with Miss Dolly had been almost instantaneous. She soon entered into his fantasies with complete intimacy, and he was spellbound by her stories of the gaiety and beauty of Mediterranean life. They would play dressing-up games together, and enacted all his favourite historical scenes. She helped him with his French, too, and taught him Italian words with lovely sounds; she praised his painting and helped him to make costume designs for some of his 'characters'. With Miss Marian at first there had been much greater difficulty. She was an intensely shy woman, and took refuge behind a rather forbidding bluntness of manner. Her old-fashioned military airs and general 'manly' tone, copied from her father, with which she approached small boys, reminded Johnnie too closely of his own father. 'Head up, me lad,' she would say, 'shoulders straight.' Once he had come very near to hating her, when after an exhibition of his absentmindedness she had said, 'Take care, Johnnie head in the air. You'll be lost in the clouds, me lad, if you're not careful.' But the moment after she had won his heart for ever, when with a little chuckle she continued, 'Jolly good thing if you are, you'll learn things up there that we shall never know.' On her side, as soon as she saw that she had won his affection, she lost her shyness and proceeded impulsively to load him with kindnesses. She loved to cook his favourite dishes for him, and give him his favourite fruit from their kitchen garden. Her admiration for his precocity and imagination was open eyed and childlike. Finally they had found a common love of Dickens and Jane Austen, which she had read with her father, and now they would sit for hours talking over the characters in their favourite books.

Johnnie's affection for them was intensely protective, and increased daily as he heard and saw the contempt and dislike with which they were regarded by many persons in the village. The knowledge that 'they had been away' was nothing new to him when Mr Codrington had revealed it that afternoon. Once Miss Dolly had told him how a foolish doctor had advised her to go into a home – 'For you know, caro, ever since I returned to these grey skies my health has not been very good. People here think me strange, I cannot attune myself to the cold northern soul. But it was useless to keep me there, I need beauty and warmth of colour, and there it was so drab. The people, too, were unhappy, crazy creatures, and I missed my music so dreadfully.'

Miss Marian had spoken more violently of it on one of her 'funny' days, when from the depredations caused by the village boys to the orchard she had passed on to the strange man she had found spying in her father's library and the need for a high wall round the house to prevent people peering through the telescopes from Mr Hatton's house opposite. 'They're frightened of us, though, Johnnie,' she had said. 'I'm too honest for them and Dolly's too clever. They're always trying to separate us. Once they took me away against my will. They couldn't keep me. I wrote to all sorts of big pots, friends of father's, you know, and they had to release me.' Johnnie realized, too, that when his mother had said that she never knew which was the keeper, she had spoken more truly than she understood. Each sister was constantly alarmed for the other and anxious to hide the other's defects from an un-understanding world. Once when Miss Dolly had been telling him a long story about a young waiter who had slipped a note into her hand the last time she had been in London, Miss Marian called Johnnie into the kitchen to look at some pies she had made. Later she had told him not to listen if Dolly said 'soppy things' because being so beautiful she did not realize that she was no longer young. Another day when Miss Marian had brought in the silver-framed photo of her father in full-dress uniform and had asked Johnnie to swear an oath to clear the general's memory in the village, Miss Dolly had begun to play a mazurka on the piano. Later, she, too, had warned Johnnie not to take too much notice when her sister got excited. 'She lives a little too much in the past, Gabriele. She suffered very much when our father died. Poor Marian, it is a pity perhaps that she is so good, she has had too little of the pleasures of life. But we must love her very much, caro, very much.'

Johnnie had sworn to himself to stand by them, and to fight the wicked people who said they were old and useless and in the way. But now, since that dreadful tea party, he could not fight for them any longer, for he knew why they had been shut up and felt that it was justified. In a sense, too, he understood that it was to protect others that they had to be restrained, for the most awful memory of all that terrifying afternoon was the thought that he had shared with pleasure for a moment in their wicked game.

It was certainly most unfortunate that Johnnie should have been invited to tea on that Thursday, for the Misses Swindale had been drinking heavily on and off for the preceding week, and were by that time in a state of mental and nervous excitement that rendered them far from normal. A number of events had combined to produce the greatest sense of isolation in these old women whose sanity in any event hung by a precarious thread. Miss Marian had been involved in an unpleasant scene with the vicar over the new hall for the Young People's Club. She was, as usual, providing the cash for the building, and felt extremely happy and excited at being consulted about the decorations. Though she did not care for the vicar, she set out to see him, determined that she would accommodate herself to changing times. In any case, since she was the benefactress, it was, she felt, particularly necessary that she should take a back seat, to have imposed her wishes in any way would have been most illbred. It was an unhappy chance that caused the vicar to harp upon the need for new fabrics for the chairs, and even to digress upon the ugliness of the old upholstery, for these chairs had come from the late General Swindale's library. Miss Marian was immediately reminded of her belief that the vicar was attempting secretly to blacken her father's memory, nor was the impression corrected when he tactlessly suggested that the question of her father's taste was unimportant and irrelevant. She was more deeply wounded still to find in the next few days that the village shared the vicar's view that she was attempting to dictate to the boys' club by means of her money. 'After all,' as Mrs Grove at the post office said, 'it's not only the large sums that count, Miss Swindale, it's all the boys' sixpences that they've saved up.' 'You've too much of your father's ways in you, that's the trouble, Miss Swindale,' said Mr Norton, who was famous for his bluntness, 'and they won't do nowadays.'

She had returned from this unfortunate morning's shopping to find Mrs Calkett on the doorstep. Now the visit of Mrs Calkett was not altogether unexpected, for Miss Marian had guessed from chance remarks of her sister's that something 'unfortunate' had happened with young Tony. When, however, the sharp-faced unpleasant little woman began to complain about Miss Dolly with innuendoes and veiledly coarse suggestions, Miss Marian could stand it no longer and drove her away harshly. 'How dare you speak about my sister in that disgusting way, you evil-minded little woman,' she said. 'You'd better be careful or you'll find yourself charged with libel.' When the scene was over, she felt very tired. It was dreadful of course that anyone so mean and cheap should speak thus of anyone so fine and beautiful as Dolly, but it was also dreadful that Dolly should have made such a scene possible.

Things were not improved, therefore, when Dolly returned from Brighton at once elevated by a new conquest and depressed by its subsequent results. It seemed that the new conductor on the Southdown – 'that charming dark Italian-looking boy I was telling you about, my dear' – had returned her a most intimate smile and pressed her hand when giving her change. Her own smiles must have been embarrassingly intimate, for a woman in the next seat had remarked loudly to her friend, 'These painted old things. Really,

I wonder the men don't smack their faces.' 'I couldn't help smiling,' remarked Miss Dolly, 'she was so evidently *jalouse*, my dear. I'm glad to say the conductor did not hear, for no doubt he would have felt it necessary to come to my defence, he was so completely *épris*.' But, for once, Miss Marian was too vexed to play ball, she turned on her sister and roundly condemned her conduct, ending up by accusing her of bringing misery to them both and shame to their father's memory. Poor Miss Dolly just stared in bewilderment, her baby blue eyes round with fright, tears washing the mascara from her eyelashes in black streams down the wrinkled vermilion of her cheeks. Finally, she ran crying up to her room.

That night both the sisters began to drink heavily. Miss Dolly lay like some monstrous broken doll, her red hair streaming over her shoulders, her corsets unloosed and her fat body poking out of an old pink velvet ball dress – pink with red hair was always so audacious – through the most unexpected places in bulges of thick blue-white flesh. She sipped at glass after glass of gin, sometimes staring into the distance with bewilderment that she should find herself in such a condition, sometimes leering pruriently at some pictures of Johnny Weismuller in swimsuits that she had cut out of *Film Weekly*. At last she began to weep to think that she had sunk to this. Miss Marian sat at her desk and drank more deliberately from a cut-glass decanter of brandy. She read solemnly through her father's letters, their old-fashioned, earnest Victorian sentiments swimming ever more wildly before her eyes. But at last she, too, began to weep as she thought of how his memory would be quite gone when she passed away, and of how she had broken the promise that she had made to him on his deathbed to stick to her sister through thick and thin.

So they continued for two or three days with wild spasms of drinking and horrible, sober periods of remorse. They cooked themselves odd scraps in the kitchen, littering the house with unwashed dishes and cups, but never speaking, always avoiding each other. They didn't change their clothes or wash, and indeed made little alteration in their appearance. Miss Dolly put fresh rouge on her cheeks periodically and some pink roses in her hair which hung there wilting; she was twice sick over the pink velvet dress. Miss Marian put on an old scarlet hunting waistcoat of her father's, partly out of maudlin sentiment and partly because she was cold. Once she fell on the stairs and cut her forehead against the banisters; the red and white handkerchief which she tied round her head gave her the appearance of a tipsy pirate. On the fourth day the sisters were reconciled and sat in Miss Dolly's room. That night they slept, lying heavily against each other on Miss Dolly's bed, open-mouthed and snoring, Miss Marian's deep guttural rattle contrasting with Miss Dolly's high-pitched whistle. They awoke on Thursday morning, much sobered, to the realization that Johnnie was coming to tea that afternoon.

It was characteristic that neither spoke a word of the late debauch. Together they went out into the hot July sunshine to gather raspberries for Johnnie's tea. But the nets in the kitchen garden had been disarranged and the birds had got the fruit. The awful malignity of this chance event took some time to pierce through the fuddled brains of the two ladies, as they stood there grotesque and obscene in their staring pink and clashing red, with their heavy pouchy faces and blood-shot eyes showing up in the hard, clear light of the sun. But when the realization did get home it seemed to come as a confirmation of all the beliefs of persecution which had been growing throughout the drunken orgy. There is little doubt that they were both a good deal mad when they returned to the house.

Johnnie arrived punctually at four o'clock, for he was a small boy of exceptional politeness. Miss Marian opened the door to him, and he was surprised at her appearance in her red bandana and her scarlet waistcoat, and especially by her voice which, though friendly and gruff as usual, sounded thick and flat. Miss Dolly, too, looked more than usually odd with one eye closed in a kind of perpetual wink, and with her pink dress falling off her shoulders. She kept on laughing in a silly, high giggle. The shock of discovering that the raspberries were gone had driven them back to the bottle and they were both fairly drunk. They pressed upon the little boy, who was thirsty after his walk, two small glasses in succession, one of brandy, the other of gin, though in their sober mood the ladies would have died rather than have seen their little friend take strong liquor. The drink soon combined with the heat of the day and the smell of vomit that hung around the room to make Johnnie feel most strange. The walls of the room seemed to be closing in and the floor to be moving up and down like sea waves. The ladies' faces came up at him suddenly and then receded, now Miss Dolly's with great blobs of blue and scarlet and her eyes winking and leering, now Miss Marian's huge white mass with her moustache grown large and black. He was only conscious by fits and starts of what they were doing or saying. Sometimes he would hear Miss Marian speaking in a flat, slow monotone. She seemed to be reading out her father's letters, snatches of which came to him clearly and then faded away. 'There is so much to be done in our short sojourn on this earth, so much that may be done for good, so much for evil. Let us earnestly endeavour to keep the good steadfastly before us,' then suddenly, 'Major Campbell has told me of his decision to leave the regiment. I pray God hourly that he may have acted in full consideration of the Higher Will to which...'; and once grotesquely, 'Your Aunt Maud was here yesterday, she is a maddening woman and I consider it a just judgment upon the Liberal party that she should espouse its cause.' None of these phrases meant anything to the little boy, but he was dimly conscious that Miss Marian was growing excited, for he heard her say, 'That was our father. As Shakespeare says "He was a man take him all in all", Johnnie. We loved him, but there were those who sought to destroy him, for he was too big for them. But their day is nearly ended. Always remember that, Johnnie.' It was difficult to hear all that the elder sister said, for Miss Dolly kept on drawling and giggling in his ear about a black charmeuse evening gown she had worn, and a young donkeyboy she had danced with in the fiesta at Asti. '*E come era bello, caro Gabriele, come era bello*. And afterwards... but I must spare the ears of one so young the details of the *arte del' amore*,' she added with a giggle, and then with drunken dignity, 'It would not be immodest I think to mention that his skin was like velvet. Only a few lire, too, just imagine.' All this, too, was largely meaningless to the boy, though he remembered it in later years.

For a while he must have slept, since he remembered that later he could see and hear more clearly though his head ached terribly. Miss Dolly was seated at the piano playing a little jig and bobbing up and down like a mountainous pink blancmange, whilst Miss Marian more than ever like a pirate was dancing some sort of a hornpipe. Suddenly Miss Dolly stopped playing. 'Shall we show him the prisoner?' she said solemnly. 'Head up, shoulders straight,' said Miss Marian in a parody of her old manner, 'you're going to be very honoured, m' lad. Promise you'll never betray that honour. You shall see one of the enemy punished. Our father gave us close instructions – "Do good to all," he said, "but if you catch one of the enemy, remember you are a soldier's daughters." We shall obey that command.' Meanwhile Miss Dolly had returned from the kitchen carrying a little bird which was pecking and clawing at the net in which it had been caught and shrilling incessantly – it was a little bullfinch. 'You're a very beautiful little bird,' Miss Dolly whispered, 'with lovely soft pink feathers and pretty grey wings. But you're a very naughty little bird too, *tanto cattivo*. You came and took the fruit from us which we'd kept for our darling Gabriele.' She began feverishly to pull the rose breast feathers from the bird, which piped more loudly and squirmed. Soon little trickles of red blood ran down among the feathers. 'Scarlet and pink a very daring combination,' Miss Dolly cried. Johnnie watched from his chair, his heart beating fast. Suddenly Miss Marian stepped forward and holding the bird's head she thrust a pin into its eyes. 'We don't like spies round here looking at what we are doing,' she said in her flat, gruff voice. 'When we find them we teach them a lesson so that they don't spy on us again.' Then she took out a little pocketknife and cut into the bird's breast; its wings were beating more feebly now and its claws only moved spasmodically, whilst its chirping was very faint. Little yellow and white strings of entrails began to peep out from where she had cut. 'Oh!' cried Miss Dolly, 'I like the lovely colours, I don't like these worms.' But Johnnie could bear it no longer; white and shaking he jumped from his chair and seizing the bird, he threw it on the floor, and then he stamped on it violently until it was nothing but a sodden crimson mass. 'Oh, Gabriele, what have you done? You've spoilt all the soft, pretty colours. Why, it's nothing now, it just looks like a lump of raspberry jam. Why have you done it, Gabriele?' cried Miss Dolly. But little Johnnie gave no answer, he had run from the room.

# Alan Wykes

## *Nightmare*

Before I met Dr Frazer my life was a long nightmare of persecution. I am a naturally timid man, and from childhood onward people edged on to this not uncommon sensitivity and took a delight in seeing me build up my secret fears. That element of derisive cruelty is common too. Quite ordinarily pleasant people indulge in it, though they'd be horrified if you accused them of it and would certainly deny it. But I know. I've experienced it. There's no mistaking the breath of malevolence; it becomes audible and visible as you grow older, and there comes a time when you perceive it as an aura. Someone at a party will turn from a conversation, and you will believe that the sneer on his lips is for you; or you will hear your name spoken by total strangers in a theatre foyer; a footstep will sound in the night below your bedroom window, a curtain will twitch as you pass the house of supposed friends; and a hand, surreptitious beneath the table, will prepare a few grains to be slipped into your drink.

You see, it builds up. The intent of malice lies everywhere. One's nearest and dearest are most culpable because of course they know one's fears thoroughly; and they always have the advantage of being able to be quite convincing about acting for your own good. They have explanations on hand for everything; but after a time you see that each is more suspect than the last. And in the end they become curiously misted as physical figures, and their voices drone on in unrecognizable terms that have only the connotations of evil.

They have merged into a nightmare backcloth, and only the aura of malevolence is recognizable. Voices, shadows, sniggering laughter, pursuit – these are the elements of persecution. And all you have to balance them is a bitter longing for revenge on your persecutors – a revenge which you are quite unable to implement because of your natural timidity.

That, then, was how it was with me. I was slowly edging forward over the borderline of insanity. I dared not go out; but it came to the point where it was not sufficient to lock my door; *they* would get in… somehow. Barricades were useless – indeed, they proved so, for, finally, I was taken, cringing in a corner of the room that was my last retreat from the world.

Of that actual day I remember nothing clearly. No doubt the details were unpleasant – they could hardly be otherwise. But they are unimportant. What is important is that I then met Dr Frazer.

We understood each other. 'You're absolutely safe here,' he said quietly; and although it was the same phrase many others had falsely used to me, I knew that this time it was true. There was no need even for him to demonstrate security by leaving the door open or giving me *carte blanche* to investigate the room for hidden contrivances. True, I crept furtively about, touching the bare walls and turning sharply to surprise the shadow that I had come to expect to be creeping up on me. But there were no shadows, and I smiled a bit shamefacedly at Dr Frazer as he sat at his desk.

'All right?'

He stood up and shook hands with me. It was a gesture of friendship, not a greeting or farewell. We were much of a height – both tall and lean, though at that time my constant fears had given a twist to my neck and shoulders that had stamped me with the slightly obscene horror of all those who believe they are hunted, while Dr Frazer was tranquil, aquiline, and dignified. But I felt none of the customary inferiority even when he looked down at my hand held briefly in his own, and saw the swollen and ragged cuticles where for years I had picked and bitten at them in an habitual reaction to my fears.

'Such finely shaped hands,' he murmured gently. 'We must make them better.'

He was *with* me, you see. From the first he understood all my difficulties; and although at that first meeting he didn't even begin the work of release, he gained my confidence.

Of course I had my own quarters in the Home – and a very comfortable suite it was. And I was absolutely free to come and go as I wished. But I preferred not to go beyond the walls surrounding the grounds. For some time I just wanted to enjoy my new-found safety, and in any case it would have seemed ungrateful to want to go beyond the walls that contained the pleasant and extensive park – almost as if I wanted to escape from escape.

As for the cure, I can tell you little of that. Every morning Dr Frazer and I used to talk – that was the heart of it. I would tell him things – almost whatever he asked. Sometimes not. Then he would say, 'We'll enjoy a light sleep'; and after that it would seem as if I'd told him what he wanted to know, even though I couldn't actually remember doing so. You see? It was as easy as that. Just lie down on that perfectly comfortable sofa and answer Dr Frazer's questions – which were always put in such a way that they scarcely seemed like questions at all, but more like ordinary to-and-fro conversation really. He never seemed to be prying, he was just interested, man to man.

Then peace. Gradually but certainly all my anguish disappeared. I had no fears of any kind. 'Look at yourself in the glass,' Dr Frazer said; and when I looked I saw that my shoulders had become noticeably less hunched because now I was no longer constantly looking behind me; and my eyes no longer had the terrible shiftiness of eyes trying to follow the movements of ubiquitous enemies. My hands, too, had begun to heal up. At first I sat on them while Dr Frazer and I were talking; but after a time he made me look at them steadily, and I found I could do so without revulsion. As he said, it was all a matter of facing up to things. 'That you can now do,' he added. 'But stay a few weeks longer. Go out and about, get used to things in your own time. Many a cure's been spoilt by too sudden a transition.'

'I really am cured?' I asked. I just wanted the security of hearing it again. 'You really are,' he said.

You can imagine my delight on entering my new life. Free of enmitous whispering and disjointed implications of torture, I went about with what must have appeared to be a very childlike gaiety; though in that place innocence and experience were frighteningly and terribly combined. But since, cured or not, all of us there looked inward upon ourselves rather than outward at our companions no one remarked as extraordinary my new-found happiness.

Happiness. I speak of it as that. And you would think that for one just released from the persecution of a world of enemies, able to seek love instead of enmity in people, there would be unlimited vistas of joy. But in my case it was not like that.

Indeed no.

The first time I realized this was on the third day after Dr Frazer had given me my pass into a world free of enemies. I felt as I can only suppose any normal man would feel if he had just recovered from a long illness and been granted a new lease of life. All the colours, sounds, and smells of the world were intense and clear. People were just people—I could talk with them if I wished, enjoy the normal intercourse of civilization.

I walked down the hill to the village. Faintly astonished by my new-found daring, I went straight into the public bar of an inn, reminding myself that before I met Dr Frazer nothing would have driven me into a room where people were gathered. I would have distorted them into vicious enemies, their derision misting the air and their secret laughter droning like voices heard in a sick sleep.

In the pub I nodded cheerfully but not too deliberately to the company and ordered a ginger-beer shandy. The buzz of conversation stopped for a moment. I crossed one ankle over the other and leant against the bar. My drink came and, as I paid, I heard a man who was sitting at one of the small tables say to his woman companion:

'He may be skinny, but 'e's a devil for strong drink.'

It was an unfunny remark and meant only to impress the woman that the speaker was 'a lad'. I accepted it as such. There wasn't a flicker of resentment in me, even when I heard the woman respond with a stifled snigger.

No resentment; no horror. I had been momentarily in the presence of real, not imagined, derision, and it had left me unmoved, perhaps even a little disappointed. Frazer had almost, one might have said, given me a completely new personality.

Calmly I left the pub, my nod of farewell including the man who had mocked me, and walked back up the hill, seeing myself in my mind's eye as the poor hunted creature I had been. I smiled with easy self-contempt as I imagined myself running, running, my breath gasping, pursued wherever I went by that baleful evil with which all my tormentors had been invested. It was amusing to consider that for so long I had, in a way, been sustained, as a cancer is sustained, by the malignant accumulation of a malevolence I had created for myself. Now there were no shadows, no baleful voices.

Lasting happiness, one would have thought. But strangely, in a little while I found that, lacking the sustaining power of torment, I was, so to speak, starved. I needed the torture of persecution to feed me. Now I had nothing – nothing.

This realization was built up over many weeks. I began to seek persecution with the same intensity I had fled from it. I dressed and acted eccentrically in the village, wearing an old-fashioned Inverness cape, laughing and talking to myself and in general inviting comment. But I realized all too clearly that the surreptitious remarks people made about me were impelled by humour and compassion rather than derision. There was no malice in them.

Dr Frazer was of course delighted with my progress. He saw that now I ventured into every lion's den. I didn't tell him that my venturings had become desperate searches for the sustenance of torment. I had begun to feel stirrings of resentment towards him, for it was he who had brought about my growing despair; but being in many ways a weak man and in every way a timid one, I couldn't find the kind of courage that was needed to tell him of my resentment. Such courage as I possessed was needed to face the emptiness of my tranquil life.

Then, at the end of autumn, a thin, bitter malice once more attacked and persecuted me.

This time it was in the form of a nightmare.

In the dream there was an intense heat and light surrounding me – the kind of sunshine in which you're forced to screw up the eyes to avoid being blinded. But in the centre of all that light was an oasis of shadows, columns.

And among the shadows a figure stood, cloaked and still, watching me.

Watching, I say. But that isn't quite accurate. For when the figure moved a little, a turn only, I knew that it had no face.

It wasn't, I hasten to say, a Gothic facelessness, a ghastly impression of shredded flesh or glaring eyesockets or mangled bone. I might have felt my scalp prickle, I might have been faintly amused or disgusted by such a dream vision. But this was a subtle refinement of facelessness, a void that, hooded though it was by shadow, turned and watched. And this watching, even though it was expressed by neither eye nor mouth, was nonetheless clearly malevolent, the malevolence of asps was hooded there. It seemed, in fact, the very void from which malice might have been created.

In the dream I felt, very clearly, that my search for the sustenance of torment was over.

I screamed of course. But the scream was at once aborted in that special dream atmosphere of fungoid oppressiveness, and escape was equally impossible.

Then, waking at last from this nightmare, I felt quite certain that it was no single visitation of horror. It would recur again and again, like a new lease of torment. Awake, I screamed.

I proved myself right in my apprehension: it was a recurring nightmare. Night after night I found myself within the confines of that sunlit purlieu with its heart of darkness; night after night the faceless figure turned all the intensity of its darkly burning malice upon me.

I say 'night after night', but that isn't strictly true. Even I, with so many years of persecution behind me, could not have borne that. The nightmare was frequent though, and it was, in a curious way, progressive. I mean that the blinding, stifling light and heat that formed its atmosphere, and in which I found myself trapped, oppressed, immobile, diminished somewhat in intensity with each recurrence. I wasn't aware of this until I had dreamed the nightmare many times; but at last I realized that there seemed also to be an increasing clarity about my cloaked and hooded tormentor, almost a promise of revelation. Still no eyes looked out, and not even the thinnest of lips were folded back from the vicious breath of malice – in fact, my familiar's malevolence remained bitterly inscrutable, even though I gained, as you shall see, a hint of his identity. But nonetheless there was a definite feeling of progression – whether towards revelation of my tormentor's identity, or disaster, or both, I could not be sure. But a gathering excitement attended my recurrent visits to the benighted Asphodel of my nightmare.

Outwardly, the effect on me was appalling. I was rapidly falling back to the state that had brought me to Dr Frazer.

He, naturally, was puzzled. 'This will never do,' he said jovially. 'You must tell me what has happened. I can't have a triumph turning into a failure.'

I cowered back in my chair, biting at the skin round my fingernails. I would say nothing. He rose from his desk and came towards me. I whimpered, backing away into the corner.

'Please,' he said. 'We're friends.' He seemed to be standing amid columns and shadows, a lean figure, watching me. I must have cried out, for he said quickly: 'Ah, an hallucination.' This conclusion seemed to satisfy him, and he sat down again behind his desk. 'It's a dream you've been having. You must tell me about it.'

'No!' I shouted. I could feel my mouth quivering with fear and frustration. With all my heart I wanted to reveal my nightmare to him; yet to me the loss of its defilement would be like the draining away of life. I had already experienced the emptiness of tranquillity.

I had enough cunning to be careful. I calmed myself.

'Stop that giggling,' Dr Frazer said harshly.

I hadn't realized I was laughing. I felt humiliation burning through me like fire.

'Now,' he said kindly again, 'you have only to tell me your dream. You know you can trust me. Didn't I exorcize your fears before? I can again – even in a dream.'

'No,' I said. I was putting on the brave front I used to put on, pretending. 'I don't dream, ever.'

'Then you're the only man in the world who doesn't,' he answered dryly. 'Some dreams are remembered, some not; that's all.'

'I don't remember, then.'

He shrugged. 'All right. Today you won't remember. Tomorrow perhaps. Shall we see? I can assure you I'll have your dream from you sooner or later. Sleep now. You'd like a little something to help?'

'No!' I shouted again. The thought of the malevolent persecutor of my dream was more than I could bear.

Yet I moved onwards through time towards night and sleep with a fascination combining horror and lust. If my assignation with my familiar was cancelled out by a dreamless slumber, I endured the interval between that night and the next with a relief which, paradoxically, I found almost unendurable. The persecution that was destroying me had become a necessity.

For several days Dr Frazer tried to prise my nightmare from me by gentle encouragement. But his persistence was unavailing. I had too much to lose. He had robbed me of one source of existence; I didn't intend that he should steal the other from me. My resentment towards him grew. I longed for revenge upon him for cornering me as he had, for, after all, whom else could I blame? But, as I have hinted before, I am not the sort to plan or execute overt reckonings.

Secret, introverted vindictiveness, though, is another matter.

One morning he said with weary patience: 'Well, if I can't take your nightmare from you by request, I shall have to have it by extortion.' Then I recalled that when I had first come under his care he had overcome my reluctance to reveal the details of my earlier tormented life by putting me into an hypnotic trance.

'Tomorrow morning,' he said softly, 'we will try a little sleep.'

I wanted to shout out in frenzied rage, but I covered my trembling mouth with my hand.

'Quiet, now,' he said. 'Quiet.'

I could feel his eyes burning into my back as he had me led back to my room.

That was yesterday.

Last night I dreamed again, but with a subtle difference.

The blinding light and scorching heat had diminished and had been replaced by a thin sweating chill, and it was into this that I entered the nightmare. My familiar watched me, shadowed, anonymous, hooded, and ubiquitous in the sense that when I forced myself to shut out his sinister faceless malevolence I found the cloaked silent figure still watching me, full of a malicious surprise that I should have been so naive as to seek escape by a mere closing of the eyes. For the nightmare went endlessly tunnelling inwards through countless reflections of eyes reflected in eyes.

And this time I experienced also a strange duality. I seemed to have been drawn into a dreadful impersonation of my watching tormentor, so that I was myself looking outwards facelessly from the shadowed hood, and observing with immense glee the surprised horror of the tall, lean figure which chokingly screamed and closed its eyes in a ridiculously abortive effort to escape the malignant evil I embraced him with. The recognition of myself as a creature eaten by malevolent persecution, yet at the same time triumphantly and vindictively *projecting* malevolence outwards, should have been more than I was capable of bearing.

But I regret to say that I knew a wholly lustful orgasm of

satisfaction in that moment of recognition. Vindictiveness of a secret kind is, as I have said, easier than overt revenge.

When I awoke I felt as if I had experienced some strange metamorphosis. I looked at myself in the glass. No change there: my head was still hunched on my shoulders in the familiar attitude of the persecuted, my eyes were shifty with fear. Yet I felt calm – not calm in the way I had felt when Dr Frazer had released my previous fears from me, but, rather, calm with the satisfaction of achievement.

I chuckled to myself and rubbed my hands pleasurably together. They sounded unusually dry and papery.

When I knocked at Dr Frazer's door there was no answer. I knew he was inside, though. I pushed the door silently open and stood there, watching.

Dr Frazer was at his desk. The room was filled with sunshine – the cold pale sunshine of a winter morning. The thin nightmare chill was with us.

Dr Frazer looked up. Beads of sweat glistened on his forehead. He, too, had suffered a metamorphosis. He was not, as yet, a creature completely derided by terror; but the silent erosion of fear and malice within his skull had begun. The horror of this realization was clearly upon him. His lips and fingers trembled. His eyes looked wearily out from beneath his fine brows, and in them I could see my own, warily hooded, watching him, and his in mine, endlessly reflected back and forth.

'For God's sake, what is going to happen now?' he whispered.

I did not answer him. I was very well aware that he sought the comfort of my assurance: *Why, surely you're going to exorcize my dream, Doctor? Isn't that what I'm here for?* But it was no longer necessary for him to discover my dream: he already knew it. Nor was it necessary for him to tell me that last night he had experienced the first long nightmare of persecution, in which the lean cloaked faceless figure stood watching him – just as I watched him now, malevolent and sinister, his familiar always.

*Permissions Acknowledgements*

Every effort has been made to contact copyright holders of material reproduced in this book. If any have been inadvertently overlooked, the publishers will be pleased to make restitution at the earliest opportunity.

Joan Aiken 'Jugged Hare' © Joan Aiken 1959. Reproduced with permission on behalf of The Estate of Joan Aiken.

A. L. Barker 'Submerged' © A. L. Barker. 'Submerged' from *Innocents*. Reproduced with permission on behalf of The Estate of A. L. Barker.

Oscar Cook 'His Beautiful Hands' © Campbell Thompson & McLaughlin Ltd on behalf of the copyright owner.

Peter Fleming 'The Kill' © the Estate of Peter Fleming, 1936. Reproduced with permission of Johnson & Alcock Ltd.

C. S. Forester 'The Physiology of Fear' © C. S. Forester 1959. Reproduced by permission of PDF on behalf of The Estate of C. S. Forester.

L. P. Hartley 'W. S.' © The Society of Authors as the literary representatives of the Estate of L. P. Hartley.

Hazel Heald 'The Horror in the Museum' is reprinted by permission of Arkham House Publishers, Inc. and Arkham's agents, JABberwocky Literary Agency, PO Box 4558, Sunnyside, NY 11104-0558.

Fielden Hughes 'The Mistake' © Fielden Hughes. Reproduced by permission of The Estate of Fielden Hughes.

Nigel Kneale 'Oh, Mirror, Mirror' © Nigel Kneale. Reproduced with permission of The Agency on behalf of The Estate of Nigel Kneale.

Seabury Quinn 'The House of Horror' is reprinted by permission of Arkham House Publishers, Inc. and Arkham's agents, JABberwocky Literary Agency, PO Box 4558, Sunnyside, NY 11104-0558.

Flavia Richardson 'Behind the Yellow Door' © Campbell Thompson & McLaughlin Ltd on behalf of the copyright owner.

Muriel Spark 'The Portobello Road' © Muriel Spark. 'The Portobello Road' from *The Go-Away Bird*. Reproduced with permission of David Higham Associates.

Angus Wilson 'Raspberry Jam' © Angus Wilson 1959. Reproduced with permission of Curtis Brown Group Ltd on behalf of Estate of Sir Angus Wilson.

www.panmacmillan.com